Bride
by
Blackmail

Moonlight and Magnolia Series

D0877749

DEBBIE LYNNE
COSTELLO

By Debbie Lynne Costello

Published by Wakefield Press

ISBN: 978-0-9861820-9-9
E-Version ISBN: 978-0-9861820-8-2

All Scripture is taken from the King James Version of the Bible.

Edited by:
Louise Gouge https://louisemgougeauthor.blogspot.com/
Cover Design by: Carpe Librum Book Design, Evelyn Labelle
https://www.carpelibrumbookdesign.com/

Wakefield
Press

Endorsements

Two things you can count on with a Debbie Lynne Costello book, a heart-swooning romance and a fast-paced adventure. Just my kind of book! *Bride by Blackmail* is no exception. What's not to love about spies, villains, unrequited love, danger, and romance? I guarantee you will be enthralled with every page, just as I was.
MaryLu Tyndall, author of the award-winning Legacy of the King's Pirates

Best-selling author Debbie Lynne Costello has a deep love for Charleston which reflects in her work. Christian historical romance readers will be swept away to another time and place with this exciting story!
Carrie Fancett Pagels, Award-winning and best-selling author

A whirlwind courtship fails to sweep the lass off her feet, so a handsome, wealthy Scotsman uses less conventional means to achieve his objective. He's a King's agent who always gets his man, but will he lose the queen of his heart? This riveting and tempestuous romance keeps the suspense high and the pace fast, concluding in a crescendo for the sweet happily ever after you won't want to miss!
Kathleen L. Maher, author of Sons of the Shenandoah series

Rarely has a novel by a newer author caught and held my attention as did this story by Debbie Lynne Costello. The warmth and charm of the South shines through on every page of this story of love and courage, wounded hearts and redeemed lives. I didn't want to put it down until I reached the satisfying conclusion.
Laurie Alice Eakes

Acknowledgements

Books are the efforts of so many people and this book is no different. I always want to give God the glory first and foremost as He gave me the desire in my heart to write and the story to put on paper. He is my Rock and my Comfort. I want to thank my wonderful husband who was the first person to encourage me to write a book. He always encourages me and believes in me. Thank you, Joe. I love you always and forever! I'd like to thank Kathleen L. Maher who saw this story as all my stories in its raw and unpolished form and fell in love with it. She has walked every step of this road with me, critiquing Bride by Blackmail every time I got a crazy notion to rewrite it again. Her insight has been invaluable and her friendship irreplaceable. I'm so thankful God put us together. My life is richer because of it. Thank you, dear friend. You'll never know the impact you've made. Thank you to my other critique partner, Carrie Fancett Pagels, whose edits on etiquette kept me from committing historical faux pas, her phone calls keeping me straight, and most importantly her friendship and prayers. You've been a great encourager. Thank you for believing in me, my friend. I want to thank the ladies of my street team who help me get the word out about my new books. You ladies are amazing! And a special thank you to my two beta readers, Connie Ruggles and Lynda Edwards. Your eagle eyes for errors were a huge blessing.

Lastly, I want to thank my family who stood by me, cheered me on, and believed in me. You'll never know how much that means to me.

This book is dedicated to my
daughter, Kacie Jo.
You are beautiful inside and out.
I love you
and am so proud of you
for all you've overcome and all you have
accomplished.

Scottish Word Glossary

Aboot – About
Aye – Yes
Bonnie – Pretty
Dearling – Darling
Dinna – Do not
Fash – Worry
Guid – Good
Ken – Know
Kent – Knew
Nay – No
No' – Not
Och – Express surprise, emphasis agreement or disagreement
Oot – Out
Skellum – Scoundrel

Historical Note: The Jackson's home is based on some of the 19th Century Charleston homes—a two-story home which features stairs leading to the second floor where the main living quarters are. The lower level holds the family's bedrooms.

Husbands, love your wives,
even as Christ also loved the church,
and gave Himself for it.
Ephesians 5:26

Chapter 1

Charleston, South Carolina, 1880

Charlotte Jackson maneuvered through the crush of partygoers with her sister, Nellie, latched on her arm. Having weaved through the archway, the two stepped into a spacious great hall where white walls shimmered beneath the glow of crystal chandeliers. Charlotte scanned the room for Frank as Nellie released her arm.

The room overflowed with small groups of mingling people, adding to the heat of the October day. Charlotte let out a sigh. The humidity was sure to frizz her hair and make her look like a wire-haired terrier.

She rose on tiptoes and searched the room, wishing she were taller. Dresses of every color and shade filled the room, reminding her of an array of flowers, only these didn't give the room a smell quite so sweet as azaleas did.

"Do you see him?" Nellie turned her head in the direction of Charlotte's search.

"No." Her gaze swept across the room once again. "Oh! There he is."

As if he'd heard her, Frank Sorrell turned dark eyes her way. She loved the way his black hair brushed his collar, which pushed it into the slightest curl. The full mustache he sported dropped down below the corners of his lips and covered sun-kissed skin. She glided toward him.

Frank scowled. Her heart hiccupped before plunging to her stomach and forcing her feet to a halt.

Nellie, following close behind, bumped into her. "Is something wrong?"

"I-I don't know."

In Duncan Mackenzie's book, Frank Sorrell was a scoundrel of the lowest kind. How dare the man snub the lass? He wished he hadn't seen the pain that flickered across Miss Jackson's face, for it went straight to his heart. A woman as fine as Charlotte Jackson deserved much better than that *skellum*. As a spy for Scotland, Duncan prided himself on reading people—and Frank Sorrell was an open book.

The stringed quartet finished their first set as a young man claimed Charlotte's sister and the two headed off toward the veranda and away from the crowded room. Duncan grinned and proceeded toward Charlotte.

"'Tis guid to see you, Miss Jackson." He exaggerated his bow.

Miss Jackson glanced in the direction of Sorrell. "Hello, Mr. Mackenzie."

"Please tell me you've saved a dance for me." He gave her his most charming smile.

A rosy hue filled her cheeks. "Apparently I have."

Duncan grasped the card she held out to him and opened it. Not a single name was listed. He scrawled his name beside two of the waltzes, pleased to see the absence of Sorrell's name. The man's intimidation might have caused the younger bucks to steer clear of her, but it didn't bother him—no ring graced Miss Jackson's finger. And if one was going to be there, he might just make it his.

"Your sister seems to have disappeared."

Miss Jackson glanced toward the open terrace. "She went outside to get a breath of fresh air."

"I can stay with you while you await her return."

Her lips turned up, but disappointment painted her eyes. "It isn't necessary, sir."

"'Twould be an honor, and some say I'm even guid company." He smiled.

She shot another quick glance toward Sorrell. "You are kind."

"You look beautiful tonight."

Miss Jackson glanced down at the blue gown, her fingers skimming over the gathers. She peered in the direction of Sorrell again, then returned her attention to Duncan. Mischief sparkled in her eyes. She leaned toward him as if to conspire. "I had to sneak out of the house with it. Mama tells me it is time to hand it down to my sister."

Duncan chuckled. "'Twas a bonnie choice. The color becomes you." *Och*, this woman delighted him.

The dancers weaved in and out, playing their part in the reel. The younger Miss Jackson returned to her sister's side. Duncan excused himself, promising to return for his dances.

Spotting Tavis Dalzell standing near the refreshment tables, Duncan sauntered toward his good friend as the song ended. Sorrell stepped into his path, blocking his way.

"I'm sure you found the coquette's dance card empty. I haven't seen any *other* man approach her." Sorrell's shrill laugh grated on Duncan's nerves. "Charlotte's in love with me, you know," Sorrell continued. "She's probably pining away, waiting for me to sign my name beside all the sets."

The ladies that Sorrell left moments earlier stood only a few steps away, tittering. Sorrell glanced their way and smirked before returning his attention to Duncan. He lowered his voice. "When I catch a bigger fish, I'll be happy to throw Charlotte to you. You, being a ship merchant, understand, don't you, Scotty?" The man snickered.

Duncan flexed his hands into fists, fighting the urge to cause the man as much pain as he'd seen flicker across Miss Jackson's face earlier. Instead, he straightened to his full height and glowered. "You dinna deserve a lass as fine as Miss Jackson. And for future reference, my name is no' Scotty. You'd do well to remember that." He turned on his heel and strode away before his impulse to hurt the man overcame him.

Duncan had seen too many of Sorrell's crooked dealings in the months he'd been in the States to hold any respect for the man. Sorrell was an opportunist whose latest venture was an investment of substandard building equipment. Perhaps his scheme left him out of money and needing to marry a wealthy lass. Duncan ground his teeth. It would be the bonnie Miss Jackson over Duncan's dead body.

Releasing the tension in his balled-up fists, he continued over to Tavis as a plan shaped in his mind.

Tavis slapped him on the shoulder. "It's good to see you, Duncan."

"Weel, 'tis guid to see you." He'd known Tavis since they were boys, before they'd both ended up in the States. "I need a guid friend to keep me oot of trouble."

"Och! I'm good at that, as we both know. I kept us out of the woodshed as lads."

Duncan rubbed his hand along the side of his clean-shaven face. "'Tis no' the way I remember it. As I recall, you caused us a few lashings with sticks *from* that woodshed. My backside stings just thinking aboot it."

Tavis raised his blond brows. "Just toughening you up, ole friend."

"Aye. That it did." Duncan snatched a rose from an arrangement on a nearby table and breathed in its sweet scent before tucking it into his lapel. "I have a favor to ask of you. I'm on a mission to help a damsel in distress."

Tavis grinned. "I'm always willing to play the gallant hero. And who is the lucky lady?"

Duncan took in his *braw* friend, with his blond hair, broad shoulders, and startling blue eyes—a man who could garner any woman's attention. He shrugged. Tavis would never steal his woman.

"I'd like you to ask Miss Jackson for a couple of dances."

Tavis rubbed his chin thoughtfully, sweeping the room with his gaze. "Which Miss Jackson?"

Duncan's mind drifted. What was he thinking? *His woman?* He came to America for one reason, and that reason did not include Miss Jackson. His mission—find a murderer, a traitor to Britain, then return to his beloved Scotland with the traitor. He just wished to help the lass out, he reminded himself.

Tavis's attention on Miss Jackson surely would knock down Frank Sorrel's high opinion of himself. He chuckled and punched his old pal on the shoulder.

Tavis rubbed his shoulder and swept the room with his gaze. "Miss Nellie Jackson?"

Duncan glanced at Miss Charlotte. Medium ash blonde curls cascaded in waves about her face. How long would her hair be if not pulled up in back? Deep brown eyes heavy with thick lashes and distress made him wish he could bear her burden. Och! She was bonnie.

"Duncan!" Tavis's voice brought him from his reverie.

Duncan turned back to his friend. "Miss Charlotte Jackson."

"Isn't she Frank's lass?"

"Not for long."

"You know I'm always ready to help you out." Tavis gave him a rakish smile and headed in the lady's direction, not giving Duncan time to change his mind.

Suddenly he wasn't so sure that had been a good idea after all. Tavis stopped in front of Charlotte and started working his charm on her. A smile lit her lips. Duncan had to remind himself that he trusted his friend even if they had liked some of the same lasses growing up. He shook his head. What was wrong with him? He needed to focus on his mission, which was finding a traitor, not winning a lass.

Getting his mind off Tavis, he moved on to explore the rest of the room. He spotted a young lad nearly a foot shorter than himself. Before striding to him, he took in the man's measure and deduced he was shy and unsure of himself. He gave him a slap on the back. "What's your name, lad?"

The boy had barely sprouted whiskers on his chin. Looking up at Duncan's height, the boy's Adam's apple bobbed. "Ch-Charles. C-Cook."

"Charles Cook, I have a favor to ask of you. I'd like you to go sign your name on Miss *Charlotte* Jackson's dance card."

Young Charles shuffled his feet and glanced down. "I don't much care for dancing, sir. And if I did, I'm sure it wouldn't be with her. I value my life."

"You need no' fear Frank Sorrell." Realizing this wasn't going to be as easy as he thought, Duncan threw back his shoulders so the young lad would not want to tell him no.

"That would be e-easy for you to say, sir. No disrespect intended."

"None taken." Good thing he had brought some money. He reached inside his jacket and pulled out one dollar, not quite a day's wage. Easy enough money for a dance. "Maybe this will give you the courage."

The lad's chin wobbled before any words came out. "I don't think so. I won't live long enough to spen—"

Duncan pushed the bill in the lad's hand and nudged him forward. "Go on. I'll see Sorrell doesn't give you any problems."

Charles took several steps and stopped before glancing back over his shoulder. Duncan drew his brows down and crossed his arms in front of his six-foot-three frame. "Is the lass no' to your liking?"

"No, sir. I mean, yes, sir!"

"Guid. Then make that two dances and be sure you keep this to yourself." He disliked resorting to intimidation, but it had worked for Sorrell. And this *was* a greater cause. He'd free Miss Jackson of the scoundrel.

Charles swung back around and sped toward Miss Jackson.

Duncan hurried on to the next target. He patted the pocket that held the remaining bills and hoped all the young men didn't require as much persuasion. Perhaps some assurance that Sorrell wouldn't bother them would suffice. The lass was bonnie enough for most to risk the threat of trouble, although her intelligence and wit might have scared a few off.

Making his way around the room, he picked the young men he felt sure wouldn't catch the eye of Miss Jackson, all the while refusing to ask himself why it mattered. When he'd finished his mission, he leaned his shoulder against the wall, folded his arms, and grinned as the young men swarmed around her. Yes, this should definitely make ole Frankie Boy angry.

A twinge of guilt struck him, remembering the fear on several of the young men's faces when they'd realized they would make either him or Sorrell unhappy. One even opted to leave the ball. But Duncan reminded himself it was all for a good cause.

Chapter 2

"Frank acts as if I'm not even here. How could I have misunderstood his intentions?" Charlotte nearly wept on her sister's shoulder.

Nellie lifted the dance card that dangled on Charlotte's wrist and ran her finger down the sets, grinning. "Even so, the dress seems to have gained you plenty of attention."

Charlotte glanced down at the filled lines in disbelief. Since she walked in the door of the Barrows' home, she had tried to garner Frank's attention, but he had ignored her with the efficiency of a man avoiding a duel. Yet one eligible male after another had grabbed her card and scrawled his initials upon it. True, they were rather young, which was even more puzzling. Frank usually scared off the men wanting to dance with her. She wouldn't entertain the thought that his lack of reaction could mean he'd lost interest in her.

Charlotte started to sigh, but her corset, painfully tight to accommodate the gown, forbade a deep breath. She stuck out her lower lip instead just as the Scot returned to claim his first dance.

"Pigeon's going to roost." He flicked a forefinger at her protruding lip.

Despite her disappointment, the corners of Charlotte's mouth twitched with amusement as she fought a smile. The man thought himself funny. Her eyes shifted to where Frank stood talking with two women.

Mr. Mackenzie tipped his head toward the trio that had earned her attention. "Come, lass, let me take your mind off that trouble." Grasping her elbow, he guided her to the floor before she could utter a word of protest.

His large hand rested on her back with the gentlest of touches. Jade-green eyes gazed down into hers, and his lips tipped up in a self-assured smile. His square jaw was covered in the slightest hint of shadow. Her stomach did a quick flip. His smile grew. He took her right hand in his and twirled her around the room and away from Frank.

Frank disappeared into the crowd. She glared at Mr. Mackenzie. Every Sunday at church, he would intrude upon her and Frank just when they'd found privacy to talk. He had a knack at pulling them apart. She chalked it up to his being from Scotland and not educated in American propriety. And yet, when he approached her for a set, in his fitted black tailcoat, white waistcoat, and necktie, he appeared the perfect gentleman.

And oh, how that gentleman could dance. He glided across the floor as if there were air beneath his feet, and not so much as a falter in his step. This was no backward highlander. There was more to this Scotsman than she had thought. She glanced up at him to find him smiling and appearing to be enjoying himself as much as she.

No, no, no. She did not enjoy herself tonight, and she mustn't let this Scotsman take her mind off the fact that Frank had ignored her. She wouldn't allow herself to take pleasure in this dance even if Mr. Mackenzie did move fluidly and she seemed to fit right into his arms.

Her tall partner guided them around another couple as he bent his head near her ear. "Have you been enjoying yourself, lass?" His breath disturbed the fallen tendrils of hair, tickling her skin.

Charlotte fought the urge to tuck back the offending strand. Wasn't this just another of Mr. Mackenzie's interruptions? If she drank refreshments right now instead of dancing, perhaps Frank would have come over to her. "It's a beautiful ball. I know my sister and I would have been thrilled to have such an affair for our sixteenth birthdays."

"Ah, but you avoid my question."

He held her with such confidence, as if he had danced a thousand times before. *She must stop this.* He probably *had* held a thousand other women this way. "*You* seem to be having a fine time this evening."

"Aye, and it just got better." His eyes twinkled with amusement.

"I'm sure you say *that* to all the young ladies." Her words came out on a curt tone, and she winced inwardly.

Mr. Mackenzie chuckled.

As the song wound to a close, he pulled her closer. Charlotte gasped. What would people think of him holding her so close? But as the heat of his body began to infuse her clothing and the strength of his hand held her tight against him, she found herself strangely comforted. She wanted to lean into him, to enjoy this moment and close her eyes and pretend he cared about her. Charlotte shook herself from her daze. What would Frank think if he saw them dancing so close? The music ended, and she pushed away and glared.

"That, sir, was uncalled for."

Mr. Mackenzie tilted his head to the side. "And what would that be, lassie?"

Charlotte lifted her chin and thrust her balled hands on her hips. "You know perfectly well what I'm talking about. I'm not going to give you the satisfaction of saying it out loud."

His brows furrowed as he straightened and ran a hand through his umber hair. "I dinna ken what you are referring to, lass, but if I have offended you, it's sorry I am." He offered his arm to escort her off the floor.

Charlotte wanted to ignore it and walk away. As much as she disliked his tactics, she'd rise above the urge to return his rudeness. After all, the Bible did teach to turn the other cheek.

She wrapped her gloved hand around his arm and glanced at him out of the corner of her eye. He seemed truly perplexed. Perhaps the rules of how close a man could hold a woman weren't as strict in Scotland. She released a sigh. "No, it's I who am sorry. I must have misunderstood. It's just that I'm unaccustomed to being held like that."

A smile spread across Mr. Mackenzie's face. "Naught to be sorry for then. I thank you for the dance, Miss Jackson, and

I'll look forward to our next set." He winked at her. "And I'll try to behave more to your liking."

He returned Charlotte to her sister, gave a slight bow, and departed. Fiddling with her fan as she awaited her next dance partner, she couldn't keep herself from searching for Frank's whereabouts. Her breath caught as she glimpsed a sneer marring his handsome face. He shifted his gaze from her to the retreating back of Mr. Mackenzie.

What did Frank expect her to do? Wait around all evening for him like some desperate wallflower?"

"Nellie, do you think Papa might be changing his opinion of Frank?"

"Why do you ask such a random question?"

"It isn't random at all. Papa always allowed Frank to come calling and even invited him to dinner a few times in the eight months we've courted. But now, whenever Frank's name is mentioned, Papa scowls. Haven't you noticed that?"

Her sister raised her finger to her cheek and tapped it thoughtfully. "I cannot say that I have, Sis. Maybe they are too much alike. I've heard that can cause people not to like each other."

At the moment, Papa stood with his back to them in a small alcove off the main room. Charlotte sent up a quick prayer. *Lord, please help Papa to like Frank.*

She sniffed. "Frank is nothing like Papa. For all his faults, Frank allows me to make my own decisions."

Nellie let out a short giggle. "And when, pray tell, did the man ever do that? Papa makes the decisions for all of us."

"Well, he would allow me if we were married. Of that I'm certain."

"If Papa doesn't like him now, you can forget—"

"I don't want Papa picking my husband. He'd probably choose someone just like him—old-fashioned. Someone who believes the only place for a woman is in the home. And someone who believed that no respectable woman should hold a job."

"You are right there, Charlotte. Papa believes all those things."

"Times are changing. Maud Young is a botanist and author of the Texas's first botany textbook. And Lydia McPherson is a newspaper publisher and started the Whitesboro *Democrat*. Women are being hired for every job imaginable now."

"You don't have to convince me, Sis."

"If I could just marry Frank." If she did, she'd see to it that her sisters didn't have to follow her father's dictates. They could marry anyone or be anything they wanted. Surely, Frank had enough money to help them since Papa would never allow her to become interested in a man without means. Could that be why her father shunned him of late? These speculations were all nonsense. Borrowing trouble, as her mother would say.

As the evening progressed, Charlotte's dance partners claimed their sets, one after another. She barely returned to her spot next to Nellie before another dragged her back to the floor. So, when one gentleman failed to come for her, she took great pleasure in the chance to relax.

She sucked her stomach in to gain a little relief. "Sweet mercy, I'm miserable. My feet ache, and I can hardly breathe."

Nellie rolled her eyes. "You don't suppose it's because your gown is too tight? Mama did tell you to give me that dress."

With a flip of her wrist, Charlotte opened her fan and waved it before her, sending cool air over her face. "Be nice to me or I won't introduce you to Frank's cousin when he gets here."

Nellie giggled. "Oh, Charlotte, you wouldn't be so mean. I was only teasing."

Charlotte pressed her lips tightly together until the urge to smile passed. "You'll have to behave yourself. I'm sure all the girls will be anxious to meet a war hero."

Nellie sighed.

Charlotte snapped her fan together. "He's too old for you anyway."

"He's only a little older than Frank, and you're in love with *him*."

"A little. He's four years older, and I am almost nineteen."

"Well, I'll be eighteen in seven months. Besides, what are a few years when it comes to love?"

Charlotte burst out laughing. "Love? You haven't even met Mr. Sumpter."

"I have too."

"You were barely walking."

Nellie shrugged. "I love everything I've heard about him." Her voice exuded the confidence of a smitten young woman. "He's tall, blond, handsome, kind, and brave. How noble of him to have joined the war at only fourteen years old. What else could one want in a husband?"

"You know some tease him that he joined the war just in time to get wounded and the war to end."

"Well, it isn't nice to tease a hero."

Charlotte shook her head. "Gracious, Nellie, you talk like you already have the man's promise of marriage. The man nears thirty. Don't get ahead of God."

"Me? You're the one who thought Frank was going to propose tonight. Don't you think he would ask Papa first?" Nellie looked down and brushed her hands over the front of her pristine gown as if smoothing wrinkles.

"I'm sure Frank feels he's too old to have to ask Papa's permission."

"Frank may be old enough, but I'm sure Papa would say you are not, and if he thinks he can propose to you without speaking to Papa first, he is not the man for you." Nellie gave a sharp nod of her head for emphasis.

"You sound like Mama. Besides, who's to say Frank hasn't spoken with him?"

"Because Papa would have come to you and asked your feelings on it."

Mary Barrow, the sixteen-year-old birthday girl, strolled up beside Nellie, interrupting their conversation. "Are you enjoying yourselves?"

Charlotte smiled. "It's a lovely party. Thank you for inviting us."

Nellie took Mary's hand. "Oh yes. We're having a grand time. I'd have been in heaven to have such a party. The decorations are beautiful."

Mary's eyes twinkled. "Thank you. Mama and I have been planning this for weeks."

Charlotte glanced behind her at the furniture lining the wall to make space for the dancers. An empty chair called her name. If it wasn't for the hope of talking with Frank she'd like to go home.

As if her thoughts made him materialize, Frank's black hair caught her attention. Ignoring her aching feet, she excused herself from the two ladies and set in his direction. Now was as good a time as any to learn why he'd avoided her all evening. The crowd shifted, and she lost sight of him. Determined to speak with him, she worked her way toward the spot she had last seen him. Her line of vision swallowed by more people, she pushed through the throng, hoping to close the distance, hoping he was still there.

Breaking through the crowd, she saw him—with June Wagner, the wealthiest belle at the ball.

June's face turned scarlet as she glared at Frank. "Mr. Sorrell, I wouldn't permit you to call on me if you were the last man on earth."

Chapter 3

Duncan searched for Miss Jackson. The protectiveness the woman caused in him was a wee bit troubling. His mind needed to stay focused on his mission for the Crown, not a bonnie lass. While they were dancing, he'd caught sight of Sorrell and, with a sudden desire to protect her, pulled her tight. And irritation had grown within him as he'd watched her dance with partner after partner. A battle raged inside. He set the plan in motion for her to dance with all these men. The plan had worked as he had hoped. Sorrell was angry and didn't get so much as one dance with the lass—so why did his gut twist?

Unable to get the lass off his mind, Duncan shoved his hands in his pockets as he assessed the room. His traitor could be here, dancing, drinking refreshments, or playing cards. His eyes fell on Sorrell speaking to Miss Wagner. Duncan recognized her as one of the man's earlier prey. She didn't appear to be taken with him. She looked more like she wished to flee at the first chance. Duncan chuckled.

A flash of familiar blue taffeta moved into Duncan's peripheral vision as Miss Jackson approached Sorrell. Duncan scowled and made his way to intervene. Why couldn't she leave the man alone? It was hard to believe she didn't see past Sorrell and his lies.

Och! He couldn't stand the thought of her getting hurt again. He grumbled to himself as he stalked toward her. If the lass could just follow his plans.

What was wrong with him? He came here because of Queen Victoria. Not Miss Charlotte Bay Jackson.

When the queen had summoned him for this mission, requesting he find this turncoat, Duncan couldn't say no. Not because she was the queen or a friend of his mother's, if one could call a queen friend, but he did it for his brother. So his death on that battlefield would not be wasted. He loved his country and would die for it, but he loved his brother more. And for brother and country he would do whatever required of him. Owning merchant ships gave him cover for his mission and an introduction into Charleston society.

Duncan sped up his step, his mind still ruminating on a course of action. Should he intercept Miss Jackson and increase the risk of raising her ire, or should he rescue her along with Miss Wagner by taking Sorrell away? Before he had to make his decision, Miss Jackson and Miss Wagner made it for him. Duncan had caught Miss Wagner's parting words to the man and, by Miss Jackson's reaction—she flinched and turned away, he guessed she had, too.

Duncan continued on to Sorrell. He might as well keep the man occupied. If Sorrell ran out of bigger fish, he may decide to look up Miss Jackson again.

"How aboot we head to the men's lounge, Sorrell?"

Sorrell glared at the retreating back of Miss Wagner. He spun on his heels and continued walking past Duncan. "Yes, let's hit the tables."

Duncan smiled. Catching Charlotte's gaze as he turned, he gave her what he hoped was a sympathetic look before making his way out of the great hall and lengthening his stride to catch up with Sorrell.

"You look a mite bit annoyed. Something bothering you?"

Sorrell seemed to be measuring his sincerity, so Duncan slapped him on the back in an assuring gesture.

"Nothing that a stiff drink and a good hand won't cure."

Duncan squeezed Sorrell's shoulder. "Lassie problems, eh?"

Sorrell snorted. "The little coquette is hardly worth my concern."

Duncan dropped his hand off Sorrell's shoulder and drew in a deep breath. "The lass has a name."

Sorrell turned his head toward Duncan and tripped. He lurched forward, sprawling spread-eagle over the marble tile.

What had caused Sorrell to go plunging to the floor Duncan didn't know but determined God must have a sense of humor.

He bent down and gave Sorrell his hand, attempting a look of concern while he swallowed down amusement. "Perhaps you should avoid that stiff drink." Duncan pulled the man to his feet. "Let me help you brush off."

Sorrell jerked his hand away as soon as he had his balance. "Keep your hands off me, *Scot.*"

Duncan raised his right brow in a slow, calculated manner. "You say that as if it were an insult." Most people found his Scottish birthright intriguing. He clenched his back teeth, not wanting a fray, but too proud to let the slight pass. "Much of this part of your country was settled by Scotsmen. Maybe even your kin."

Sorrell gave him a quick onceover. "Meant nothing by it. Just forgot your name."

"'Tis Duncan. Duncan Mackenzie. The same man who speaks with you every Sunday."

Sorrell laughed. "All right then, Mackenzie. Let's get to the tables so I can relieve you of your cash.

"How aboot we sit and talk?"

Sorrell sneered. "No backbone, huh?"

Duncan wasn't fond of playing cards. That was a good way to lose hard-earned money. "Why dinna we take a stroll outside?"

He'd really only wanted to get Sorrell away from Miss Jackson. He hadn't wanted to spend the evening with him, but he'd do what he needed to accomplish his goal.

"Thanks, but I think I'll pass." Sorrell turned into the parlor where a table and a few chairs were set up for men in need of a diversion. Duncan assumed the limited number of seats were to keep too many men from escaping the ball. It would defeat the ladies' purpose if all the men huddled in the parlor waiting for the ball to end.

With nowhere else to go, Duncan sauntered back into the ballroom. Leaning his shoulder against the archway, he observed one young man after another dancing with Charlotte as the evening wore on. It hadn't ended up costing him too much money. Most of the men he approached only wanted assurance that Frank Sorrell wouldn't take it out of their hide afterward. That was easy enough to do.

Another song ended and, as she had every other time, Charlotte seemed to search for someone in the crush of people. Duncan knew who that someone was.

"E-excuse me." Charles Cook stood beside him.

Duncan turned his attention away from Miss Jackson. "Yes?"

Charles held up his dollar. "I'm returning this."

Duncan's brows shot up. "Why? I thought I saw you dance with her."

"I-I did. But with all the men dancing with her tonight, I'm the least of Frank Sorrell's problems. Besides, I've never danced with someone so beautiful. I wouldn't want it said I had to be paid to do it."

Duncan grinned. He liked this lad. He folded the bill and tucked it in his pocket as another set got claimed on Miss Jackson's card. Duncan pushed off the wall, tired of wishing he danced with the lass instead of watching all these young bucks do so.

He strolled on back, passing where he'd left Sorrell. He hadn't seen even a glimpse of him in the past hour. Not that he had missed him.

Sorrell's slurred words blasted into the hall. Duncan stopped, backed up, and glanced in the parlor to find Sorrell still there. He eyed him from the doorway. The man was loud and obnoxious.

Sorrell stuck his hands in his pockets and pulled them out. "I'm outa casssh. Where's Sssharlotte." He shoved back, and his chair tumbled over with him in it.

The men sitting at the table with him roared with laughter but didn't move to help. Duncan sighed. He'd like to leave him lying on the floor, too, but more than that, he wanted him home and away from Miss Jackson.

He sauntered in and gave Sorrell his hand to pull him up. He slipped Sorrell's arm around his shoulders to steady the incapacitated man as he made his way from the room. With every part of his being, Duncan wanted to walk away. He didn't like him and had a hard time pretending he did. But the sooner he got him out of this place, the better off everyone would be. Maybe with Frankie Boy gone, the lass would stop looking for him. "I think it's time you go home and sleep this off."

"Youtookallmymoney." Sorrell's words were hard to understand.

Such a fool to be drinking *and* gambling. "You're lucky you only lost your pocket change." Duncan looked up and locked eyes with a seething Miss Jackson. She glared at him from the hall. Duncan stepped out of the room, and Sorrell leaned heavily on him.

She crossed her arms, her glare burning through him. "How dare you get him drunk so you can steal his money?"

"Lassie, I could no' force him to overindulge any more than I could make my horse drink water. If you will excuse me, I need to get him to his carriage and on home."

Sorrell lifted his drooping head. "Home? I'm not goin' home." He smiled at Miss Jackson. "I haven't gotten my dansss with her yet. Are you ready to dansss, my dear?"

Duncan wanted to let go of him and let him fall on his face in front of the lass. But even that probably wouldn't convince the drunkard he was in no shape to dance. "I believe Miss Jackson's card is full."

Sorrell lifted his wobbly head. "Isss that true? You didn't sssave me a dansss?"

The lass shuddered and stepped back, bringing her open fan to her nose. "I'm afraid you are in no condition." She turned to Duncan and narrowed her eyes to slits. "And shame on you, taking advantage of him. Why, as long as I have known Frank, I've never seen him in such a state."

Duncan stared at the lass. Did she believe what she said? He opened his mouth to ask her just that, but decided better of it and snapped it shut.

"If you will excuse me, lass? I need to see my friend oot." He moved around her and headed for the door.

"You haven't seen the last of me, Mr. Mackenzie." The lass raised her voice as he exited the door.

Duncan admired her devotion, misguided though it was. He couldn't help himself when he mimicked her. "You haven't seen the last of me, Mr. Mackenzie." He chuckled. No, it wouldn't be the last time he saw her. It had to be getting close to his second dance, and he didn't plan on missing it.

Chapter 4

As Mr. Mackenzie audaciously repeated her words, Charlotte fumed, while her glare followed the two men out the door. The nerve of the man. With a staggering Frank leaning heavily on him, the arrogant Mr. Mackenzie attempted to get them both out the door. They were two peas in a pod, as the old saying went—both disappointments.

And how could Frank have done this to her? He'd made her believe this evening would be special—that he would ask for her hand. Then he'd spent the entire night playing cards and getting intoxicated. She'd suffered the entire evening squeezed into this blue dress just for him because he liked her in this color. Why, she could barely breathe. Nellie had to pull the corset so tight, she thought surely the laces would snap. And all because Frank had bidden her to wear it.

A dress that he never even noticed after he'd made the request. She sniffed and looked down at her hand, imagining what the engagement ring would look like on her finger—the ring she'd hoped he'd give her. At least her torment in this dress hadn't been wasted. The young men had appreciated the trouble she'd gone to enough to stand in line waiting for a dance. Something that hadn't happened to her since Frank began to court her.

Too bad the gown was so painful. It truly must look good on her. Charlotte sighed. Her mother would never change her mind about passing it to Nellie.

She came around the corner in time to see Mr. Sumpter, Frank's cousin, and a hero of the War Between the States, step into the hall.

Charlotte rushed to him. "Mr. Sumpter. You came."

He grinned. "I had some business that kept me. But I didn't want to miss seeing the prettiest belle in town. Frank had better be careful, or I'll be vying for your attentions."

"I think he may have left." Charlotte looped her arm in his. "By the bye, my sister has pestered me to death wanting to meet you."

Mr. Sumpter smiled. "If she's anything like you, I look forward to it."

His words pleased her—especially after Frank's rejection. Mr. Sumpter kept the pace slow, which helped conceal his hero's limp.

"I wish I'd thought to save you a spot on my dance card, but rest assured Nellie has saved you a dance." Truth was her sister had saved her last two.

Mr. Sumpter chuckled. "Someone must have built me up bigger than life. I hope I don't disappoint."

"No, I would say she has a fairly good assessment of you. You are a man to be admired."

A ruddy hue rushed to Mr. Sumpter's cheeks, and Charlotte took pity on him. "Perhaps I can scratch the last name off my card and put you in. I believe he has left as well."

And good riddance to Mr. Mackenzie, as far as she was concerned.

Mr. Sumpter raised his brow as he cocked his head. "Frank has allowed you to fill your dance card? At the last ball, if I remember correctly, he had every buck intimidated so much that I became the only other man permitted to dance with you."

"He seemed to have other things on his mind tonight. So tell me, how long will you be staying in our lovely city?"

"Haven't really decided yet, but with such a beautiful lady holding me in such high esteem, I'd be a fool to leave." He winked at her. "Unless of course you play with my heart when you tell me of your sister."

"Why, Mr. Sumpter with a hero's heart. But you haven't seen my sister since she was knee high to a mosquito. Can you be sure she is still as lovely as when she was a child?"

"I have but to look at her sister and know."

"Ah. Now you flatter me."

Mr. Sumpter grinned and placed his hand over hers, resting on his sleeve. "Where is Thomas these days?"

"My brother is in Virginia trying to win the hand of a woman who has stolen his heart."

Mr. Sumpter burst out laughing. "He's going down without a fight, eh?"

"I'm afraid so."

Inside the ballroom the musicians left the flower-bedecked refreshment tables and returned to their instruments. Servants busied themselves behind the table serving punch to thirsty guests.

Charlotte let her gaze drift around the room until she spotted her sister in her lime-green gown. "There's Nellie." Charlotte waved, and Nellie rushed toward them. "See how anxious she is to meet you? Now tell me you're sorry for suggesting such a thing as me exaggerating."

Mr. Sumpter stopped and turned to face Charlotte. He clutched his chest playfully. "My dearest Miss Jackson, please forgive me for being presumptive."

"You are forgiven, sir." She curtsied. "Now behave so I can present my sister to you."

Nellie stopped abruptly in front of them, eyes sparkling and lips turned up in a grin. Charlotte tried not to smile at her sister's enthusiasm. If Mama had seen her practically running across the floor, she'd accuse Charlotte of teaching Nellie bad manners. "May I introduce you to my sister, Miss Nellie Jackson."

He gave a slight bow. "It's a pleasure to meet you, Miss Jackson."

"Nellie, this is—"

"I know who this is. I'm so happy you could make it." Nellie clasped her hands together in front of her and gazed up at him. Quickly realizing her mistake, offered him her hand.

The music began. A young man bore down on Charlotte—her next partner. She grinned at Nellie. "I was telling Mr. Sumpter that you may have saved a dance for him."

Nellie looked down at the floor, her face coloring. "I believe I have one or two open."

Kindness filled Mr. Sumpter's eyes. "I'd be honored to pen my name on one. I may not be as smooth as some, but I still enjoy dancing with a beautiful woman."

"Excuse me, Miss Charlotte," Charlie interrupted.

Charlotte laid her hand on Mr. Sumpter's sleeve. "I'll leave you in the capable hands of my sister."

While the band played a quadrille, Charlie led her to the floor for their second dance. Mr. Sumpter and Nellie followed. As the couples moved forward, Charlotte glanced at her sister. Her smile warmed Charlotte's heart. She needn't feel coming to the ball a waste of time after all, even if Frank had disappointed her.

Charlotte joined hands with her dance partner and Nellie, and the foursome turned like spokes on a wagon wheel. One more dance and she would be on her way home. Realizing that last dance was the very one she'd offered to Mr. Sumpter and the second dance her sister had kept open on her card, Charlotte determined to beg off, claiming exhaustion.

The music ended and the musicians set down their instruments for one last break before the final song. Charlotte gave a slight curtsey to her partner before he escorted her off the floor. Offering to fetch a glass of lemonade, he disappeared into the crowd, giving her a chance to catch her breath and decide how to tell Mr. Sumpter she couldn't dance the last dance.

The subject of her thoughts came into view. Mr. Sumpter and Nellie strolled around the room, laughing. If Nellie had thought she was in love before, there would be no help for her now. The stories her sister had heard about Mr. Sumpter had her practically swooning at his feet before she even met him. Now that she had, goodness. Charlotte would never hear the end of it.

Someone tapped her on the shoulder. She whirled around expecting Charlie but finding Duncan before her, refreshment in hand.

"Your lemonade." He handed her the glass.

Drat. She'd hoped he'd gone home. "Thank you, Mr. Mackenzie." Charlotte took a sip of her drink to avoid smiling at him.

"You look a wee bit tired."

The lemonade suddenly soured on her stomach, and she placed the glass on the tray of a passing servant.

Though she'd just noted that very thing, annoyance prickled over her at his saying so. "I'm quite fine, sir."

A few minutes later the musicians returned. Duncan placed his hand on her upper back and grinned. "I believe this one belongs to me."

Her mind jumped to his inappropriate embrace earlier, and she tensed. He guided her to the floor and the dance began. That he'd chosen a waltz twice sent more prickles down her skin. But as they moved around the room, his kindness nudged away the burrs and turned them to downy thistle.

Why couldn't this be Frank? She released a heavy sigh. As if her sigh were a cue, Duncan's hand caressed her back. She nearly swallowed her tongue before stilling the shiver that wanted to shimmy through her body. This pleasure she felt was wrong. She loved Frank.

Frank, Frank, Frank. She must remember why she needed him and not Mr. Mackenzie. Although Mr. Mackenzie had the requisite wealth, he was not what she required to save her sisters from her father's will. Frank knew her sisters. Surely that would make him more apt to help them fulfill their dreams.

"You seem lost in thought, lass. You dinna still blame me for Frank's behavior, do you? I just happened by and helped him."

With some effort, Charlotte managed to smile. "You wouldn't be feeling guilty, would you, Mr. Mackenzie?"

Duncan raised his thick brows. "Guilty?" He laughed, then lowered his lips to her ear. "Aw, lassie, there are many things I may feel guilty aboot, but Frank Sorrell being a drunk is no' one of them."

Charlotte sucked in her breath and swung her head to look him in the eyes. "Fra—Mr. Sorrell is not a drunk. Something...perhaps your stealing all his money, caused him to overindulge this evening."

"Nay. I wasn't with *your* Frank. But I can assure you a mon chooses his own destiny. No one can make him do what he does no' want to."

She wanted to be mad at him for his remarks about Frank, but she couldn't find the anger, knowing his words were truth. She looked away as they glided around other couples. This evening had left her with one disappointment after another.

The music ended, and the couples lingered on the floor talking. Charlotte stepped back as Duncan loosened his hold.

"Thank you for the dance." She curtsied and hurried away in search of Nellie and her parents, whom she found waiting near the door.

On the short ride home, Nellie entertained them with chatter about Mr. Sumpter. While her sister's hopes soared, Charlotte's plummeted. Home was the only place she wanted to be right now. Where she could crawl beneath her covers and forget this evening.

Nothing had gone as she'd thought or hoped it would. The evening had ended without a chance for Frank and her to talk. What had provoked him to request she wear this dress if he wasn't going to bother to dance with her? She'd thought he'd had something special planned. Ha! He probably wanted to see if she would do as he requested. Well, she was no man's fool. She might do it once, but never twice.

The carriage headed down Meeting Street to Broad before finally turning onto Church Street and slowing to a stop in front of her family's two-story home. Built shortly after the war, the home sported four large pillars that ran from ground to roof, broken by an upstairs balcony that extended the length of the front. A wide set of steps went to the second floor and the entrance door. Candlelight filtered from the six-foot windows like a friendly beacon welcoming her home. The driver jumped down and stood by ready to assist. Charlotte slid from the seat and stepped from the carriage. Hurrying toward the many steps and the entrance, she fought back tears that seemed to come from nowhere and pricked the backs of her eyes, begging to fall. She looked down, pretending to brush something off her gown as she scurried past the servant holding the open door, all the while hoping no one would see her glassy eyes. Servant gossip was the last thing she wanted.

Instead of going down to her room and her soft bed on the first level, where Nellie headed, she stayed on the main floor, the study her destination. Picking up the silver candle holder from the hallway table, she entered the room and pulled the door closed behind her. The windows were open, allowing a faint breeze to waft through the room. She placed the lit candle on the desk. Exhausted, she dropped onto the sofa and lay down, her stiff stays digging into her sides.

What a dreadful evening. Memories of Frank's aloofness brought a knot to the pit of her stomach. She released the tears she'd kept pent-up since his rejection. What did she see in a man who could so easily brush her aside as if she were nothing more than a pesky debutante? Up until this evening, he'd showered her with the attentions of a man in love.

Frank's dark brown eyes, his best feature, burned in her memory. He was a handsome man. Unfortunately, he knew it—such a shame he didn't know a little humility along with it.

She sniffed. Funny how she'd never noticed those things before. It would do her well to think of all his unbecoming traits along with his behavior tonight. He'd never ignored her before. Then again, she'd never seen Frank when he was around Mr. Mackenzie, either, other than church. The man obviously had a bad influence on Frank.

Her eyes grew heavy. She'd rest them for a moment, then go down to her room. Perchance things would look better in the morning. The lightheadedness that comes as sleep overtakes crept in along with the vision of one very handsome man—Duncan Mackenzie.

She woke with a start. Lifting her head, she forced away the fog. Was that a man's voice? She tipped her head toward the window. The slurred words from an angry Frank Sorrell poured in through the open window. She pushed to her feet. The candle had burned down to a nub, shedding a small amount of light into the room.

Carefully, she crept over to the large open window and peered out. The full moon gave sufficient light for her to see Frank stooped over, fighting to keep his balance as he lost the contents of his stomach on her front lawn. She turned away in disgust but not before she saw a shudder wrack his body. He didn't look like the man of her dreams now.

"Psst...Frank. What are you doing here? Why aren't you at home sleeping this off?" She leaned out the upstairs window and struggled to keep her voice low and still have it reach Frank's ears.

He staggered over and raised his gaze to the window she leaned from. "Sssharlotte, come out here. I wanna talk to you." His words slurred together, and his body wavered as he stood with feet planted apart on the grass.

"You're drunk. Go home before you wake my family and the servants."

"No." He sounded like a spoiled child. He tripped. With what seemed to be great effort, he remained on his feet and tottered forward. "I'm not leavin' until you come down."

Charlotte closed her eyes and drew in a deep breath. "I don't wish to see you like this, Frank. Go home."

"I sssaw you wasshing me tonight, Sssharlotte. You want me as musssh as I want you."

He took several unsteady strides toward the house. "If you don't come down here, I'll come up there."

Charlotte took a step back. "You would disgrace me?" Her voice came out strangled. "Drunk or not, I would expect more from you, Frank Sorrell."

"As would I."

At the booming voice of her father, Charlotte spun around to face his fury.

Chapter 5

Charlotte's heart leaped in her chest with the same urgency as a frog trying to escape her little brother's pail. Papa fairly steamed with anger. Heat scorched her from his smoldering eyes and fuming breath.

"Papa, I…I, it isn't as it appears. I fell asleep on the sofa and woke to—"

Papa moved to stand in front of her. "I am well aware of what has transpired, as is the whole household."

Charlotte wilted under her father's disapproval. If he heard the whole of it, then why did he sound angry with her?

"I pray the neighbors haven't heard, too. This spectacle could lose us our good standing. And that could have my customers finding another bank for their business."

Tears pricked the back of her eyes. Why should Papa's words surprise or hurt? His business always came first.

Papa moved around Charlotte and over to the window. "Frank Sorrell, I suggest you find your way back home. If not, I'll come down and give you a personal escort to the police station where you can sleep this off."

He closed the windows and turned around. "Young lady, get to your room."

"But, Papa, I had no idea Frank would come by here tonight. I fell asleep on the sofa and woke to his voice."

"Charlotte Bay Jackson, it doesn't matter what you know as the truth or what I believe happened. What matters is only what others think." Her father strode to the door and waited.

Chastised and burning with indignation, Charlotte understood the silent command to follow him. She turned from the room and sailed down the hall toward the stairs, her stays still digging into her sides, reminding her she hadn't intended to fall asleep.

She glanced over her shoulder to see her father heading off in the other direction. She slowed her pace. A heavy sigh deflated her. Papa would never approve of Frank now.

♥♥♥

Did she even know this man? Charlotte left the breakfast room with the same thing on her mind that she woke with—Frank. After going to her room, she'd spent a good part of the night in prayer. His lack of character had stunned her. It pained her to admit it, but he wasn't the man she had believed him to be. She'd thought him all that was good and honorable. There was no way she could love someone who willingly dishonored her, whether from drink or not.

A shiver ran through her as she realized how thankful she should be that she saw who he *really* was before she married him—if he'd ever gotten around to proposing.

She passed her father's study. He sat behind his dark walnut desk, its top glistening from excess polish. Immaculate, only a fountain pen, paper, and oil lamp adorning it.

"Charlotte!" Her father's voice roared into the hall.

Her feet stuck to the floor. She turned around and peeked into the room. "Sir?"

"Come in here and take a seat." He tapped a pen held between his two fingers on the desktop as he waited. "Close the door behind you."

Charlotte tugged on the knob, and the door banged shut. She winced. "Sorry, Papa." She padded to the chair opposite him and sat. Lifting her gaze to his, she swallowed, trying to moisten her suddenly dry throat.

Her father took off his glasses and began twirling them between his thumb and finger. "Charlotte, I've given this a lot of thought. What happened last night cannot happen again. It could ruin us. I'll not have your mother and sisters living in disgrace because of your infatuation with a man. You are forbidden to see Frank Sorrell again."

Charlotte gasped. "You cannot mean that."

"I can, and I do."

"How can you hold one indiscretion against him? It isn't fair. I love him." As the words left her lips, she doubted the truth of them.

"You might as well learn now, Charlotte, that there are many things in life that are not fair. This fascination with Frank will pass, and someone new will take his place. And let us hope that you will choose more wisely next time."

Something inside her rose up. It didn't matter that she was coming to the same conclusion—Frank was not the man for her. She gritted her teeth at her father's belittling suggestion that she make a better choice. She wouldn't let him know that Frank's action had her thinking along the same line. It was wrong, she knew it, but it didn't matter. She wouldn't acquiesce now.

She drew in a deep breath, knowing that this type of behavior was part of what her mother loathed. "I love him. I can't walk away because of one small mistake. Doesn't the Bible tell us not to judge but to forgive?"

Her father's brows drew down, leaving deep wrinkles between them. "Don't be foolish. Think about your sisters. Your mother."

"What about *my* happiness? Doesn't that matter?"

"You'd never be happy with Frank Sorrell."

Secretly, she agreed. Why couldn't she admit it? It'd make things easier. But her father's words stung and made her want to retaliate even if she didn't want Frank anymore. "May I be excused Papa? I must finish readying myself for church."

He put his glasses back on and looked down at the newspaper. "Think about your family. Could you live with yourself if society shunned them? If we were reduced to poverty because of your poor judgment or if your sisters couldn't find good matches? I strongly advise you not to be a foolish girl. I would hate to send you away, Charlotte, but if you force my hand, I will." He lifted his head, and his gaze burned into her. With a quick raise of his hand and a flick of the wrist, he dismissed her from the room.

Charlotte took her leave, gliding out of the room and down the hallway. She should have told him, put his mind to ease that she agreed with him, but she couldn't make the words leave her tongue. She wasn't blind to Frank's character any longer. Somehow she had known deep within that he would never make her happy, but she was willing to accept that if it would help her sisters. But with each prayer she had prayed last night, God impressed upon her that she wasn't to be yoked with Frank Sorrell. She supposed she deserved Papa's threat, but she found it still hurt. She hadn't been a bad daughter, just a little more headstrong than most. Surely some man would find that appealing.

♥♥♥

She intrigued him. Duncan stared at the flames dancing from log to log in the fireplace. Stretching his legs before him, he leaned back in his chair and let the previous night run through his mind. Miss Charlotte Jackson was a bonnie lass. She'd first caught his eye at church. The lass sat prim and proper—engrossed in every word the preacher spoke. Sunday after Sunday, she would sit in rapt attention as if drinking in every word. How could anyone enjoy going to church and listening to the pastor drone on about something that happened thousands of years ago? He certainly wouldn't be there if he didn't need to establish himself in the local community.

But it was important that he become part of them, made them think he was fulfilling a dream and gain their trust. After all, the turncoat was here in Charleston. He could feel it in his bones, beside the fact that all the information he'd received pointed to the same conclusion. Whoever the man was, he needed to feel at ease when Duncan showed up.

He'd do whatever it took, including sitting through a lengthy church service every week, if it meant finding the turncoat who led a thousand men to their deaths, including his brother, who had served as an officer in the campaign. Duncan was one of the best at what he did—finding a traitor. He hadn't been surprised when Queen Victoria had summoned him. His reputation for espionage had earned him commissions from the

Crown before, but this time his brother's death was his driving force. He was not so naïve that he didn't realize the queen knew that as well.

Would things have turned out differently if Britain had partitioned Afghanistan off among multiple rulers, as some in Parliament had urged? Or what if they had placed Ayub Khan on the throne instead of his cousin Abdur Rahman Khan? Would Ayub have revolted as Abdur did at Miawand? And would his brother still be alive?

The longcase clock announced the passage of time and shook Duncan from his thoughts. He rose from the chair, wanting to get to the church early so he could offer Miss Jackson a ride home. After last night, it was obvious the lass wasn't smitten with him. He had some work on his hands if he wanted to win her over. Money and possessions would not persuade her into marriage, not if she fancied herself marrying ole Frankie Boy. Duncan heaved a sigh. Miss Jackson was not his mission, and he must be careful not to allow her to cloud his vision as to why he was here.

Duncan opened the door and gave a yell. "Stuebing."

The valet appeared in the room. Duncan shook his head. It was nothing short of amazing the way Stuebing always seemed to be within a few feet when he needed him.

"Help me get my coat on. I am off to impress a lass."

Stuebing stood a good ten inches shorter than Duncan. His silver hair had receded, and he combed it back, emphasizing his balding pate. Coffee-colored eyes ringed with blue stared up at him.

Duncan grinned. "'Tis glad I am you followed me halfway around the world."

Stuebing pulled the coat over Duncan's shoulders. "You pay well, sir."

"I would have paid you more if you were a Scot instead of a Sassenach." Duncan turned to face his valet, pulling the coat together in the front.

Stuebing raised his eyebrows.

"It was a joke, Stuebing."

The corners of his valet's lips quivered in an attempt at a smile. "Ah, yes. Very funny, sir."

Duncan chuckled. As Stuebing braced himself to keep from vaulting forward, Duncan slapped him on the back.

"I shall attempt to enchant the lass with my charm and your superior ministrations to my appearance. Though we need to work on your sense of humor."

His valet remained silent as he stood back and eyed Duncan up and down. With a nod of his head, he gave Duncan his approval.

Duncan strode out of his chamber and ran his hand along the painted wall. He'd be a wee bit sorry to leave this place and its luxuries when it was time to return to Scotland.

America, he had to admit, had its own beauty, but his homeland held his heart. A heart that was no closer to his adversary than the day he arrived. He could be here for years. One thing was sure. He would find the man he came for, or he would not return home. He shook off the thought. He *always* got his man, and this time would be no different.

Detouring through the kitchen, he picked up an apple, tossed it in the air, caught it, and stuck it in his pocket as he continued out the door.

Once outside, he headed for the stables and Aberdeen, his unruly stallion. He brought an apple for him, as he did every day, to calm the horse's skittish behavior. The coal black color fit the stallion's mood most of the time. Duncan approached the small fenced area and broke the apple apart with his hands. Aberdeen pawed the ground with his hoof and bobbed his head up and down.

"You are no' so fierce an animal. Now come get your apple." Duncan held his hand over the wooden fence.

Aberdeen moved forward. Duncan held his ground by the fence while his horse took the apple from his hand. He chewed the fruit, never taking his eyes off his new owner.

Duncan reached up and scratched behind the horse's ear. "You and I need to come to an understanding. You want to get oot and feel the wind through your mane as you gallop along the river's edge. I need a guid swift horse to get me where I need to go. Now we can work together, or you can stay cooped up in this pen, and I will continue to take my carriage."

He leaned up against the wooden rail and took a bite of the other half of the apple, then held it out until Aberdeen's mouth wrapped around the red skin and pulled the juicy fruit from his hand. Duncan gave the horse's nose a quick pat and swiveled to meet the approaching curricle. The footman turned the reins over to Duncan, then took his place on the back of the vehicle.

Duncan had never bothered to employ footmen, but 'twas the only way to get what he wanted.

He drove the team of two along the dirt road, glancing down at the fine gray dirt settling on his clothes. He gave little notice to the passing countryside until the church steeple came into view. There he slowed the rig, and as he neared the small building, he began dusting the road dirt off his coat.

He perused the families who stood outside visiting in the warm October sunshine. He took notice of each person, looking for any newcomers and noting with whom each person spoke. His traitor would try to fit in to society.

No one had yet parked under the tall oak tree, so Duncan pulled in and steered his horses around to its shade. He tied the reins to the bar and jumped down while his footman snatched up the lead rope and tied it to the tree.

Duncan's long legs brought him across the churchyard to where Tavis swung off his mount. In this land where every other person seemed suspicious of him, he could always count on his friend. "You disappeared on me at the ball last night. You danced with Miss Jackson, and that's the last I saw of you."

Tavis's one hand rested on the horn of the saddle. "Sorry about that. Something came up, and I had to leave. You seemed to have survived. Did any of the mamas foist their wallflowers on you?" He pulled the reins to the front of the horse and tied him to a fence post.

Duncan couldn't keep from grinning. "Nay. I spent most of my time keeping Sorrell away from a certain lass I have my sights on."

"Is she aware of your intentions?"

"Nay. But neither was I until last night."

Tavis stared at the approaching carriage containing the Jackson family. "She is bonnie, but I understand a bit bookish and possesses rather unconventional ideas."

"'Tis what I find so intriguing aboot her."

With Tavis beside him, Duncan started toward the Jacksons' slowing carriage. "Mr. Jackson is the president of Charleston Brotherhood Bank. Seems a bit stuffy. But then I will no' be spending time with him, but his lovely daughter."

"Are you sure about that? I think you'll have a fight with Sorrell on your hands. From what I have seen, she and he seem to be the next pair to be walking the church aisle."

"Charlotte is too guid for the likes of Sorrell."

"By the way, I ran into Alan Ferguson the other day." Tavis changed the subject.

"Aye, I saw him no' too long ago. What's he doing here? I never had a chance to ask him?"

Tavis shook his head. "He said his family lost everything they own to a fire, his father lost his job with the government, and they never seemed to be able to recover. His father committed suicide, and his mother died grieving his loss."

"What of his sister?" Duncan wasn't sure he wanted to hear the answer.

"Alan said she is staying in Edinburgh with an aunt and uncle. He came to America to start over. I invited him to church."

"Odd the three of us from the same town run into each other here in America." Duncan lowered his voice as he and Tavis reached the Jacksons' carriage. Arthur Jackson had just finished helping the last of his four daughters down.

Duncan stuck out his hand. "Guid morning."

Jackson grasped Duncan's hand in a firm shake. "Good to see you at church this morning, Mr. Mackenzie. You're becoming a regular. Finally adjusting to our American ways, are you?"

Duncan nodded his head. "That surely would be the truth. Naught like a brisk drive to church on a Sunday morn. I'd like to introduce you to my friend. This would be Tavis Dalzell."

Tavis's broad shoulders dwarfed the banker's. He thrust out his hand.

"Arthur Jackson." The banker gripped Tavis's hand and pumped it. "Nice to meet you, Mr. Dalzell. Haven't seen you at church here that I can recall. You new to the area?"

"I've visited here a few times. Usually slip in and out quietly."

"I hear a bit of a Scottish accent. You know Duncan from there?"

"Aye, we were childhood friends until my parents went on the mission field."

Duncan grinned "'Tis why the mon no longer sounds like a true Scotsman."

Duncan glanced behind Jackson as the man's wife, Charlotte, other daughters, and his youngest son began to move toward the church building.

"Before you head off to catch your family, I'd like to request the honor of driving your oldest daughter home after the service."

Chapter 6

"What are your intentions?" Jackson gave Duncan a hard stare.

The man was no fool. He had to know Sorrell's character, and he had to see his daughter's infatuation with the man. What father would want his daughter to marry a man of Sorrell's ilk?

"I'm fond of the lass and would like to spend a wee bit of time with her. However, she's stayed pretty weel occupied of late." *Occupied with a man who comes up short even against riffraff.*

As if his thoughts had conjured him up, Sorrell rounded the side of the building and headed for Charlotte. Jackson's gaze seemed to track his movement. That, Duncan was confident, worked in his favor.

"Do you have a footman with you?"

"Aye."

"Then you have my permission to see my daughter home. I'm sure Charlotte will be honored to accompany you. Now please excuse me. I need to escort my family in and seated."

Duncan trailed behind the Jackson family. He climbed the three steps to the old wood frame building and stepped through the opening to make his way to his seat of choice—back row, next to the aisle, on the left hand side.

The location gave him several advantages—he could slip out as soon as the service ended. He didn't have to feel the preacher's eyes on him. And best of all, it gave him a perfect view of Miss Jackson, who also seemed to have a favorite seat, right up front and center.

Duncan dropped down onto the oak pew and stretched his legs in front of him as his eyes sought the lass. Tavis took a seat beside him and opened his Bible. Six of the tall windows' shutters had been pushed open, letting in enough light for him to see clearly as he awaited the moment her father would reveal that he would escort her home.

Her quick glance back to his favorite seat left him taken aback. Not a hint of irritation flashed across her face. If he didn't know better, he'd have thought it looked more like relief, and a bit of curiosity.

The congregation stood before Duncan realized he'd daydreamed the entire church service away. He chuckled to himself. His thoughts must have stayed within the bounds of decency because God hadn't sent any lightning bolts to strike him down. After all, a church was God's house, which made it holy. Tavis raised his brows in question.

"'Tis nothing. I need to get outside."

"Always in a hurry to get out of church. I see nothing has changed, my friend. You can't run from God."

Duncan grinned. "I have a bonnie lass I dinna want to miss."

Stepping into the aisle, he decided to wait for Miss Jackson outside. He hustled down the steps and made his way over to a tree and leaned his back against the rough bark, settling in for what he assumed would prove to be a long wait. Women could talk for hours about absolutely nothing. He bent down, picked a piece of grass, and stuck it in his mouth just as Miss Jackson exited the church.

Duncan crossed his arms in front of him and observed the congregants as they exited.

Most could not be the traitor he searched for, but did they know the man, or had they ever crossed paths with him? Duncan shook his head. He had his work cut out for him. In a city as large as Charleston, a person could be anywhere. With as little as he had to go on…a tattoo, the ship he traveled on, his nationality… It could take weeks or months or years to find him.

♥♥♥

Charlotte stood at the bottom of the church steps, clutching her Bible to her chest while searching for Mr.

Mackenzie, her ride home. She was anxious to be on her way before Frank could seek her out. He'd gotten tied up with two elderly ladies who thought he didn't look well and were taking their time cajoling him and pressing their hands to his brow, when she slipped from the pew in front of him.

She spotted Mr. Mackenzie just before he pushed away from the oak tree. With a few long strides, he moved alongside her and offered his arm.

Papa had not left any room for argument when he told her she would be escorted home by Mr. Mackenzie. If truth be told, she was thankful he had asked her father—not necessarily because she desired to ride with him, but because it saved her from having to deal with Frank Sorrell. Although Papa would never have let Frank around her after last night.

Charlotte sighed. Mr. Mackenzie raised his brows, and she regretted making the sound. "It's nothing. I realized I needed to take care of something that I'd rather avoid."

"'No' with me I hope."

She laughed at the seriousness in his voice. "No, not with you. As a matter of fact—" She stopped herself before she said too much. She didn't need to share her personal problems with him. Besides, wasn't she still supposed to be mad at Mr. Mackenzie for allowing Frank to become so intoxicated? Mr. Mackenzie's words came rushing back to her. *Lassie, I could no' force him to overindulge any more than I could make my horse drink water.* That was true. No one but Frank could have gotten Frank drunk. Mr. Mackenzie hadn't signed up to be Frank's keeper, nor had he shown a hint of drunkenness himself.

Mr. Mackenzie stared at her, apparently waiting for her to finish her sentence. "Thank you for the ride home." She glanced around for his carriage. "Papa had a meeting with the pastor, so I would've had a long wait."

"'Tis my pleasure." He helped her up into the curricle while his footman untied the horses.

Placing her Bible in her lap, she settled onto the leather seat and glanced around the handsome carriage with its polished wooden trim.

Mr. Mackenzie climbed up next to her. He cut a fine figure—his fawn tweed jacket pulling across his broad shoulders as he reached forward.

"Are you ready, lass?"

"Quite."

A single eyebrow rose as if making some sort of statement. Instead of giving in to the urge of explaining herself, she faced forward and waited for him to direct the horses.

"Thank you for accepting my invitation. I dinna think you would. The last time we spoke you seemed a wee bit irritated with me."

"To be forthright with you Mr. Mackenzie, I really had no choice. It seems Papa thought we should be more neighborly."

Duncan reined the horses around and down the road. "Ahhh. But you dinna seem too upset. Did you think you should be neighborly, too?"

Heat crept up her face but not from embarrassment. She cocked her head and gave him her most severe glare. "What, sir, is that supposed to mean?"

Duncan frowned. "Did I say something to offend you again, lass?"

Charlotte searched his face for the truth and some clue as to whether this burly Scot truly didn't mean to imply anything. Determining he did not, she smiled. "My apologies, sir. I must have misunderstood." As she turned her head away, she glimpsed his lower lip quirk before his face turned placid, and he looked forward. She held back a scowl. The man obviously shouldn't be trusted.

"You seem to have a habit of that." He continued to stare ahead.

"Of what, may I ask?"

"Misunderstanding me." The corner of his mouth twitched as before. "I enjoyed our dance, lass."

She lifted her chin. "And which dance would that be?" Doubtless the one he held her too close.

"Both. I look forward to our next."

"I doubt there will be a next, Mr. Mackenzie."

He slowed the horses. "There will be, make no mistake." Charlotte sniffed. "You're terribly confident of something *you* have no control over." She tightened her grip on her Bible.

He chuckled. "Now, lass, dinna you be going and getting upset with me again. Did I no' behave to your liking on the last dance?"

Charlotte clenched her teeth and recited *this too shall pass* several times in her head. The ride couldn't be over soon enough. "There are no balls planned. There won't be until the Christmas season arrives." She looked off in the other direction, hoping he'd let the subject drop.

"There you are mistaken. I'm throwing a ball in less than a fortnight, and your father has already consented to bring his lovely daughters." Duncan's thick brogue rolled off his tongue with pride. "Ah, but now I have gone and spoiled your father's surprise."

Charlotte swung her gaze around. Duncan's grin looked nothing short of mischievous. She glared at him, hoping beyond hope that he would get the message, but knowing he was playing some game and enjoyed it very much. She'd never deliberately gone against her father's wishes, at least that she could remember, but this well could be the first occasion.

She was forever the dutiful daughter, although she doubted her parents felt that way. But it was true. She might not agree with her parents' choices, might argue that they didn't live in the 1850s anymore, and might just voice her opinion when it wasn't wanted, but she never deliberately went against their wishes. "We shall see. It's possible that one daughter may have a previous engagement."

His brow shot up. A habit, she realized, he used to intimidate. She smiled at him to let him know it was ineffective.

"I like your spunk. Reminds me of the lassies back in the Highlands." Duncan eased the horses to a stop in front of her home.

Mr. Mackenzie was down and around the carriage waiting on her as she stepped down. "I thank you again for the ride home, Mr. Mackenzie. I'd ask you in for a cup of hot tea, but with my family not home yet, I'm afraid it would be inappropriate. I won't keep you. Have a good day, sir." Charlotte headed for the door, her gaze focused on the handle she would turn to get away from him.

As the first horses' hooves hit the paved road, his voice floated through the air. "I look forward to our next dance, lass. I shall be counting down the days. Oh, and be sure to bring your blue dress. I couldn't take my eyes off you." He chuckled and snapped the reins, prompting the horses into a canter.

Charlotte refrained from turning around to glare at him. The man was nothing short of infuriating, and she had a feeling it was not by accident. He seemed to enjoy ruffling her feathers.

The door creaked as she pushed it open and slipped in. The smell of roast beef and fresh baked bread wafted up to greet her. Ignoring her stomach's sudden gnawing, she hurried toward the library. Did he really think that he could manipulate her into attending his ball? It wouldn't take much to outwit the man. She'd simply wait until her father announced the ball, then cry out on it, explaining she had planned to go visit her aunt down in Savannah that same evening. Mr. Mackenzie had said it would be a fortnight, so she needed to send a letter off straight away to her aunt, securing the whole weekend. That would be the safest approach because she couldn't be certain which evening he would choose for the ball.

Drawing open the door of her father's study, she was greeted by the pleasant smell of leather books and polished furniture. Wanting to run her hand along the book bindings and lose herself inside the contents of one, she forced herself to stay focused and went directly to her father's desk, where she pulled out a sheet of linen paper. She sat down, picked up the pen, and began to write. As she finished the letter, she sighed. Now she needed to get this to her aunt. First thing tomorrow morning she would see it posted. Leaning back in her father's chair, she waited for the ink to dry.

The click-clack of shoes crossing the oak floorboards brought her from her seat. Directly, she folded the letter and stuffed it in an envelope. Her father stepped into the room.

"Papa. You startled me. I thought you had a meeting with Pastor Aldridge."

He motioned for her to sit down in his chair as he pulled an upholstered one closer. "Did you think I'd give Mr. Mackenzie permission to bring you home if I wasn't going to be *right* behind you?"

Charlotte sat back down. "I did wonder about that."

Papa took his seat. "I can't have my good name besmirched."

It was always about what people thought. For once why couldn't he be worried about her? She forced a nod.

He leaned back in his chair as if he were settling in for a long stay. "I'm glad you're here. I wanted to talk to you."

Charlotte held her breath.

"I was speaking with Mr. Mackenzie today. The man seems like an honest enough fellow. He comes from money and has traveled to America to expand his wealth."

"If he's wealthy, why not stay in Scotland and invest there?"

"He's a ship merchant, and America has unlimited opportunities. People come from all over the world to start new business ventures here. We're a powerful nation. I know it's hard for a woman to understand these things. You'll have to trust me on this."

Charlotte bristled at his comment but was careful with her tone. "Women can understand anything a man can if they're only given the opportunity. Why, women are becoming doctors, lawyers, and even dentists. I've read all about them, and I think it's wonderful that we are finally being given a chance to contribute to society."

He snorted. "Contribute? Women in a man's workplace will contribute nothing but problems. Mark my words, Charlotte Bay, *nothing but problems.* That's why I will see that my daughters marry well and do what they were called to do—become wives and mothers. I never should have let you read all those laissez-faire books."

They had had this conversation many times before. She couldn't win with her father. He was set on the idea that a woman's place was in the home. She certainly didn't see anything wrong with a woman making her own way in the world. But he frowned on her desire to be an accountant despite her aptitude with numbers, stating that was a man's job. How could she achieve her goal of helping her sisters reach their dreams if she had no funds and Frank was no longer in the picture?

Effie, fifteen, could draw beautiful pictures and hoped to work for a magazine. Charlotte was determined to see her dream come true. Her sister's eye for detail and her execution of it rivaled the artists in Charleston's newspaper, *The News and Courier.* If she continued to draw, which Charlotte knew she would, someday she'd be the best in the Charleston area.

Pearl aspired to be a doctor. Every sick animal she could find she nursed back to health. Charlotte once suggested she become a veterinarian, but Pearl, thirteen, told Charlotte she'd rather care for the next sick person. With Mama as her competition for caring for ill family members, she never did have any volunteers.

"Why the interest in Mr. Mackenzie, Papa?"

"He is coming down to the bank later this week to speak with me about moving his money over. I won't bother your pretty little head with the particulars, but I will say it is a substantial amount. He'll be quite a catch for our bank, not to mention to some lucky young lady. Which brings me to the reason I wish to speak to you. Mr. Mackenzie has requested our presence at a ball he's holding in two weeks."

Charlotte ran her fingers over the edge of the missive she'd finished writing. "I'm sorry I won't be able to make it

Papa. I just wrote Aunt Sara a letter." She tapped the envelope to bring attention to the mail in her hand. "I told her I would come visit her in two weeks."

She held her breath. Papa hadn't told her when the ball would be. If she'd asked him about visiting Aunt Sara, he'd have squashed the idea immediately. But up until this moment, she'd never had the courage to tell Papa she couldn't do something.

Papa pushed himself up from the chair, which usually meant he was finished discussing things.

She almost let out a sigh of relief, as victory was almost hers.

"I'm glad I caught you before you sent the letter, because *you will be coming*. Mr. Mackenzie's planned a weekend full of entertainment, and we are one of the families he's invited to stay at his home. I told him we'd *all* be there. All being you, Nellie, your mother, and I, of course Pearl is too young, and Effie will stay home with her and your brother. I've given my word we'll all come. Therefore, you will accompany us." He walked to the door and paused. "After all, I doubt very much it's us that he wishes to spend time with. You can visit your aunt another time."

Charlotte walked past him, and he stuck out his hand. "I'll take the letter. You won't be needing it."

Chapter 7

Would a traitorous scoundrel attend church every Sunday? Duncan scrutinized his reflection in front of the mirror as he reminded himself what his priority was and was not. He did need to fit in, he told himself, even if the man he sought chose not to attend the Lord's house.

Duncan stuck his head out of his bedroom door and gave a yell. "Stuebing." He returned to his stance before the mirror. A week had passed since he'd seen Miss Jackson, and he found himself anxious to see her.

"You called, sir?"

Duncan spun around to see Stuebing standing behind him. "How do you do that?"

His valet raised his brows.

"Och! Never mind. Just help me get this ridiculous thing tied. Whoever designed these things should be drawn and quartered."

"A bit harsh, wouldn't you say, sir?"

"Just get me looking spiffy. I have an important day." Duncan shifted his weight as his valet fussed over him.

"Sir, it would help if you would remain still."

Duncan chuckled. "So you've told me."

"Yes. If only it would sink in, sir."

"Why, Stuebing, I believe that was humor."

Stuebing's expression remained staid. "No sir, just truth."

His valet brushed his hands down the front of Duncan's coat, smoothing the invisible wrinkles and keeping a stoic face.

"What would I do without you?"

Stuebing shuddered. "Let us hope we never have to face that, sir."

"For once I am in agreement with you, my friend." Duncan smiled and gave him a friendly slap on the back. "Do I meet your approval? 'Tis important, since there's a box lunch after the service, and I want to look my best for Miss Jackson."

And like it or not, he couldn't stop thinking about the lovely Miss Jackson becoming his wife.

Stuebing gave his customary nod of approval and turned to the door. "I wish you luck, sir."

Duncan patted his money pocket. "'Tisn't luck I'll be needing." He picked up his derby from the pole of his bed and placed it at a rakish angle.

Stuebing straightened the hat. "Much better, sir. You did say you wanted to meet my approval."

Duncan chuckled. "Aye, I did that."

Wanting to arrive early to church, he hurried down the stairs and out of the house. It was imperative that he find Albert Jackson, Miss Charlotte's brother, before the service started and unbeknownst to anyone.

She hadn't seemed too pleased with him when he'd dropped her off last week, so she most assuredly wouldn't give him any hints about her lunch box—at least correct hints. However, her little brother had recognized a quick way to make a dollar, and Duncan was happy to oblige him. He chuckled. After all, the money would eventually all be in the family.

He climbed into the carriage and urged the horses into a trot. He'd never been to a box lunch auction before, but it sounded like grand fun. The promise of coin made Charlotte's little brother quite happy as well.

He only hoped winning her lunch pleased the lass. The thought that she really didn't like him was troubling. Everyone liked him. Everyone that is but Miss Jackson.

And that made her all the more desirable.

Today he would impress her with how far he was willing to go to win her box. Perhaps when the bidding started to slow, he'd bid a rather large sum. That should astonish her and lift him up in her eyes since the money was going to a good cause—new hymnals to replace the old tattered ones with missing pages.

By the time Duncan had maneuvered his horses over to his usual spot under the tree, Albert had spotted him and ran to meet him.

Duncan jumped down and secured the animals. The lad slowed as he approached, and he offered him a smile. "Glad you arrived early. Where is the rest of your family?" Albert looked up, craning his neck. "I rode with the Millers so no one would see me meet you. Papa would tan my hide if he knew I gave away my sister's basket colors, especially for money."

"You're a smart lad."

A smile spread across the boy's face, and he stood a little taller. "Yes, sir. I like to stay as far away from the switch as possible."

Duncan rubbed Albert's head, mussing his hair. "Weel, you best be telling me what your sister's basket looks like before your family arrives."

Albert glanced around. "It's a square basket with a twisted handle and a big blue ribbon tied to the side of the handle near the base."

"And what color would the basket be?"

"The basket is made from sweetgrass."

Duncan scratched his head. "Sweetgrass? Now I'd no' be knowing what that is."

The lad's chest puffed up like a strutting rooster as he explained to him the thin green and cream reeds. Duncan bit back a smile at the child's pride of knowing something an adult didn't.

"So, you see, Charlotte's basket will be made of a mixture of the two color grasses. I'll stand where you can see me. I'll nod if it's hers."

Duncan reached in his pocket and pulled out a dollar coin and flipped it up in the air toward the lad. Albert caught the coin and ran a finger over it reverently.

"Thank you for the information. Now, you'd best run along before someone sees you talking to me. Remember, 'tis our secret."

Albert shoved the coin into his pocket and ran off as he yelled over his shoulder. "Oh, don't worry about that. Your secret is safe with me. Don't forget to watch for my nod."

Duncan had thought the sermon would never end. The church had been packed, and he couldn't even see Miss Jackson to help pass the time. Now he stood in the midst of a mob of men, whispering back and forth and pointing to the pile of baskets. He recognized several of the young studs as boys he'd coerced into dancing with Charlotte at the ball.

He strained to see the basket Albert had described but couldn't pick it out of the wealth of containers. The first box was placed on the table and the bidding began. Friendly banter between the auctioneer and the men kept the crowd entertained. He held the basket up and turned it from side to side as the bidding slowed. "This is a beautiful basket and, remember, this goes to a good cause. Will anyone raise the bid to one dollar?"

Someone behind Duncan raised his voice. "Just sell it to the man and let's get on to the next."

The auctioneer frowned at the intruder but gave a resounding. "Sold! For seventy-two cents."

Duncan scrutinized each basket that came up for bidding. His heart beat a little faster each time the auctioneer went to retrieve a new dinner from the shrinking collection, and each time, regardless of what the food was housed in, Duncan's eyes shifted to Albert and watched for his nod.

When the next basket was placed on the small table, Duncan knew he had his meal. A smile spread across his face. He recognized the description of sweet grass, and sure enough, a blue ribbon sat on top of the handle. His heart thudded in his chest at the thought of a bidding war.

Someone started the dinner bid at twenty-five cents. Duncan raised it ten cents. The man across from him bid fifty cents. Duncan bid a dollar and his opponent countered with one dollar and twenty-five cents.

Did the man know on whose box he bid? No matter. He would pay whatever he needed to win the dinner and Charlotte's company. Duncan yelled, "Two dollars."

The other bidder wavered as he glared at Duncan.

The auctioneer looked at the man. "Do I hear two dollars and five cents?

The man yelled, "Two dollars and eighteen cents."

Duncan shook his head. Men should not bid away something they did not have—even if it was for charity.

The auctioneer looked to Duncan this time, and Duncan's blood rushed through his veins as victory drew near. "Two dollars and seventy-five cents." The bid had barely left his lips when Sorrell, who had been standing two men down from him, swung his head around, gathering Duncan's attention. Their eyes locked.

Sorrell yelled, "Three dollars. I'll give three dollars for the basket."

This was going to be even more fun. He never thought he'd be bidding against ole Frankie Boy. Duncan smiled to himself and raised the stakes. "Three dollars and fifty cents."

Sorrell lifted four fingers. "Four dollars."

"Four dollars and twenty-five cents." Duncan wanted to drag this out as long as possible. He hadn't had this much fun since…since he danced with Miss Jackson.

Sorrell glanced in Charlotte's direction, drawing Duncan's gaze to her. Sorrell smiled. "Five dollars."

The lass's eyes grew round. Duncan chuckled. She looked like her brother when he had offered him one dollar for information on his sister's basket. "Five dollars and fifty cents."

Sorrell swung around and glared at him. "Six dollars."

Murmurs amongst the men surrounding them commenced as giggles and gasps came from the woman standing opposite. They had kept the bidding so active the auctioneer couldn't keep up.

Duncan hesitated, waiting on the auctioneer to do his job, adding to the tension of the moment. Everyone seemed to wait on bated breath to see if he would raise the bid. Commotion came from the right and the left sides of the table. On the left, a middle-aged woman appeared to be in the process of swooning. Duncan raised his voice. "Twenty-five dollars." As the words left his mouth the frantic waving on the right caught his eye—Albert's hands beckoning his attention and shaking his head.

A rock sunk to the pit of his stomach as reality struck. He hadn't once looked to see if the lad had given his nod of approval.

Sorrell turned away, and the auctioneer hollered. "Sold!"

The women crowded around the distressed lady. The auctioneer raised his voice above the crowd. "Would the lady who owns this basket please come and claim your dinner partner."

The thirty-something-year-old distressed woman steadied herself and walked out from amongst the women huddling around her. She shifted her gaze to Duncan, then waddled forward to claim her basket.

Sorrell threw back his head and roared with laughter. Duncan swallowed. The other men began to snicker and then to hoot. The woman glanced over the men, stopping at Duncan, and hesitating before dropping her head. His heart clenched. These men had humiliated her.

Duncan stepped from among his fellow bidders and stuck a smile on his face. "Lass, I'm mighty hungry, and I believe I can smell that delicious meal from here. Are you ready to spread a blanket and commence to eating?"

Her head swung up, and she returned his smile. He went to her and took the basket. Extending his arm to escort her, he asked her where she would like to sit. He held back a sigh as he had to lean down to hear her whispered reply. The lass dropped her head back down to study the ground.

She looked like a wilting flower compared to Charlotte. But then so did all the other lasses. Well, he would have food to satisfy his belly. With such a robust figure, she no doubt had an ability to cook. The aroma of fried chicken and fresh bread wafted up to his nose. He smiled. Aye, she could cook. He spread their blanket amongst the crowd of people already indulging themselves with their meal and in the shade of a live oak covered in sage-green moss. He smiled at her.

"I'm Duncan Mackenzie. I dinna believe we've met, lass."

Her voice was so light, he again had to lean forward to hear. "Miss Campbell."

A sincere smile spread across his face. "You'd be of Scottish blood then?"

She nodded.

"Have you ever visited the fair land of Scotland, lass?"

She shook her head.

"Och! You are in for a treat then. I would be pleased to tell you aboot my, excuse me—" He grinned. "Aboot *our* lovely country."

Miss Campbell laid a spread that made his stomach rumble in anticipation. She lifted her eyes and waited. Duncan frowned. What was she waiting for? "Go ahead, lass. If you let me go first I may no' leave enough for you."

She cleared her throat. "Would you please ask the blessing, Mr. Mackenzie?"

"Oh, Aye." Duncan bowed his head. "Thank you, Lord, for the food we are aboot to partake. Amen."

She gave him a gentle smile. He waited for her to fill her plate before he indulged himself.

As he lifted a piece of the fried chicken to his lips, Charlotte's voice floated through the air. "I really don't want to sit here, Frank."

"Well, I'm the one who paid for the food, and this is where I choose to sit." Sorrell spread the blanket on the ground.

Duncan caught the smirk on Sorrell's face as he picked the basket—almost identical to the one Duncan had bought—off the ground and placed it on the blanket next to Miss Jackson. One slight difference between the two, the bow on Miss Jackson's was placed on the side of the handle near the base like Albert had described. Why hadn't he remembered that detail? Miss Campbell's bow sat on the top of the handle. Duncan almost groaned. Nay, he would make the best of it. 'Twas obvious the lass had gone out of her way to prepare a wonderful meal for her beau, a plan which he had inadvertently sabotaged. He would try to make it up to her by entertaining her with the wonders of Scotland.

As the meal progressed, Miss Campbell became more talkative. To his delight, he was not the only one doing the entertaining. She regaled him with the antics of her grandfather running the hills and moors of Scotland. He laughed so hard at times he had to wrap his arms around his middle. The afternoon had turned out quite enjoyable even if he had bid on the wrong basket and spent the day with the wrong lass.

He smiled. That was the first he'd thought of Miss Jackson in over an hour. His eyes swept to where she sat, and she quickly looked away.

Duncan put the empty dishes and containers back in the basket. He had all but licked them clean. "'Twas a delicious meal and charming company."

"Oh, Mr. Mackenzie, you need not pretend. I am, shall we say, many years your senior. It didn't pass me by that you and Mr. Sorrell thought you were bidding on Miss Jackson's basket. I must say that I'm much relieved you won the bid, although it was definitely to your disadvantage."

"Dear lass, 'tis true I thought I be bidding on another's fare, but I assure you whole heartedly that I have no' one regret. Your company has been a breath of Scottish air. You brought me back to the land that I love, if only for an hour."

A rosy hue crept up Miss Campbell's cheeks. "Then God has blessed us both this day. However, I am afraid I have spoiled Miss Jackson's day."

"Nay, dinna fash yourself aboot that. It takes all Miss Jackson can do to tolerate me."

Miss Campbell glanced over to where Miss Charlotte and Sorrell sat. "I think you are mistaken. I could not help but notice Miss Jackson's frequent glances your way."

It took Duncan a moment to appreciate what she had told him. Perhaps, Miss Jackson was more interested than she appeared. "And have I upset the applecart with your beau? Even as I speak, I see the other mon I outbid leaning against yonder tree, glowering at me."

Miss Campbell giggled. "Mr. Hewitt has no room to *glower*. He has been courting me for two years now. Plenty of time to see to it that *every* meal I cooked he partook of."

Duncan burst into laughter and grasped Miss Campbell's hand. Beyond Miss Campbell, Sorrell and Charlotte both turned to look. "Shall we light a fire under him? Perhaps if Mr. Hewitt thinks someone else may steal his—"

Hewitt stomped up. "Let go of her hand."

Duncan released his hold and pushed himself up, now looking down on Hewitt from his superior height. "I believe 'tis my meal here, no' yours. So be on your way."

"I ain't goin' nowheres till you take your hands off—" He looked down at Miss Campbell and back up at Duncan. "Well, you shouldn't of been holdin' her hand."

Duncan turned to Miss Campbell and winked. "And why shouldn't I? 'Twas my bid that won the lady's basket."

Hewitt's gaze bounced back and forth from Duncan to Miss Campbell. "W-well, 'cause I was going to ask her to marry me. You bought a meal, not the right to fondle her hand."

Duncan smiled. "Weel then, I'll stand here while you ask her and see if she wants to marry you. If she does, I'll leave. If she doesn't, then you'll leave." Duncan crossed his arms and waited.

Hewitt turned to Miss Campbell and started to speak. Duncan placed his hand on the man's shoulder and pushed him down. "You propose on bended knee, you knave."

Hewitt scowled over his shoulder at Duncan. Duncan held back the chuckle that was threatening to erupt.

"M-miss C-campbell, I'd be mighty honored if you'd agree to be my wife."

A smile spread across Miss Campbell's face. "It would please me very much."

Duncan pulled both of them up from the blanket. "Let me be the first to congratulate you, Hewitt, and the first to give Miss Campbell a hug."

Hewitt stepped in between them. "I don't think so. I believe you said if the lady said yes you would leave."

Duncan nodded. "So I did. So I did. Then I'll bid you both a guid day, and I will be on my way. It has been a pleasure, lassie."

Duncan swooped down and scooped up his hat. "If he ever gives you a problem, you ken where you can find me, lassie."

Whistling the tune "Within a Mile of Edinburgh Town," he headed for his carriage.

He released the horse's reins and leaped up onto the seat of the curricle. A small stone hit his arm, and he looked down. Albert crouched beside the carriage.

"What are you doing down there? 'Tis a guid way to get run over."

Albert stuck his hand in his pocket and fumbled around, finally withdrawing the dollar. He peered over the edge of the carriage and ducked his head. Moving forward, the lad reached his hand up. Between his thumb and finger, he held the coin. "Mr. Mackenzie, here is your money back."

Duncan frowned at the lad. "Now why would you be giving me the money back?"

The boy dropped his head. "You didn't get to eat with my sister."

Duncan leaned over and patted Albert's head. "And whose fault would that be? I forgot to look and see if you gave me the nod. You did what you said lad. The coin is yours."

Albert's eyes widened. "Honest?"

Duncan grinned. "Honest."

As he rode away, he threw a glance over his shoulder. Charlotte busied herself putting things back in the basket as Sorrell hovered around. Next time, he would come out on top...Next time.

Chapter 8

Mr. Mackenzie's carriage headed down the dusty road and soon disappeared from Charlotte's view. If she never saw the man again, it would be too soon. She put the plates and silverware into her basket and glanced over at her father, who stood by the church talking to the pastor. She hurried to fold the blanket. "Frank, could you please help me with this?"

Frank stood next to the basket and snickered. "I bought the meal, not the work."

Charlotte narrowed her eyes to slits. "And just *how* did you know which basket was mine?"

"That wasn't difficult. I watched to see which one that Scot bid on. When he bought the wrong one, I knew the other had to be yours."

Charlotte let out an unladylike "humph" and continued folding the blanket.

"Did you see the Scot making a spectacle of himself? If I had bid on the wrong basket, I'd have refused to pay. I wouldn't have eaten with that woman. Just looking at her would have set my stomach roiling."

"I think what he did was noble. Miss Campbell is a very sweet lady. And you should be ashamed for saying that."

Frank guffawed. "Don't you know that's what they say about all ugly women?"

Charlotte finished folding the blanket and walked toward the basket. "She is a kind and thoughtful lady."

"Exactly. And ugly."

As she reached the basket, her toe caught on a raised live oak root, throwing her forward and into Frank's arms. Charlotte squealed and fought to right herself, but Frank held her close.

She wrenched herself away and almost fell backwards, but strong arms caught her. Strong arms she recognized without turning around.

Papa's voice was tinged with ice. "Mr. Sorrell, I will say this only once. Keep your hands off my daughter. I allowed you to eat this meal with her because the money went to a good cause, but don't think this gives you access to her now. You have shown your true colors, and whether Charlotte agrees or not, I demand that you stay away from her."

She wanted to say she did agree, but once again Papa had thought the worst of her. He believed she couldn't see what Frank had become, and because of Papa's blindness and lack of trust in her, she refused to agree with his suspicions. She clutched the blanket to her as she picked up the basket, and then marched to their carriage.

The same words she always heard when he was displeased spilled from his lips the whole way home and then again after the evening meal when Albert asked a question about Frank. Image was everything. The truth didn't matter, only what people thought.

She claimed exhaustion and went to bed early.

Charlotte glanced over to where Nellie lay staring at her.

"It's about time you woke up." Nellie stretched her arms above her head and yawned.

"I don't want to be awake. I'm so tired of Papa's rants." The morning rays streaked fingers of light across her bed. Another beautiful October day, but she didn't want it to be morning.

Nellie sat up and scooted back, leaning against the headboard. "You shouldn't say such things about Papa. He emphasizes his beliefs because he cares."

Charlotte watched the progress of a ladybug as it crawled across the ceiling above her and flew away. Oh, to have the freedom to fly. She would lift her wings and flutter away to a place where someone appreciated her. "I speak of it as I see it. He never even asks my opinion or asks for my side of the story. He might actually find that I agree with him if he would only inquire. Besides, how many days does he have to continue to harp on something?"

Nellie folded her arms across her chest. "He can't read minds, you know. Maybe you should tell him what you're thinking."

Charlotte sat up and swung her feet off the bed. "Why? I want him to trust me because of who I am. I want him to have faith in the daughter he raised, to trust my judgment. To believe in me."

"It might help if you gave him an inkling of what's going on in that head of yours." Nellie's voice softened. "I do think he has faith in you. He doesn't want to see you make any mistakes that you will regret is all."

Charlotte smiled at her sister's always-positive attitude. "Regardless, I think I'll wait up here until he leaves for work."

"Papa has left. I heard Jeffrey leave and return thirty minutes ago with the carriage."

"I'm starving." Charlotte jumped off the bed and grabbed her robe. "Let's go get something to eat." She sailed from her room and followed the smells of bacon and coffee to the dining room. She filled her plate from the sideboard and took the seat next to her mother. Mama sipped her coffee and flipped through the latest *Harper's Bazar Magazine*.

Charlotte bowed her head and asked the blessing over her food. Nellie took the seat across from her.

"Good morning, Mama," Nellie said.

"Good morning, girls." Mama looked up from reading. "I'm glad to see you're up. We have a lot to do this week to get ready for the trip to Mr. Mackenzie's."

"Oh. Mama, couldn't you talk to Papa?" Charlotte unfolded her napkin and laid it across her lap. "I don't want to go. I'd much rather go visit Aunt Sara."

"I don't believe that's an option, dear. Your father is quite adamant about your attending." She reached over and tucked a curl behind Charlotte's ear. "He has already mentioned to me that you may try to convince me you shouldn't go."

Charlotte continued to fiddle with her napkin. "But Mama—"

"No, dear, this isn't going to become a debate. Your father's words are final."

"Yes, Mama." She picked up her fork and stabbed at her bacon.

Mama's gaze shifted to Nellie. "You're awfully quiet. I don't hear you complaining about the ball."

"Complain? I love balls, Mama. And Mr. Mackenzie is throwing two. I can't wait to go."

Her mother smiled at her younger daughter, then turned to Charlotte, who still hadn't taken a bite of food.

"Perhaps this will cheer you, Charlotte. I told your father that, with giving up your blue dress, you would have to have a new gown before we left. So you and Nellie can go shopping today. Nellie, you can purchase a new hat. I've tried everything I know to get the dirt out of yours, but I'm afraid when those horses ran it over, they as good as dyed it mud red."

"Thank you, Mama."

"You're welcome, dear. Now you two hurry and eat. I'll instruct Jeffrey to have the carriage brought around."

A few hours later Charlotte and Nellie strolled down King Street peering in the shop windows. As they approached My Lady's Apparel, Nellie moved toward the door. "Let's go in. They always have the latest styles."

Charlotte followed her in, feeling not in the least like shopping. As the door banged shut, the bell rang. The clerk and Miss Campbell turned their heads toward them. As their eyes met, a smile spread across the woman's face. "Hello, Miss Jackson." She gave Nellie the same smile. "Miss Jackson. I am having a time deciding which color dress to choose for my wedding. Could you two give me your opinions?"

Miss Campbell pulled a dress the color of lilacs from the rack and handed it to the saleswoman, then pulled out a light-yellow gown. "These are the ones I've chosen. Which do you like?"

Charlotte fingered the lavender dress. "I believe I like this one, although both are lovely, and you would look beautiful in either one."

"I agree," Nellie chimed in.

"Thank you." She turned to the clerk. "I will take this one. I'll return tomorrow for a fitting."

Nellie wandered toward the hats.

Miss Campbell moved toward Charlotte. "Miss Jackson, I wanted to tell you how much I appreciated all that your…Mr. Mackenzie did for me last Sunday. I know it was your basket he thought he was bidding on. He's one of the most gallant men I've ever met. If I were a few years younger and not already smitten with Mr. Hewitt…" She smiled at Charlotte. "Well, suffice to say, I'd do my best to be your competition."

Charlotte gulped. "Oh, Miss Campbell. You misunderstand. There is nothing between Mr. Mackenzie and me."

She patted Charlotte on the shoulder. "Well, I must be on my way. I have a wedding to plan." She grinned. "Perhaps you'll be planning one too in the near future."

"I assure you, Miss Campbell, I have not set my sights on Mr. Mackenzie."

With a twinkle in her eye, Miss Campbell leaned forward. "As you say, dear."

Charlotte wanted to ask Miss Campbell what Mr. Mackenzie had told her. She would never admit it to him, but his chivalry at the box lunch auction warmed her heart. There weren't too many men who would have done what he did. That was obvious from the snickers and taunting.

Though he might be honorable in some ways, he was an absolute thorn in her flesh—always trying to aggravate her. He could be insufferable at times. She had every right to avoid the man.

Nellie made her way in front of Charlotte. "I said, how long are you going to stand there daydreaming? Do you like this hat or don't you?"

Charlotte didn't bother to look. "It fits you perfectly."

"You haven't even looked at it."

The bell rang, and Charlotte turned as Miss Campbell disappeared. Whatever caused her to think of such a ludicrous idea? To imagine her and the Scotsman as a couple. Humph! That day would never happen. No, never.

"Ouch!" Charlotte rubbed her arm where Nellie had pinched. "What did you do that for?"

"You're not listening to me. Should I buy this hat?"

Charlotte finally looked at the hat and burst out laughing. Feathers of all colors stuck in every direction from the back of the hat—several of which came up over the top, waving in front of her sister's nose. "Well, one thing is for sure, it will go with any color dress you want to wear."

Nellie took the hat off and placed it back on the shelf. "Do you want to look at some gowns?"

"No. Let's go eat."

Nellie giggled. "You can't be that hungry already."

"I'm not trying to fit into a blue dress anymore." She shot a quick smile at her sister.

"Not going to wear it to Mr. Mackenzie's soiree?"

"No. Mama gave it to you. But, as a matter of fact, I was thinking about wearing the yellow dress Aunt Sara sent instead of buying a new one."

Nellie's giggles turned into a snort, and she slapped her hand over her mouth.

Charlotte raised her brows. "What? You don't like the dress?"

"Charlotte, the dress looks terrible. It's way too big, and Aunt Sara's eyes must be failing because I have never seen a poorer sewing job in my life. Not to mention that yellow makes you look sallow."

For all she was worth, she fought the grin threatening the corners of her mouth. She turned her head away and fumbled with the dress hanging in front of her. "But wouldn't Aunt Sara be so pleased to hear I wore her dress to the ball? Besides, it would serve Mr. Mackenzie right after he told me he hoped I would wear the blue dress." It was Charlotte's turn to slap her hand over her mouth. Nellie's eyes doubled in size. "Oh!" Charlotte gave in to the urge and stomped her foot. "I didn't mean to let that slip."

"Charlotte Bay Jackson! You wouldn't dare. You know as well as I why he said that. And if you wear that yellow dress, as ugly as it is, God may punish you for your rebellious spirit."

"Pfft! Punish me?" She should be like her rebellious older brother, who left to follow his dream and his sweetheart. She could follow her dream. She could be an accountant for a bank and then be able to help her sisters. If Papa didn't want her at his bank, she could go to a bigger bank. She was better than most men with numbers.

"Well, those stitches are so poorly done, you could be in the middle of a dance and half your dress could fall off."

That tickled Charlotte a little too much, and she burst into a gale of laughter. "Oh Nellie, could you see the look on everyone's face? And Papa's?"

"Papa's? What about Mama's?"

Charlotte let the dress fabric slip from her fingers. "Of course I could never show my face again. But at least I wouldn't have to dance with Mr. Mackenzie."

"Now you're sounding like a spoiled child. It isn't as if Papa is making you marry him. I swear Charlotte, ever since we went to Mary Barrow's birthday party, you haven't been yourself."

Her? Spoiled? Rebellious?

Well, if she had to go to Mr. Mackenzie's, she'd make the best of it. She'd find the prettiest dress possible, one that would make all the single men want to dance with her, and she'd dance with them all. All except for Mr. Mackenzie, that is. He could look all he wanted, but she wasn't about to give him a second of her time.

"You're right Nellie. I am acting like a child." Charlotte smiled. "Help me find the most beautiful dress on these racks. I want to be the belle of the ball."

Chapter 9

E vening shadows darkened the windows of Duncan's office as he sat at his desk staring at a painting of his homeland. How he longed to walk again through those rolling hills and smell the lovely fragrance of heather. Waiting for Tavis, he flipped the page in his logbook. His small office sat on East Bay Street, several blocks from his warehouse on the Cooper River. He needed to get down to the docks and see about two of his ships. *The Scottish Lass,* his pride and joy, and the only one of the three schooners he'd purchased in America, had sailed down the Cooper River and out to sea a little over a week ago. He didn't expect her back for a few more weeks. *The Moor,* he'd just seen sailing to the wharf. He wanted to talk to Gilbert, his captain, before meeting Tavis. While he was at the docks, he could make sure *The Thistle* had received and loaded the cargo for the trip up the coast to Maryland tomorrow. The only drawback was that every time he saw his ships, the desire to return to his homeland and his family plagued him.

This longing had grown until he decided he must leave the espionage business, which required frequent extended trips away from home and the keeping of too many secrets. He wanted to be the real Duncan Mackenzie. He wanted to settle down in a quiet hamlet nestled in the hills not too far from Dundee where he could see to the running of his business. But things didn't always go the way one planned. Sacrifices had to be made. And he'd made the choice to accept the queen's call to come to America.

Now he had work to do.

The door swung open and Tavis stepped in, bringing him out of his reverie.

"You ready?" Tavis stood in the open door.

Duncan shut the book. "Aye. Let's go."

By the time they fetched their horses and reached the Sailors' Galley Saloon, darkness had covered East Bay Street. The water lapped at the shore, but as Duncan pushed open the doors of the saloon, the loud ruckus drowned out the mesmerizing rhythm of the water. Evening activities were in full swing as they crossed the threshold, with men already halfway to being inebriated. As he peered around the large room, he readjusted his thinking. Many *were* in a stupor. Packed booths lined one wall. Several men sat at the middle table deeply involved in a card game.

Duncan pointed to an empty table, where they sat down.

Tavis leaned forward and laced his fingers together on the surface. "Okay. So *why* are we here? I know you're here to find information. I'd be a fool not to see that. Do you want to tell me why you keep dragging me down here to these godforsaken stink-holes?"

He'd speak vaguely to gauge his friend's response. "I'm here on a mission as a favor for Her Majesty. I'm looking into some things that she requested of me concerning Afghanistan."

Tavis's brows rose. "The queen herself? Afghanistan? Would this have anything to do with the massacre?"

Duncan hesitated. "Aye, it does."

"What has Her Majesty requested of you?"

"She has asked me to find the turncoat who caused such senseless loss of lives."

Tavis scooted his chair in closer. "And you think this traitor is here…in Charleston?"

"You dinna sound surprised. How did you hear aboot our adversary?"

Tavis's hands drew into tight fists on the table. "My brother, Bruce, died in that battle. I make it my business to know."

"I understand your loss, and I'm sorry."

"And how do you propose to find him? Do you have any information on him?" Tension emanated from Tavis as he rubbed his shoulder.

His friend's eagerness to know more information both encouraged and troubled Duncan. But why wouldn't he be interested? Tavis's loss was as great as his. Duncan leaned in and lowered his voice. "The mon we're looking for was spotted talking to an Afghani only days after the massacre. Our British troops pursued and the mon was shot. He eluded their capture, but they were able to track him down through the process of elimination. They ken he had to have medical treatment, so they searched all doctors and hospitals in the area. They finally found the physician who had performed the surgery. He gave a vague description of the mon. Six-foot-tall, blue eyes, a bullet wound on his right upper arm and a tattoo of a cross with a thistle. He wore a turban, so we dinna ken the color of his hair."

Tavis sat across from Duncan, gaze glued on him as if drinking in every word. "How can they be so sure this man is the traitor?"

"When he met with the enemy, they were approached by our troops. They ran, and both were shot. The turncoat escaped with his life. His conspirator was no' so lucky."

Tavis seemed to let the information sink in. "And the tattoo. Many men have these things etched into their arms. That will not be an easy undertaking."

"Aye, but no' many will have a thistle."

Tavis nodded his head slowly. "Nay, not many. Anything else to help us find him?"

"'Tis all I have for the time being."

Tavis massaged his shoulder as his eyes met Duncan's, and he gave a wry smile. "Where do we start?"

"Tonight, we mingle."

"Unless the opportunity presents itself, I think that's the safest plan to follow." Tavis stood. "So then, I am off to circulate among the heathen."

Duncan nodded. "Your shoulder bothering you?"

"Aye. My horse threw me a few days ago. Been giving me problems since."

Duncan winced. "I'll give you riding lessons sometime."

Tavis grunted as he sauntered away. Duncan followed his lead, walking around chatting with friendly men about everything from the price of cotton to who was hiring down on the docks. At midnight, they left the establishment and ran into Alan Ferguson, who approached on horseback.

The strawberry-blond man dismounted and shook hands with Duncan and Tavis.

"What brings you out so late?" Tavis retrieved the reins of his horse, holding the leather straps in his hand.

"Just oot for a guid time."

Duncan grinned. "You both will be at the ball I'm throwing tomorrow night, won't you? 'Tis guaranteed to be a guid time."

"I wouldn't miss it. I'm looking forward to seeing if you can sweep the lass off her feet." Tavis slapped the reins across his palm.

"Aye, I'll be there. What lass is this?" Ferguson raised his brows.

Duncan stole a glance at Tavis. "Och! No one to concern yourself with. We need to be on our way. I'll see you on the morrow, then."

As Ferguson made his way into the tavern, Duncan and Tavis mounted their horses. Duncan had not learned a thing while mingling with the cliental, but he was making some headway. The locals were becoming comfortable around him. Tomorrow he would prepare for the ball. So many irons in the fire, but they all tied together to the one greater goal.

Tavis turned his horse at the intersection. "This is where we part ways."

"'Twas guid seeing you." Duncan continued toward his home. The moon lit the road, making an easy ride.

By the time he reached his destination, his body called for the soft comfort of his bed. He handed off his mount to Langley, a sleepy stable worker, and took the steps leading to his front door two at a time, belying his tired bones. At last he stepped over the threshold. Leaning against the foyer wall, he slipped his boots off and quietly made his way to his room, a habit he had acquired as a lad, trying not to wake the whole household, and one that seemed hard for him to break even if only servants lived there.

His door stood ajar, and he snuffed out the last wall lamp before he slipped through the opening. A lit oil lamp sat on the table beside his bed, where the covers were pulled back. Duncan tossed his coat on the chair and gave a sigh as he sank onto the mattress and started stripping off his shirt.

"Will you be needing anything, sir?"

Duncan shot off his bed and grabbed for a gun that wasn't there. Luck was with Stuebing this night.

"Crevvens, Stuebing. Dinna do that. You are either going to be the death of me or the death of you."

Stuebing's lips twitched. "Yes sir. I made sure there was no weapon within your reach before I spoke. That would just leave the death of you then, sir."

Duncan couldn't pull his eyes away. Was that humor on the old chap, again? "I prefer to live, also."

The valet didn't flinch. "As do I, sir. I would hate to have to look for another employer. Do you need anything?"

"No, no' tonight."

Stuebing pivoted around and disappeared from the room. As the door closed behind him, Duncan burst out laughing. The man was developing a sense of humor. Though his ability to slip in and out was a wee bit unnerving. Perhaps he should check his valet's arm for a tattoo.

Chapter 10

Papa surely fumed by now. Charlotte slipped on her shoes and went to the mirror for one last look to see if everything was in order. She turned to Nellie. "Are you ready?"

Nellie smiled from where she sat on the bed. "Only for about an hour now."

Charlotte bit her lip to keep from smiling. "I suppose we should go." She led the way down to the waiting carriage. "Just want to be fashionably late."

"I think Papa is getting a bit tired of your *fashionably late*."

As usual, Papa stood holding the door, tapping his thumb against his pocket watch. Right on cue, he stuck it back in his waistcoat pocket. Charlotte grinned at Nellie, who only shook her head.

Papa assisted her and Nellie into the carriage where Mama waited. Papa took his own seat, rapped on the top, and the horses jerked the carriage forward. They were on their way.

The leather two-seater carriage rolled along, hitting the occasional rut and sending Charlotte bouncing and bumping into her sister. She slipped the thin ribbon of her fan onto her wrist to prevent it from falling to the floor. "I don't know why someone doesn't fix these roads."

Papa, who had been leaning back with his eyes closed, flicked them open. "Because with all the rain, no one could keep the holes filled. They would just continue to wash back out."

Charlotte braced for Papa's usual litany.

He sat forward. "Everything costs money, girls. The sooner you realize that, the better off you'll be. You can't have everything you want. Men work hard for the money to provide for their families. It's expensive to purchase clothes and food.

Not to mention shoes and—" He paused and looked at the fan still clasped in her hand. "—the other ridiculous trinkets you women think you need."

Charlotte sighed inwardly. She loved Papa, but she could probably recite his speeches verbatim, and this one would see them all the way to the outskirts of town and Mr. Mackenzie's estate.

And it did.

Charlotte peered out the window. "Looks like we're not the only late arrivals."

"No. This time I got the last laugh." Papa grinned. "We told you the wrong time. We are actually here precisely on time."

Mama giggled, and Nellie joined in. Charlotte looked from one to the next and finally gave into her mirth. "Well, you can't say I didn't try."

The carriage pulled to a halt and the door swung open. Her father stepped down. "No one is accusing you of that, daughter."

Charlotte stood on the carriage step and looked at the stately home. It was by far grander than what she'd expected from a bachelor. The home had to be twice the size of her family's. Four pillars adorned the front. Both the upper and lower levels had porches that wrapped around as far as she could see. Large windows covered the front on both levels, reminding her of the elegant houses in town. The manor was magnificent. Winding around the home, well-groomed paths were lined with assorted flowers still holding their color.

Nellie nudged her from behind. "Are you going to keep standing there, or are you going to move so I can get out of this carriage?"

Charlotte turned to answer Nellie, but not before she saw Mr. Mackenzie watching from an upper window.

She raised her chin and stepped to the ground.

Nellie drew up beside her. "Gracious. This is much nicer than I had expected."

Charlotte couldn't help but smile at her sister's enthusiasm because it mimicked her own thoughts. "It is grand, isn't it?"

"Oh my, yes. I heard Mama and Papa talking. Apparently the house had been in need of repair from the War of Northern Aggression. Mr. Mackenzie hired poor folk and those out of work to restore the house."

"Pfft! Why doesn't that surprise me? He is obviously very rich and comes here to America to take advantage of our poor. Well. I'm glad Papa knows this. Now he won't think so highly of Mr. Mackenzie."

Nellie giggled. "I am afraid, dear sister, you are wrong. Papa may think highly of him now that he has seen this place. I know Papa told Mama that Mr. Mackenzie paid his workers quite handsomely."

She gave an unladylike *humph*. "He may have been generous in this instance, but I'm sure he has many flaws. There is a reason the Bible says it is hard for a rich man to get to heaven."

"You really shouldn't take scriptures out of context. You're still angry because he told you to bring your blue dress. I think he's a kind man, and you're lucky you've caught his eye."

"Shhh." Charlotte lowered her voice. "I wish I hadn't told you that."

Nellie grinned, then whispered back. "You didn't willingly. You slipped."

The large double doors swung open, and Mr. Mackenzie strode out with a smug smile on his face, his gaze set on her. "'Tis glad I am to see you and your fine family." He shifted his gaze to Papa.

Papa advanced and stuck out his hand. "Mr. Mackenzie, it's good to see you. Fine home you have here."

As the men clasped hands, Charlotte sniffed before she could stop herself. She covered with a slight cough. Mr. Mackenzie's brow went up. Nellie's eyes twinkled, and Charlotte prodded her with her elbow, holding back her own smile.

Mr. Mackenzie gave Papa's hand an extra pump. "Call me Duncan. Please." He bowed and extended his arm for Charlotte and her family to pass by and enter his home. With Nellie by her side, Charlotte sashayed past him and into the vestibule. Her breath caught. She'd thought she'd entered the vestibule, but the room where she stood was too large and too beautiful to be called a vestibule. It was more like a grand ballroom. The marble-paved floor glistened beneath her feet. Beautiful oil paintings hung on each wall, depicting a different time in history of what she could only assume was his homeland. Hunters and their ever-faithful deerhounds bringing down the mighty stag with antlers as wide as a man is tall. A castle and the men gathered in full armor ready for battle. Glens and moors and sheep scattered in the fields covered the canvases. Pillars framed the fireplace on both sides and extended to the ceiling, drawing Charlotte's gaze up to the plaster heights that held intricate lacework patterns. The room was magnificent.

Mr. Mackenzie looked pleased. He turned to meet her approaching parents. "Let me show each of you to your rooms, and I'll have the staff bring your things up straightaway."

They followed him up a wide, open staircase, and at the top Mr. Mackenzie turned to the left and proceeded down a hallway. He opened the first door and ushered her parents in. "I hope you will find the accommodations satisfactory."

Mama gave him a smile. "It's lovely. Thank you."

"Your daughters will be in the next rooms." Mr. Mackenzie took a step toward the door and stopped. "You're free to explore the house and gardens. There are many flowers still in bloom."

Nellie and Charlotte followed him out of their parents' room and into the next. Mr. Mackenzie faced Nellie. "Miss Jackson, this will be your room."

Nellie's face lit up. "Oh! A room to myself." She looked at Charlotte. "Not that I mind sharing with you."

"I understand, but you'll miss me." Charlotte fluttered her lashes at her sister, then looked at Mr. Mackenzie.

"I assume my room is next door?"

"Aye, lass that it is." Mr. Mackenzie moved into the hall. Charlotte frowned at the distance between her and Nellie's doors. He turned the knob and pushed the door open and waited as she walked in. The room was twice the size of her sister's room and her parent's. She spun around and met his gaze. "There must be some mistake."

"Nay mistake, lass. 'Tis the room I have chosen for you." Blue window dressings and a bed covering the color of her dress, the one she'd given to Nellie, adorned the room. A coincidence? She doubted Duncan Mackenzie ever did anything that wasn't calculated. Two could play at his game.

"Such an exquisite color." She strolled over to the bed and ran her hand over the silky blend of fabric. "It reminds me of my blue dress." She swung around to reconnect with his gaze and then smirked. "Or I should say Nellie's dress."

The recognition was there. She smiled to herself. It wasn't what he had expected. "Speechless, sir?"

A grin crept across his face. "Did the lass bring it?"

She hesitated. "Yes."

"Perhaps you could borrow it. You looked verra bonnie in it."

She drew herself up. "I begin to think my first impression of you was correct."

Mr. Mackenzie cocked his head. "And that would be?"

"You have the manners of a sheep farmer."

Mr. Mackenzie burst out laughing. "And what would you ken aboot a sheep farmer's manners, lass?"

She sputtered. "Well, I can surely imagine."

"Could you now? Would you like to share some of those visions?" His chortle that followed his rude remark grated against her nerves.

"You sir, are a beast."

"A beast with the manners of a sheep farmer." He moved out of the doorway and into the hall still chuckling. "You and I, lass, have much in common."

Charlotte scowled.

"Enjoy the room, lass. I'll have your bags sent straight up."

Blessed silence filled the room. She took a deep breath, giving her heart time to calm. At least he was gone. From the hall outside her room another roar of laughter met her ears. The man was insufferable.

Dropping onto the side of the bed, she listened to Mr. Mackenzie's chortles grow fainter. They were alike? *Indeed.* The nerve of him. They were no more alike than oil and water. And she would avoid mixing with Mr. Mackenzie and all temptation the man may cause her to fall into.

Charlotte threw her shoulders back. She would do her best not to let him raise her ire, but it would take a lot of prayers. The man deliberately tried to provoke her.

Noise from outside the window drew her, and she hurried across the room and tugged back the curtain. New arrivals pulled up on the circular driveway. The servants scurried around, helping women alight and pulling trunks and bags from the vehicles. Craning her neck to see the front entrance, she saw no sign of Mr. Mackenzie. Apparently he didn't greet every carriage as he had her family's.

A light tapping on the door made her understand why he didn't greet the new arrivals. What did he want now? God must be testing her patience. She didn't budge. "Yes?"

"Your bags, miss."

Relieved it wasn't Mr. Mackenzie, Charlotte hurried over to open the door. "I'm sorry. Please, put them over there." She pointed to the end of the bed.

A tall, ebony-skinned man brought in her luggage and placed them on the floor where she pointed. "Is there anything you need, miss?"

"No, thank you."

"Mr. Mackenzie asked me to give you this message." He placed an envelope in her hand and bowed before he left.

When the latch clicked shut, Charlotte sat in the chair by the window and slid open the note.

Bride by Blackmail

Dear Miss Jackson,
Would you do me the honor of sitting beside me at the noon meal? No response is necessary. I look forward to your dining with me.

Humbly Yours,

Duncan

Who did he think he was? Her father? Telling her she would be sitting beside him for the midday meal. And there was nothing humble about the man. Humph. Duncan Mackenzie just might drive her crazy. The last thing she needed was to sit next to him. Didn't God's word say if your eye caused you to sin to pluck it out and throw it away, or if your hand caused you to sin cut if off and throw it away?

She'd be happy to throw him in the rubbish heap. She was sure the anger he caused her crossed over into sin. She should flee from this place. When the midday meal came, she would sit with her family. After all, that was what an obedient daughter would do—sit with her parents.

There was only one way she would get through this weekend. *Oh, Father, what am I to do? I am here and I don't see how I can avoid him all the time. Please help me be civil to Mr. Mackenzie. Help me to be pleasing to you and give me patience to get through this weekend.*

Charlotte opened her eyes. She would do best by staying as far from Mr. Mackenzie as possible.

Another knock at the door set her heart thrumming. "Yes?"

"It's me, Nellie. May I come in?"

"Yes." Before Charlotte had finished her answer, Nellie slipped through the door opening and across the floor.

"Oh, how beautiful. My room is too, but not nearly as large. The chamber I am staying in is yellow. So very bright and cheerful. I love the color of this one." She pirouetted and glanced around at the furnishings. "It reminds me of the blue dress you gave me. You don't suppose he put you in here because of..."

Charlotte winced at the mention of the blue dress. For heaven's sake, couldn't people forget about that? Though she did seem to make a big impression that night. Never had she had so many men clamoring to dance with her, and their requests certainly assuaged her wounded ego somewhat after Frank's snubbing.

"...and to think a man as kind as he could have all this wealth. After all Papa has said, I'd have expected him to be rather pompous, coming from Britain and money." Nellie stopped and skimmed her hand over the taffeta coverlet on Charlotte's bed. "Yes, I would say he was telling you something by putting you in this room. Amazing how he can say so much with so few words."

"Nellie, do you want to stay in here? Because if you do, please stop going on about Mr. Mackenzie." Charlotte huffed and went to the mirror to check her hair. It was almost time to freshen up anyway. "Are Mama and Papa still in their room?"

"No, I believe they went down to 'admire the landscape,' as Papa said."

"More than likely to see how wealthy his new customer is, if I know Papa." Charlotte tucked a stray strand back into her coiffure. "Are you ready to go down to eat?"

"Yes."

After asking busy servants for directions, they found their way to the dining room. Many guests had already taken their seats. Charlotte was glad to arrive a midst the business so she could quietly join her parents.

Nellie rose on tiptoes. "Look. There's Mama and Papa." She raised her hand and waved with excitement.

Charlotte chuckled and waited for the response she knew would come from Papa. He always attempted to stifle Nellie's enthusiasm. She continued to flail her arm until she caught Papa's attention. As usual, he rolled his eyes and drew his lips down. He spoke something in Mama's ear, and she looked up, straight-faced, but her eyes danced. With a subtle shake of her mother's head, Nellie brought down her arm.

"Let's go sit." Nellie took two steps into the room and studied the elegantly set tables. "Name cards." Her shoulders dropped, and she let out a sigh. "I assume we are to sit with our parents. I would much rather sit with someone our own age."

Charlotte's gaze shot around the room, then to the chair at the head of the table. Duncan hadn't arrived. She grabbed Nellie's hand and pulled her in that direction. If she could snatch her card from its place and replace it with someone else's, Mr. Mackenzie would not be able to do a thing. He certainly wouldn't make the person move when their name card designated the seat next to him. She grinned and picked up her pace. The card was there, as the note had said it would be.

Nellie squealed. "There's my name."

Charlotte cringed as people's heads turned. She seized her name from the table but wasn't able to move. Nellie stood on her dress. Charlotte swung around and spoke in a low voice. "Nellie, you are standing on my dress."

Nellie didn't look at her. Her sister was looking over her head with wide eyes. The hairs on the back of Charlotte's neck prickled. She slowly turned around and gazed at the buttons of a very fine black dinner jacket. Her eyes followed the buttons up to peer into the twinkling eyes of Duncan Mackenzie.

"Glad I am to see you received my note and found your place." He moved around and pulled out her chair.

Charlotte glanced back at Nellie, who hadn't moved a muscle and still gawked steadily at the large Scotsman. "Nellie." Charlotte drew in a deep breath and raised her voice. "Nellie."

Nellie pulled her focus away and looked at her sister. "S-sorry."

"You are still standing on my dress."

Nellie giggled and sidestepped.

Charlotte huffed and pulled the gown from beneath her sister's raised foot. Mr. Mackenzie continued holding the chair, a droll smile on his lips. She moved to the seat and wanted to flop down in it, but her eye caught her parents' ever watchful gazes. She stopped mid-fall to sweep her hands beneath her gown and tuck it neatly under her before lowering herself into the chair.

Mr. Mackenzie proceeded to Nellie's chair and pulled it out. Nellie's feet didn't move, and her gaze was once again fixed on Duncan. She bit her bottom lip. "I believe your shoulders are as wide as my uncle's prize bull."

Duncan Mackenzie threw his head back and roared with laughter, drawing the guests' interest. Charlotte wanted to disappear under the table. She didn't fancy being the entertainment for this party.

Mr. Mackenzie, however, seemed oblivious to the stares and snickers that the clamor had brought. "Let me get this straight. Your sister likens me to a beast and a sheep farmer, and now I remind you of a prize bull. I believe I will take yours as a compliment." Duncan shifted his gaze to Charlotte. "This should prove to be a verra interesting weekend."

Chapter 11

How did a man win the obstinate Miss Jackson? The recreation room had finally emptied out and there Duncan pondered the night's events. Tavis took a seat across from him. "You've been in deep thought, my friend." Duncan took his focus from the fire's flickering flames and turned it onto his friend. "Do you ken the lass doesn't like me?" A grin spread across Tavis's face. "I'm guessing you are speaking of Miss Jackson. Aye, I was beginning to get that impression. What did you do to her?" Duncan scratched his head. "I dinna do a thing. I've done everything right. All females like to dance, so I threw a ball. They like the most important seat, so I sat her at the head table. And doesn't every woman want her best friend included? So I invited her sister and sat her beside Charlotte."

"Perhaps it is the way you have done it, Duncan. Maybe the lass would like more talking."

"Any attempt to engage her in conversation to let her ken I have taken notice of her is rebuffed. All she will do is answer my questions in a civil manner and turn back to Nellie." Duncan replied in frustration.

"You mean to tell me you have lost your silver tongue?" Tavis goaded.

Duncan ignored his friend's comment and continued to lament. "It is no' as if I am a pauper. Most women are drawn to a mon with money no matter his age or looks. And it isn't as if I am a homely mon. I'm certainly no' scrawny or sickly."

He could see Tavis was having a difficult time holding in his laughter. "Beauty is in the eye of the beholder, my friend."

Duncan glared at him. "What does she find lacking in me?"

"I am afraid only she can answer that question. Perhaps you should ask her or pursue another lass. Her sister is every bit as bonnie."

"Aye, I have thought those verra same things. Nellie is bonnie, but I canno' stop thinking of Charlotte. 'Tis like no other lass will do. Her zest for life and the fire within her draws me—mesmerizes me."

"Well, Duncan, I think the chase has much to do with her appeal. You aren't used to not getting what you want."

"I think the lass is blinded by Frank Sorrell."

"I can't believe I'm seeing this with my own eyes." Tavis guffawed, placing his hand on his chest. "It's with heavy heart I tell you that perhaps you'll have to lower yourself and do what most men have to do."

"And what would that be?"

"You, my dear friend, are going to have to woo the lady."

Duncan pushed himself from the chair. "'Tis what I've been trying to do."

Tavis shook his head. "Then you'll have to try harder."

That he would. And with the dinner hour close at hand, he left Tavis and made his way to his room to ensure he looked his best. Stuebing waited near a chair pulled to the center of the room with Duncan's coat lying over it. Duncan's trousers and shirt lay on the bed.

His valet came forward and helped him from his coat. Duncan cleaned up and dressed while Stuebing busied himself in and out of the room.

"You can have the honors of the tie. 'Tis the most aggravating piece of attire I have yet to encounter."

With a few twists and snaps of his fingers, Stuebing finished with the tie. He pulled Duncan's coat off the back of a chair and held it out. Duncan slipped his arms in and shrugged it on as the short Englishman circled him, eyeing his attire. "I have to look my best." Duncan grinned. "A lady, again."

Stuebing made a noise that sounded like a half-sniff and a half-grunt. "I *always* dress you to look your best, sir."

Duncan chuckled and took his leave.

Standing at the entrance of the ballroom, he studied the room with all the trappings he'd ordered to make this a memorable event. Welcoming the guests as they entered, he then directed the ladies to a table laden with dance cards.

It appeared most of the guests had arrived—all but Charlotte and her sister. Duncan grunted. How long could it take the lass to prepare? Certainly, she would not be so bold as to skip the ball.

Five minutes later, Duncan still stood waiting at the entrance of the room. With a motion of his hand he summoned a servant. Just as he tipped his head to speak, he spied Charlotte and Nellie approaching. Duncan sent the man back to his post and awaited the ladies.

He pulled two dance cards from his jacket, glanced at them and stuck one back in his pocket. Nellie greeted him as she stopped before him. He tied the card on her wrist before leaning down near her ear. "Be sure and save me a dance, lass."

He was rewarded with a beaming smile.

"It will be my pleasure, sir."

Charlotte, wearing a moss green gown, stood behind her sister. As she moved in front of him, Duncan pulled the remaining dance card from his pocket and tied the ribbon on her wrist. "You are a wee bit late, are you no'?"

Charlotte raised her chin. "Fashionably so." She gave him a nod and sashayed into the ballroom.

His gaze followed her as in regal form she swept across the room to her parents. He didn't want to miss the moment when she opened her card.

Tavis sauntered over.

Duncan straightened his tie. "I think that was aboot the end of the guest list. Are you ready to fill up some of these lasses' dance spots?"

"That I am." Tavis's eyes glimmered with eagerness as he gazed on the festooned room and the fair ladies within.

The band warmed up, and Duncan strolled into the room toward Charlotte. Mr. Sumpter approached her, and she radiated with delight. Jealousy prickled Duncan's insides. He shrugged it off, desiring to see her smile at him that same way.

She slid her dance card off her wrist and lifted the cover, allowing Mr. Sumpter to pen his name on one of the dances.

"Encouraging." Duncan mumbled.

"What's that?" Tavis's gaze followed his friend's.

"Miss Jackson had little response when she opened her dance card."

"And what did you do?" Tavis eyed him carefully.

"Just penned my name on a couple of dances, 'tis all."

"I will assume the dinner dance was one."

"Aye."

Tavis shook his head. "And this is how you woo? You don't even ask?"

"Nay. She could have said no."

"You, my friend, need lessons on wooing." With that Tavis strode away and toward a fair lass.

The crowd closed in, and he lost sight of Charlotte, so he moved in her direction. Before he could reach the other side of the room, Miss Nellie crashed into him, losing her balance. He clasped hold of her arms and steadied her. "Where do you go in such a hurry, lass?"

A pink flush filled Nellie's cheeks, and she gulped in air. "I am terribly sorry, Mr. Mackenzie. I was..." She stopped and caught her breath. "I was trying to get over to Will...Mr. Sumpter."

"I dinna think he will be going far."

"But I wanted to get to him before he signs his name to someone else's dinner dance."

Duncan let go of her arms. "If he's already asked you for the dance, lass, I dinna think you have to concern yourself. He'll still honor it, signature or no'."

Duncan observed with interest as her pink flush turned a bright red.

Nellie's lashes fluttered down. "He hasn't asked me. That is, I was hoping he would ask."

Her sigh spoke volumes, but the slump in her shoulders tugged at his heart. What was it about these Jackson women that stirred something in him? Heaven help him when he got to know the other three sisters. "I have a small matter to discuss with your sister. Why dinna I walk you over to them, and perhaps I can clue Mr. Sumpter in that you dinna have a dinner partner."

"You'd do that for me? Oh, thank you."

She appeared about to throw her arms around him, but then blinked, apparently thinking better of it. He offered her his arm, and they proceeded through the ballroom. "Aye, I am happy to help you oot. But you have to save one dance for me."

She tipped her head to the side and smiled at him—the same smile as Charlotte's. But never had Charlotte bestowed that smile on him.

Nellie squeezed his arm slightly. "Which dance would you like?"

"I would be honored to have the third dance. That is, if it is still open."

"Most of mine are open. Charlotte wanted to be the last one to arrive. She always is. Says it's fashionable. Not for me when I'm trying to get dances secured."

He chuckled. "Once the men ken your card is no' full, they'll be standing in line." The vision of the men crowding around Charlotte at the last dance flashed through his thoughts.

"Do you wish to discuss the dinner dance with my sister?"

Duncan coughed. "Aye, it is that." They reached the small party standing together. "May I?" He took the pencil and scrawled in his initials on the younger Miss Jackson's card.

"I'll look forward to our reel." Nellie turned to Mr. Sumpter and smiled. "Good evening, Mr. Sumpter."

"A delight to see you, Miss Jackson." Mr. Sumpter bowed.

"Are you enjoying your visit to Charleston?" Duncan asked Sumpter.

Sumpter flicked a glance at Nellie. "I certainly am. So much beauty within the city."

"That it has." Duncan's eyes shifted to the sisters.

Charlotte whispered something in Nellie's ear. Duncan could imagine what that was. But it gave him the opportunity to hint to Sumpter that Miss Nellie would make a fine dinner partner. The sisters separated as the musicians struck up their first number. Charlotte tensed.

Duncan gave her a slight bow. "I believe this is my dance." The Virginia reel music began, and he led her to the floor. "Come now, lass, I am a verra guid dance partner. I weel no' shame you."

Charlotte lifted her chin. "I have no doubt you can dance the reel as well as you do a waltz."

Duncan grinned. "You think I waltz weel, then?"

The reel started and the couples lined up. Duncan and Charlotte drew together. He bowed, and she curtsied, then they returned to their row. Next, they met, he took her hands to shuffle sideways down the center of the two lines, while he admired the way her skirts rippled and shimmered under the light of the chandelier, and the becoming rose of her cheeks.

"I didn't say that." Charlotte paused as they switched directions and shuffled back to their places. "I said you could dance. I didn't mean to imply anything. Just that you could." They reached the end of the line and went back to their positions.

Duncan never walked away from a challenge, and Miss Jackson was assuredly that. The reel continued, but with no more conversation. Each time they came together in the dance, she looked every other way but his. As the song ended, Charlotte tucked an unruly strand of hair behind her ear and, before he could offer her his arm to escort her off the dance floor, rushed away.

He made his way around the hall speaking with each of his guests, dancing with a few of the lasses that seemed to have become wallflowers along the way. He wasn't interested in any of the other ladies. Especially the ones who batted their eyes at him, acted coy, and played games with their fans. Nay, just one attracted him this night, and she obviously preferred to avoid him.

Dancing with Nellie revealed very little despite his continued efforts to find out Charlotte's thoughts. The most he got from her was to be patient with her sister.

Sauntering over toward the refreshments, Duncan stopped short of the table to speak to Miss Campbell and Mr. Hewitt. "Good evening."

Mr. Hewitt nodded, and Miss Campbell smiled.

Duncan glanced at Hewitt, then at the lass. "Miss Campbell, you are looking bonnie this evening."

She giggled. "Thank you."

He turned to Mr. Hewitt. "How are the wedding plans coming along?"

Hewitt started to shrug and must have thought better of it. "You would have to ask my betrothed."

Duncan tipped his head down and let his eyes rest on Miss Campbell as he waited for her reply.

"Everything is coming splendidly." She looked at him with mischief in her eyes. "I ran into the Jackson sisters while shopping for a dress. They're both lovely ladies."

"As are you, Miss Campbell." Duncan's gaze swept the room at the mention of the sisters and stopped on Miss Charlotte. Her head bobbed as laughter flowed from her plump pink lips. A mixture of golden and ash curls spilt down her back. Duncan forced his attention back to his guests.

"What a beautiful place you have here," Miss Campbell said.

Duncan smiled. "Thank you. Do you have any dances open?"

Hewitt threw back his shoulders and put his hand on Miss Campbell's elbow in one swift movement. "No, she does not."

Duncan smiled at Hewitt. Perhaps the man had learned to value the lady. Nothing wrong with being protective. He'd take his leave and relieve the man's worries. "Then, if you will excuse me, I need to see to my other guests." He took Miss Campbell's hand and squeezed it. "I'll be expecting a wedding invitation soon."

Duncan finished the short trek to the refreshment table and picked up a glass of punch to quench his parched throat. The musicians finished up a quadrille, and the dinner dance would follow. If it went anything like the first dance, he'd be doing all the talking while Miss Jackson did everything she could to avoid his gaze.

Duncan clunked his glass down on the table and strode toward Charlotte. She remained steadfastly in the same place she'd been when last he looked for her as he spoke with Miss Campbell. His eyes narrowed as he drew near. Tavis had suddenly come to capture Charlotte's attention. She patted her fan on Tavis's shoulder and shook her head as a grin teased her lips. Tavis chuckled and her face lit up with amusement. She shook her head again and her gaze met Duncan's. The smile faded. He would have given anything to see it return. However, that was unlikely when he was the reason it disappeared.

Despite his disappointment, he gave her a courtly bow. "I believe this is my dance."

Chapter 12

Barbaric. That was the only word Charlotte could come up with to describe a man who would have the audacity to write his name in on a lady's card without her permission. Not once but three times. What would people think? Sweet mercy. Every man in the county would think she had her sights set on Mr. Mackenzie or, worse, that they were promised to each other. Didn't he know there was protocol to follow? Why did the man have to attach himself to her? He was worse than a leech.

With a sigh of resignation, she let him escort her onto the dance floor. She had hoped Tavis Dalzell would ask her for the dinner dance. It wouldn't take much to strike a line through his name and write in Mr. Dalzell's. Mr. Mackenzie could learn much about manners from his friend.

The tall Scot's arm wrapped around her waist, interrupting her thoughts as she gave him her hand. Within a few steps of the waltz, she was reminded that Mr. Mackenzie could waltz better than most. She didn't even have to think as they moved around the room because he guided her with such expertise.

"You're lovelier than the heather that adorns the Highlands." His breath tickled her ear and caressed her neck.

Her belly fluttered, and she frowned at its betrayal. "I'm sure you say that to all the ladies."

Mr. Mackenzie's grin grew. "Nay. Only the bonnie ones."

"Humph."

They glided around the dance floor, and he raised his arm as she twirled under it. The music filled the room while couples wove in and out about the dance floor. A smile touched her lips when they passed Nellie and Sumpter. Charlotte couldn't help herself and wiggled her brows at her sister. Nellie giggled, and Sumpter swept her away. Charlotte noted the extra sway in his step due to his injury, and so proud of her sister for falling right in with Mr. Sumpter's unusual rhythm.

"I hope you are enjoying yourself in my humble home."

Charlotte raised her eyebrows. "There is nothing humble about your home. False modesty doesn't become you, sir."

"There you're wrong, lass. I would take you to my Scotland estate where you would see this is merely a modest abode." Duncan pulled her closer.

She stiffened her arm and tried to force their bodies apart. "I shall have to take your word for it, sir. I have no intention of traveling across the ocean."

"I have a bonnie ship, and I could see to your utmost comfort."

Charlotte leaned her head back to examine his face. Was the man daft? Worse yet, was he serious? His strong arm tugged against her waist as she fought against it and tried to keep her step with the music. She wouldn't trust this man. Everything within told her he wasn't what he pretended to be. Let him find another female to pursue, one who was willing. "Sir, you insult me if you think I would *ever* consider such a proposition. Do you understand nothing of propriety?"

She bit her bottom lip. There was no reason to let him believe something that would never happen. "I don't mean to be rude. However, you need to understand I am not now, nor will I ever be, interested in you. You're wasting your time. I'm sure there are many young ladies whom you can win over with your home, wealth, and…" He raised his arm and gently guided her as she twirled beneath it. Oh, the man could move with such grace. Her mouth engaged before her mind. "… your dancing ability."

A dazzling smile spread across his face. She drew in a deep breath. Of all the times to let Nellie rub off on her. She should have kept that thought to herself. It wasn't what she meant to say. His smile not only remained, but it spread to his eyes. As if she had revealed some secret about herself.

"But what if I dinna find any other lasses to my liking?"

She had to discourage this incorrigible, irrational behavior of his. They were as different as she and her father. "I would say you need to search a little harder. We share nothing in common."

The dance ended. At the front of the hall the musicians set down their instruments. Duncan offered his arm and laid his hand over hers as they made their way ahead of the exodus of dancers heading for the dining room.

"As I said earlier, lass, I think we have much of the same interests. You just dinna want to see it."

That prickled her temper, but prudence told her not to jump at his bait. He goaded her, and she would not respond to it. She stole a glance at him as they continued through the crowd and couldn't help but notice the corner of his mouth seemed to want to curve upward.

"Mr. Mackenzie, believe what you wish. But it couldn't be any further from the truth."

Duncan guided them to the head of the table, and he pulled out her chair. She swept her gown beneath her and sat. The aroma of spices and herbs from a well-prepared meal tantalized her senses.

He took the seat beside her, then beckoned her sister to come. Nellie rushed forward with Mr. Sumpter's hand cupping her elbow. A flicker of respect lit in Charlotte's heart for Mr. Mackenzie, but she quickly snuffed it out.

Without a doubt, Mr. Mackenzie was a master chess player. He only invited them to sit by her to win her admiration, something she was loath to give him. He was not the man for her, and the sooner he made up his mind to that fact, the better. She would be more careful not to let him see her approval of his actions.

Sumpter drew Nellie's chair out. Nellie tilted her head toward her. "I'm having a marvelous time. How about you, Sis?"

Duncan's one eyebrow rose, almost daring her response. She gave him a mutinous glare and set her gaze back on Nellie. "How could I answer any other way than you have, dear sister, when my dinner partner is none other than our host?" She gave her biggest smile and let him decipher what she meant by that.

Duncan grinned. The man was incorrigible.

The guests grew louder as the meal progressed. Nellie leaned forward to be heard. "Your home is very beautiful, Mr. Mackenzie. I would love to see all of it."

Their host had lifted his fork full of roast beef to his mouth and hesitated. "I thought I made that clear, lass. You are welcome to wander around inside and oot. Make yourself at home."

Nellie wiggled in her seat. "You have so many things I'd love to ask you about. Do you think you could give us a tour?"

Charlotte blinked. Did she say *us*? What was she thinking? Charlotte lowered her head and picked at her food. She prayed she was speaking of Mr. Sumpter.

Nellie nudged Charlotte with her elbow. "We'd love that, wouldn't we, Charlotte?"

Charlotte refused to raise her head for fear she'd see that one brow raised in challenge again.

Nellie prodded her once more. "Isn't that so?"

"Weel, if it would mean that much to you lasses, I'd be more than pleased to take you around." His voice sounded strained.

Charlotte raised her eyes to see what ailed him. He was doing all he could to keep himself from laughing. The man was insufferable. It was no secret to him that she had no wish to take the tour. She wasn't getting through to him at all.

She frowned. Tomorrow she'd have to cry off from the event. She could have Nellie bring her a roll from breakfast and something at the midday meal to hold her over until dinner. Surely he'd take her sister around his home before evening. That settled in her mind, she picked up her fork and began to eat.

Savoring the taste of the fried okra, she chewed it slowly. There was a lot of food on the table tonight, and she'd fill up so as not to be too terribly hungry in the morning.

"As soon as you are all finished eating, I'll show you my home." Mr. Mackenzie dropped his silverware on his plate and shoved it away. "Sumpter, would you care to come along?"

Charlotte choked. Not now. There was no time to come up with an excuse. If he'd waited until later or tomorrow, she could have disappeared for a while. She reached for her water and gulped it down, having to stop in between coughs.

Nellie pounded on her back.

"I'm fine, Nellie. You can quit beating me now." She coughed again.

Duncan's face creased with concern. "Are you sure you're well?"

"Yes. I just choked. Nothing for anyone to worry about."

Nellie wrapped her arm around Charlotte and drew her near for a hug. "You scared me. Gracious, all I could think about was when great Aunt Emma took that big bite of meat and—"

"I don't think anyone wants to hear about that, Nellie."

Nellie glanced around the table at the people staring at her. Her gaze dropped. "No, I don't suppose they do."

"I would no' mind hearing your story sometime, Miss Jackson," Mr. Mackenzie said.

Nellie looked up and smiled as she stood. Charlotte had to admire the way he came to everyone's rescue. He didn't seem to like to see people ill at ease. Anyone but her, that is. He didn't mind putting her on the spot.

Charlotte took her time finishing her meal. She'd barely swallowed the last bite when Mr. Mackenzie pushed back from the table and stood in a fluid motion. "You coming with us, Mr. Sumpter?"

Mr. Sumpter, whom Charlotte had heard hardly a word from all evening, got out of his chair. "I'd be delighted to escort Miss Jackson anywhere. Wouldn't want to leave you with the two loveliest ladies here, Mackenzie. That is if it pleases you, Miss Jackson."

"I'd love to have you escort me." Nellie sighed.

Debbie Lynne Costello

Charlotte rolled her eyes. Mama really needed to have a talk with Nellie, because *she* wasn't getting through to her.

They passed the bedrooms her family stayed in. She noted several more closed doors along the way and he mentioned guests stayed in them.

He stepped into a large room. "The drawing room." He swung his arm out for them to pass.

The small group entered. Carpeting with deep burgundy and gold tones covered the floor. A fireplace drew her gaze to the far wall where a painting of a ship in a storm hung above it. Her mind went quickly back to the many books she'd read about ships. She'd love to travel on one someday. Several sets of upholstered chairs with tables in between were placed around the room. A gas chandelier hung from the center of the ceiling, illuminating the room.

"Such a beautiful room." Nellie's enthusiasm was not shared by Charlotte.

"Thank you, Miss Jackson." Duncan seemed genuinely pleased at her compliment.

It hadn't taken a terrible amount of time for their small group to make its way through Mr. Mackenzie's home. Their last stop—the library, a large, inviting room.

Once inside, Charlotte breathed in the smell of leather books and chairs that permeated the room. She ran her hand along the bindings as she strolled down the row, looking at the titles. Her gaze left her sister as she moved into the room, enjoying its ambiance. The library reminded her of her father's study—her favorite room. Two dark leather chairs sat facing a stone hearth. She made her way over to them. The fire popped, sending an array of fireworks up the chimney. Bagpipes hung on the wall, beckoning her. She wandered over to inspect the strange apparatus. She'd never seen one but recognized it from pictures. Hanging beside it was a woolen tartan that someone had painstaking pinned with pleats to create a kilt.

Nellie spoke from the other side of the room. "Mr. Mackenzie, do you have anything by Wilkie Collins?"

"I have *The Moonstone.*" Duncan's voice drew near.

"I've never had the opportunity to read it."

"You are welcome to borrow it."

Mr. Sumpter made his way over to Nellie and began to search for the book with her. Their light voices and exclamations of obvious treasures found carried through the room, enticing her to look through the titles. Before she could move, the smell of sandalwood wafted toward Charlotte, causing the hair on her neck to rise.

"'Tis my clan tartan."

Charlotte nodded and trailed her fingers up to a gold pin in the shape of a sword and shield. "And this?"

"That has been passed down from generation to generation. 'Tis a kilt pin and one of the few things I own that I cherish. 'Twas my great-great grandfather's. The thistle you see raised up in the center of the shield is the Scottish flower."

Charlotte moistened her lips. "A weed? A prickly weed is the only thing Scotland has to call a flower?"

His brows drew down, and she could have shouted with glee at the disgruntled look on his face. Of course, she knew they had heather and other lovely flowers, but he didn't know her love for books and that she knew much about many places.

"'Tis no' a *weed*. Every Scot from the time he is in swaddling clothes is told the story of how the thistle saved the Scots."

How she wished she could raise one brow as he did when he wanted to challenge her. Instead, she raised both brows and cocked her head.

"I tell you true, lass. King Haakon of Norway landed on the Coast of Largs at night, his goal to conquer the Scots. 'Twas dark, and his plan was to surprise the sleeping clansmen. To do that the Norsemen removed their footwear to move aboot quieter. But the area surrounding the clan was covered in thistle and one of the Norsemen stepped on it and let oot a yell, warning the sleeping Scotsmen o the impending attack. Needless to say, we Scots won."

Charlotte burst out laughing. "Really?"

Duncan chuckled. "'Tis true."

Nellie strolled over to them. "What's so funny, Charlotte?"

"Oh, nothing. Did you find the book you were looking for?"

Mr. Sumpter walked up behind Nellie with the book in his hand. "Got it right here."

"Oh, thank you." Nellie nudged Charlotte. "Come now, Sis. Tell me what amused you so."

"We were discussing the thistle and the beautiful heirloom that has been in Mr. Mackenzie's family for years. I suppose we should get back. We still have dance promises we must fulfill." Charlotte hooked her arm through her sister's and started toward the door.

Nellie sighed. "I didn't get my last dance filled."

Charlotte grimaced. "You can have mine."

Mr. Sumpter rushed ahead of them and drew the heavy oak door open. "What's that you said Charlotte?"

"We haven't much time."

Charlotte's gaze shifted to Mr. Mackenzie. By the way his brow rose, he must have heard her the first time. The room suddenly felt very warm, and she flicked open her fan to cool herself. What did she care if he heard her? She hadn't agreed to the dance with him.

Guests milled around the dimly lit halls as they made their way back to the ballroom. The sounds of the musicians' instruments floated down the passageway, gaining in volume the closer they drew.

"There you are, lass. I've been looking all over for you." Mr. Dalzell intercepted Charlotte as she entered the ballroom.

"I hope I didn't miss our dance." Charlotte took his offered arm.

"You're just in time." He guided her to the crowded floor as the music for the quadrille began and the people lined up.

They came together and clasped right hands as they turned in a circle. Mr. Dalzell smiled. "You and Duncan seem close. I'd thought you were fond of Mr. Sorrell."

Gracious, the man was impudent. "That is rather presumptuous of you, isn't it?"

He gave her a crooked grin. "How else am I to find out what your intentions are?"

Chapter 13

Women and traitors had much in common. They both kept Duncan awake at night. He lounged in the sitting room outside his bedchamber, his gaze resting on an oil painting of heather-covered hills. Legs extended, Tavis sat across from him in a golden tapestry chair. The guests had long retired for the evening and the halls had quieted. A deep yearning filled Duncan's belly for the moors and glens he'd left behind. Knowing he had no time frame to return added to the urgency. He was ready to do what had to be done so he could return to Scotland.

Tavis yawned. "I tried to get the lass to talk to me tonight. But she was unwilling to share."

Duncan stretched and rested his head against the chair back. He hadn't accomplished a thing tonight with Miss Jackson. The more she avoided him the more he wanted her. He laughed. "And you expected more."

Tavis shrugged. "I asked her if she still cared about Frank Sorrell. But she skirted the question. Sorry, my friend."

He leaned forward and tented his fingers. "I need to get my mind off the lass and direct my energy toward finding this turncoat. I've been thinking, maybe a trip down to the High Seas Shipping office would be helpful."

Tavis held a watch fob, twisting the chain and letting go, watching it spin. "I thought you'd already gone down to see them, and they denied your request to look at the books. Weren't they concerned with you stealing their business?"

"Aye, I've been down there several times, and it's the same thing every time."

"Then why do you think this time will be different?"

Duncan gave him a lazy grin. "Because this time I'm no' going to ask."

Tavis sat up and leaned forward. "You're going to steal what you want?"

"I've tried to be patient, but my patience has run oot. I dinna plan to actually take anything. I just need to see the books and find oot the names of the men who booked passage on that particular day. With all these guests here, the earliest will be the beginning of next week. Tuesday night, perhaps."

Tavis's face took on a sober appearance. He stuck his dangling watch into its pocket and raised his eyes to meet Duncan's. "You'll need help."

"Are you offering?"

"I'm busy all week, but Ferguson is always looking for excitement."

"Do you think he'd ask a lot of questions?"

"I think you could tell him anything."

"It'd be guid to have someone as a lookout. If we're caught…"

Tavis nodded. "There's always the chance the man didn't use his real name. Would you have?"

"I wouldn't. Neither do I ken what this mon was thinking. Did he even expect that someone would follow him across the ocean? I have to leave no stone unturned." Duncan stood. "I'm turning in. Could you plan to stay through Sunday night? 'Twould give us more time to go over this."

"I can."

♥♥♥

Turning the lass's head rather than locating a turncoat dominated Duncan's thoughts as he closed the door of his bedchamber. The fire flickered, throwing heat and a small amount of light into the room as he readied for bed. He reclined, clasped his hands behind his head, and stared at the undercover of his bed canopy. A vision of Charlotte danced on the ceiling with the shadows from the hearth's flames. The feelings she stirred within him gnawed at his sleep-deprived thoughts.

He shook his head and punched down his pillow. Who was he trying to fool? She wasn't going to look his way anytime soon. The lass could barely speak to him in a civil tone. He rolled to his side and stared at the wall. An idea formed in his head and he sat up, energized.

He would use her father's worries to his advantage. The man placed too much importance on appearance, but that would help his scheme. Sitting on the edge of his bed, he shoved his hand through his hair. If the plan unfolded as he hoped, Mr. Jackson would feel compelled to convince his daughter to marry him.

His heart drummed a wild beat in his chest. She might not want to marry him now, but after they were wed, she'd learn to respect him. Just like his mother respected his father. Time was all he needed—time to win her over. Duncan reclined back onto the bed. He'd set the plan in motion tomorrow and enlist Tavis's help. The only other person he would trust was Stuebing, but he'd need to catch his valet unaware to have surprise show on his face. He doubted Stuebing could pretend. As he closed his eyes, a flicker of hope eased his sleep.

Morning didn't come soon enough. The sun's rays peeked through the tiny opening in his curtains and sliced across his bed and into his eyes. His feet hit the floor, and he was in mid-stretch when Stuebing tapped on the door and stuck his head in.

"Your clothes, sir. I took the liberty of having them pressed."

Duncan scrubbed his morning shadow. "Thank you, Stuebing. You can place them on the bed."

"Do you need assistance?"

"Nay, I can see to it myself. Are there many guests up?"

"The young lady, Miss Jackson, came down early and went back to her room." Stuebing said no more.

Duncan smiled to himself. His valet knew him well.

"I take it you speak of the older sister, Miss Charlotte. Is Tavis moving around yet this morning?" Duncan splashed water onto his face.

"Yes, Miss Charlotte Jackson. And I haven't seen Mr. Dalzell, although I believe I've heard him stirring in his chamber." Stuebing laid out the clothes in the fastidious fashion he always did, all the items placed in the order they would be put on and spaced equal distances apart.

Duncan lathered and pulled out a straight blade. "That will be all I need for now. However, please stop and tell Tavis I need to speak to him."

"I'll do that straightaway, sir." Stuebing pulled the door shut as he exited.

Shortly after Stuebing left, Tavis appeared. Duncan bid him enter and quickly laid out to him the plan that had hatched in his mind late last night. He explained in minute detail what was expected of him tonight and tomorrow. If Miss Jackson responded in a positive way this evening, he would request permission to court her and abort the plan he'd revealed to Tavis.

The day progressed without a glimpse of Charlotte. By evening Duncan was a bit frustrated as he bathed and readied for the evening. He slipped his arms into the evening jacket Stuebing held for him. She'd not come to dine for the morning or noon meals. He'd been tempted to approach one of the Jacksons but refrained. If she was ill, he would have heard from one of the servants. News among the help traveled like water rushing down a riverbed.

Duncan shook off his wet hair, sending little droplets of water showering down on Stuebing and his coat. His valet's staunch expression never wavered as he continued to fuss over the jacket.

All day his mind wandered to his plan. 'Twas obvious the lass was avoiding him. If she didn't show for this evening's ball, he would speak to her father. She had to be out of the room for him to proceed with the plot. He sighed. Wooing her didn't look possible with the way she had holed up in her room. She'd obviously made her mind up and wanted no part of him.

Removing his pocket watch, he pressed a small button. The cover flipped open. The ball started in less than half an hour. Replacing the watch, he headed to the hall to welcome his visitors as they entered.

He stepped from the room and a young servant girl bobbed a curtsey, then scurried ahead, lighting the hallway gas lamps. Once downstairs, he encountered small groups gathered throughout the lower level, speaking in hushed tones. Duncan stopped briefly and spoke with various guests before striding into the hall where musicians warmed their instruments.

It'd been a temperate day for autumn, yet heat still lingered in the house. The chandeliers, lit with hundreds of tiny gas flames, threw excess warmth into the room. He glanced at the few guests milling around and found none of great interest so took his place by the door.

Slipping his hand into his pocket, he ran his fingers over the two dance cards.

Alan Ferguson, with his strawberry-blond hair, came in and shook Duncan's hand.

"Och! You made it. 'Tis glad I am to see you made it back for this evening's ball."

Ferguson grinned. "Weel, I had some business to take care of, but never do I miss dancing with a bonnie lass if at all possible."

Duncan chuckled. "I hoped to speak to you tonight."

"Does it have anything to do with what Tavis mentioned?"

"I would imagine. Are you interested? I can pay you for your help."

"Oh aye. I'm always game for adventure and can use a few dollars in my pocket, to be sure." Alan looked over the gathering horde of people entering the ballroom.

A flash of peach caught Duncan's eye, and he turned away from Ferguson to greet the guests…and came face to face with Charlotte.

"Good evening, Miss Jackson. 'Tis guid to see you. No' seeing you today, I had worried you may be under the weather."

"I am quite well, thank you."

"That does please me. And you are fashionably early." Duncan chuckled, pulled the cards out of his pocket, and opened one. "I have your card right here, lass. Let me help you tie it on."

Two wrinkle lines formed between Charlotte's brows. "If you don't mind, I believe I'd like to pick my own from the table."

The sound of a throat clearing brought Duncan's attention to the man behind Charlotte. Mr. Jackson stood there frowning at his daughter. Duncan's gaze shifted back to Charlotte. She sighed with great theatrics and lifted her hand.

He couldn't stop the grin that spread across his face. When she looked up, he had expected to see a little acceptance, but what he saw looked more like defiance than anything else. She would be pleasantly surprised when she discovered he'd only signed two of her dances—the dinner and the last.

Mr. Jackson shook his head before guiding his wife over to Mr. Sumpter. Nellie, by Mr. Sumpter's side, wore the blue gown he'd last seen on Charlotte.

"You look lovely this evening, Miss Nellie. I hope you dinna mind, but I took the liberty of signing my name to a dance."

Nellie's gaze flickered to where Mr. Sumpter stood talking to her parents and back to Duncan. "I'm honored to dance any set with you, Mr. Mackenzie."

Duncan chuckled. "I left your dinner set open. I thought you might have someone special you'd like to save that for."

Her cheeks blazed brilliant red, and her gaze dropped to the floor. Mr. Sumpter moved away from her parents almost on cue and made his way over to Nellie. "May I escort you to the refreshment table, Miss Jackson?"

As the couple walked away, Duncan pulled the watch from his coat and glanced at it. A quick look into the hall revealed his friend leaning against the wall. Duncan shoved the watch back into his pocket. Tavis gave him a mock salute and headed for the stairs. His friend would set the scheme into motion.

His chest constricted. If he had calculated Mr. Jackson's response correctly, this would all but ensure that Charlotte would become his wife. The brown-eyed lass had originally caught his attention because of her beauty, but admiration for her passion and her fierce loyalty to those she cared for soon overshadowed how bonnie she looked. His thoughts were interrupted by a deluge of guests forming a line to speak to their host before entering.

Speaking with each guest before they entered the ballroom—cementing, he hoped, his friendships and allies within the community. With any luck it would still the wagging tongues as to why he was here in the States.

After greeting the last guests, Duncan smiled as the band struck up their first song. Things were already falling into place.

Tavis strolled up. "You're sure about this?"

Duncan nodded toward a secluded area in the ballroom. Large urns filled with plants stood in pairs, blocking two doors. They made their way over and stood between the set sheltering them from all eyes.

"Aye, I am."

"What if something goes wrong?" Tavis tilted his head.

Duncan folded his arms in front of him. "I have faith that her father will do exactly what I expect."

"I hope you're right. Otherwise it could get messy if they wanted to call in the authorities."

Duncan shook his head. "Nay, that would be up to me." He peeked around one of the urns. "Weel, I need to get back to my guests."

"And I have a dance coming up."

Duncan parted from Tavis and strolled around the room signing his name on the cards of wallflowers. One young lady he led to the floor giggled nervously every time he spoke to her. To save them both from discomfort, he abandoned all attempts of conversation and tried to enjoy the dance. Wishing he were with Miss Charlotte, Duncan found himself seeking her out. He groaned. She was missing again.

Chapter 14

Oh, how she wanted to crumple the dance card Mr. Mackenzie had given her. The arrogance of the man irritated her like a stone in her shoe. He used everything to his advantage, including hosting the ball. *And* somehow he knew she wouldn't raise a fuss over his blatant misuse of her dance card. Charlotte made her way out of the ballroom and down the east hall to the library. She found the room empty. Thankful she'd left a couple dances open so she could slip away and not be missed, she dropped into a chair. Her fan, still attached by a string to her wrist, fell to her lap. Knowing the dinner dance came next was enough to make her want to escape the clamor of the ballroom for a few moments.

She'd prayed last night that Mr. Mackenzie wouldn't embarrass her again by putting his name on her card three times, and God had answered her prayer with one fewer. Only now she wished she had asked God for no dances with the man. It was better that way. The tall, broad-shouldered Scotsman with his thick brogue caused her stomach to do strange things.

She sighed. He thought too much of himself, and surely she could never care for someone like that. The insufferable grin of his face had wedged in her mind's eye to the point of distraction. And that single brow, cocked impudently at her with no other purpose than to make her knees weak—but apparently not too weak to dance.

Well, he'd best enjoy it, because it would soon be over for good. The evening was near half-finished, and her time here was ticking away with every dance step she took. She need only get through the night. In the morning she would pack her bags and bid Mr. Mackenzie good day. The thought almost made her giddy.

She'd survived most of the weekend. She could make it through the rest.

This room didn't hold the blessed silence she sought. The noise from the evening activities carried down the hall. But being there gave her a chance to catch her breath. Before long the click of shoes on the hall floor grew closer, drowning out the ball ruckus. The door swung.

A man of medium height with strawberry-blond hair strolled into the room. Charlotte jumped up from her comfortable seat.

He tipped his head. "Would you be Miss Charlotte Jackson?"

Charlotte glanced from him to the door, knowing she'd have to pass him to escape. She edged away from the chair. "Yes, I'm Miss Jackson."

"I have a message for you."

Charlotte stiffened.

"I'm sorry. I didn't mean to startle you. My name is Alan Ferguson. I ran into Frank Sorrell while getting a breath of fresh air."

Charlotte's throat went dry. She attempted to speak, but her voice would not cooperate. The only sound that came out was a squeak.

"Are you ill, lass?"

Charlotte reached for a pitcher on the table near her and poured some water into the glass sitting next to it. Her fan still dangled from her wrist, and she removed it, laying it on the table before taking the glass. Several gulps later she forced her words out. "No, I'm well. Now, did you say Mr. Sorrell? I was under the assumption he hadn't been invited."

"Invited or not, he is in the garden."

Charlotte pursed her lips. "Why would he come *here?*"

"That I don't know, miss. He asked me to fetch you. He said you only need to come down the sidewalk path."

She did want to say something to Frank. He needed to leave her alone. But her father would be none too happy if he found out she had spoken with him. "I'd appreciate it if you wouldn't share this information with anyone."

"Your secret is safe with me, miss."

Charlotte hurried past him and exited the library. What would bring Frank this far and this late at night? It must be important—not a death or he would have summoned Mr. Sumpter. She didn't dare risk going upstairs to her chamber to get her shawl. If someone saw her with it, there would be no explaining why she needed it when the rooms were warm. However, if she just slipped out the door, perhaps no one would notice.

She stood back and waited for the entrance hall to empty of guests before passing through. Her body tensed. Wisdom said *don't go unescorted.* It was folly. She should return to the ballroom. But instead she dashed to the door. Just before she pulled the door shut, the rumble of a man's voice she didn't recognize was joined by the titter of a young woman.

The sun had gone down, and the evening air held a chill. A shiver crept up her spine. Whether it was from the night's damp air she'd stepped into, the idea of being found out, or the fact that she knew she shouldn't go alone, she didn't stop to consider. With arms folded around her, she fled down the steps. Quickening her pace, she followed the winding walk.

Lamps lit the way along the path. The music floated from open windows. She glanced up at Mr. Mackenzie's house, her eyes drawn to the large windows and partygoers inside. She never should have come alone. If one person saw her... she spun around to retreat back to the warmth and security of the inside.

Strong arms wrapped around her, trapping her against his hard body. Chills swept through her. She opened her mouth to scream. Her attacker's mouth came smashing down on her lips. She twisted her head away and gasped.

"Don't be afraid. It's me." Frank's finger caressed the bare skin on her arm. "Heaven knows I've missed you."

Anger surged through her. She squirmed and tried to free herself. His grip tightened. "What do you want, Frank?"

"I want you. I miss you. I love you." He turned her to face him.

Her heart thudded hard enough to hear the blood pound in her ears. "Are you drunk again?" How she had longed to hear those three small words. But no longer.

"No, I haven't had a thing to drink."

Charlotte frowned. "I don't believe you."

"Okay, I had one or two, but I'm not drunk."

"So if you're not drunk, why are you here?" She had to tip her head back to be able to look into his face.

"I came with news about that Scot. I should have known he was out to steal my woman." He pulled her against him again. His fingers dug into her arms.

"Frank, you're hurting me." Tears stung her eyes. For the first time in her life, Frank frightened her.

"I'm sorry, darling. I didn't mean to." His grip remained firm. "It's just when I think of what that no good–"

"Frank." Charlotte all but yelled his name.

"Oh, darling, it makes me so mad when I think about him." He buried his head in her hair. "I'd like to call him out."

Charlotte wiggled again and thrashed her head. "First of all, I am *not* your darling. You gave that up the night of Mary Barrow's ball. And you sealed it the day of the box lunch auction. You treated me so poorly."

Frank jerked his head up and glared down at her. "Maybe you'll change your mind when you hear what your Scot did."

"He is not *my* Scot. Frank, please release me."

He shook his head. "No. If I do, you won't listen. You'll run back inside."

"I promise. I'll hear you out. Just let me go."

"I like you this close to me." He loosened his hold enough to ease the pain in her arms.

She fought the trembling of her body. "What do you want to tell me? I'm due in for the next set, and if I'm nowhere to be found, someone will come looking for me."

Frank sneered. "Let me open your eyes to what *really* took place at the Barrows' ball."

Charlotte looked up into his eyes. "Excuse me?"

"Do you also remember that before I could put my name on your dance card you were bombarded with men asking for dances?"

An uneasiness crept through Charlotte and nestled itself in the pit of her belly. "Y-yes."

"Didn't you wonder why so many men were suddenly interested in you? I surely did. I had thought I'd made it clear to them about you." He laughed.

She couldn't answer that. How could she say she thought they had found her irresistible in her blue dress? That they thought she was worth making Frank angry. She swallowed the lump in her throat. "Go on, Frank. I'm running out of time." One of the tears she fought to hold back trickled down her cheek.

"Upon a little investigating, I discovered that Duncan Mackenzie *paid* each of those men to dance with you." He snorted and laughed condescendingly. "Imagine. He had to *pay* someone to dance with you. That's a lot of money. Don't get me wrong, Charlotte. I think you're worth a dollar. But to have to pay someone." His shrill laughter bubbled up again.

Charlotte squared her shoulders for show. "That's what you came to tell me? You rode all this way to tell me that?"

"That and to tell you I love you, and I want to marry you. Don't you see that the Scot is trying to take you from me? He doesn't care about you."

Her heart ached. How long had she waited to hear those words come from Frank's lips? And now they weren't as sweet as she'd once imagined. Instead, it was bitter milk from a dandelion. She wanted to rip her hands free and run away. Run until her legs could take her no farther and then fall down and cry until the tears would come no more. But she wouldn't. She would put on the good appearance her upbringing demanded.

"I heard what you had to say, now let me go." She tried to step back.

"No."

She pulled, trying to free herself. "What do you want from me?"

He jerked her forward. "I want you to tell me you love me and you'll marry me."

The ache inside threatened to undo her. "Too much has passed. I can't go back to where we were."

He squeezed her tighter. "You're wrong. We can work through this. I know you love me." His breath blew across her skin as he reached in for a kiss.

She squirmed and turned her head.

The music inside stopped. Fear shot through her chest, threatening to take the breath from her. The dinner dance was next. She had to get inside before they came looking for her. "No, we can't, and I don't love you."

A glint appeared in Frank's eyes. "Oh, darling, I need to hear it. Tell me you love me."

She tried to push, but to no avail. His lips came down on hers again, but they didn't linger. She turned her head away.

He whispered in her ear. "Tell me you love me, and I'll let you go."

She looked up into his eyes. "I don't love you."

"I don't care. Just say you love me, and I'll let you go. I need to hear it one last time."

Hot needles burned the backs her eyes. She was in this situation because of her own foolhardiness. Why didn't she listen to that small voice that had warned her not to come outside? "You promise?" Her voice came out in barely a whisper.

He shifted his eyes from her to the walkway and back to her. "Yes, yes. Just say it. Say it now."

Had Frank lost his mind? "Why? I wouldn't mean it if I said it."

Frank's hands dug into her upper arms as he pressed her to him.

Charlotte gasped for the breath that her lungs were being denied. "Please." She whispered. The tears began to flow. "You're hurting me."

"Say it." He growled the words next to her ear.

She swallowed, hoping the words would come out. "I-I love you."

He threw his head back and laughed a boisterous laugh, as if they'd shared some funny tidbit, then bent back down to her ear. "I could hardly hear that. Come now, darling, say it loud enough so that I can hear it, and you are free to go."

She drew in all the air she could. "I love you."

"Louder." He whispered.

"I love you." She yelled it at him.

"I love you too, darling." Frank smirked.

Charlotte's voice came out a strangled whisper. "Frank, you promi—"

His lips crashed back down on hers.

"What's going on here?"

Relief swept over her. She twisted in Frank's grip to try to catch a glimpse of her father. She couldn't see him. "Papa?"

"Take your hands off the lass, Sorrell." Mr. Mackenzie's voice demanded compliance.

Charlotte drew in a shaky breath. Sweet mercy. How many others stood behind her? Frank's arms loosened, and she dipped down under them, spun around, and ran toward her father. Mr. Mackenzie flew past her, his feet pounding the pavement. She turned to see his fist slam into Frank's jaw. Frank's head snapped back, and he crumpled to the ground. She stared at his body, then looked up at Mr. Mackenzie. He shook his hand, turned on his heel, and strode past her without a word.

"What were you thinking, daughter?" Her father's voice boomed through the still night air.

Charlotte's bottom lip trembled. "He said he wanted to talk to me."

"So you came outside to meet a man who was not invited. A man you knew your father did not approve. A man who is a drunk. And all this without the bother of a chaperone? Charlotte, what our host must think of you right now." He shook his head. "What we came upon didn't look like talking. Frank Sorrell's hands all over you and his mouth on yours infuriates me. If Duncan Mackenzie hadn't knocked him to the ground, I think I may have. And to hear you declaring your love for that scoundrel at the top of your lungs is nothing short of shameful." Papa clasped her elbow and guided her back toward the house. "I can't even imagine what all must be going through Mackenzie's head right now. He invited us here because of you. I wouldn't blame the man if he told us to pack our bags and leave tonight.

"You know word of this is going to spread. People will talk. I passed several couples on my way here. I pray to God that it doesn't affect my business. And I certainly hope I can still find a good match for you after this fiasco."

"I didn't do—"

"I don't want to hear your excuses. I just hope I didn't find you too late."

Curious, Charlotte turned to her father. "How did you know I was out here?"

"Mr. Mackenzie noticed you missing. He became worried and came to me to see if you had retired early with an illness."

"But how did you know I was outside?"

They had ascended the steps, and her father stopped short of opening the door. "Some guests saw you leave. Others saw *someone* out on the sidewalk in front of the ballroom."

Charlotte wanted to defend herself, but he would believe she was only attempting to justify her actions. Besides, it *was* her fault that she had gotten into this predicament. She had no one to blame but herself.

"I want you to go directly to Mr. Mackenzie and apologize to him."

Charlotte's head shot up. "What do I have to apologize to *him* for?"

Her father thrust his finger in her face and wrinkled his brow. "I think you know full well, young lady, what you need to say. The man is our host. He has been nothing but generous and kind. And don't forget, he is a client of mine now. I won't have him thinking that any daughter of mine has loose morals."

"So I am to apologize to him for going outside unescorted? What you saw there was not what it appeared." Maybe she would defend herself after all.

He started to speak, but Charlotte continued. "I know you won't believe me. It's all about what you think you saw. But I did nothing wrong besides being foolish enough to speak to Frank alone. What he did was without my consent."

"What I heard and what I saw went hand in hand, daughter. Are you going to deny those words?" He growled. "Did he force those from your lips?"

Chapter 15

The splintering pain that shot through Duncan's hand as he connected with Sorrell's jaw helped ease some of the anger that had stirred within him when he witnessed Charlotte in the man's arms. He wouldn't be surprised if he loosened a tooth or two. It would serve the miscreant right. He had a lot of nerve showing up uninvited. There weren't too many men Duncan had no use for, but Sorrell was at the top of that list. The man cared only himself and would walk over anyone in his way to get what he wanted.

Duncan stomped to his library and shut the door. The window beckoned him, and he pulled back the curtain with his uninjured hand, peering into the darkness. No moon or stars to give light, and he had yet to install yard lanterns on this side— a dark void. Much like what he felt inside. He released the cloth, and it fell back over the window. He hadn't anticipated Sorrell's arrival or the emotion it stirred within him. Did she love him? He heard it from her lips. The memory caused an ache in his chest. Sorrell treated her so poorly and Duncan would do anything for the lass. Why couldn't she feel that way about him?

As he settled into the overstuffed leather chair, the scent of lilacs reached his nose. It was the same fragrance he always noticed when he was with Charlotte. If he could smell her perfume when she wasn't around, the woman was getting to him a little too much.

He ran his throbbing hand through his hair and winced. A lacy white fan on the table caught his attention. He picked it up, and the scent of lilacs permeated the air. He ran the fan under his nose and closed his eyes as he breathed in Charlotte's scent.

She had caught him in her snare without even trying. Without even wanting him. He laughed to himself. What was it about the lass?

She consumed his thoughts. When he should be working on ways to flush out the traitor, he instead found himself doing things to win Charlotte's heart, like the ball. The idea of forcing a marriage between him and her should be given up. He should go to Tavis and have him retrieve the heirloom pin from Charlotte's bag and return it to the place of honor on his clan's tartan. Tomorrow should pass seeing his guests off with no further ado.

But it wouldn't. Because he'd have Charlotte at all costs. Once she was away from that scoundrel Frank and treated with respect and devotion, she'd come to return that respect—maybe even care for him. At least he prayed she would.

Humph! *Prayer?* His prayers were never answered. Not unless he made it happen. And he'd make this happen. He would win the heart of the bonnie Miss Jackson. He didn't need to pray to a God who had favorites and wouldn't save his brother.

He pulled his watch from his pocket and glanced at the time. The meal was well underway by now, if not over. He snapped the lid shut and stuffed it back in the pocket. Food didn't sound good to him right now. The only thing that appealed to him at this moment was out of reach.

A light tapping came from the other side of the door. He ignored it. Maybe they would go away. Then voices.

"No one's answering. He must not be in there." Charlotte's voice.

Duncan sat up.

"Knock again. And louder this time." Charlotte's father.

Duncan cleared his throat. "Enter."

The door pushed open. With some hesitation, Miss Jackson stepped in. Duncan dropped the fan onto the table and stood. She glanced from the fan to him. Crimson filled her cheeks.

Perhaps they were leaving. Jackson was all about propriety and image. This may have been more than her father could bear. It would be easier to slip out tonight rather than face the multitude of questions that could crop up tomorrow—especially if the identity of the embracing couple spread. He gave a nod of his head. "Miss Jackson. Mr. Jackson."

She stopped inside the threshold. Her father gave her a nudge. Lifting her chin, she strutted in the room and stopped near him, but not before she reached over and plucked her fan off the table. "I've come to apologize for…" She stopped and looked back at her father. "What is it I am apologizing for again, Papa?"

Mr. Jackson choked, and Duncan thought he might have to run to his rescue and pound him on the back. But the man recovered and glared at his daughter.

She smiled. "Oh yes. Now I remember. I'm sorry I missed our dance."

Jackson cleared his throat.

Charlotte took a deep breath. "And for worrying you and causing you to search for me."

Mr. Jackson shuffled his feet. Charlotte stood with her shoulders squared and her hands clasped in front of her. Her father cleared his throat again. If Duncan hadn't cared for her so much, he could have found the whole thing amusing.

She let out a huff. "And for causing any talk about impropriety." She glared at him.

At him! Duncan blinked. What did he do to deserve that? It was her father who had prodded her, not he. And it was she seen kissing a man.

"That will be all, daughter." Mr. Jackson took a step backward and pulled the door open.

"No, Papa, it is not. I wish to hear Mr. Mackenzie's apology."

Mr. Jackson gasped and quickly shut the door.

Duncan wasn't sure what he was supposed to apologize for unless it was for contributing to Sorrell's sudden nap, and he wasn't about to say he was sorry for that.

Jackson got a hold of himself, although his face flushed and his eyes blazed. "Charlotte Bay Jackson, I want you to go find your mother and sit with her. Now."

Charlotte turned to her father. "Papa, I'm sorry, but this has to be said." She turned back to face Duncan. "I want to hear Mr. Mackenzie tell me he's sorry for making a mockery of me at the Barrows' ball."

Duncan cocked his head. "I'm verra sure I dinna understand, lass."

"Charlotte, you apologize this instant." Jackson's voice boomed across the room.

Duncan raised his hand. "'Tis all right. I'd like to hear what the lass has to say."

"I understand you paid many men to dance with me. Do you have any idea how that makes me feel?" Her voice wobbled, and Duncan's heart dropped into his belly. She lifted her chin. "Did you think I wasn't capable of procuring my own dance partners? That I was such a pathetic case that you must give men money to spend three minutes of their time with me?" Her voice caught. She turned to her father. "You are right, Papa. I should leave."

She grasped her skirt and fled the room through the door her father once again opened. Duncan and Jackson stood staring at the door.

Jackson broke the silence. "This is not like Charlotte, I assure you, sir. I don't know what to say except please accept my deepest and most sincere apologies for her dreadful behavior. I can only attribute her conduct to this connection she has with that rogue, Sorrell." His gaze slid to the floor.

Duncan couldn't stand the man's groveling any longer. "Nay apology is necessary. The lass has a right to be angry with me."

The older man looked up. "She does?"

Duncan scratched his cheek. "Aye, I'm afraid she does. She only has part of the information, and I'm sure that partial knowledge would make any lass upset. I shall try and straighten it oot with her later when she has cooled down a wee bit. But I'd like you to know, sir, that what I did, I did because I was trying to keep her *away* from Frank Sorrell."

Jackson smiled and stuck out his hand. "I like you, Mackenzie. We think alike, you and I."

Duncan shook his hand and returned the smile. Were they really similar?

"I had better track down that daughter of mine and see that she has gone to find her mother. You're a good man, Mackenzie."

After he left the room, Duncan collapsed back into the chair. Crevvens. How did Sorrell find out about that? He was sure the man had told Charlotte. Didn't these men have better things to do than gossip? And if they were going to gossip, they could at least get the story straight. He had only ended up paying a few. Apparently, Sorrell's job didn't keep him busy enough if he had time to turn the rumor mill and mix it with lies. Duncan heaved a sigh. Now he had something else to work on to win the lass. But at least he knew what he did wrong this time.

Perhaps all this wasn't such a bad thing after all. Sorrell just went to the bottom of the cesspool in Jackson's eyes. And if he read Arthur Jackson right, Duncan went up to the top—a near saint. Duncan settled back in the chair and smiled. Yes, this very well could be a blessing.

He'd best not let any more time pass before he showed himself to his guests. He pushed out of the chair and strode to the dining room, finding he was hungry after all.

When he entered, the room wasn't as empty as he'd expected. The aroma of fresh bread still lingered along with the blended spices of anise and cinnamon used to cook the meat. Dozens of people conversed over half-finished dinner plates and dessert. Duncan took his seat.

Tavis sat to his right. "Is something amiss?" He smiled. "It's not like you to be late for a meal."

A servant placed a plate of food before Duncan. "Nay. All is well. I was delayed, that's all. And I think 'tis going to be weel worth the wait."

"Miss Jackson seemed a mite upset. She came in here and spoke to her mother in whispers. When her mother tried to persuade her to sit down and eat something, she proclaimed she couldn't eat if her life depended on it and left for her room."

Duncan took a bite of the roasted duck cooked in white sauce. "'Tis a guid place for the lass. Tomorrow will be a most disturbing day for her."

Tavis took a drink of lemonade. "You're still set on going through with this, then?"

"Oh aye, more so now than ever. 'Tis for the lass's own good."

Tavis laughed. "You mean your own good. It's what you want, not the lass."

"Nay, if you had witnessed what I did, Sorrell with his hands on her, kissing her…"

"Sorrell is here?" Tavis stole a quick glance at Duncan.

"He was. May still be. I left him on the sidewalk. But I have a feeling he'll no' be staying around." Duncan put the fork back down without taking another bite. "What baffles me is how the lass kent he was oot there. Someone must have seen him and told her."

Tavis pushed his chair back and stood. "I'm sure that will come to light. I hate to leave you sitting here by yourself, but I have a bonnie lass waiting on me for this dance."

Duncan finished eating his meal in silence, then made his way into the ballroom. Dancers glided around the room unaware of what had preceded the meal. Circling the room, he chatted with men, apologized to a lady with whom he'd missed a dance, and danced with a few of the others on whose cards he'd signed his name. He heaved a sigh when the last song of the night ended. His dance partner never came back down, but he didn't expect her to. Leaving his guests to mingle, he strode through the gaslit hall, his feet thumping on the floor. Taking the stairs two at a time, he nodded at a couple descending and hurried on to his chamber. With the door shut behind him, he pulled at the tie around his neck.

"Can I help you, sir?" Stuebing's voice resonated through the silent room.

"Crevvens. Stuebing, you're going to take years off my life."

"Sorry, sir. Let me help you with your coat."

Duncan shrugged from the garment. He pulled his tie off and tossed it to his valet, then dropped onto the chair and let his mind wander to what the morrow would bring. He could envision the lovely Miss Jackson's haughty expression. What he wished he could change was the icy glare she would give him when it was announced that she would be his bride.

Chapter 16

If Charlotte weren't so angry with Duncan Mackenzie for the humiliation he had caused her by selling her dances, she would actually have found comfort in his chivalrous act of defending her honor. Hitting Frank may not have been the best way, but it left her with a warm feeling inside to think someone had cared. In fact, Mr. Mackenzie might have been willing to listen and believe her if only she'd tried to talk to him, unlike her father.

Papa showed no concern for Frank's actions. Never questioned the decorum of his showing up uninvited and unwanted by their host. He didn't ask what Frank was doing with her, didn't get angry with him for the kiss that was forced upon her, though her father didn't know that because he wasn't willing to listen. The only thing that mattered to Papa was how things looked and how it would affect his work. The pain inside her grew until it pulsated within her head with each heartbeat—a pain with no respite.

The morning light streamed in through the window as birds sang a melodious tune outside. Charlotte rolled over in the bed and covered her head with a pillow. She didn't want to get up and face the day. If only Papa had not forced her to come here, none of last night would have happened. How she longed for a father who believed in her. The whole incident was bad enough, but then to have Papa believe the worst of her left her empty inside.

She flung the pillow off her head and opened her eyes. Perhaps she could find some comfort in going home today and getting on with her life. After this weekend, it was apparent she needed to make some different plans for her future. She swallowed the lump in her throat, recalling the dream that had slipped away. She prayed her sisters never had to go through some of the things she had—having the man she loved turn into a pawing animal.

She rolled out of the bed and slid to the floor on her knees. Clasping her hands and resting them on the bed, she closed her eyes to keep the tears at bay.

God, please take away this pain. Help Papa to believe in me. A sob escaped her. *Allow Mr. Mackenzie to see through the things that took place last night. I don't want either of them to think badly of me.*

A firm rap sounded on the door, and Charlotte sprung up from her knees and wiped away her tears with her sleeve. Strangely, she did feel somewhat better. She cleared her throat. "Yes."

"Your mother and I are going down for breakfast. Are you dressed?" Her father's voice filtered through the crack.

"I'm not hungry. Please go down without me, Papa."

"Open your door."

Charlotte dried her eyes one last time before scurrying to the door and opening it.

He frowned. "Your sister hasn't finished readying herself, either. Get yourself together and meet us downstairs. We need to be on the road shortly if we hope to make it to church on time."

Charlotte bit her bottom lip and considered telling him she really didn't think she could eat a bite, but his next words put a stop to them.

"You can't hide yourself forever."

She fought the burning in her eyes, but the tears won. A single drop trickled down her cheek. Charlotte swiped it away. "I'll go over and dress with Nellie."

Her father's stern features softened. "I know this is hard for you, Charlotte, but avoiding people won't stop the talk. We must meet it head on and squelch it before it gets out of hand." He placed his hand gently on her cheek. "Don't despair. I'll do everything in my power to find a good match for you. I'm sure there will be people who will never hear about your indiscretion."

A second tear followed the same trail down her face. "I don't care if I never marry. I don't want to be thrown to any man you can find for me just because of a misunderstanding." She wrapped her arms against her. "And I know you don't believe me, but last night *was not* what it appeared."

Papa let his hand fall to his side. "If Duncan Mackenzie were the only one that had witnessed the incident, I think he would have kept quiet. But I'm sure others saw you from the windows. Frankly, I'm surprised he allowed us to stay after what he saw and heard."

"Papa, you are not listening. *I* did nothing wrong."

Her father patted her on the shoulder. "Don't fret, daughter. I will figure a way to save our good name. But I've wasted enough time talking. It won't look good if we aren't in church. Get your sister and hurry down." He started to leave and turned back. "Don't forget to gather your bags. Place them on the trunk at the end of your bed so the servant can easily find them and bring them down."

Charlotte gathered what she needed and hurried over to Nellie's room with her church dress flung over her arm. When they had finished dressing, they headed for the dining room. It was empty except for her parents. "Are we that early?"

"One family has left, but I think most are just waking after the late night." Her mother smiled and patted the seat beside her. "I don't think many staying here will be attending church today."

Charlotte strolled over to Mother and sat.

"I'm glad it's time to go home." Charlotte peeked around Mama to see her father push away from the table and rise.

"I'm going to find a servant to load our bags. You ladies finish up so we can be on our way." Her father snatched his hat off the side table as he strode from the room.

Charlotte turned back to her mother. "Mama, there is so much I need to explain to you. Last night…well, I made some foolish mistakes, but you must believe me when I tell you things were not as they seemed. I know how bad it looked." She blinked the tears away. "I did nothing other than go outside to speak with Frank, and I did that because I feared something was wrong."

Mama reached over and squeezed Charlotte's hand. "I believe you. When we get home, you can tell me all about it."

"Will you talk to Papa and explain to him what I told you? He won't listen to me."

Her mother laughed. "What makes you think he'll hear what I have to tell him?"

"There is a better chance if it comes from you."

Her mother squeezed her hand again and then stood. "You aren't going to eat anything?"

"No. I'm ready to be on our way."

Nellie popped her head up, taking a break from eating a poached egg covered in hollandaise sauce. "I wonder if they'd mind if I took a few of these scones with me. They are wonderful. And these eggs are the best I've ever eaten. No offense, Mama. Maybe Mr. Mackenzie's cook could give the recipes to our cook."

Her mother's eyes grew round. "Nellie May! You will do no such thing. Gracious, your father would have apoplexy if you took some of those scones from here. But I'm sure I can send a note and ask for the recipe." She moved around the table toward the hallway. "I'll see you girls shortly. You don't want to make your father wait."

"No worries about that, Mama." Charlotte assured her. She couldn't wait to leave this place, as lovely as it was. And good riddance. She hoped to never have to darken the door again.

Nellie took her last bite of egg, then shoved the rest of the pastry in her mouth. With one side of her mouth full she gave her a lopsided grin. Charlotte shook her head, a glimmer of a smile tugging at her lips, and headed toward the doorway.

Nellie hurried ahead of her. Situated next to the serving table, the servant handed Nellie a bulging cloth napkin as she passed. She stopped.

"A gift from your host. I'm sure he'd approve." The tall man winked at Nellie.

She unwrapped a corner of the package to discover scones. "Thank you. I'll put them out of sight in my pocketbook." She winked back.

Charlotte giggled, enjoying the carefree moment, and gave her sister a slight push. They hurried to catch up with their mother, who stood outside next to their carriage.

"Where is Papa?" Charlotte gazed at the carriages down the tree-lined drive.

"Your father went to tell Mr. Mackenzie we are leaving. He'll be here shortly." Her mother took the driver's hand and climbed into the vehicle.

Nellie entered as the two men came around the corner of the house. Charlotte scrambled into the carriage behind her sister. She straightened her gown and leaned back. A long sigh escaped her lips. Finally they would be on their way. Maybe not home yet, but after this weekend in the devil's den, it would feel good to take refuge in the house of the Lord.

Several minutes passed, and Charlotte turned to see what was taking so long. A third man had joined her father and Mr. Mackenzie. Their voices traveled through the air, but she couldn't make out the words. The third man turned, allowing a glimpse of a servant as well. He hurried off, followed by the servant, while her father and Mr. Mackenzie continued toward them. Charlotte inclined her ear toward their conversation and strained to hear.

"The heirloom has been passed on for many generations." The thick burr in Mr. Mackenzie's words floated on the breeze.

Charlotte frowned. Why were they talking about that now when it was time to leave? She disliked hearing only part of a conversation. The men stopped about ten feet from the carriage and looked in the direction of the disappearing servant.

"What are you looking at?" Nellie twisted around and glanced in the same direction.

"Just wondering what's holding Papa up. He was the one who was so anxious to be on our way to church. Not that I'm not." Charlotte let out a sigh.

"Girls, it's not polite to stare." Her mother reprimanded them.

"They don't know we're staring." Nellie grinned at Charlotte.

"Nellie and Charlotte." Mama's voice was stern.

Charlotte swung back around, and Nellie settled into the seat.

A few minutes later the servant returned with a young maid. He pulled off one piece of Charlotte's luggage and set it on a small stand.

"Is this the bag you saw it in?" Mr. Mackenzie's servant asked the maid.

"Yes, sir. It was tucked in a bit, and I caught a glimpse of the pin. I didn't think much of it until I heard your heirloom pin was missing."

Charlotte stuck her head out the door. "Papa, is there a problem?"

"Everything is fine."

Charlotte stepped down from the carriage and stood by Papa. She glanced at the servant speaking to the maid. The man straightened and turned to Mr. Mackenzie.

"It is the same bag, sir."

Mr. Mackenzie nodded, and the servant excused the maid. Charlotte frowned as the young woman walked off.

"That bag contains my daughter Charlotte's clothing."

"What is the meaning of this, Papa?"

Nellie and her mother moved out of the carriage as well and stood beside her.

Her father tried to smile. "We are attempting to sort that out, Charlotte."

Charlotte folded her arms in front of her and glared at Mr. Mackenzie. "I can assure you, sir, you will find nothing in my bag. You insult us all by this."

"Charlotte, Mr. Mackenzie is our host, and that is not how you speak to him." Her father's tone sent a warning.

Why, Mr. Mackenzie was nothing short of accusing them. One minute the man sent her heart aflutter. The next she'd like to drop her trunk on his foot.

Mr. Mackenzie's gaze rested on her and he raised his brow—the single brow he used to intimidate her. She tipped her chin.

"Sorry I am, lass, but two of my employees saw the pin in your bag."

With arms still folded, Charlotte drummed her fingers on her upper arm. "Well, you're wasting—found what in my bag?"

"My family's heirloom pin. The one you admired."

Charlotte stared at the pin the servant handed to Mr. Mackenzie. The very one she'd run her fingers over days earlier. She shook her head and opened her mouth, but her words had left her. How could this be? There had to be some mistake. She whipped her head to face her mother and father, hoping beyond hope they'd defend her. Instead, her mother gasped, and her father showed no emotion. She wished she'd been prone to swoons so she could escape the mortification seeping a horrified numbness down into her very bones.

Chapter 17

Duncan knew what to expect from the lass. She'd been so confident they wouldn't find anything, it practically permeated the air. He presumed she'd tip her chin so high she'd have to look down her nose. Insinuating she took the heirloom would certainly have stirred fire in her veins. He anticipated Miss Jackson's fortitude would come forward as she defended herself with the anger that was rightfully hers. But instead, she looked confused and vulnerable. Her head shook in disbelief, but not a word left her lips. A pang of guilt hit Duncan, but the sweet taste of success quickly devoured it.

Mr. Jackson broke the lingering silence. "Charlotte. I can't believe this of you."

Duncan didn't remove his gaze from her. He wanted to see her every reaction. Her mouth opened and closed, and finally she gathered herself together.

"I didn't put that in there, Papa." Her voice was pleading.

"Then how did it get there, *daughter?*"

Duncan cringed at Jackson's use of 'daughter,' stealing a good part of his enjoyment in the scene.

"I-I don't know. But I do know I never touched it. Well, I touched it, but that was in front of Mr. Mackenzie. And when I walked away it was still there." She turned to their host. "Isn't that right, Mr. Mackenzie?"

Jackson didn't wait for a response. "Don't bring our host into this scandal. He has nothing to do with it, other than he was looking for his heirloom pin. You shame our family and you shame our name, Charlotte Bay Jackson. Stealing! What will people think? The daughter of the bank's president, stealing. Oh, heaven help us."

Charlotte's color drained from her face, and a tear trickled down her cheek, quickly followed by a second and third.

"Perhaps somehow it fell in the bag." Her words were barely a whisper, and no one else seemed to hear.

Duncan's chest constricted. He hadn't expected this. He'd thought she would fight like a cornered badger. He hadn't meant to hurt the lass. It took all he had to restrain himself from stepping forward and saying it was all a mistake. He had to stop the man from berating Charlotte.

"Mr. Jackson, can we talk in private? I'm sure we can work something out." Duncan held his breath as the next part of his plan teetered in the balance. Jackson must agree to come willingly if Duncan was to convince him to hand over his daughter for marriage.

Jackson looked from his daughter to Duncan and back again. He drew himself up. "Lead the way. I fear, sir, I am at your mercy."

Duncan escorted the man back inside his home and to his study. Not wanting to intimidate him, Duncan avoided sitting at his desk because then Jackson would have to sit in the chair across from him, possibly an intimidating arrangement. If things went well, this man would be his father-in-law. He wanted Arthur to feel as if Duncan had helped him out.

"Have a seat." Duncan gestured for the older man to sit in one of the leather armchairs that faced the fireplace.

Jackson sat, keeping his body rigid. "How much do you want?"

Duncan took the seat opposite him. He'd never thought that Jackson might think he wanted funds. "I want no money."

"Then what do you want?"

"It's a little more complicated than that."

"I'm listening." Jackson continued to sit stiffly in the chair.

"Can I get you something to drink, Arthur?" Using his Christian name should make Duncan appear friendly, willing to work things out.

"No. Just tell me what you have to say." The man's eyes bore into Duncan's.

Duncan leaned back, resting his elbows on the chair arms and tenting his fingers before him. "I see what a dilemma this poses for you, sir. The way this will affect your reputation in the banking community. Then of course the prospects of marrying your daughters into guid families...it's all in jeopardy now. I feel badly for you. May I propose a solution to your predicament? The lass pleases me, even though in her youthful impetuosity, she may have committed some ill-advised mistakes. Mistakes that could make it even harder to find her a good match. 'Tis hard to say how many people saw the incident with Frank last night. We both know that Sorrell is beneath her, and neither of us wants to see her throw her life away with a cad like him. What I'd like to offer to help you out of this quandary is to accept your daughter's hand in marriage. I ken that probably sounds like an unusual request after all that has transpired here this weekend. However, as I said, the lass pleases me. She has the spirit of many of the lasses in Scotland. 'Tis time I find a wife. This arrangement would benefit you and me and would save Charlotte from the possibility of marrying beneath her."

Jackson sat back in his chair. "Frank Sorrell will never get my approval for marriage. He's already been told to stay away. Although you can see he didn't heed my warning. I fear for Charlotte's future. She is in love with the idea of being in love. I suppose that is another of the foolish ideas she's gotten from the books she reads."

"Aye. I fear as slick as Sorrell is, he will lure the lass regardless of your wishes."

"I had hoped my daughter possessed more sense than that."

Duncan leaned forward and rested his forearms on his knees. "Let me be more to the point. I have everything a mon could want. I own a shipping company and a fine home here and in Scotland. I live in America, but I want a wife. No man wants to live alone. I'd be guid to Charlotte. She could have anything she desired. And it would erase all the damage her indiscretions have done to you, to her, and to your family if you are seen to marry her off well."

Jackson scratched his slightly graying beard. "Let me get this straight. You say my daughter took a priceless heirloom from you and now you want to marry her?"

"Aye. 'Tis what I'm telling you."

"I know you are from Scotland, and you are not familiar with our southern ways, so I will excuse the accusation against my daughter. I don't know how that pin got in her bag, but one thing I do know about Charlotte is—"

"Charlotte is a fine woman, or I wouldn't be offering for her hand." Duncan interrupted seeing his chance slipping away. He needed to get back to the subject of Frank. Hadn't he known deep down that her family wouldn't believe she'd stolen the pin? But that was just a ploy to get Jackson sitting right where he was sitting so Duncan could convince him he was the answer to finding a good match for Charlotte. "The real question here is do you want to take a chance on her ending up with Frank Sorrell? Especially after what transpired here this weekend."

"And you want me to believe you'll be good to her? First last night with Sorrell and now this accusation?"

Duncan narrowed his eyes. "I gave my word. I'm no' angry with the lass. I look at this incident as God putting an opportunity in my path and perhaps saving Charlotte from a life with a scoundrel." A twinge of guilt bit him for the lie he spoke, but he brushed it off. God never did anything for him, but maybe He did for Charlotte.

Resting his gaze on Duncan as if weighing his words, Jackson shook his head. "She'll never say yes."

To his dismay, Duncan saw his chance disappearing once again. He had to make the man want this as badly as he did. "Think aboot what the repercussions of all this weekend could be. It is no' just Charlotte. You have other daughters who are nearing or at marriage age." He'd use the man's own words to make him realize he needed to convince Charlotte to marry him. "You ken how people are. It's aboot how things look. No' everyone wants the truth of things. But I will no' try to force you into something you are no' comfortable with."

"N-now I didn't say we couldn't make this work." Jackson stuttered. "I just said if you walk out there and ask, she'll decline. The only way I know to get her to agree is by giving her a choice in which she likes the alternative even less."

"Do you have something in mind?"

Jackson stood and paced the floor with hands clasped behind his back. His forehead furrowed with lines of concentration. "Let me first say that I *do* believe my daughter. Charlotte is not a thief. She may have crazy ideas about what women should be allowed to do, thanks to some of the books she's read, but she didn't steal the pin. Now why someone would put your pin in her baggage, I don't know. Perhaps to sully our good name. Perhaps it was a jealous young lady seeking revenge. That being said, this whole thing with Frank Sorrell worries me. The man seems to have some sort of a hold on her. It would be disastrous for our family should she get it into her head she is going to marry the man regardless of my wishes. So I will tell her that you have offered for her hand in marriage. I'll explain to her that this will be a fine match."

"She won't choose marriage. No' when it is to me." Not without some sort of encouragement from her father.

Jackson continued as if Duncan hadn't spoken. "She of course will object to the whole idea. I will then give her the second option." Stopping in front of his chair, he sat back down and rubbed the back of his neck. "I think even as taken as Charlotte is with Frank, she will still do what I ask of her. And if I'm wrong, calling the authorities and reminding her that her behavior has jeopardized her sister's chances of marrying well will secure the right decision."

It was Duncan's turn to get up and pace. "I dinna like it. What if she chooses the authorities over marriage?" Perhaps he hadn't thought this through well enough.

"If I am wrong, which I don't believe I am, I will convince her to do the right thing."

"I hope you ken your daughter."

Jackson pushed himself up from the chair. "We have an agreement, then?"

Duncan stuck out his hand. "Agreed."

Chapter 18

Her father marched from the manor stiff as a soldier. Charlotte lost faith with each step he took. What he had to say would not be good.

Mama had insisted they return to the carriage to await Papa's return. When Papa reached them, he told the driver to give them some privacy and then climbed up, taking his seat across from Charlotte. He glanced from the window to lock his dark eyes on her. "You know this doesn't look good."

Charlotte leaned forward. "Papa, I told you I did *not* take his pin."

"Servants and Mr. Mackenzie saw it pulled from your bag, and that is what matters. How many times must I remind you of these things?"

"I know, Papa, but I don't care what people think. I know I didn't take it."

"Charlotte, I've talked with Duncan Mackenzie. He's an honorable man. He has agreed to forget this ever happened if you agree..." Papa hesitated and looked at her with pleading eyes.

"What must I do, Papa?"

Papa's voice softened, and he reached over and took her hand. "If you agree to wed him."

Nellie grasped her arm. Charlotte blinked and searched his face for something that would tell her he was making fun with her. But the somber expression on his face destroyed that hope. "You can't be serious. Why would I want to marry him? Better yet, why would he want to marry me?"

"He wishes to marry, and you are the woman he has set his sights on. If you agree to wed, he won't press charges for the stolen heirloom. Mr. Mackenzie assures me that if you were to become his wife, he would treat you well."

"I don't want to marry him. I hardly know the man."
Charlotte wanted to put all this behind her and go home. Nellie wiggled beside her as if she too were anxious to leave. "I won't marry him."

Papa sat back and crossed his arms in front of him. "I expected as much. As I see it, Charlotte, since you won't marry him, you need to go in and beg his forgiveness. Tell him that you took the pin to gain his attention and that you are terribly sorry for such a foolish prank. Every man likes to think he's desirable, and if he thinks you took it to obtain his notice, it may be enough that he will let you go with the apology. It's that or jail."

Nellie gasped.

"Why would I do that? I didn't take it." Charlotte lifted her chin. "I won't lie and say I did. That would be wrong."

Her father drew his brows down and drummed his fingers on the armrest. "Listen to me, young lady. We are in a precarious position here. Mr. Mackenzie is being more than generous. He's a good man. A wealthy man. The way I see it, you have to make your decision. What you do will not only affect you, but it will determine what kind of a match I can make for your sisters as well. Don't just think about yourself. Think about your family—the shame you would bring on your mother and me. Not to mention finding you a suitable match after this fiasco will be a daunting task. Probably impossible."

Her sisters. She mustn't forget about her sisters. If she were to refuse, and some unspeakable disgrace befell her family, whom would Papa find to marry her sisters? Would her refusal really make it hard for them to find good husbands? She couldn't allow her father to force them into unhappy marriages with older men. But she couldn't lie to Mr. Mackenzie either and say she had stolen the pin. She didn't want people to think she was a thief or the type of woman who would play reckless games to gain a man's attention.

Charlotte suddenly felt like retching. As if things hadn't been complicated enough with Frank. Now, to be put in a situation where she must make a choice between marrying a man she didn't love or ruining the futures of her sisters was more than she could bear. Was God angry with her? Was He testing her?

Yes, maybe He *was* testing her to see if she would do the right thing. Like the time He tested Abraham and told him to offer his son Isaac as a sacrifice. Then perhaps, just as God stopped Abraham from plunging the knife into Isaac, God would stop this marriage before it took place if she was willing to sacrifice herself for her sisters.

Her father slapped his leg with a loud *thump*. "What is your decision?"

Nellie, still sitting next to her sister, jumped at the noise. Charlotte reached over and squeezed her sister's hand. "Are you not going to give me time to think and pray about it?"

"I'm sorry, daughter, but we cannot leave this place until you have given your decision."

The growing lump in her throat made it almost impossible to answer. Regardless of her decision, lives would be changed. Glancing at Nellie gave her the courage she needed. For all the books she'd read, for all her talk about equality for women, the truth was she loved Nellie and her younger sisters too much. Papa was right. Those books about women's rights and freedom were nothing more than the dreams of fanciful women. She looked back at her father. "I will marry Mr. Mackenzie."

Nellie gasped and pulled her hand from Charlotte's, then gripped her arm again. "No, Charlotte, you mustn't. You've always said you would marry only for love. You've even made me promise that I would hold out for love."

Fighting the tears her sister's words brought, Charlotte turned to her. "You must still marry for love, dear sister." Her voice came a whisper.

Nellie dropped her head on Charlotte's shoulder and began to cry. Charlotte patted her head. "It will work out. God will take care of me. I put my trust in Him."

Nellie sniffled, and Charlotte glanced at her father as he leaned from the carriage and handed Mr. Mackenzie's servant his card. Her father sat back in his seat. Their eyes met briefly, and he jerked his gaze away. That was when she realized the card was some sort of a message to Duncan Mackenzie. The churning in her stomach continued. "Do you believe me, Papa, that I didn't take the pin?"

He hesitated, then slowly turned his gaze back to her as if a tug-of-war went on inside him. "Yes. I believe you." Charlotte waited. That was it? *Yes. I believe you. No I'm sorry this has happened?* Or *Who could have done this?* Or *I'll get to the bottom of this.* Charlotte leaned her head against Nellie's and closed her eyes. Her life was in God's hands. She could only pray He would show her mercy.

♥♥♥

Late Monday afternoon, Duncan sat behind his desk trying to focus on the paperwork from his shipping business...with little success. He couldn't keep his eyes from wandering to Arthur Jackson's card, which lay nearby. The lass may have agreed to marry him, but she clearly didn't wish to.

A loud wrap on the door tore his attention from the card and Charlotte. The door creaked open and Gibson, a lanky servant, poked his head in. "You have a guest, sir."

"Send him in."

The door pushed open, and Arthur Jackson stepped through—uncertainty written on his face. Duncan stood and smiled to assure the man of his good intentions.

"Good afternoon, Jackson. Come in. Sit down." He waved a hand toward one of the chairs facing his desk.

"Good afternoon. Please. Call me Arthur. I hope I'm not interrupting anything." Jackson shook Duncan's hand.

Duncan's heart skipped a beat. "What can I do for you, Arthur?" He hoped Arthur wasn't there to tell him that Charlotte had changed her mind.

Arthur cleared his throat. "I thought we should talk about a marriage arrangement. I'm told there is much to do to prepare for these things. I know they can be quite expensive." He cleared his throat again and shifted in his chair. "I would like to know what your expectations are in that respect."

"You needn't concern yourself with the wedding. I'll see to all of it." Duncan felt certain the family wasn't hard pressed, but this would help win over his new father-in-law.

"Excuse me. Do you mean to say you'll be paying for the wedding? That is just not done. Why, what would people say?" Duncan smiled at the man's bewildered look. "No' done? Weel, that may be so, but I'm no' a man who always follows social protocol or takes no for an answer when it comes to my wedding with Charlotte. I want the best of everything for her. I want this to be a day she'll always remember. I'll see to the arrangements and pay for the wedding. Your daughter is worth every penny I'll spend. 'Twill be a wedding no one will forget."

"I can give my daughter a nice wedding, Mr. Mackenzie. You need not." The man squirmed a bit in his seat.

"I will no' take nay for an answer, sir. 'Tis a gift I wish to give Charlotte."

Jackson paled.

"You want the best for Charlotte, aye?"

"Of course." The man straightened in his chair and lifted his chin.

Duncan smiled inwardly. He could see where Charlotte got that from. "Would you deny her that when I can give it to her?"

"When you put it that way…" Jackson's shoulders slumped.

"Guid to hear. So we are in agreement then." Duncan reached forward and extended his hand again.

Jackson leaned in and grasped it with a firm shake. "Thank you, Mackenzie."

"Call me Duncan. We will soon be family."

Arthur smiled. "Duncan. I'm not sure what to think of you. But I like you more every time I meet you."

A half hour later, his future father-in-law left. A date had been settled on, and now Duncan had two weeks until Charlotte Jackson became Charlotte Mackenzie.

As promised, he took on the full responsibility of preparing for the wedding and then happily handed it over to Betsy, who oversaw his female servants. Evelyn, who not only ran the kitchen but also proved to be indispensable while they prepared the ball a few weeks ago, would work beside Betsy. Both reported to his valet. He could only hope that Stuebing and the ladies could see eye to eye when it came to the upcoming event.

The next day, Duncan took a trip to *My Lady's Apparel* dress shop in downtown Charleston. A bell clanged against the door as he walked into the small store. A middle-aged woman emerged from a door hidden by hanging dresses. "Can I be of assistance to you, sir?"

He glanced around the room hoping to see what he looked for. "Aye, I'm looking for a wedding dress. I saw in your window you have some from Paris. I'd like to see them."

"Certainly." She bustled off into another room and then poked her head back through the doorway. "I'll be right back with them."

The clerk returned before Duncan could make his way across the floor to the shoes.

"Here we are, Mr.—?"

"Mackenzie." Duncan took a long box from the woman's arms and set it on the counter.

The woman turned and scurried toward the back room, all the while talking. "I have two more for you to see. Do you know which one your special lady liked?"

Duncan raised his voice as she had disappeared. "She dinna say." He pulled the lid off the box and knew immediately he wouldn't need to see the others. The pale blue damask silk he held in his hands was of the finest quality he'd ever seen and the color of many a Scottish wedding gown. The modest scoop neck would leave some men grumbling. The bodice came down to a *V* below the waistline. Tiny pearls were sewn into the embroidered Brussels lace outlining the neckline. Morning glory flowers splashed across the skirt fabric that draped and gathered into a bow on the one side.

"Here we are, Mr. Mackenzie." The clerk carefully laid down the two other boxes.

Duncan looked at the other two gowns because she had gone to the trouble of getting them, but knew full well he wouldn't change his mind. He placed the tops back on the boxes. "I'll take this one."

"Would you like to know the price?"

Duncan strode over to the shoes. "Nay. 'Tis the dress I want." He glanced over the shoes and picked up a blue satin pair with embroidery and a heel. "Add these. Do you have other sizes?"

The woman hurried over and picked up the shoes. "Yes. I have several. And when would the young lady like to come for her fitting?"

Duncan thought about Charlotte. The lass surely had enough to do without having to come for a fitting. "I'd prefer you go to the lass. I'll pay you for your trouble."

She nearly dropped the shoes as she scurried back to the counter. "No trouble at all. I'm so pleased that you're…I mean to say, that you found something you think will please her. Now, what is your betrothed's name? I'll send her a note."

"Charlotte Jackson."

"Oh! You must be the Scotsman Miss Campbell spoke so highly of to Miss Jackson. I didn't put the two of you together. But Miss Campbell did say she thought there may be a wedding in the future for you two."

Duncan couldn't hold back the grin that tickled his lips. "Did she now? And what was my betrothed's response?"

The clerk tilted her head and frowned. "As I remember, Miss Jackson tried to convince Miss Campbell that was not the case."

"Weel, I hadn't yet proposed." A veiled tiara caught Duncan's eye. He picked the headdress up and laid it on the box. "How much do I owe?"

♥♥♥

Charlotte poked her needle through the fabric in her embroidery hoop and looked up at Mama, then glanced at her three sisters before deciding whether she wanted to bring up the topic. Her youngest sister Pearl took the choice from her. "Why is the lady coming here for you to pick out a wedding dress? I want to go shopping. I never get to go to town."

Effie set her hoop in her lap. "What makes you think you'd be going along? Charlotte is the one who needs a wedding dress, not you."

Pearl glared at her sister. "She would take me." She glanced at Charlotte. "Wouldn't you, Charlotte?"

Charlotte smiled at her little sister. "I would if Mama would allow it."

All eyes turned to Mama, whose patient smile favored each one in turn "It's of no concern, because the fact of the matter is, Miss Sawyer is coming here."

"I don't know," Charlotte said, "why Mr. Mackenzie felt the need to take it upon himself to send someone to our home. It's ridiculous that the woman has to take time away from her dress shop to bring who knows how many gowns here for me to choose from. And what happens if I don't like any of the dresses? Gracious. I hate to think about that possibility. Besides, I could have gone to town days ago and had this whole ordeal behind me."

Nellie tied a knot in her thread. She picked up a pink strand and began to thread her needle. "You can always pick out a dress for me." Nellie batted her lashes. "I'm sure I can find something I'll like."

Charlotte giggled. "I like that idea. Then I could wear that dress from Aunt Sara."

Nellie laughed, shaking so hard she stabbed her finger with the needle. "Ouch!" She stuck her finger in her mouth.

"When Aunt Sara came to stay with us while you were at Mr. Mackenzie's house party, she did ask if you'd worn that dress." Effie gave her a look of conspiracy.

Charlotte stilled her hands. "And what did you tell her?" She couldn't bear to think of hurting their kind aunt.

"I told her you had wanted to wear it to the ball, but it wasn't dressy enough."

Nellie burst out laughing.

Charlotte turned to her sister. "You told her I said that?"

Nellie pulled herself together. "I didn't know it was a secret."

"Charlotte Bay! Sometimes I wonder if you are really my child." Mama tried to hide her smile.

Effie sighed. "I think it's romantic."

"Me wearing Aunt Sara's dress?" Charlotte put her needlework aside.

"No, silly. I think that Mr. Mackenzie buying your dress is romantic. I don't care what you think. I'd marry him."

Charlotte's smile faded. "Well, I don't think it's romantic, and if I could give you the right to marry the man, he'd be yours. I don't want a man taking my freedom away. He didn't ask my opinion. He took it upon himself to send this woman here. What if I didn't need a wedding dress? Or what if I wanted to go to Savannah to buy my dress? Who is he to decide where I go? He's already picked the wedding date without consulting with me. We aren't even married and he's trying to control my decisions."

Nellie pulled her finger from her mouth, her eyes full of sympathy. "I'm sorry, Charlotte. You have a week until the wedding. Surely it isn't too late to change your mind. Tell him you don't want to marry him."

Charlotte immediately regretted her words. She would do anything for her sisters. Making Nellie feel bad about her marriage wasn't going to help. "No, it'll be fine. I'm frustrated, that's all. But I'm trying to trust that God will work things out."

Pearl's eyes brightened. "I'll be here tomorrow. Can I watch if I'm good, Mama?"

Effie giggled. "You're always here, Pearl."

"Girls!" Mama set her embroidery down on the table beside her. "I think Charlotte and I will manage without the rest of you. Now, go wash up for dinner."

Charlotte began to follow her sisters out of the room and stopped. "I'd like to have Nellie with me, if that would suit you, Mama."

"That's all right." Mama nodded. "Charlotte, I'd like to speak with you."

Charlotte sat back down and folded her hands in her lap. "Yes, ma'am?"

"You haven't said much to me about your wedding. I feel as your mother I need to say a few things to help your marriage go smoothly. You're going to need to bite your tongue and try to keep the peace between you and Mr. Mackenzie. I know you, Charlotte, and you like to say what you think. I promise you won't agree with everything your husband says. There will be times you will want to speak your mind. It's best to try to talk with him, and if he doesn't agree with you, give it to God and pray your husband makes the right decision. There is nothing worse than a woman who constantly nags her husband. And whatever you do, don't remind him of his mistakes. I assure you he remembers them. If you do nag, it will drive a wedge between the two of you."

Charlotte stared at her mother, trying to decide how much to say to her. She decided only the truth would do. "Mama, the reason I haven't spoken to you about my marriage is because I don't plan on marrying Duncan Mackenzie. Ever."

Chapter 19

Charlotte perched on the end of her bed. "Nellie, I do believe I nearly sent Mama to an early grave." She giggled. "I don't think she expected to hear me say I didn't plan on marrying Mr. Mackenzie. Even after I explained that I believed God would intervene, I thought she would swoon."

A servant scurried past the sitting room to answer a knock at the door. Charlotte glanced up at the clock on the mantel. Miss Sawyer was right on time. *If only the lady hadn't been able to come today.*

"What did Mama say?" Nellie joined Charlotte on the settee as the footsteps approached.

"She told me not to get my hopes up. I think she fears I will refuse to marry. But I gave my word to Papa, and unless God shows me mercy, I will do as I promised."

"Maybe he would marry me instead. I would do that for you, Charlotte."

Tears welled in Charlotte's eyes. "You are a dear, but I want you to marry for love. And what of Mr. Sumpter? He's your hero."

Nellie's breath hitched. "I want you to love your husband. You're the hopeless romantic. I've learned it from you. It breaks my heart to see you throwing away your chance for true love." A small smile touched Nellie's lips. "And as for Mr. Sumpter, though I would be honored to be his girl, I am well aware that he was being kind to me at the balls. It is as you've said. He is much older than I."

"Mr. Sumpter's a man, not some boy just out of school. You must win his affection. Besides, Duncan Mackenzie has made up his mind that he wants me."

As Mama and Miss Sawyer entered the room, Nellie leaned over and whispered, "Little sister Effie did offer to marry Mr. Mackenzie. She was quite taken with him."

Charlotte giggled. "Would serve him right if we could switch brides unbeknownst to him."

"Charlotte, Miss Sawyer is here." Her mother announced cheerfully.

She stood to greet the woman. "It's nice to see you again, Miss Sawyer. I'm sorry you had to come all the way over here. I'd have been happy to come to your shop." She needed to keep in mind it wasn't Miss Sawyer's fault that Mr. Mackenzie had made the appointment. The lady was quite nice.

"It's no problem at all. I'm thrilled to be a part of your happy day."

Charlotte held back a sigh. The best she could think to do was to be indecisive. She didn't want to have to buy a dress if she wasn't going to marry the man. She'd narrow the choice down to two or three gowns and then tell Miss Sawyer she would have to think about it. And she'd come into her shop when she decided.

A young lad followed behind Miss Sawyer, his arms stacked full of shoe boxes. He set them down, then hurried out and returned with more. Charlotte fought the urge to roll her eyes. It would have been so much simpler had she went down to My Lady's Apparel. Next, the boy brought in a long box and set it near the shoes. He left again and returned, this time with a sewing box. When he had set the box down, Miss Sawyer excused him.

Nellie leaned over and whispered in her sister's ear. "What are you supposed to be picking out today? Shoes?"

Charlotte grinned. "It would be fine with me if that was all I had to do."

Her mother turned away from speaking with their guest. "What's that, Charlotte?"

"Nothing, Mama. I was just wondering where the rest of the dresses are."

"I'm sure they'll be in here shortly. They may be too heavy for the boy." She glanced at Miss Sawyer. "Would you like a servant to help the boy bring in the rest of the gowns?"

Miss Sawyer busied herself with the boxes. "There are no more gowns. Did Mr. Mackenzie not explain to you?"

Charlotte shifted on the settee.

Mama hesitated as if unsure she'd heard correctly. "We never spoke with Mr. Mackenzie. He sent a note telling us to expect you, and then we received your missive. If you're not here for a wedding dress, why are you here?"

"Oh, yes, I've come about Miss Jackson's dress."

"And shoes," Nellie added.

Charlotte giggled and could have kissed her sister for alleviating the awkward situation. Mama frowned at Nellie.

But Miss Sawyer just smiled. "Yes, shoes, too."

"Well, then, where are the dresses?" Mama gazed toward the door.

Miss Sawyer picked up the large box lying on the floor and placed it on the sofa. Using great care, she lifted the lid and pulled out the gown.

Exclamations came from both Nellie and her mother. Charlotte pinched her lips together and remained seated. The gown indeed was beautiful, but she saw no reason to get excited about a dress when she didn't plan to wear it.

Nellie hurried over to touch the gown. "This is lovely."

Miss Sawyer beamed. "It's from Paris."

Mama ran her fingers lightly over the fabric. "This one is sure to outshine the other dresses. Can we see the others?"

Miss Sawyer continued to hold the dress before her. "This is the only gown I brought."

"How is my daughter to pick a wedding gown if you only brought one?"

"I'm sorry. I thought you understood. I'm not here to show you other gowns." Her voice softened, and she glanced at Charlotte with sympathetic eyes. "I'm here to have the wedding dress Mr. Mackenzie purchased fitted to Miss Jackson."

Charlotte gasped, and her insides trembled. Duncan Mackenzie had picked her dress? Even her father allowed her to pick her own garments. She'd never met a man as controlling as he. Could her betrothed be worse than Papa? She closed her eyes and attempted to still her shaking body. She drew in a deep breath to steady herself. *Father, give me the strength, courage, and faith to trust You. I know Your Word says to trust You with all my heart and that all things work together for good for those who love You, but right now I'm having a hard time seeing how anything good can come of this. And I'm having doubts that You will rescue me from this marriage.*

Nellie scurried over to Charlotte and gave her a side hug. "It is stunning. I'm sure he didn't mean to upset you." She looked back at Miss Sawyer. "Did I hear you say Mr. Mackenzie bought the dress?"

"Yes, miss."

Nellie squeezed Charlotte's arm. "Well, at least he is allowing you to pick your shoes."

Even with Nellie's attempt to ease her woe, Charlotte couldn't find much encouragement.

Miss Sawyer forced a weak smile. "The truth is, he purchased those, too. The boxes you see are different sizes. Mr. Mackenzie purchased your wedding gown, shoes, and veil. I'm here to fit you and do any alterations that may be needed."

Mama straightened and caught Charlotte's eye. "He did a fine job. The design is lovely, and the fabric is some of the finest. And from Paris. My, the ladies will be jealous of you."

Charlotte looked back at the dress and burst into tears. Had she really given her word to marry this man? Nellie patted her shoulder as Mama rushed over.

"Maybe we can—" Nellie was interrupted by her mother "There, there," Mama said. "I know you are so overcome with joy. Sometimes all the excitement and happiness of a wedding can cause such tears. Isn't that right, Miss Sawyer?"

The willowy woman smiled, but her knowing eyes revealed she understood so much more. "It's not uncommon at all."

♥♥♥

Duncan Mackenzie buttoned up his black coat as he waited on a late Alan Ferguson to show up, half tempted to go alone to the shipping office that held the book with the traitor's name. The docks remained quiet apart from an occasional drunken sailor. It was after two in the morning. A bit perturbed, Duncan ground his back teeth. He'd planned on being home at two.

Just as he had decided to go it alone, Ferguson finally rode up.

"Where have you been, mon? I was aboot to head there without you."

Ferguson swung off his horse and tied it next to Duncan's. He pulled his coat together, but not before Duncan caught a glimpse of a knife tucked under his belt, its curved blade like those the Afghanis carried. The gemstone-covered handle had flickered briefly in the streetlights. "I had something I had to do."

Duncan frowned. Why hadn't he told him that when he first asked him?

They started toward High Seas Shipping. Moving away from the gas lamps that lit much of the streets, Duncan was thankful for the overcast sky and moonless night. Reaching the office, they flattened themselves against the back of the building, edging their way down the alley to the back door. A lone dog barked in the background, and Duncan tensed. Music and laughter from a nearby saloon floated on the evening air. He let out a breath.

When they reached the entrance, Duncan grasped Ferguson's arm and strained to hear anything that might indicate they weren't alone in the alley. Hearing only distant noise, he pulled out a crowbar and forced it between the frame and door. He pushed against the bar with his weight. Instead of a loud crack and splintered wood flying everywhere, the door swung open. He stared into the dark building.

Alan gave him a slight nudge, and he moved into the pitch-black room. He pulled a candle from his pocket as Ferguson closed the door. "I didn't want to stand there and risk getting caught."

Duncan lit the wick. "'Tis fine. I hesitated because the door opened with only a wee bit of effort."

"Count it as a blessing then. Let's do what we came to do and get out of here."

Duncan lifted the candle and peered into the office. He'd paid special attention to where the ship's logbooks were when he had stopped by and requested to see them. Having his own made them easy to spot as he had stood and tried to convince the man behind the counter to allow him to look at them. Duncan moved toward the shelves that held the logs and scanned the years. "It's gone." His heart sank as he thought of this lead being a dead end.

Ferguson came along beside him. "What do you mean, gone?"

"It's no' with the others. Maybe they left it sitting oot." Duncan turned and glanced at the counter, holding the candle up so the light would shine farther. A small table, an oak desk, a smoking stand, and the bookshelves were the only furniture. Duncan walked around the room.

Ferguson strode over to the desk. "I'll check the drawers of this desk." He began opening them. "If it isn't in these, I don't know where it could be."

Duncan went back to the bookshelf and searched again.

Ferguson pushed the last drawer shut. "Not here."

"I don't see it lying around anywhere."

"We're wasting our time. We should leave."

Someone pounded on the front door, and Duncan snuffed the candle's flame. He and Ferguson hurried to the back exit. Duncan cracked the door open and peeked outside. He could still hear the pounding on the front door. He slipped into the alleyway with Ferguson close behind. They crossed to the other side and slid between two buildings, bringing them out one street over.

Their long strides ate up the distance toward their mounts. When they had made it down another street, Ferguson broke the silence. "It was probably a drunk who saw the light through the window."

"Aye. I heard them down the street when I was waiting for you."

"So, what now?"

Duncan thought for a moment. "I dinna dare go back in there myself. I'll send a servant down and have them request to see the logbook. If it's been stolen, perhaps they will say something."

♥♥♥

The next day, Duncan took an early morning ride. His churning thoughts had kept him awake, so he hadn't slept well. Whoever the traitor was, he remained a step ahead of him. And that troubled him. The crisp morning air cooled Duncan's skin. Aberdeen threw his head from side to side as if to show his displeasure when he slowed their pace. The bright sun sent streams of light through the tall oaks and drew lines on the dusty road. Duncan sat up straight and stretched the muscles in his back.

Realizing his attempt to relax had failed, he urged Aberdeen on with a nudge of his feet, then let him have the reins. He'd finally won the animal's trust and enjoyed the sensation of the magnificent horse beneath him, but even the morning ride couldn't expel the feeling that the traitor knew Duncan was in America looking for him.

Once home, he hustled up the stairs to his room. "Stuebing." He reached for the doorknob.

He tugged the door open and got one foot in the room.

"You called, sir?" Stuebing stood in the room a few feet from the threshold.

Duncan stumbled backwards.

Stuebing turned. "I shall try to announce myself from now on, sir. What is it you need?"

Duncan frowned. Blast the man. Sometimes he thought Stuebing would make the better spy. "I want you to find a lady's maid for my betrothed."

"*Me?*"

Duncan glanced around the room. "You are the only one in here."

"But I know nothing about finding a lady's maid."

"You are the only one I trust wholly to do this. The woman you pick will be a gift to Miss Jackson. They'll most likely spend much time together."

Stuebing paled. "Wh-what if she doesn't like whom I hire?"

Duncan watched in fascination at the transformation in his valet. He'd never seen the man anything but sure of himself. Until now. "You'll do just fine. That's why I chose you."

As if someone slapped him across the face and he finally got a hold of himself, Stuebing drew himself up. "I shall see what I can find, sir. Remember, we aren't in Britain anymore."

Duncan chuckled. "Stuebing, you're so pompous."

"Merely being civilized, sir. However, this wild country makes it difficult at times."

Chapter 20

The aroma of fried bacon lost its appeal. Charlotte glanced around the breakfast table at her siblings and parents. Papa dominated the head of the long table while Mama sat at the end nearest the kitchen door. The first chair to the right of her father was assigned to her, and to the left of her father was Nellie. Effie, Pearl, and Albert were seated around the table according to their ages, as per her father's rules. The only one missing was Thomas.

These were the last days she would eat here with her family if God didn't intervene soon. Her faith that He would rescue her from this unwanted marriage receded like the strong tidewaters, drawing shells, sand, and driftwood out to sea. Charlotte's hopes seemed pulled from her, setting her adrift in waters too deep to touch ground. The close of each day took a piece of her faith farther out to sea. Like a castle made of sand, her life crumbled around her, and she was helpless to stop it without repercussions to the people she loved most. It wasn't fair.

Papa set his fork down beside his plate. "Your mother tells me you had a fitting for your wedding gown last week."

Charlotte squirmed under his perusal. What exactly had Mama told him? She glanced to the other end of the table, but Mama had busied herself with Albert. Charlotte dragged her gaze back to her father. "Yes, Miss Sawyer came by."

"Mr. Mackenzie has graciously paid the expense of your gown. Although I do worry how that will look, the man left me little choice."

"And veil and shoes too, Papa." Pearl's eyes gleamed with excitement.

He pushed his chair back and folded his hands over his rounded stomach. "Very generous, this future husband of yours."

Charlotte shoved the food on her plate around with her fork. Silence hung over the room, and she forced herself to meet Papa's gaze. He obviously wanted her to respond, but she saw Mr. Mackenzie's purchase anything but generous. "I would have preferred to pick the gown I'm to be married in."

"Isn't the gown from Paris? It's far more than we could afford."

"That it's from France matters not one whit to me. What right does he have to tell me what I will wear on *my* wedding day?"

Papa leaned forward, his brows drawing to a *V*. "When you became his betrothed, you became his concern. I'm not saying I have no right to supersede him. I do until you say your vows. But unless I disagree with his actions concerning you, he can make the decisions."

Charlotte gritted her teeth and wrestled inwardly with the Bible's commandment to honor her mother and father.

"But, Papa." Nellie broke the silence…and one of Papa's rules about contributing to a conversation without being invited to first. Her voice quivered. "A wedding day is a very special day in a woman's life. Do you find it unreasonable that Charlotte would want to choose the dress for that special occasion? A woman only marries once."

Papa turned cold eyes on Nellie. "I was speaking to Charlotte. But just so you understand me, I will answer you. If Mr. Mackenzie had wanted her to wear a rag, I would step in. But he has purchased an expensive gown and, I repeat myself—one we could not afford. There is no good reason Charlotte should *not* wear the dress. Do I make myself clear?"

"Yes, sir." Nellie looked down at her plate.

Charlotte wanted to reach over and squeeze her sister's hand to let her know how much she appreciated her support and words. But she couldn't. Her father would see that as insubordination on both of their parts.

Later, when they had finished eating, her father dismissed everyone from the table. Charlotte followed Nellie out of the room.

"Charlotte, meet me in my study in five minutes."

Charlotte stopped in mid-stride and turned. "Sir?"

"I wish to speak to you in private."

Charlotte glanced at Mama, who once again fiddled with something so she need not look at her. Charlotte sighed. "Yes sir."

She left the room in search of Nellie but didn't have to go far. Nellie stood on the first step waiting on her.

"Did you hear?"

With wide eyes, Nellie nodded and whispered. "What do you think he wants to talk to you about?"

"The same as always, I'm sure. 'Be the dutiful daughter. I wouldn't want people to think badly of us.' But Nellie, I'm not trying to go against Papa's wishes. I don't want to be married to a man like…well, a man who doesn't allow his wife or children to make any of their own decisions. And the more I learn about Mr. Mackenzie, the more I am beginning to think the man is not to my liking."

"Papa does love you, Charlotte. I'm sure he wants what is best for you."

"Just like he wanted what was best for me two years ago when he told me I was going to the picnic with that awkward Jack Thompson?" That had been a humiliating day. Charlotte could have died when Papa told her Jack had asked to take her to the picnic and that he'd said yes for her. Papa hadn't considered her when he'd agreed. The other girls had hidden their giggles and gossip behind their fans as she and Jack sat on the blanket together.

Nellie giggled. "It wasn't that bad, was it?"

Charlotte shoved her hands on her hips and scowled. "Why, he spilt the tea all over the blanket and then, while he was trying to clean it up, his hand came down on the spoon in his strawberry shortcake, sending it flying through the air and landing on my neck, then sliding down into the bosom of my dress. To make matters worse, he felt it his duty to clean it off. Need I remind you, Nellie, that only made the girls titter all the louder."

No, Papa didn't care about her feelings. He only cared about getting business for his bank. If Jeremiah Thompson hadn't been Jack's father and recently come into money...Charlotte sighed. No sense dredging up that memory.

Nellie attempted to look serious but failed. "Papa did apologize. He never expected Jack to try to take liberties like that with you."

The memory sent a shudder up Charlotte's spine. "I don't want to think about it. I despise remembering that day."

A rap of the brass doorknocker resounded through the foyer and down the stairs, pulling Charlotte's attention away from the conversation at hand. Nellie glanced up the stairs. "I wonder who that could be this early in the day. We don't usually get visitors before ten."

Charlotte's demeanor brightened. "No, we don't. Perhaps something important has come up and will take Papa away before he can speak with me."

Nellie leaned against the banister and ran her hand over the smooth wood of the rail. "It will only delay the inevitable. He'll speak with you when he gets home from work."

"If he has to leave now, it lends to hope. And right now that's more than I had a minute ago. I'd best go up even if he can't talk to me. I need to be in his study on time. Wish me luck." Charlotte picked up her skirt and went up the stairs. She crested the top step and rushed down the hall. Up ahead of her, Papa crossed to the foyer.

"What do you wish to see my daughter about?" Papa's voice echoed in the small room.

Charlotte slowed her pace and peeked in as she passed. A young servant stood with hands folded in front of her, probably terrified by her father. Continuing on at a leisurely pace, she took a few more steps and heard the young woman introduce herself as Vivian. The sound of crinkling paper reached Charlotte's ears. She hesitated. The woman must have brought some sort of a missive and handed it to Papa. She leaned back to hear.

"I'm sorry, sir. This explains everything. Mr. Mackenzie sent me. I am Miss Jackson's new lady's maid."

Charlotte spun around and headed for her father's study, fuming. He sent her a lady's maid. What kind of man did these things without asking her opinion? She drew in a deep breath in an attempt to contain her anger. She slipped into the room and sat down, knowing she'd have a few minutes to collect herself before her father came in.

As she waited, she drummed her fingers on the arm of the chair. At least she wasn't the one who would be late to the meeting. She sighed as the minutes ticked by. Talking with her father about Mr. Mackenzie was one of the last things she wanted to do because she knew what would be said and how it would end.

"Charlotte." Her father spoke her name as he entered his study.

"You wanted to speak to me alone, Papa?"

He went around his desk and sat. "I wanted to speak to you without interference from one of your siblings. I'm late because I just left the foyer where I was speaking with your new lady's maid whom your fiancé has obtained for you. Thoughtful man. I know you, Charlotte, and I can see that defiance in your eyes. Mr. Mackenzie is a good man. You are lucky he wanted to marry you after all that transpired this past weekend. By marrying you, he has redeemed your good name. Don't ruin this for yourself and your sisters."

"The man is insufferable, Papa. A lady's maid. He picked *my* lady's maid. He didn't ask me what kind of person I would like, just as he didn't ask me what kind of wedding dress I'd like." Still incensed from Duncan's latest *gift*, the words flew out before she gave much thought to whom she spoke. At the frown on her father's face, she almost groaned.

"This is exactly what I'm talking about, Charlotte. Do you know how many wives would like to have their own lady's maid? Most women would be thrilled to have their husband hire help. Your mother for one. Yet you find fault in everything your fiancé does for you. I'm warning you, Charlotte, do not hinder this wedding. You'll not get a better match. You need to be thankful for what the good Lord has given you."

♥♥♥

His marriage would take place in two days. Duncan stood at the Battery looking over the gray ocean water. He hoped it would fill the emptiness inside him. For the vast part of his adult life he'd chased after fulfillment, only to find it lasted a short amount of time, and then he would be off again, seeking it somewhere else. If he were honest with himself, he'd admit that when the queen asked him to return to work, he'd needed the distraction as much as the Crown needed him. The loss of his brother had left him hollow and aching, but despite his quiet life in the Scotland hills, he found himself yearning for purpose.

A mission usually gave him an objective and filled the meaninglessness of his life. But this time it was different. As busy as this search had kept him, he wanted more. He prayed Charlotte could fill the void in his life. He shouldn't say pray. It was a useless waste of words and thoughts. God in His greatness never showed favor on him. He hoped that God's displeasure didn't transfer over to Charlotte when she became his wife.

Was he being selfish forcing the lass to marry him? A cinch wrapped around Duncan's heart. Could he risk causing her such unhappiness to gain his own? He'd already hurt her with his deception. He'd been the person who'd brought the pain he'd seen. The cinch tightened and his heart stumbled. Should he postpone the wedding until he won her love?

Chapter 21

Charlotte halted inside the church door, fighting the urge to bolt. Her father tugged on her arm, compelling her to move forward, but her feet remained fastened to the floor. Bouquets of sweet autumn clematis, oriental lilies, and confederate jasmine tied to the end of each pew decorated the sanctuary. The urge overpowered her to spin around, throw off her veil, and run. She turned. Her father's hand tightened on her upper arm.

The fear that began several days ago when her lady's maid arrived and she realized she might have to go through with this loveless marriage now exploded into full-fledged terror. She tried to tell herself that Abraham had to raise the knife above Isaac's body to prove himself obedient before God intervened. But even that couldn't calm the tremor that engulfed her whole body. What if there were no substitute ram in the thicket for her? She could almost feel the cold steel of the knife at her skin.

Pain brought her mind back to the present. Her father's grip, which was sure to leave bruises, dug into her arm. She swallowed and focused her eyes ahead. Not only were the pews decorated with bouquets of the fragrant blossoms, but not a place at the front of the church had been left unadorned. The gaiety all around her stood in contrast to the bleakness engulfing her heart.

Forcing herself to take the steps down the aisle, Charlotte sent up short prayers. *Have mercy on me, Lord.* She took several more steps and stared at the vase filled with white blooms interspersed with pale yellow ginger lilies sitting on a pedestal ahead of her. *Rescue me.* Her steps tightened as she closed the distance to the front. The fragrance from the moonflowers woven into her tiara added to the sweet scent filling the room, making her queasy. *I beg you, God.*

The pianist continued to play Mendelssohn's "Wedding March." The music resonated through her memory of other brides who had walked the aisle—happy brides. Only an arm's length separated her from her betrothed and where she would stand. Dragging her eyes from the decorations, she forced them onto Duncan.

A white linen shirt peeked out of a black velvet jacket pulled taut against his broad shoulders. Shiny silver buttons ran down the front and sleeve cuff. Duncan's belt included a large buckle and a thin chain draped over his hips. At the end hung a small fur pouch. Farther down his garment, her perusal stopped on the item that had brought her to this day—the heirloom pin attached to his kilt. She glanced down at white socks pulled up to his knees and secured with a ribbon that matched the red in his kilt. Tucked into one sock was a knife. Charlotte's mouth went dry as she attempted to swallow.

Once again, she was torn from her thoughts by her father's stern grip. She made herself look up and into the eyes of her betrothed. Mr. Mackenzie stood with a slight smile on his face. His best man, Tavis Dazell, stood beside him.

Mr. Mackenzie offered her his hand, but she didn't take it. A slight push on her back moved her forward. She peered over her shoulder to see Papa had let go of her arm and urged her up the final distance with another nudge. Mr. Mackenzie wrapped his hand around hers.

Charlotte turned to her sister, who now stood beside her. Nellie's eyes pooled with tears. Sorrow etched her delicate features. Charlotte yearned to take away the sadness on her sister's face.

"Dearly beloved, we are gathered here…" The reverend began to speak.

Charlotte drew her gaze away from the sister she would no longer sleep beside each night.

♥♥♥

Duncan's heart slowed to its normal pace as he guided his new wife out of the small sanctuary and into cool autumn air. The wind blew through the trees, and the leaves whispered their secrets. The moss swayed on the live oaks that shaded the small white church. When Charlotte had finally looked at him, he hadn't been sure she would repeat the vows. The lass had seemed as if she were staring down the barrel of a gun.

Duncan stopped long enough to brush the back of his finger across her cheek, then tuck a stray strand of hair behind her ear. She flinched and glanced at him from the corner of her eye. He smiled and tried to ease her fears. But still no smile touched her. They passed through the crowd of well-wishers. Charlotte seemed so ill at ease that he hurried her toward the carriage, and soon they headed for the manor and the reception.

With his wife on his arm, he led her into her new home and down the echoing halls to the ballroom where the reception awaited. He pulled out Charlotte's chair and took his own. The servants brought the food to the tables. Duncan hungered. Not for the fine delicacies that were being brought to the table, but to hear the voice of the woman beside him.

He removed from his pocket a package wrapped in fine purple velvet and tied with a bow. "Open it." He paused, waiting for her to do so. "Please."

Charlotte unwrapped the small gift to find a silver spoon with detailed engraving. She gazed at the present.

"'Tis a Scottish custom for the husband to give the bride an engraved spoon. It symbolizes we will never go hungry."

A slight nod was all she gave him. His chest clenched. She looked woeful. "I ken you canno' read Gaelic, but it says, 'You have my devotion.' Duncan placed his hand over hers and the spoon. "'Tis true, lass, and I will do all that's in my power to make you happy."

He had to make her happy. Calling off the wedding had entered his head but only for a few minutes. His heart wouldn't let him. Instead, he had promised himself he would see her contented and never wanting for anything.

Charlotte lifted her head. Her bottom lip quivered, but she managed a slight smile. The gesture, though small, touched him. The band around his chest tightened. He hadn't been fair to her. He should have wed a woman who wanted him. The only thing he could do now would be to earn her love. If it took until his last breath, he would do it. He rubbed his thumb in a circle over her gloved hand. "I ken 'tis hard for you, but you are strong. My hope is you will find me more to your liking."

A thought that had never crossed Duncan's mind hit him like a charging horse. What if even on his deathbed she never cared for him? What if she remained fearful and recoiled from his touch?

He studied Charlotte's pale complexion. Dark lashes batting over large brown eyes stared back at him. Crevvens, the lass had stolen his heart, and the only thing she felt for him was revulsion. He wished he could pull her into his arms, kiss her, and make her feel the love he had for her. He wanted to run his fingers through her hair and promise he'd protect and love her. But he'd just said that in his vows and she still looked frightened.

"Everything will work oot, lass." He smiled. When she didn't respond, he released her hand. "I'm famished."

Charlotte glanced down at the food in front of her. "It looks delicious."

Duncan could have gotten up and danced a jig. She hadn't said much, and there was a quiver and weariness in her voice, but she had at least spoken to him. And there was no condemnation in her tone.

Once the meal was finished and the music opened with a waltz, Duncan led his bride to the floor. Tavis as the best man and Nellie as the maid of honor followed. Slowly the area filled up with dancers. Duncan wanted to draw Charlotte close to him, but the memory of her last reaction to nearness kept him from indulging that impulse.

As they moved around the floor, the stiffness in her eased. He hoped she was relaxing. The music ended, and Duncan led her back to their seats. Tavis pulled up two chairs, and he and Nellie sat across from them.

Tavis gave a friendly grin to Nellie and turned to Charlotte. "If Duncan ever gets out of hand, you let me know, lass. I'll straighten him out. We go back a long way."

Ferguson sauntered up. "I'll be happy to help."

Charlotte sat back in her seat and folded her hands in her lap. "All of you were friends? Just how far back do you go?"

Tavis leaned forward and put his forearms on the table. "We grew up together as lads. Duncan was always getting us in trouble. I'm telling you, lass, you'll have your hands full with this mon."

Charlotte smiled and glanced out of the corner of her eyes at Duncan. "You came to America together?"

"Nay. It was fate that brought us together again. Tavis arrived around the same time as I did." Duncan glanced at Ferguson. "When did you say you arrived in the States?"

"'Tis been a while." The band struck up another song. "A bonnie lass awaits me." Ferguson grinned and hurried away.

Duncan turned to Tavis. "When *did* he arrive?"

Tavis shrugged.

Duncan returned his attention to his wife. "Tavis's parents were missionaries, and when we were still lads they up and moved their family away."

Charlotte straightened in her seat. "Your parents were missionaries? Do you remember the places you went?"

"I can't forget them. And some I wish I could. They were pretty dangerous." Tavis's voice lost its usual light humor.

"Oh, that must have been so frightening for a small boy. How sad. Yet how honorable of your parents. Not many are willing to give up all they have and take their families to remote places where they don't have the luxuries of everyday life. You must be very proud of them."

Tavis nodded. "They're good people. I didn't like some of the places where I grew up, but now that I'm older, I can appreciate the experience."

"That must be why you've lost most of your Scottish accent. It would be hard to guess where you're from."

"Och, 'tis true, don't you ken." Tavis wiggled his eyebrows.

Charlotte laughed. "So it's down in there somewhere I see."

"Aye, 'tis there when I want it."

"Are your parents still on the mission field?"

"They are home in Scotland, enjoying the moors and heather for a few months. Then they will return to Africa." Tavis scooted back his chair.

Duncan gazed at the transformation in Charlotte. She chatted, smiled and laughed. The conversation continued, with her sister joining in. The longer they talked, the more troubled Duncan became. How could they talk of God as if He cared about everyone? They spoke as if He loved all people the same. That wasn't what he had experienced. He shook his head. No one really knew God, and if he knew nothing else, it was that God did have favorites.

"Weel, Mrs. Mackenzie, can I persuade you to dance with the best man?" Tavis winked and gave her a big grin.

"It would be my pleasure, sir." Charlotte stood and moved onto the floor.

Nellie fidgeted in her seat, then smiled at Duncan. The lass wanted to dance. Dancing with anyone but Charlotte was not something he desired. However, at her expectant gaze, he squelched the sigh petitioning to be released and asked her. She rewarded him with a smile that caused little dimples to dent her cheeks.

"Oh! I'd love to. My first dance with my new brother-in-law." She hooked her arm into his as they moved onto the polished wood floor.

The best spot was right beside Tavis and Charlotte. It may have been a little crowded in that corner, but it was a good place to watch her. Of all the sets for Tavis to request, it would be a waltz. Duncan grumbled to himself. Couldn't he have chosen a reel?

Tavis leaned down and whispered something in Charlotte's ear. She giggled and tilted her head to the side. Duncan tensed.

Nellie tipped her head up. "Charlotte is beautiful. I can understand why you are jealous of other men around her."

Duncan frowned. "I dinna say I was jealous."

"Yes, you did. It just wasn't in words."

He grunted.

Nellie leaned back and caught Duncan's gaze. "Do you cherish my sister?" The seriousness in her voice startled him.

"I do."

"Hmm. That's good you care for her. I hope you will be mindful of her feelings."

"I like to think I have always and will always be mindful of my wife in all ways." Guilt assailed him. If that were true, he'd not be married right now nor dancing with his new sister-in-law.

The evening wore on, and at the end of the last dance, Arthur Jackson came forward with his wife on his arm and wished them happiness. Their departure seemed to be a signal for others to follow. Charlotte's four younger siblings said their goodbyes to her.

Effie sighed. "You are the luckiest girl, Charlotte."

Duncan did his best not to grin. He certainly felt like the luckiest man.

Nellie hugged her sister as if she would never see her again. "Charlotte, I'm going to miss you so much." She laid her head on Charlotte's shoulder.

"I'm going to miss you, Nellie." Charlotte sniffed and wiped at her eye.

"Lass, you can come see your sister any time you'd like. You are always welcome."

Nellie lifted her head and smiled. "Thank you, Mr. Mackenzie."

"We are family now. You can call me Duncan." He smiled at her.

He took Charlotte's hand and led her to the entryway while people formed a line to thank them and wish them well.

The last couple stopped before Duncan and Charlotte. Duncan recognized the woman as one of the local gossips. She smiled. "And where are you taking your new wife on her bridal tour?"

Duncan had hoped this question would not come up. "Weel, if I tell you, it wouldno' be a surprise for my wife."

The woman tittered. "How romantic." She turned to her husband. "I don't remember you ever being that romantic."

Her husband shook his head. "Nope, and I don't plan on starting now. Duncan, you're going to give us husbands a bad name."

Duncan chuckled.

When they had walked away, he gazed around the room, which now held busy servants cleaning up after the departing guests. He offered his arm to Charlotte. "Let's stroll. I'd like to speak to you." As they sauntered down one of the long hallways, he turned to her. "'Tis the honeymoon I wish to address. I have important business here in town. I'm no' sure how long it will take. It could be a week, a month, or more."

Charlotte looked on ahead.

"I canno' take you away until my business is completed. But I want you to think aboot where you would like to go. I will take you anywhere. You just say where."

♥♥♥

Charlotte couldn't bring herself to look at her husband. He'd take her anywhere? The only place she wanted to go was home. She wanted to run after her father and mother. But she was stronger than that. As much as she might wish to flee, she wouldn't. God had not rescued her from saying her marriage vows.

Perhaps if this *business* of his took a while, she could get to know him better and tell him she preferred money. Right now, she must find her courage and move forward as Mrs. Charlotte Mackenzie. It didn't matter that her husband's presence unnerved her. She was married and that couldn't be changed. But hopefully with the help of Mr. Mackenzie's money, her sisters would have a real choice of whom they married and what they did with their lives. If Papa tried to force them into something they didn't want, Mr. Mackenzie's wealth would surely allow her to help them.

"Where do you think you would like to go?" He was persistent, she would give him that.

"Right now I'm trying to adjust to the fact that I'm married and in a new home, Mr. Mackenzie. A honeymoon does not sound appealing to me."

Duncan patted her hand, which lay gently on his sleeve. "You can call me Duncan now, lass."

"I suppose I can." She refused to look his way. That is, until he turned and led her up a flight of stone stairs. A quick glance out of the corner of her eye told her nothing. But as they continued down the hall, she couldn't help but notice that all the rooms off the hall were bedrooms.

Suddenly, she realized that the only light came from the lamps flickering on the walls. It was evening...on her wedding night. Her throat went dry, and she tried to swallow, but it stuck together. A servant passed by and curtseyed.

"Excuse me." Duncan stopped the servant. "Would you find Miss Vivian and send her to our chamber?" The woman scurried away in search of her lady's maid.

Duncan stopped outside a closed door and pushed it open. "I'll let you have some time with your maid. I'll be back shortly."

Charlotte's insides quivered, and her mind spun with the realization. "No hurry."

Duncan chuckled and retraced his steps down the hall. Charlotte closed her eyes and leaned against the door for support. How would she get through this night?

Chapter 22

Charlotte stretched and opened her eyes. Married. She shot up and glanced at the side of the bed where her husband should be. It was still made. She swung her feet to the floor and dropped her head in her hands. How did she get into bed? Vivian had helped her get into her nightclothes. After stoking the fire in the fireplace, her lady's maid had giggled and excused herself. Charlotte had curled up in the chair to wait for her husband. That was the last she remembered.

The fire had died to coals during the night. The chill from the evening remained in the room. She wrapped her arms around her sides. Where was her trunk? She needed to get dressed so she could leave the bedchamber. The sooner she left the room, the better. She tiptoed over to the heavy oak door and gave it a tug until it opened far enough to stick her head out. The hallway was empty. She quickly shut it and turned to the only other closed door in the room. The one she assumed was an adjoining bedroom such as some of her friends' parents had. There was only one way to find out, so she darted across the room and put her ear to the wooden slab. Silence. She opened the door a crack and peeked in.

It was indeed an adjoining room, and in it sat her trunks. She flung the door open and rushed in. At least she could get to her clothes. The gown she wore yesterday was beautiful, as much as she hated to admit it, but it was too fine for daily wear. She flipped open the lid of the trunk and took out the tray, setting it on the floor. She knelt down and began looking through her belongings for a dress.

"Good morning." Duncan's voice reverberated through the room.

Charlotte squealed. Her quick movement caused her to lose her balance, and she landed on her backside. Duncan chuckled from across the room. Charlotte drew her brows down and narrowed her eyes as she turned her head to find him.

"Do you find it funny startling me?" The edge in her voice was apparent, but she didn't care. She found no humor in the situation.

"Weel, if you want me to be honest, aye." He sat in a chair with his foot crossed over his knee.

Charlotte pushed herself back onto her feet, bent forward over her trunk, and returned to her search. The awkwardness of her position dawned on her. She stood before him in her nightclothes. Jerking up the dress as she pulled it out, she pressed it to the front of her body. "Y-you shouldn't be in here." She glanced around the room and remembered this wasn't where she'd slept. "I mean I shouldn't be in here." She rose to her feet and began backing to the door.

Duncan raised his brow.

"You won't intimidate me with that." She bumped into the wall.

"Lass, I'd no' be trying to intimidate you. I wondered why I or you shouldno' be in here."

"If you were a gentleman, you'd have left the room as soon as you saw me come in. Especially dressed like this." Charlotte swept her arm through the air and down the front of her.

Duncan's brow rose even higher. "Do you forget we are husband and wife?"

"Yes. I mean no. I-I need to get dressed." The heat surged up her neck and spread to her cheeks and ears. She looked from her husband to the trunk, trying to think if she needed anything else from it. If she put the gown on, at least she'd be modestly covered.

"Do you need any help?"

"As a matter of fact, I do. Thank you. I was actually looking for my lady's maid when I peered in this room."

Duncan rose with the grace of a cat—a big cat—and stalked toward her.

"What are you doing?"

Duncan smiled. "I'm going to help you."

Charlotte went to back up, but the wall hindered her. "No! You can't."

"I'm your husband. I can."

Charlotte shook her head fiercely. "I wish for my maid." She turned and fled into the other room, slamming the door and then throwing the lock. Her heart drummed an erratic beat in her chest.

A chuckle came through the crack. "You win, wife. I shall go find your maid."

Charlotte pressed her ear to the door and listened for the outer door to close. When it did, she sagged against the wall.

Once her courage returned, she marched over to the oval mirror that hung on the wall. She first tried to raise her right brow. But the only thing she managed to do was shut her eye and scrunch her face. She attempted raising her left brow. It wouldn't cooperate either. She couldn't keep her eyes open, her mouth shut, and her face from contorting. After several minutes of trying, she sighed. It would take practice, but she would get it. One of these times when Duncan raised that brow at her, she would raise hers right back.

♥♥♥

Duncan continued to chuckle as he searched for Vivian. He wouldn't expect any less modesty from his new wife, but her feisty spirit encouraged him. When he had come back to their room shortly after leaving her last night, he found her curled up in a chair, fast asleep. The uncertainty, nay, the fear he had seen in her eyes before, during, and after their wedding pricked his heart. She needed rest more than he needed her. After pulling the covers back, he'd laid her on his bed and tucked the covers around her. Then he'd leaned down and kissed her forehead. He had yearned to brush his lips over hers, but he feared he'd wake her. Fighting the urge to lay down beside her, he left his room and went to sleep in the adjoining chamber. He snorted. A fine way to have spent one's wedding night—in separate beds.

Duncan glanced at the large clock hanging at the end of the hall. As if to confirm the late morning hour, his stomach protested its lack of food. Waiting for Charlotte to waken, he'd put off his breakfast and was glad he had. Perhaps over the morning meal, when it was only the two of them, she would relax a wee bit.

The sound of female chatter floated up the stairs. Duncan headed down toward the voices. As he crossed the threshold to the library, silence filled the room, and two young ladies' eyes trained on him. The one held the feather duster in mid-swing.

"Would you please find Vivian and have her sent to Mrs. Mackenzie? She'd like to dress. And tell Vivian to show her mistress to the breakfast room."

The young maid without the duster gave a curtsey. "Right away, sir."

Duncan followed her out of the library, then turned down the hall to wait for Charlotte. He'd have a cup of tea in the meantime.

About a half hour later, Charlotte graced him with her presence. The lass looked timid. He must feel like a stranger to her. He'd spent too many hours thinking about the lass for him to feel the same way. Perhaps he should have gone and visited her some after their betrothal was announced. But he had thought to give her time alone with her family. After all, she would spend the rest of her life with him. "Come lass. Sit beside me so we can talk."

Her gaze went to the chair he'd pulled out and stood behind.

She sauntered over and sat down. "Thank you."

"You are verra welcome. Did you sleep weel?"

She stared at the plate in front of her. "Yes."

Duncan took his seat. "You have nay reason to be embarrassed or fearful of me." She continued to examine her empty plate, so Duncan continued. "'Twas my choice no' to wake you. I am no' an unfeeling mon. I ken yesterday was hard on you, lass, and you were tired. I chose to let you sleep."

She lifted her head, eyes questioning.

He prodded her. "What do you wish to ask me?"

"You aren't angry with me? What will the servants think? I'm sure they all know by now. Even if you were to warn them to remain silent, one will tell, and the word will get out."

He couldn't believe she worried about this. "I care no' what people think or what they say. My servants are loyal to me, but if one does gossip, it is no' my concern. I'm no' ashamed of my decision. And if that mind of yours is running wild, let me tame it a wee bit by saying the *only* reason I dinna wake you last night was because of my concern for you."

Charlotte blinked. "You don't care what people think? I got the distinct impression that you did."

"And when did I ever give you that notion?"

"I don't remember."

Duncan reached over and laid his hand over hers. "Weel, lassie, I have an idea. What would you say to forgetting everything you think you ken aboot me, and I will do the same? Let's start our marriage oot anew with no preconceived ideas."

♥♥♥

Charlotte had thought him so much like her father. Maybe not in all ways, but just like her father, he didn't allow her to make her own decisions. He proved that with their wedding. But if he wasn't like her father in everything, he might listen to reason. The vows had been said, and she was married. Why not try to make the best of it? She would be living with this man for a long time. "That sounds like a reasonable idea, Mr. Mackenzie. I shall endeavor to forget the past and look forward only to each new day."

"You make me a happy mon." Duncan began tracing a small circle on her bare hand with his thumb. "Now, I have a request. Would you call me Duncan?"

Charlotte chewed her bottom lip. "My mother still calls my father Mr. Jackson or 'your father' if she is talking to one of us children."

"But I'm no' your father nor are you your mother. I wish to hear my name on your lips."

"I'll try to remember…Duncan."

A smile spread across his face and lit his eyes. "I thank you, Charlotte, for giving me a chance."

She wanted to believe that Duncan could be the kind of man her heart desired and that God knew best when He didn't stop the marriage. What if Duncan was the man God had chosen for her and he was everything she wanted? She almost laughed out loud at the thought. She was letting her imagination run away if she believed that. How could Duncan be the man she wanted when she was given no choice in the marriage? She didn't understand why God had ignored her pleas, but He had.

But there were many people in the Bible who had prayed and the answer they got was no. Why would she be any different? Paul was a mighty man of God and begged God to take away his affliction, but God never did. She should be thankful that her husband did seem to crave a peaceful marriage. She must put her trust in God. He would see her through everything.

Charlotte smiled back. "Our marriage will be much happier if we try to get along."

"Aye, that it will, lass." Duncan waited for the food to be served and the servants to leave. "Is there anything you need or would like to do? Perhaps a tour of your new home."

"That would be nice." She wanted to say she'd had one. The first time she'd seen the heirloom pin. But that would not seem like she was seeking a peaceful marriage.

He scooped some food on his fork and guided it toward his mouth as she waited with hands in her lap.

She cleared her throat. "Would you like to pray over the food, or would you prefer I do?"

Duncan set his fork down on his plate. "I see I have a new ritual to remember. If you dinna mind, I'll give you the honor."

Charlotte bowed her head. "Thank you, Father, for this beautiful morning and for loving us even when we don't deserve it. God, I ask you to guide me and my new husband in our marriage. I pray You will always be the center of our union. I ask You to bless this food to the nourishment of our bodies. In Jesus' precious name. Amen."

Duncan raised his head. "The house servants will start reporting to you. I have business that will take me to town for the next wee bit. If you have a question, you can ask my valet, Mr. Stuebing."

"And what kind of business takes you to town so often?"

"Just business. Nothing for you to fash yourself aboot."

She stiffened. So much like her father.

"Och! Lass, I dinna mean that as it sounds. I have some new clients I need to see. I dinna want to talk aboot work with you today on the first day of our marriage."

It was going to take some effort not to compare her husband to Papa. Duncan seemed more sensitive to her feelings this morning.

Once the meal was finished, the servants lined up in front of Duncan and Charlotte to introduce themselves and explain their duties.

Duncan guided her through each room and gave her little details. The bedroom he showed her was his. He walked over to a large chest and yanked on a drawer. Retrieving a wooden box, he tipped it for her to see. "If you are ever in need of funds and I am no' around, you can find what you need here."

"Thank you, but I don't foresee that happening."

"You never ken, lass."

They moved on. When they crossed the threshold into the library, Charlotte couldn't stop herself from seeking out the heirloom pin to see if it had been returned to its place of honor. The reason she'd been forced to marry. Her feet guided her to the same place where she'd stood only weeks before.

How did that pin get in her bag? Could it have somehow caught on her sleeve when she'd reached up and touched it? But she was sure she'd seen it still on the tartan when she'd spoken to Nellie. Perhaps someone tried to play a practical joke—a joke that went terribly wrong.

A gentle brush of Duncan's finger over her cheek caused her to turn to him. He looked down at her, eyes full of compassion. "Charlotte, I hope you dinna always think of this room and my pin in a negative light. I'm sorry, lass. I wish this was no' so hard on you. I'll be guid to you, lass. I give you my promise."

She closed her eyes, angry for the way her body enjoyed his skin against hers. He didn't seem nearly as frightening as before. "I don't dislike either of them. I was remembering that this was the beginning of..." She opened her eyes. "Sorry? What are you sorry for?"

He tensed. Dropping his hand lightly to her shoulder, he looked away before breaking the silence he'd allowed to linger. "I dinna like to see you hurting." His eyes moved back toward her. "I'm verra pleased to call you my wife. My pin will forever be much more special because it brought you to me."

Duncan's face was only a few inches from hers, his eyes fixed on her lips.

She turned away. "You're very kind."

He brushed the back of his finger over her cheek. "You make that easy. I wish I did no' have to, but I have to go down to the docks."

She didn't want to be alone. The house was so large, and she didn't know anyone.

As if he read her mind, Duncan nodded toward the wall and the books filling the shelves. "Pick yourself oot a book to read. I'll try no' to be gone any longer than I have to."

A few minutes later she stood alone in the room with the item that had sealed her fate. She turned her back on it and strolled from the room.

♥♥♥

Many hours had passed, and Duncan hadn't returned. Waiting for him in the parlor, Charlotte busied herself with the needlework she'd brought from home. The evening meal, which she'd eaten alone, had long passed. Darkness had fallen and the curtains had been drawn. She'd spent most of the day with Vivian, trying to learn her way around and becoming acquainted with the large staff. She'd met Mr. Stuebing. He didn't seem terribly friendly, and she hoped she wouldn't have to ask him too many questions.

She secured her needle in the embroidery cloth, then set the hoop on the table next to the lamp. It was late and time to go to bed. Once she'd slipped out of her clothes and dismissed Vivian for the night, she stood in front of her mirror and attempted to get her brow to rise. She was sure she had gotten every other muscle in her face to do great contortionist feats— all but the one brow. With a sigh, she turned away. The house was too quiet for her. With five siblings, her home was always noisy. She thought of Nellie. Did she like having a room to herself? She swallowed a sob. She felt so lonely, and she'd only been gone one day.

Once in her bed, she snuggled down beneath the covers to ward off the chill. She closed her eyes, but sleep didn't come. When slumber evaded her at home and Nellie had drifted off, she would talk to God. Charlotte opened her eyes and stared into the darkness. "Lord, I'm lonely. I hope Duncan won't be gone every day. I'm still not sure why You made me marry him. But You did, and I know it was You, because we both know that I didn't steal that pin. I'll do my best to be a good wife. He seems like a good man, and I have prayed for many years that you would send me the man You wanted me to marry. So I'm trusting you, Lord, that Duncan is that man. Help me to love him. I love you, God. Amen."

As she drifted off to sleep, her door latch clicked, but her eyes were too heavy to open and see if someone had walked in.

Chapter 23

Duncan pulled the door shut. Her prayer weighed heavy on his heart as he sank onto the bed where Charlotte had slept on their wedding night, except tonight she had fallen asleep in the bed he'd slept on. The irony.

She thought God had caused them to marry. He hoped she never found out that it wasn't God, but he that brought this marriage about. She might never forgive him if she knew the truth. He shuddered. And she was lonely. He could take care of that.

He undressed and lay down on his bed with hands clasped behind his head. The second night of marriage and once again he slept alone. When Charlotte had asked God to help her love him, his chest cinched, stealing his breath. He hoped God would answer her prayer.

He rolled to his side, and a hint of lavender wafted up from the pillow that Charlotte had slept on the previous night. Duncan groaned. It was going to be a very long night.

The distant bark of a dog woke him. The sun greeted him, peeking its rays through his window, as well as Charlotte's faint humming. He rolled over and stared at her door where the melody flowed through the cracks and imagined her readying herself as she hummed the song.

He quickly dressed, stuffed a small package in his pocket, a special gift for her, and tapped on the adjoining door. "Are you hungry, lass?" The door opened and Charlotte stood before him dressed in a gown as green as the Scottish hillside. "You look bonny."

She looked down at herself as if to check and see what she was wearing. A light laugh flowed from her lips. "Thank you. But I don't believe you. I've had this dress forever."

"Weel, you still look bonnie in it." He took her arm and guided her to breakfast.

Once seated at the table, he pulled the box from his pocket. "This is for you. It was my mither's."

Charlotte opened the decorative metal box and gasped. "It's beautiful." She removed the chain with an amethyst thistle charm hanging from it. Small diamonds formed the stem and emeralds the leaves. "I can't accept this. It had to be terribly expensive."

"My mither gave that to me years ago to give to the woman I married. She wanted to make sure it was passed down." Duncan's gut twisted as he thought of his brother who would never have a wife to give his heirloom to. Nor would he have children to carry his name. He shook off the melancholy threatening to steal the joy of this moment.

"It's the most beautiful thing anyone has ever given me." She turned her back to him and held up the necklace. "Would you fasten it for me?"

"It would be an honor." Duncan brushed her hair from her neck and secured the chain. He gave in to temptation and ran his fingers through her hair as he let it fall down her back. The same lavender scent that tortured him during his sleep last night rose and filled the air. He closed his eyes and breathed in. Perhaps tonight…

♥♥♥

She couldn't have been more wrong—marriage to Duncan was rather sweet. She sat on the blanket with her legs tucked to the side. The sun shone from the west, its reddish rays sending heat, warding off the nip in the air, and warmed her. Duncan sprawled across from her, legs stretched out, head resting on his balled-up jacket, and a long piece of grass in his mouth. It was a pleasant end to a good day.

After breakfast they had walked the grounds. He'd taken her down to the stream where they sat on the bank and talked. He told her about his youth in Scotland and his family. He missed them both. She could hear it in his voice.

They had come back to the house and had lunch. He had a few things to do pertaining to his business, and she went upstairs and took a nap. When she'd awoken, he'd had a picnic basket packed and the carriage ready by the front door.

"I'm having a lovely time, Duncan." She made a point to use his name.

"As am I. The company could no' be better. Nor the weather."

"Hmmm. I agree." She glanced beyond the carriage and field, where a copse of trees stood near a curve in the road. A mounted figure emerged from around the bend. "Are you expecting someone?"

Duncan leaned on his elbow and turned his head to see. "Nay." The horse and rider drew nearer. "'Tis Tavis."

Charlotte fluffed her gown making sure her feet were covered. "Mr. Dalzell? What in the world is he doing out here?"

"We shall soon see." He swung up to a sitting position and draped his arm over his bent leg as he waited.

Duncan's friend jumped from his horse. His feet hit the ground with a thud that must have jarred his body. "Are you enjoying your time alone?"

Duncan frowned. "We were."

Charlotte giggled. "It's good to see you, Tavis." She tipped her hat, blocking the sunshine. "What brings you our way?"

"Only the prettiest lass in Charleston." Tavis dropped down across from her and Duncan.

Charlotte shook her head. "Now I *know* you two grew up together. You both use the same flattery."

Duncan reached up and tucked a wayward strand of hair behind her ear. "Wrong you are, lass. When two men agree, it must be the truth."

The simple yet familiar gesture warmed her insides. "You, Duncan, are full of yourself." Charlotte turned back to Tavis. "Is there trouble that you come and seek us out?"

Tavis shifted his gaze to Duncan and then back on Charlotte. "All is well. I have a wee bit of business I need to discuss with Duncan tonight. If you can spare him." Charlotte let her shoulders relax. "He has entertained me all day. I would be selfish to insist he continue to do so." Duncan flicked the piece of grass at Tavis. "Do I get a say in this?"

Tavis grinned. "If you insist."

"I will meet with you after Charlotte has gone up for the night. I'm no' leaving her to sit by herself this evening."

Charlotte gazed at Duncan. His kindness and self-sacrifice touched her. Thus far, he had proven to be everything she thought he was not. "Really, Duncan, if you have business, I can find something to do."

"You are more important than business. It can wait." Duncan gave her a meaningful look. "But now that we have unwelcome company, we should head back."

She gathered everything and put it back into the basket while Duncan folded the blanket. They loaded the carriage and headed home. Once there and settled in the library, they played checkers. After losing two games to Tavis and winning a game with Duncan, she let the two men play. Duncan won the game before Tavis could get one king.

She feigned shock. "You let me win. How could Tavis beat me twice and I beat you, yet you beat Tavis?"

Duncan looked up from the board. "Och! You distract me with your beauty, dearling. I couldno' concentrate."

She watched him win another game and had to smile to herself. Covering her mouth, she yawned for the third time. "If you two don't mind, I'm going to go up to my room." Both men stood, and Duncan walked her up to her chamber door. She opened the door and turned. "I had a wonderful day today. Thank you."

He reached out and once again tucked the stray strand of hair behind her ear. His hand lingered, cupping her cheek. She gazed up into his eyes, and the tenderness she saw in them caused her stomach to flutter.

He leaned forward, bringing with him his musky cologne scent. She closed her eyes and held her breath, waiting for their first kiss. His lips, so soft and smooth, brushed hers, not demanding, but gentle and oh so sweet. Her lips tingled, and she found herself not wanting it to end.

When he pulled back, he smiled with hooded eyes. "I have wanted to do that since I met you." He kissed her on her forehead. "You get a guid night's sleep."

Charlotte held onto the door frame, enjoying the memory of her first kiss as he disappeared down the hall. She nearly floated to the chair and collapsed in it. Her first kiss. The one that Frank had forced upon her didn't count. It had been appalling and had made her sick. But this one, it was different. It made her whole body feel strange things. And this time it was enjoyable. She touched her fingers to her lips. If he made her feel like this, maybe she could love him.

Vivian came and helped her ready for bed. "You seem a bit dreamy-eyed this evening."

"Oh, just thinking things are not as bad as I had first thought."

Vivian gave her a knowing smile.

"What is that grin for?" Charlotte attempted to sound offended.

Vivian helped her out of her deep azure dress. "Oh, nothing, ma'am. Just happy things are better than you had hoped."

Vivian finished helping Charlotte ready for bed. After she left, Charlotte snuggled down into the covers as she did every night. The fire burned in the fireplace, casting an orange glow around the room. The crackle of the wood didn't lull her to sleep like it had the last six nights. Sleep eluded her even after she had prayed. Voices outside drew her attention. She tiptoed to the window and peeked out.

Duncan sat on his horse, ready to leave. And though she could see only the back of the other rider, she knew it had to be Tavis. They were speaking with another man on a horse. When they finished speaking, Duncan and Tavis spurred their horses on down the road.

♥♥♥

Duncan couldn't think about Charlotte, the kiss and how much he wanted to follow her into her room. He needed to concentrate on the mission. This could all be over tonight, and then he and Charlotte could live out the rest of their days together—that was a whole new problem. How was she going to feel about moving to Scotland and leaving her family?

He spurred his horse on and glanced over his shoulder to see Tavis keeping pace. Thankfully someone was looking out for them tonight. The sky was clear and the moon bright. He could travel the road at a good clip.

Fillman, the man he had paid to snoop around the docks for any information that might lead to finding the traitor, had sent a message. He had some information and requested Duncan come immediately to the Sailors' Galley Saloon.

By the time they reached the saloon, their horses heaved. He tucked his pistol and a dirk under his belt. "Have you any weapons?"

Tavis held up a revolver. They dismounted and sauntered into the establishment as if they owned the place.

Apparently it worked, because when he started asking questions people talked. Fillman had stepped outside, and no one had seen him since.

"We need to search around here. If he asked to meet us here, he wouldno' have gone far." Duncan motioned to Tavis. "You go to the right, and I'll go left. Give a whistle if you find him, and we'll meet back here."

Tavis gave a nod and took off at a jog. Duncan went the opposite direction. Pulling the dirk from his belt, he turned down an alleyway. Finding it empty, he returned to the road and made his way to the next alley. He got halfway through and nearly tripped over a man sprawled on the ground. Duncan knelt and he pulled him up to a sitting position to get a good look at his face. "You see a mon come down this way?"

The drunk only stared at him and passed back out. Duncan got up and let him slump to the ground. A shrill whistle pierced the air. Duncan took off at a full run. Turning the corner from the alley onto the road, he looked ahead. Tavis wasn't in front of the saloon. Duncan sped past the door and slowed as he came to the first alley Tavis would have gone down. Another whistle, this one was broken in mid-sound. He sprinted on, realizing his friend was farther away than he had thought. He glanced down the next lane as he passed.

Darkness loomed between the tall buildings, but as he slowed again, he could make out the silhouettes of two people. One on the ground and the other leaning over him.

Duncan dashed forward and did a quick surveillance before dropping down to his knees and tucking his knife away. He leaned over the body and tried to make out the face. It was Fillman.

"What happened?" Duncan lifted the man into his arms and stood.

"I came down here just as someone stepped out and attacked him. I couldn't get to him fast enough." Tavis gasped. "When I reached him, he collapsed against me."

Duncan took long strides into the street and laid the man down. He felt for a heartbeat, then for breath. Blood saturated the man's shirt. He moved his hand, trying to feel for the lifegiving pulse. "He's dead." Duncan wanted to slam his fist into something. "Did he say anything?"

"I had a hard time hearing him. I think he said, 'not who I thought.'"

"That doesno' make sense. He never told me he suspected someone." Duncan couldn't believe his ears. They'd come so close to catching this villain, and it had cost an innocent man his life. And what had they found out? Nothing. "Why wouldno' he give us a name? Who did he think it was? It doesno' make sense." Duncan continued to stare at Fillman as if he could still tell him something.

"I don't know."

Duncan looked up for the first time and saw his friend. Blood covered his shirt. "Are you wounded?"

Tavis shook his head. "Must be Fillman's blood."

"Weel, I think 'tis time to call the authorities in."

Tavis stepped back. "Duncan, I'm not too far from my place. Do you think you can handle this? I have something I need to see to."

Duncan looked around and saw a small crowd from the Sailors' Galley gathering. "Aye, I can take care of it." The last thing he wanted was to speak with the authorities, but they couldn't both leave. And too many people had seen him. Best he stay.

By the time Duncan had explained what had taken place to the authorities, it was late. He considered stopping at Tavis's lodgings but decided against it. He was probably asleep. Besides, he wanted to get home to his bride. Between the time spent answering the police's questions and the ride home, it was the wee morning hours. Duncan dropped his horse off at the stables and went up to his room. He shucked his boots and collapsed onto his bed.

Another night alone, and his mind wouldn't rest. He knew Fillman had a family. He'd have to see they were taken care of. And then there was Tavis, who had acted so strange tonight. Not wanting to stick around.

Duncan never saw anyone else in the alley either. But Tavis had explained that. So why was he feeling like Tavis was keeping something from him?

Chapter 24

M arried over a week and Duncan still slept in another room. Charlotte sat in front of her mirror examining herself. She leaned in. He told her she was beautiful, so it wasn't that. She put her hand in front of her mouth and blew. Her breath didn't smell bad. She smiled and looked at her teeth. They were white and clean. What was it that kept the man from her bed? She'd been more than amiable—they'd gotten along very well. With all his nocturnal outings, did he have another woman? What if he had changed his mind and regretted marrying her? If only Mother had told her a little more about these things.

Tap, tap, tap. The sound made her stop her fretting and answer the door. Duncan held a present in his hand.

"What's this?"

Duncan raised his brow. "I would think by now, lass, you would have figured it oot."

Charlotte laughed. "What I meant to say is you don't have to keep buying me presents. You've given me a present every day since we were married." Heaven forbid he was buying these out of guilt because he didn't want her anymore.

"Eight, to be exact. Nine, if you want to count the one you hold in your hand. No' that I'm counting, mind you." His eyes glimmered with mischief.

Charlotte took the heavy rectangular package and stepped back into her room. She sat in the chair and carefully unwrapped it. Words caught in her throat.

"Does that mean you like it?"

Without a thought, Charlotte sprang to her feet and threw her arms around Duncan's neck. "I love it."

His arms immediately encircled her, and he drew her tight. "Me, too."

Charlotte leaned her head back so she could see him. "You love my new Bible?"

"Aye, I do. Anything that merits this kind of a response from you, I do indeed love."

Before she could move, he swooped down and brushed his lips across hers. She melted into his embrace, and he deepened the kiss. Her heart raced as warmth tingled through her body. Maybe he did like her.

♥♥♥

Balancing a suspicious wife with working undercover for the queen was proving challenging. Duncan had gone to Sailors' Galley Saloon every night of late. It seemed all the doors had closed on him since Fillman's death. He hadn't found any more information on the traitor or who had murdered Fillman. Tavis was still being evasive in his answers. When Duncan ran into Ferguson, he'd started asking him questions about the missing book, wondering if maybe Tavis had taken it, because the two of them were the only other people who knew Duncan wanted it.

To believe Tavis was involved was as ludicrous as thinking Stuebing was. And to add to his frustration, Charlotte had been asking questions about his leaving late at night. Apparently, she was a light sleeper, something he wouldn't know much about. He didn't need her suspicious of him. So, tonight he had opted to stay in and told Tavis to go on alone. Perhaps he could quiet her apprehension about his nightly treks.

Duncan had tried to be patient with Charlotte and used his evening outings to help him. With supper behind them, his beautiful wife across from him, he attempted to teach her to play chess, but he didn't seem to be doing a very good job.

Charlotte moved her knight diagonally across the board.

"Nay, love. Your knight moves in an L shape. Your bishop moves diagonally."

Charlotte picked up her rook. "Is this my bishop?"

"Nay that is your rook. Remember, it looks like the turret on a castle? They canno' move diagonally, only forward, backward, and side to side."

"Ah, I remember now." She set her rook down and picked up her bishop and moved it.

Duncan smiled and moved one of his pawns. Charlotte stroked her queen and hesitated as if not sure what she could do with it. He bit down the urge to tell her. She let go of it and moved her rook down the board. He sighed in relief. She had likely moved the rook because he had just told her what it did. He pushed his pawn up two more squares and held his breath as her hand hovered over her queen again. Once again, she seemed unsure and chose the bishop this time to move across the board. Duncan was beginning to think he'd never relax. He didn't want to embarrass her by explaining the moves of all the pieces again. Maybe if he moved each piece, she would see how they moved.

He moved his knight. Charlotte placed her finger on the queen again, then sighed. She glanced up and smiled then moved her other bishop across the board. He moved his queen forward four spaces. Charlotte moved another rook out. With little thought, Duncan pushed his queen diagonally.

Charlotte's eyes sparkled. Duncan grinned—sure that she now understood how the queen could move. But, as she grasped her bishop again and slid him three spaces, Duncan frowned.

She beamed. "I believe that is check and mate."

He glanced up to see her biting her bottom lip and holding back a giggle. "You ken how to play chess? You little vixen. Making me believe you've never played."

She burst out laughing. "No. I never made you believe anything. You assumed I'd never played. I just never told you any different."

"You pretended no' to ken how your pieces move. 'Tis almost the same as telling me you never played." He gave his best attempt at appearing appalled by her actions.

"Perhaps I was only trying to save your pride."

"I will remember that I must be precise with you. Now would you like to play a real game of chess?"

"Only if you promise not to let me win."

He had his work cut out for him. She was a fine chess player and a good opponent. If he thought to win, he couldn't let her distract him. She made him work, but in the end, he gave in to his pride and put her king in checkmate.

She looked up from the pieces left on the board. "Next time I won't show you any mercy."

"You dinna."

She stood up and stretched. "I guess you will have to wait until tomorrow to find out."

Chuckling, he pushed back his chair and rose. The evening ritual of walking her to her room had become less uncomfortable, but after his thoughts tonight...

When they reached her room, she turned toward him. She lifted her hand and hesitated before gently touching his cheek. "Thank you for your patience and kindness. You've restored my faith. I never thought I'd say it, but I feel very blessed to call you husband."

He closed his eyes, wanting nothing to interfere with the feel of her skin on his. His heart thudded an erratic beat in his chest. He turned his head and gently kissed the palm of her hand. A slight gasp escaped her.

He knew if he opened his eyes and looked into the depths of her deep brown ones, there would be no turning back. Lowering his head, he sought her lips—just a chaste kiss goodnight. He brushed his lips over hers. It wasn't enough. He went back for more. His mouth met hers with coercion. She let out a soft moan.

There was nothing gentle in the way his mouth sought hers. He deepened the kiss. The love he felt for her overwhelmed him. She was his, and he wanted her. Combing his hand through her hair, he met pins and pulled them out. They pinged on the hardwood floor as her hair spilt down around her face and over his arm. The sweet smell of lavender drifted up and he inhaled her intoxicating scent.

With his other hand, he cupped the back of her head, controlling her movement. She was everything he'd dreamed of. Everything he wanted. The moment he saw her, he had been confident she was meant to be his and, as she melted into him, her body forming to his, he knew he'd been right.

Duncan forced himself to draw back—his breath ragged. She tipped her head, and he gazed into glazed, hooded eyes.

Heaven help him if she ever discovered the hold she had over him. "Are you ready to make this a real marriage?"

Her response was half-gasp, half-sigh. "Yes."

Chapter 25

Something tickled her nose, and she rubbed it. Now it was on her cheek. She slapped at it. A deep chuckle resonated beside her, and she snapped her eyes open. Duncan sat on the edge of the bed fully dressed, and in his hands was a fluffy black puppy with a big red bow tied around its neck. Running down the midnight nose was a white blaze that matched the four white stockings on its feet. The puffball's tail wagged like a metronome, and Duncan held it close enough so it gave little kisses all over her face.

She pushed herself up and scooted back to the headboard. "She's adorable. Is she for me?"

"I dinna have any other wife I give gifts to."

Charlotte took the puppy into her hands and snuggled it. "You'd better not have any other wives."

"Och! You are the only one for me. Dinna you ken that by now?"

Charlotte looked up from the squirming puppy. "Am I, now?" After last night she had no doubt her husband cared for her.

He raised his brow. "Aye, you are. As smart as you are, I thought you would have figured that oot by now." He smiled and kissed her on the forehead. "I've been waiting for these little furballs to get old enough. She's a herding dog from my homeland."

Charlotte kissed the animal on the head as it wiggled and sniffed her. "She's beautiful and can sleep right here next to me at night."

He shook his head. "Nay. I'll no' be sharing our bed with the dog."

Heat flooded her face at his mention of *our* bed. She looked at the furball instead of him. "But, Duncan, she'll be scared."

"I'll make her a bed, and she can sleep on the floor beside you."

Charlotte let go of her new charge, and it scampered across the bed. "Please." She attempted to inflict a pleading tone into her voice and gave Duncan a quick glance.

He chuckled. "I draw the line on animals in my bed."

"Very well. But you have to give her a nice warm blanket. It is a her, isn't it?"

He leaned over and kissed her, then stood. "Aye. 'Tis a girl. Now, I've been neglecting some business and need to go to town. Do you think she will keep you company?"

Snatching up the puppy as it ran by her, Charlotte gave Duncan her biggest grin. "Aye. The little lass and I will do quite well together."

Duncan threw his head back and roared with laughter. He closed the door, and his chuckle faded down the hall.

She snuggled the pup to her chest and closed her eyes. *Thank you, Lord for giving me a man as trustworthy and honorable as Duncan. I am so thankful that You did not give me Frank when I begged for him to be my husband. Frank was so deceitful, and you knew that, but I didn't see the big picture. I will try to trust You more.*

♥♥♥

Duncan grew weary of this cat and mouse game. He was almost to Tavis's place, and his goal was to step up the search for the turncoat. He was on the man's trail. Maybe closer than he thought if the man would turn to cold-blooded murder. Not that he hadn't already considered him that for his treachery in Afghanistan.

Duncan stopped in front of Tavis's house and dismounted from Aberdeen. The horse pranced around, and Duncan tightened his hands on the reins. He patted its neck. "I told you, you would be much happier if you were no' so ornery. Nothing like a guid long ride on a sunny morning, eh?" He tied

Aberdeen to the fence rail and bounded up the steps. Lifting the large brass knocker, he pounded it on the catch plate.

Tavis answered the door with shaving soap still on his face. "What brings you out so early this morning?"

Duncan stepped into the house. "I'm ready to be done with this. I ken we are close. I need to put a wee more pressure on, and he'll show his ugly face."

"Have a seat, and I'll be back in as soon as I finish shaving."

Duncan sat in the parlor and then remembered the errand he had asked Tavis to do. "Did you have a chance to stop by and pick up the mirror set for me?"

Tavis yelled from the other room. "It's on the dining room table."

Duncan got up and went to the other room. He spotted the silver brush, comb, and mirror set from the doorway and walked toward it. But as he neared, it wasn't Charlotte's gift that caught his eye. It was the book that lay beside it—the High Seas' logbook.

"Did you find it?" Tavis strode through the doorway, his shirt hanging open and shaving soap still on his face. "Where did that come from?"

Duncan spun around. "I'd like to ken the same thing."

"I haven't seen it before."

"Weel, is no' that strange. I found it right here next to the gift you picked up for my wife." He attempted to control his voice. "How did you get the High Seas' logbook? Did you hurry down there when you learned I planned to go?"

"Look, Duncan, I don't know how that got there. I have never laid eyes on it before in my life. Ferguson and I went to town and picked up Charlotte's gift. I left the mirror and brush set on the table when I went to get a bite to eat later that night. And I assure you it wasn't there then." Bewilderment clouded Tavis's face.

Duncan opened the book and flipped through the pages. "It walked in here by itself?"

"Oh, yes, now I remember. I put it there." Tavis's voice dripped with sarcasm, and he rolled his eyes. "No, I can't explain it. What I know is that it wasn't here when I went to bed last night, because when I got back from eating, I walked right past here. I'd have noticed something that big on my table."

Duncan looked down at the open book in his hand and the ragged edge of paper near the binding. "How convenient. The page is missing. Start talking. I'm beginning to think some things, and I dinna like what I'm thinking."

Tavis brought both his hands up in surrender. "I swear Duncan I had nothing to do with this. I hope you would know me better than that."

Duncan folded his arms across his chest. "What am I supposed to think?"

"Are you so blinded by this mission that you don't see the truth? If I did, why would I send you straight to it to get your gift?"

"Och! You have to admit, it does no' look good."

Tavis took the towel that was still draped over his shoulder and wiped off the remaining shaving soap. "Maybe it's a warning of some sort. Whoever we are looking for obviously knows we are on his trail. Why else would he put this in here? He has already killed. The man is dangerous."

"Aye. He is. More the reason I must find him quickly. 'Tis sorry I am for no' trusting you."

"Perhaps you should let me continue on. You have a family now—a wife."

"I can take care of myself. I will get this traitor if 'tis the last thing I do."

Tavis pointed his finger at Duncan's chest. "And you now need to look out for yourself so you can take care of your wife. Besides, I don't want you to meet your Maker before you know Him personally."

"I believe in God. But that isn't what this is aboot. It's aboot finding a traitor."

"You're wrong. God is what this is about. You know there is a God, but you don't *know* God. This man is a cold-blooded killer. I plan to keep you alive until you know Him."

Duncan shook his head. It was a waste of time arguing with a missionary's child, even if he was a grown man. "I am careful. Our adversary may be one step ahead of us, but I *will* oot smart him."

Tavis's eyes narrowed." I lost my brother, too. I want this guy as much as you. But more than that, I want to keep you alive."

Duncan took a deep breath. "I ken your loss is as great as mine. And I appreciate your concern for me. But I have been in this business a long time. I ken how to handle myself. I'm heading down to the wharf. You comin'?"

"Let me finish up." Tavis hustled back into his room, buttoning up his shirt, and came back out a few minutes later. "Let's go."

When they got down to the wharf, they headed to some of the local hangouts, where sailors and merchants drank away their cash and sorrows. Out of habit, Duncan felt his pocket for his weapon, again. It was there. He and Tavis made their way into the first establishment. As usual, the customers were well on their way to drunkenness. They asked around for information about Fillman. Did they hear anything about the murder? Did they see anyone else around? The ones still sober enough to talk had heard about it, but none had any leads.

By the time they made their way to the Sailors' Galley, Duncan was ready to force the information from someone. The place had few customers, many of the same they'd questioned before. He spotted a man in the corner dressed in dark pants, a long black coat, and his bowler low on his head. On the table in front of him sat a glass of ale. The top button of his white shirt lay open, and his tie hung loosely around his neck. He scanned the room, then returned his gaze to his ale. Duncan recognized the man from earlier visits, though he never saw his face. He sat at the same table with his hat pulled low over his face. Duncan had never had a chance to talk to him before. By the time he'd work his way across the room, he'd be gone. This time he'd go straight to him.

A ruckus from the other side of the room, and where Tavis had disappeared to, drew Duncan's attention. Someone had knocked a table over in protest over a card game. Duncan watched as Tavis defused the situation. Satisfied all was well, he turned back around to find his quarry gone.

Not this time. Duncan hurried to the door and jerked it open. Stepping outside, he glanced down the street in both directions, but not a soul was in sight. Frustrated, he went back in and made his way around the few patrons, learning what he already knew—the man in the corner didn't wish to talk to anyone.

Daylight had begun to fade when they left and returned to their horses to head home. Once on the road, Tavis turned off to head back to his house. Duncan stopped his horse. "Be careful."

Tavis stopped and his horse pranced in protest. "I'm always careful."

"I have a feeling we're being watched."

"Then why don't you stay with me? It'd be safer than taking that long ride home."

"I dinna like leaving Charlotte home to fash aboot me. If Aberdeen keeps a guid pace, I'll get home by dark."

Tavis pulled on the reins, and the horse stomped his foot. "I have no one waiting for me at home. I'll ride with you and stay at your place tonight."

Duncan patted his pocket that held his weapon. "I can take care of myself."

"I don't doubt it, but just to be sure, I think I'll ride along. Charlotte would never forgive me if something happened to you."

"I dinna realize you had become such guid friends with my wife."

"Och! You're jealous."

Duncan clicked his tongue and flicked the horse's reins. "You read too much into my words."

"Me thinks you are quite taken with your little wife."

"Most men are when they marry."

"If you really care for her, you should give up this hunt. It's getting too dangerous."

"I will when I catch him. And I assure you, Tavis, I will catch my traitor."

Chapter 26

Something had to be wrong. He should be home by now. Charlotte rested on the window seat and gazed over the road that led to the manor. She didn't like the way her husband disappeared for hours with no real reason for why he was gone or where he had been.

A distant clicking of horse hooves carried on the evening air. She leaned forward to get a better view. The full moon shed light on two riders coming in. Her heart skipped a beat. It had to be Duncan.

Snatching up Flora, who pulled on her dress, she nuzzled the puppy and hurried downstairs to greet Duncan. Reaching the threshold, she deposited Flora on the ground and flew to her husband, who tossed the horse's reins to the stable boy as he strode toward her.

When she reached him, he lifted her and swung her around, placing a kiss on her nose before setting her down. "I missed you today. Did you miss me?"

She leaned back, his arm still around her. "Miss you? I was so busy with my new charge, I barely thought of you. Isn't that what she was supposed to do? Keep my mind occupied?"

Duncan raised his brow. "If you were no' thinking of me, then why did I see you watching oot the window? And as soon as we rode in, you disappeared from yonder window." He nodded toward where she had sat. "And came bolting oot the door to greet me?"

"Perhaps I needed to get Flora outside quickly to take care of business." She gave him a smug look.

Duncan chuckled. "Perhaps. But you are no' convincing me."

"Hello, Mr. Dalzell. I hope all is well with you."

"After seeing your lovely face, I couldn't be better."

Her husband glared at his friend. "The man tries to annoy me."

"What have I done?" Mr. Dalzell questioned.

"You ken exactly what you do."

Charlotte looked to her husband. "Are you saying you don't agree with him, Duncan?"

He put up his hands. "Och. I give up!"

Tavis grinned.

The rattling of a carriage caught Charlotte's attention. Duncan released her from his embrace. "We met my cousin on the road home."

"Your cousin? I didn't know you had any family here."

Tavis jumped down from his mount and strode over to meet the carriage. When it stopped, he opened the door and took the hand of the woman who was emerging.

His hand on her back, Duncan gently urged Charlotte forward. "Charlotte, I'd like to introduce to you my cousin, Kirsten. Our mothers are sisters. Kirsten, this is my beautiful bride I told you aboot."

"Hello." The beautiful red-haired lady stepped forward. "I'm so pleased to meet you."

"Welcome to our home." Charlotte liked the woman right away. "I'm so happy to meet a member of Duncan's family. What brings you to Charleston? Or should I say, America?"

Duncan chuckled. "Before you start with all your questions for Kirsten, have you eaten? Tavis and I are starving." He started toward the front door.

Charlotte fell into step beside him. "No, I waited for you." She tipped her head forward to peer around Duncan at Kirsten. "I'm so glad he brought company."

"What about me?" Tavis protested.

She smiled at him. "It's good to see you again."

Delight danced in Tavis's eyes. "'Tis good to see you, too, Mrs. Mackenzie. It looks like married life is treating you well."

"It would be better if I could keep my husband home a little more." Charlotte glanced at Duncan and then Kirsten.

"Perhaps you can help me with that problem. Tavis is usually his accomplice, and I sometimes wonder if he is the instigator." Kirsten laughed. "Weel, a Scot can be verra stubborn. And my cousin was one of the worst growing up."

"We shall have to come up with a plan to stop that then." She stepped through the front door, which Duncan held open.

"Wife, remember the food?"

Charlotte laughed. "I'll have cook serve the meal while you two clean up and I get Kirsten settled."

Duncan and Tavis went on ahead of them as she walked beside Kirsten up the wide front staircase. "Did you just sail in from Scotland on one of Duncan's ships?"

"No, I came in by rail."

"Rail? You can't get from Scotland to America by rail."

A giggle escaped the woman. Green eyes, much the same color has Duncan's, danced with glee. "I dinna live in Scotland anymore. My home is in Texas."

Charlotte's eyes grew wide. "Texas! Why, that is the Wild West."

Kirsten laughed again. "No' so wild where I come from."

Charlotte stopped at a door and showed Kirsten into a guest room. "Please make yourself at home. When you're ready, just come downstairs and turn to the left to find the dining room. I will wait for you there."

Tavis entered the dining room before Duncan or his cousin. His dark blonde hair was brushed back and fell to the side. His grin held a hint of mischief as he stood behind his seat. "Your husband is a fortunate man."

"And weel I ken it, friend." Duncan walked in behind him and seated Charlotte. Then he and Tavis stood behind their chairs waiting for Kirsten to join them. When she entered the room, Tavis pulled out her chair across from Charlotte.

"Thank you, Tavis." Kirsten gave him a sweet smile. "It is guid to see you two have no' lost your manners."

"Ah, and it is guid to see you have no' lost that quick tongue of yours, cousin." Duncan chuckled.

Charlotte gasped.

"'Tis fine, Charlotte. Duncan is my favorite male cousin. 'Tis all in fun."

"Male cousin? Dinna tell me you speak of that cousin of yours from your father's side, Gillian."

"Aye, she is much kinder to me, Duncan. You could learn from her."

Charlotte smiled at their friendly banter. They reminded her of herself and Nellie.

"Tavis, will you ask the blessing?" Duncan requested.

Tavis gave Duncan a strange look before bowing his head. Duncan, Kirsten, and Charlotte followed suit. But no words came forth, and Charlotte was tempted to peek to see why he hadn't begun.

Tavis cleared his throat. "Our most gracious Heavenly Father, I'd like to thank you for our safe trip and for bringing Kirsten here safely. We know it is You who watches over us. Lord, I pray each of us here is ever mindful of Your greatness. May You be a constant reminder that we are nothing without You. It is only by You that we walk and live and breathe. I thank You for Your Son, Jesus Christ, and for the sacrifice He made that we may spend eternity with You. I pray that none of us would leave this table tonight without knowing You. Your—"

Duncan coughed, and Charlotte stole a glance at him. He continued to have his head bowed, but his brows were drawn down at sharp angles. Charlotte closed her eyes. Tavis's prayer was sounding like a sermon—and it was apparent Duncan didn't like it. Was it possible her husband wasn't saved? But he'd given her that Bible...

Tavis's voice floated over the table. "Please bless this food to the nourishment of our bodies. In Your precious Son's name. Amen."

Duncan, Kirsten, and Charlotte's "Amen" sounded in unison.

Tavis filled his plate with food. "Everything looks delicious." He licked his lips.

She took her napkin and placed it in her lap. Her understanding of Duncan's spiritual condition stirred questions she wanted answered. "Thank you. I spent part of the day in the kitchen with the cook. I can only lay claim to the cornbread and the fried okra."

Duncan stared at her. "I dinna ken you could cook."

"Apparently there is much we don't know about each other."

Duncan laughed. "I keep no secrets from you, lass, but you obviously are keeping them from me. The cornbread is delicious."

Charlotte held her fork filled with food. "Thank you."

"How is my uncle these days?" Duncan asked Kirsten before taking a bite of okra.

"He works hard and misses Mither. 'Tis thankful I am that the farm keeps him busy. But I also fash for his heart 'tis no' guid."

"I am sorry to hear that. Your da is a guid mon. Perhaps Charlotte and I can come visit sometime."

Kirsten smiled. "He would like that, and I would as well."

"So you own a farm? Do you have cows? I've heard that trouble brews over free ranging the cattle." Charlotte had read recently about the conflict in the newspaper.

"My cousin is being humble. Her father owns a rather large cotton plantation in Sunset."

"So what brings you our way?" Charlotte asked.

"When I learned Duncan was here, Da suggested I come to visit."

Charlotte turned to Duncan. "You knew she was coming, and you didn't tell me?"

Duncan shook his head. "Nay. I did no' ken until I saw her on the road tonight."

Kirsten blushed. "I guess I arrived before my letter."

Tavis piped up. "No harm done. I for one am glad to see you again after so many years."

The rest of the talk was light, and when they finished the meal, they moved to the great room. Tavis took a seat on one of the burgundy upholstered chairs, and Kirsten sat in the other. Duncan sat at one end of the heavily carved rosewood sofa, and Charlotte snuggled next to him. She chewed her bottom lip as she worked to gain her courage. Her stomach tied in knots as she phrased and rephrased the question in her head. He hadn't been with his cousin, because he'd said they met on the way home. "Where have you two been today?"

Duncan and Tavis looked at each other. Neither too anxious to answer the question. After a long pause, Duncan spoke. "We were down at the shipping docks taking care of some business. You are no' upset with me are you, lass?"

Charlotte opened her mouth to tell him no but didn't get the words out before Tavis spoke. "Och! If the lass could forgive you for putting the heirloom pin in her travel bag, I'm sure she won't hold something as small as business against you."

Chapter 27

The color drained from his beautiful wife's face, and Duncan's heart sank with it.

She turned to him, tears balancing on her eyelids. "It was you? Y-you did that? You tarnished my name and forced me into marriage? And made my family think less of me?"

"'Tis no' like that. No one thought bad of you, Charlotte." Duncan pulled her closer, but she wrenched away.

She rushed for the door. Duncan pushed up and blocked her exit. She darted around him and found her escape. As the hem of her dress swooshed from view, Duncan spun around and glared at Tavis. "Why did you mention that?" He couldn't remember the last time anger seared through him with the same geyser-like intensity.

Tavis stood in front of his chair. "You said you didn't have any secrets from her. How was I supposed to know you hadn't told her?"

Duncan glanced at his cousin, who was watching wide-eyed.

He was going to strangle Tavis. His hands fisted, and he strode the few steps toward the man, each step fanning the flames smoldering within him.

Tavis jumped over the back of the chair and raised his hands before him. "I'll not fight you, Duncan."

"It matters no' to me. I plan to give you as much pain as you have caused my wife." Duncan came around the chair.

Tavis moved backward. "I'll not raise a hand against my brother."

"If I were a brother to you, you would no' have said what you just did."

Kirsten stood. "Duncan, I dinna ken what this is aboot, but you dinna want to hit your best friend."

"Listen to your cousin, Duncan." Tavis kept the chair between him and Duncan.

"Kirsten is wrong."

"She'll forgive you, Duncan. She loves you," Tavis said.

Duncan snorted. "Nay. She has no' said those words, and you have ruined that chance."

"I'm not the one who deceived her. You are. Lay blame where it is due, my friend. You can hit me all you want, but what really is bothering you is that you have made a mess of your marriage by your deception and blackmail."

Kirsten gasped.

"It is no' like it sounds, Kirsten."

"Yes, it is," Tavis argued.

An insistent rapping on the door forced Duncan's attention away from Tavis. Stuebing stuck his head in. "Is it safe to enter, sir?"

"Come in," Duncan growled.

"It seems, sir, you have frightened some of your staff. I was handed this missive as one of them disappeared. He did take the time to ask me to give it to you. Apparently, the lad who dropped it off mentioned it was urgent." Stuebing walked over and handed the envelope to Duncan.

"Thank you, Stuebing."

"Will that be all, sir?"

"Aye."

Written in bold letters and in a hand Duncan didn't recognize was his name and address. He tore off the end of the envelope and glanced at Tavis, who still stood in the same spot, only with lowered hands. Still angry with him, Duncan turned his attention to the letter and unfolded the crisp piece of paper.

*If you value your life and those around
you, forget your mission and go back
to Scotland.*

Charlotte's feet tapped an urgent rhythm on the stairs as she sped up to her room. Her heart slammed in her chest as hard as she banged the door shut. She turned the key before rushing over to the adjoining door. With fumbling hands, she flipped the key until the tumbler fell.

Willing herself forward, her legs threatened to buckle. Duncan had put the pin in her luggage? He'd made her look like a thief, then *heroically* came to her rescue and redeemed her good name—her name that never should have been soiled in the first place? Stabbing pain penetrated her heart as if the heirloom pin was piercing her. And indeed it had, with the help of her husband.

She'd grown to trust Duncan—to deeply care for him—as a wife was supposed to. She wobbled over to the bed and collapsed, burying her face in the pillow. She never wanted him to know she'd shed one tear over him or cried for everything that might have been. She'd been such a fool to give him her heart.

How could he deceive her when he'd pledged before man and God to honor and cherish her? And he'd been so good to her since their wedding she had actually believed him. Fool. Fool. Fool. She had to be the worst judge of men. First Frank. She'd believed he was something he was not. Now…Charlotte choked on a sob. Duncan had proven himself no better than Frank. Both were scoundrels. Only this time she had married the man, and worst of all, she loved him.

She rolled onto her side and pulled a handkerchief from her gown's pocket to wipe the blasted tears she couldn't stop. Her heart had been trampled.

God, why didn't You stop my marriage? I didn't want to marry Duncan. I begged You, but You never answered my prayer. And look what has happened. I am married to a man who deceived me.

Charlotte hiccupped. It wasn't fair. She'd only had a month of marriage and less than that of it truly being happy. And now…now what would she do? Where could she go?

Papa would never let her come home. He'd march her straight back to Duncan and say, "you married him, now you have to live with him." Never mind that he dragged her down the aisle with all the guilt he'd piled on her shoulders should she decide *not* to marry Duncan. It would make the family *look* bad, and that was all that would ever matter to Papa.

She patted her eyes and cheeks with her handkerchief. With each thought of what Duncan had done to her, another needle pierced her heart. She was alone. She sat up and sniffed as she continued to dab at the tears. She'd never hurt so much in her life, nor felt so abandoned and betrayed.

A light tap sounded on the door. "Go away."

"It's me, Kirsten. I wanted to see if you are all right."

Charlotte sniffed and attempted to cover the wobbling in her voice. "I'm sorry. Thank you for asking. I will be fine. I just need time alone."

"If you need me, even in the night, you ken where you can find me."

"Thank you, Kirsten."

How humiliating. As if learning of Duncan's lies wasn't enough.

She scooted to the side of the bed as she listened to Kirsten's footfalls fade. Her feet slid to the floor, and she padded over to the oak table near the fireplace and picked up her Bible, opening it to Psalm 23. Comfort could always be found there.

Even though she could recite the familiar verses, she read through them. Seeing the words in God's holy book made them more real. She reread the last two verses.

Thou preparest a table before me in the presence of mine enemies: thou anointest my head with oil; my cup runneth over. Surely goodness and mercy shall follow me all the days of my life, and I will dwell in the house of the Lord forever.

Why didn't God show mercy to her? Hadn't she asked Him? She closed her Bible. For whatever reason, God had remained silent since Duncan had hidden that pin in her bag. He hadn't answered her prayers. If He had, this whole problem with Duncan would never have happened because she never would have married him.

If God wasn't going to direct her steps, she'd be forced to take things into her own hands.

♥♥♥

Duncan stared at the note. It wasn't the threat to his life that worried him, but to Charlotte's. The warning was clear. He either dropped his search for the traitor or risk endangering the lives of those he loved and cared for.

"What is it?" Tavis walked over to where Duncan stood.

Duncan handed Tavis the note then yelled, "Stuebing!"

His valet popped in through the door. "Yes?"

"Find the servant who received this missive, then find the lad who delivered it. I want to talk to him."

"Yes, sir. I've already sent someone after him."

Sometimes it was good to have a valet who knew him so well. "Bring me a pen and paper."

Stuebing ducked out the door and returned in a few moments. "Here you are, sir."

Duncan took the pen and paper and scrawled a note. He handed it back to Stuebing. "See that this gets to Mr. Arthur Jackson."

"Right away, sir." Stuebing disappeared again.

"Arthur Jackson? Good idea. Get Charlotte out of the way by sending her home for a visit." Tavis handed the threatening letter back to Duncan.

"I'm no' sending Charlotte back to her father. She's safer here where I can watch her. I'm sending for her sister, Nellie, to come visit. 'Tis obvious after your announcement the lass is distraught. Time is running oot to find this villain. Nellie will be guid company for Charlotte."

"Are you crazy? You'll have two of them to look after then. Send Charlotte home."

"Nay. Do you think this person does no' ken who my wife is?" Duncan shook the missive in front of Tavis. "He has stayed a step ahead of us the whole way, as if he has been privy to our conversations. The man has been trained. He thinks like I do."

"If you are off searching for a traitor, you won't be watching over the lasses."

"I will put a guard on them at all times. They'll no' go anywhere alone."

Tavis shook his head. "I hope that's enough."

Duncan sent Gibson down to the docks to bring back Captain Maher. *The Scottish Lady* would remain at the wharf for a week or two yet. If he could trust anyone, it was Maher. Duncan had yet to see a man who could stand up to his captain. Aye, the lasses would be safe with him around. And his presence would be easy to explain to his wife. Having met on a stop in Ireland years ago, they'd been friends for a long time. He'd tell Charlotte that Maher was here on business and waiting to go back out to sea. He didn't have any place to stay except the ship, so Duncan invited him to stay with them. It would all be true. He just wouldn't tell her the whole reason why Maher was staying.

A short time later, the young lad who had delivered the message was dragged back to Duncan's place and now sulked in the hallway as Duncan approached. "What's your name, lad?"

The boy scuffed his toe on the tiled floor. "Jeremy."

"Weel, Jeremy, my name is Duncan Mackenzie. And a pleasure it is to meet you."

The lad lifted his head and peered into Duncan's eyes. Duncan smiled and stuck out his hand. The boy reached up and shook it. "How much money did you earn for delivering that message?"

"Ten cents."

"How'd you like to make fifty cents?"

Jeremy eyes filled with distrust.

"I assure you, 'tis nothing illegal or bad I wish you to do."

"What is it, then?"

"I want you to tell me who asked you to deliver the message here."

Jeremy scrunched up his face. "His name is Jeffrey, and he lives in one of the abandoned buildings down near the wharf."

"Can you show me where?"

The boy nodded.

After flipping the boy a coin, Duncan took him to the kitchen and left him in the cook's capable hands. When Gibson returned with Captain Maher, Duncan explained the circumstances and what he was to do, then went to Vivian and told her she was not to leave his wife's side. He stepped into the hall and almost ran into Kirsten, whose arms were folded in front of her and her foot tapping.

"Where are you off to, cousin." She glared at him.

"I dinna have time to explain." He grabbed the weapons he'd set on the hall table.

"Make time. I dinna like what I just witnessed."

Duncan eyed Kirsten, debating on how much to share. "I am here on a mission for the Crown."

"And? That certainly does no' give you the right to hurt your wife."

"Nay. There is too much to tell. I must go. Her life is in danger."

The anger melted away, replaced by concern.

"And yours, too, as long as you are here."

Tavis popped his head in the door. "Mounts are ready."

"We have to go," Duncan said.

"Be careful. Both of you," Kirsten implored.

Night was well upon them when Duncan swung into the saddle. Tavis tossed the boy up behind him and then jumped on his own horse. Though Duncan wanted to push Aberdeen to get to the wharf in a hurry, he held himself back. From what the lad had told him, he guessed the man who gave him the missive wasn't the one he was looking for. No, his man wouldn't be living in an abandoned building. But with luck, he could lead them to the traitor.

As the horses clopped down the narrow road along the wharf, the lad pointed out the shadow of a building. Before going there, Duncan took the boy home to keep him from danger.

At the warehouse, Tavis and Duncan cobbled their horses. Sliding his hand into his pocket, Duncan gripped the cold steel as his finger curled around the trigger. Tavis drew his weapon as they approached the building. Duncan pushed the door open with the tip of his revolver. A lit lantern hung on a nail, illuminating the empty building. Torn papers and pieces of raw cotton were strewn across the floor. Empty and broken bottles lay about haphazardly. Duncan stepped in, his gaze narrowing in on what he came for. He smiled. This was going to be easier than he thought. The man they were looking for sat with his back against the wall. By the tilt of his head, he appeared to be either asleep or inebriated. A few hours of sobering him up and they would be able to get the information they needed. Duncan closed the gap between them. He stopped abruptly. "Crevvens."

Tavis ran up behind him. "What?"

Duncan swung around. "He's dead."

Deciding it wiser to send an anonymous note to the authorities than go themselves, they rode back toward Duncan's house. They hadn't gotten far when a rider barreled down on them.

"Someone seems eager to catch us." The lone man and horse drew close enough where he recognized him. Duncan tensed. What was Ferguson doing on this side of town at this time of night?

They stopped and waited for him to catch up.

"Guid it is to run into you. 'Tis bored I was." Ferguson's jovial voice rang through the quiet night air.

Duncan eyed him. "How is you kent we'd be here?"

He shifted in his saddle. "I was riding around the city looking for something to do. You don't want to break into anymore businesses, do you?"

Tavis grinned and Duncan scowled. He never should have taken Ferguson with him. Duncan kicked his horse and started home.

"Nay. We are on our way to my place."

Ferguson followed beside Tavis. "Mind if I tag along?"

Chapter 28

Charlotte woke the next morning to what sounded like Nellie's giggle. She opened her eyes. That couldn't have been her sister. Perhaps she heard Kirsten speaking. The hall clock chimed nine. She jumped out of bed and reached for her housecoat. She'd slept way too late. Her hand stopped as she grasped the garment and yesterday's memories came crashing down on her.

He'd put the pin in her bag. She sank back down on the bed.

Again, she heard Nellie's giggle not far down the hall. Had God answered her unspoken prayers and sent her family to get her? She stood and wrapped herself in the robe. Shuffling to the door, she ran her fingers through her hair.

She hadn't been out of her room since yesterday when she'd locked herself in. Vivian had sat outside her door well into the night and begged to come in. Kirsten had come by over and over to see if she could do anything for her. But she didn't want to see anyone. She stopped in front of the mirror. The puffiness in her face and her swollen eyes left no question that she'd cried too many tears. Turning away, she pulled the door open and peeked out.

It *was* Nellie. Her sister turned and ran toward her. "Charlotte, I've missed you. How are you?"

As soon as Nellie reached her, Charlotte pulled her in, shut the door, and gave her a tight embrace.

"I've missed you, too." Charlotte glanced at the door. "Is Duncan around?"

"I don't rightly know. I haven't seen him since we got back here."

"It doesn't matter." Charlotte grasped Nellie's hands. "I'm glad *you've* come. Are Mama and Papa here?"

"No, they didn't come. You know Papa. Work, work, work. And Mama couldn't leave the younger ones for very long. Nothing has changed since you left. Except that I miss having you to talk to. And I see you are sad as well."

"How did you get here? Surely you didn't come by yourself. You didn't run away, did you?"

Nellie giggled. "Of course not. Your husband sent an invitation to Papa yesterday afternoon requesting I visit and offered to send a carriage early this morning to pick me up."

"Did Duncan mention why he'd requested your visit?"

"Papa said that Duncan thought you needed me right now."

As Nellie moved forward to help Charlotte get ready for the day, her taffeta dress swished, bringing back sweet memories. Nellie chattered as she assisted Charlotte and she had to admit that waking to her sister had temporarily helped numb Charlotte's pain. If only her parents had come to take her home. She stepped into her gown and wiggled until she got it over her hips. As if the past month had never separated them, Charlotte slipped her arms through the sleeves and turned her back for Nellie's assistance. "Will you button me?" She slid her hands under her hair and pulled it up. "Is that all the letter said?"

Nellie began buttoning Charlotte's gown. "I didn't read his letter, but Duncan spoke with me this morning. He told me what he had done and how you found out. He said he never meant to hurt you."

"He told you that *he* hid his precious heirloom in my bag?"

"Yes. And he told me why he did it." Nellie buttoned the last button and turned Charlotte around. "He did it because you wouldn't give him the time of day. He could see how taken you were with Frank, and he knew Frank was a good for nothing and wouldn't treat you as you deserved to be treated."

The tears pooled in Charlotte's eyes again, so she blinked them away. She wouldn't cry again today. "Is he any better than Frank?"

Nellie pulled Charlotte over to the bed and sat down beside her, still holding her hands. "He loves you, Charlotte. I mean deep down, true love. He's hurting as much as you are right now, and he doesn't know what to do to make things better."

"Nellie you're *my* sister. You're supposed to be on my side, not Duncan's. You sound like you don't see anything wrong with what he's done."

"No, not at all. But what I do see is you are hurting because you love him, and he is hurting because he loves you."

"I never said that." Charlotte looked down at her hand clasping her sister's.

"You don't have to. It's written all over your face. When did you fall in love with him?" Nellie reached up and touched Charlotte's cheek.

Charlotte drew in a deep breath and swallowed, willing herself to keep her composure. "I don't know. It just happened. He has been everything any woman could desire. He's kind and generous to a fault. He has a sense of humor and a tenderness I never knew a man could have. It would have been impossible not to fall in love with him."

"Are you willing to throw all that away because of the pin? Aren't you willing to give him another chance?"

"That isn't everything, Nellie."

"That's what Duncan told me was bothering you."

Charlotte lifted her chin. "He doesn't have a personal relationship with the Lord." Those words were all it took. She laid her head on Nellie's shoulder and a sob broke loose.

Nellie patted her back. "Are you sure?"

"Yes, I'm sure. His friend Tavis was trying to witness to him while he asked the blessing. Duncan wanted nothing to do with it."

Nellie patted Charlotte's head. "The way I see this is you are already married to Duncan. Papa should have inquired about his spiritual state before he forced you to marry. But now that it's done, there's nothing to do. You're married. And you love him. It's your duty as a Christian to try to win your husband over by your witness."

Charlotte let out a half laugh. Flora whimpered at her feet and she swooped down and picked her up, so glad for the comfort of the little fluff ball. "And how am I supposed to do that? Remember what I just found out?"

Nellie gave Charlotte her biggest smile. "See, that's the beautiful thing about it. Duncan knows he has hurt you, and he can see now he shouldn't have gone about things the way he did. You can show him God's love by forgiving him for what he's done to you."

"What? And let him continue to control all aspects of my life? Live where I have no say, just like with Papa?"

Flora lifted her head, big brown eyes staring at her and whimpered again. Charlotte hugged the puppy to her. It was as if she knew her pain.

"I'm not saying be a doormat for your husband. You have to stand up for yourself when he is wrong. But I do think Duncan is sorry, and I think he sees he has gone about things wrong. But you have to forgive for your marriage to heal."

♥♥♥

Duncan was weary. When he started this mission, he hadn't foreseen his search causing innocent deaths. Fillman and this unnamed messenger were unsuspecting pawns in this game of espionage. Had he not come to America, they would still be alive. Then there was Charlotte to think about. He'd hurt her and didn't know how to fix it. He'd heard Nellie and Charlotte giggling last night in the room adjoining his, but his wife still avoided him. Looking back, Duncan admitted he shouldn't have gone about securing Charlotte's hand the way he had. He should have taken more time to woo the lass away from Sorrell. He understood that now.

He shook his head. Now she was angry at him and very well might still love Frank. He needed her forgiveness. Forgiveness. Such a simple word, but acquiring it from an aggrieved person wasn't so easy. His chest cinched as he thought about the hurt look on her face as she fled the room.

The sobs that she had tried to smother, but had seeped under his door, were nearly his undoing that night. It took everything he had not to barge through her door and try to comfort her. But she wouldn't want his comfort.

She needed time, and then he'd go and ask for forgiveness. That, with a little wooing, perhaps, could win her back. He hoped so.

After he completed his mission, he'd planned to return to Scotland with his new wife on his arm, but that seemed impossible now. Unless there was a miracle, she'd never go with him of her own accord, and he'd never force her against her will again.

He would give her some time, then he would ask for her forgiveness. Should he explain everything? That the queen herself had asked him to complete this mission? That it was to be his last? Or would she feel he had deceived her even more?

He dropped his bowler on the entrance table before hanging his coat on the hall tree and strode into the study. Another night with few leads, but fortunately no more dead bodies. Sinking into the leather chair, he let out a sigh. Tavis came in behind him and strolled around the room, stopping at the cherry drum table to pick up a carved ivory elephant just as Stuebing entered the room. Duncan stared at his valet. He'd never seen the man's appearance anything short of immaculate. But now Stuebing's hair looked as if he'd just woken and forgotten to comb it. "Is there anything I can get for you, sir?"

Duncan leaned forward. "Is that dirt on your shirt?"

His valet looked horrified and gazed down at his shirt. "Sorry, sir. I'll go clean myself up."

"How on earth did you get dirt on you, Stuebing? You usually keep yourself far away from anything untidy."

Stuebing's face colored. "It was your sister-in-law, sir. She requested I take the mongrel outside to play. When I told her I would find someone to do that, she got quite indignant with me. You really should speak with the young lady, sir."

Duncan chuckled at his valet's frustration. "So how did you get dirty?"

"I took the animal out as I was told, but when I tried to get it to come back inside, it ran from me. In trying to catch the varmint, I tripped and fell."

Tavis yawned. "Likely story."

Stuebing straightened to his full height. "I assure you, sir, I am telling the truth."

Tavis burst out laughing. Duncan restrained himself. "Nay, I need nothing. Go take care of yourself."

Stuebing bowed. "Thank you, sir."

Tavis continued to laugh. "You were too easy on him."

"The mon was already appalled by his appearance. I could no' add to his agony." Duncan glanced out the door. "Where's Ferguson?"

"A couple of your maids caught his eye, and he is flirting with them."

Duncan gripped the chair arms. "He'd better stay away from Charlotte, Nellie, and Kirsten or he'll quickly be finding the door."

As if his words had summoned her, Nellie stopped at the study door and gazed in. "Oh, there you are. I've been looking all over for you."

The two men rose as she entered the room. Tavis grinned and clutched at his heart. "Och! You are like sunshine on a rainy day. And to know you were looking for me."

Duncan ignored him but couldn't help notice the way Nellie's eyes danced with mirth. "Can I do something for you, lass?"

Her expression turned serious. "No, not for me. I think your captain friend is bored. He has followed Charlotte, Kirsten, and me around all day. The only time we've had any privacy at all is in Charlotte's room. Perhaps you could teach him about protocol. And I'm sure he would love some company other than the three of us, as we really don't have much in common with the man."

It took much restraint to keep from chuckling. Oh, the innocence of youth. "Why don't you ladies join us in the drawing room? We will be there shortly."

"I'm not sure Charlotte…" Nellie hesitated and glanced at Tavis before returning her gaze on Duncan. "That is to say, I believe my sister is feeling a little under the weather today."

Duncan nodded. Charlotte didn't want to see him. He eyed Nellie. He'd told her everything on their trip from her home to his manor, anticipating that she would sympathize with him. But she never gave him an indication one way or the other. She just listened. He hoped she wouldn't encourage Charlotte's animosity. Whether she did or not though, Charlotte needed her sister, and he would risk what he must to give her the comfort she needed.

"Perhaps she'll get to feeling better."

"Should I tell Captain Maher you're in here or the drawing room?"

"Send him in here."

Nellie disappeared, and he hoped she didn't run into Ferguson.

Captain Maher joined them and, finding a chair, sat and stretched his long legs before him. With the ease of a man comfortable wherever he was, he clasped his hands behind his head and leaned back.

Duncan scrubbed his hand along his jawline. "I appreciate your attentiveness to the lasses, Captain, but I dinna expect you to follow them around. Just keep an eye on them."

"I hadn't planned on it. However, when one of the stablemen said they'd seen someone poking around outside, I thought I'd better not let the ladies out of my sight."

♥♥♥

Forgiveness. Isn't that what Christ taught? Charlotte knew her sister's words on forgiving her husband were true. So why did she find it so hard? She had to forgive him but still stand up for herself. God didn't *ask* that of her. His word commanded it. How many scriptures had she memorized on forgiveness? Colossians 3:13 came to mind. *'Forbearing one another, and forgiving one another, if any man have a quarrel against any: even as Christ forgave you, so also do ye.'*

She'd forgiven her siblings time and time again and found no trouble with it. But Duncan's trespass went much deeper than anything anyone else had done to her. His betrayal of her trust had broken her heart. Charlotte closed her eyes and Christ's sacrifice on the cross became all too vivid. If God's Son could die for a sinful person like her, how could she not forgive Duncan? She knew she could say the words. The hard part would be making the words reach her wounded heart.

Father, I thank you for Your forgiveness and what Your Son did on the cross for me. I need Your help, Lord, to forgive Duncan in my heart. I know I can't do it without You. Please help me find it within myself to be more like You. I want to never look back and never remember.

Charlotte lifted her head and opened her eyes to see Nellie standing inside her room.

"Are you feeling unwell?" Nellie shut the door behind her.

"I'm fine. Just getting some things right with the Lord. When did you get so wise, Nellie?"

Nellie's eyes twinkled, and she smiled. "Oh, I think it's always been there. I've just had a hard time getting it out…What was I wise about?"

Charlotte giggled. "About Duncan, me, and forgiveness." She pushed her shoulders back. "I guess it's time to stop hiding and face my husband."

"Really? I thought I was going to have to come up here and either beg you or drag you."

Charlotte smiled. "No, I've thought about what you've said and you're right. I need to forgive Duncan. I've been praying, and God has shown me some things about myself. I'm far from perfect. I do have a favor to ask of you, though. I need your prayers."

Nellie hugged Charlotte. "It's a privilege." She kissed her sister on the cheek and took her hand. "Come. They're in the drawing room. I think Duncan may be sending up some prayers of his own."

Chapter 29

Duncan's whole body tensed. "Did they catch the culprit?" His mind flew back to the note threatening him and Charlotte. If someone was skulking around the premises, he very well might be the traitor wanting to follow through on that threat.

"Am I interrupting?" Kirsten stepped into the room.

"No' at all. Come in."

Maher unlaced his fingers and relaxed his arms on the armrests. "No. Don't believe they did. One of the old workers saw him hiding not too far from the house, but by the time he was able to get someone younger to chase him down, he was gone."

Duncan glanced at Tavis sitting at attention, then returned his focus back to his captain. "How long ago did they report this?"

"It's been a few hours now. I thought it best to stay with the women should it be a ploy to get the men away from the house."

Tavis rose. "I'll go and talk to whoever saw this character and report back as soon as I find out something."

"I'll join yo—." Duncan's last word froze on his tongue as Charlotte and Nellie strode in the room. "Good idea, Tavis. Report back when you hear something."

Tavis grinned and strode out the door.

Duncan admired the way Charlotte's body swayed as she walked into the room, causing her dress to swish from side to side.

She glanced up into his eyes. "Is something wrong?"

"Nay. Just being careful. Tavis is going oot to look around." Duncan's voice softened. "You look lovely." He searched her face, looking for forgiveness. Why would she forgive him when he hadn't asked? And didn't he really deserve her scorn now that she knew he had hidden the family heirloom pin in her bag and then forced her to marry him?

"Careful of what?" Charlotte tilted her head and waited.

Duncan wanted to tell her she needn't fash herself about it, but he had a feeling that would not sit well with her. "Someone was seen snooping around ootside. 'Tis probably nothing. I'm only taking precautions."

"Perhaps he was only hungry and in need of food."

"'Tis possible. That's why we are checking oot everything we can." He should come clean with her—tell her about his mission. But the thought of her running up to her room again stopped him. He never wanted to see that kind of pain on her face again. Especially, if he caused it.

"Captain Maher, Nellie." Kirsten stole a glance at Charlotte. "Would you accompany me to the library? I'd like to look at Duncan's books." She turned her eyes on Duncan. "With your permission, of course, cousin."

"Aye, my library is yours to peruse whenever you wish."

Duncan slid the doors shut behind them and swiveled around to face his wife. She looked at him with uncertainty in her eyes. Duncan moved forward and placed his hands on her waist and drew her to him. When she didn't tense, he gently brushed his lips across her forehead. "I'm verra sorry, lass. Can you find it in your heart to forgive me?" Her body trembled beneath his touch. "I ken I should have gone aboot this a different way. I wanted you for a wife, and you paid me no attention. Frustration stole my senses when I saw you in Sorrel's arms the night of the ball." She went rigid to his touch at the mention of Sorrell's name. "It was then I kent I had to do something, or I'd lose you to that scoundrel."

"What you *thought* you saw was not the truth. Concern is what lured me outside to speak to Frank. I feared some calamity had befallen someone I knew. By then I'd already decided he wasn't the man for me. But for him to travel so far uninvited, I believed he had important news." She stopped and gave him a sharp look. "He then proceeded to tell me how you paid the young men to dance with me. When I tried to leave, he forced himself on me. The kiss was not returned. But you left believing what you wanted to."

"You canno' deny the words I heard you say. You near bellowed them for all to hear. Would you no' believe the kiss was offered if you had heard those words?"

"I-I don't know."

"Weel, it seemed obvious to me. I was verra angry when I saw you in his arms and heard the words *I love you* come from your lips. If I had stayed, I ken I'd have hurt the mon."

"You did hurt him. You hit him. But he deserved it after what he did to me. He forced me to say those words. He told me if I would tell him I loved him, he would release me. I said it, but he made me repeat it louder. I had no idea you and my father were approaching, but I suspect that he did."

Duncan stiffened. If Sorrell were here right now, he'd pummel him good and proper. But that wouldn't bring him any closer to Charlotte. "Aye, that sounds like something Sorrell's ilk would do. But that is over. What I need to ken is if you forgive me for tricking you into marrying me? I could no' be more sorry for hurting you, lass. I promise I will never coerce you again."

"You mean blackmail. You blackmailed me to get me to marry you, and my father went along. Did he know, too, about the deceit?"

Duncan flinched. "Nay, lass, your father kent nothing. And I dinna like to think of it as blackmail."

Charlotte's brown eyes flashed.

"Why can't you admit what you did?"

"I have, lass."

"No, you haven't. Just say it."

"Blackmail sounds so harsh." Duncan's shoulders sagged. "But I understand where you could see it that way. 'Twas wrong of me. I'm sorry for hurting you so, lass." He hoped she could see the truth within him. "I care deeply for you."

That simple truth seemed to be what Charlotte needed to hear—that he did care for her. Her pinched face softened. "I forgive you, Duncan."

Relief swept through him clear down to his toes. He skimmed the back of his finger over her cheek. "Ah, Charlotte, you dinna ken how much that means."

"Do you know why I can forgive you?"

"I dinna care why. All I care is that you *do* forgive me."

Charlotte frowned. "But I want you to understand where my forgiveness comes from. If God hadn't forgiven me, I would never be able to forgive you."

"Weel, it's glad I am then that He forgave you." Duncan pulled her to him and hugged her.

"But you can find the same forgiveness."

"I only want yours. That's all I need to make me happy."

Where had she laid down her scissors? Charlotte retraced her earlier footsteps in her mind. She'd been reading in the library. Nellie had gone to get her and Kirsten something to drink. She got up and went to her room. No, she was on her way to her room when she passed by the guest room. That's where they were. As she passed the room Mr. Ferguson was to stay in, she'd gone in to see if the maid had changed his bedding. She must have set the scissors down there. She and Nellie had been working on the tablecloth for nearly a week now, and she'd misplaced her scissors as many times as she'd used them.

Charlotte rushed down the hall. Since all the men were gone, she'd slip in and get them. The door sat ajar, and she pushed it open and walked in. Mr. Ferguson swung around. Charlotte froze. Standing before her was a half-dressed man. He quickly slipped his shirt on. She lowered her gaze and started backing from the room. "I'm sorry. I left my scissors in here when I was checking to see if the bedding was changed."

"No harm done." His voice came out rigid.

Her scissors appeared beneath her gaze, and she grasped them from his hands. "Thank you." She turned and fled out the door. What had she been thinking, not knocking on the door? He was none too pleased that she had walked in on him as he dressed. Heavens, she hoped he didn't tell Duncan. That would be embarrassing to explain. Better to pretend it never happened and hope Mr. Ferguson did, too. With her scissors in hand, she headed back to the parlor.

Several hours later Charlotte stood and pressed her hands into her lower back as she stretched. "Are you two ready to take a break from this?"

Nellie glanced up from the corner of the tablecloth she embroidered. "If we keep taking breaks it won't be done by Thanksgiving."

Kirsten laughed and straightened with a wince. "A break sounds wonderful to me."

"Needlework has never been my forte. I wish I hadn't let you talk me into this, Nellie." Charlotte grinned. "Let's walk to the barn. The stableman told me the cat had kittens. He thought we might like to come and see them today."

Nellie set her work down. "The cat with part of her ear missing?"

"That's the one. I didn't even know she was pregnant. I thought she was just fat, but he said the kittens are several weeks old now. All this time I thought she was a fat *he*. Who would name a female cat Scrapper?"

Nellie grinned. "A man."

"I have to admit it fits her well." Charlotte flounced to the door and stopped, glancing over her shoulder. "She'll fight with anything that crosses her path. I'm sure that's how she lost part of her ear."

Nellie straightened and, like Charlotte, pushed her hands into the small of her back. "I suppose a small break wouldn't hurt."

Kirsten yawned. "I did no' sleep weel last night, so if you dinna mind, I'll lie down and rest while you two are kitten visiting."

The cool, late autumn air swept across her skin, so Charlotte pulled on the sweater she'd grabbed as they walked out the door. Flora darted out ahead of her. The sun had sunk below the horizon taking its warm rays with it. When they entered the barn, she headed over to the corner where she often had seen Scrapper sleeping, but she wasn't there. They walked around checking all the corners, between stacks of hay, on the loft, everywhere they could think, but the cat had hidden itself and its kittens well. "I should have asked Duncan where the kittens are." Charlotte hopped off the last step of the ladder. Nellie squealed, and Charlotte spun around to see her on her knees, her head inside an old barrel lying on its side. Flora bounced toward her sister.

Nellie pulled out a solid black kitten and held it in her hands. "I found them. Isn't he cute?"

Charlotte made her way over and pulled a gray kitten out of the barrel and Flora danced on her hind feet to see it. "I love them when they're little. So soft and cuddly." She let the puppy sniff the kitten.

"Oh, so you don't like grown cats. Did you hear that, Scrapper?"

"I did not say that, Nellie. It's just kittens are so cute and snuggly." She pressed her head against its silky fur and Flora barked.

"Looks like someone is jealous."

Charlotte bent and petted her puppy's head. "I think so."

"Too bad Papa wouldn't let me take one home," Nellie lamented.

Charlotte ran her hand down the sleek fur, and the kitten purred. "I never thanked you for talking me into forgiving Duncan. It was the right thing to do."

"You don't need to thank me, Charlotte. You'd have come around to that conclusion anyway. I just sped it up. I've wanted to ask how you two were doing but didn't want you to feel like I was being nosey."

"*Think?* I know you're nosey. We used to live together remember?" Charlotte giggled.

Nellie stamped her foot. "It isn't being nosey when you love the person and want to make sure they're doing well."

"I was teasing. I'm glad you still care for me, Sis. We are getting along much better. If the thought comes into my head, I remind myself I forgave him."

"Where are Duncan, Tavis, and Captain Maher this afternoon?"

"The captain went back to ready his ship. Duncan and Tavis are always disappearing—and at strange hours, too. I don't know what they are doing. I gave up asking."

The kitten crawled up to Nellie's shoulder, and she tightened her hold on the black fluffball. "I'm sure it's business. He probably has to be around at all hours when they arrive or leave."

Charlotte wished she could think the way Nellie did, but she'd lived with Duncan, and as much as she wanted to tell herself it was nothing, something deep down told her that wasn't true. She glanced over at her sister. She'd enjoyed this time with her. They had less than a week left together. Then Nellie would go home, and they'd only see each other for a short time on Sundays again.

"Did you hear that?" Nellie pulled the kitten off her shoulder.

"I didn't hear anything. What did it sound like?"

"It sounded like a thud and a groan."

"Maybe a branch fell from a tree. The wind is picking up." Charlotte pried the kitten's sharp nails from her gown.

"It didn't sound like a branch."

Charlotte chuckled. "Now you're imagining things."

Nellie put her kitten back in the barrel with its littermates. "I didn't imagine it. Let's go back to the house. It's getting cold out here."

Another thud hit the back of the barn. Charlotte looked at Nellie, then let the kitten down at the edge of the barrel where it skittered in with its siblings. Flora stretched her head in the barrel and let out a yipe before running back to Charlotte. "See it's only the wind blowing something against the barn." Surely, it was nothing more. A chill trickled down her spine.

Charlotte headed out of the building and rounded the first corner before Nellie caught her arm. "Let's go to the house and get one of the men. I know what I heard." Nellie's voice came in a whisper.

"Maybe someone fell and got hurt and needs us." Charlotte's voice quivered as she tried to be brave.

"Shhh." Nellie covered Charlotte's mouth with her hand and whispered. "Or maybe it's that man they saw snooping around here last week."

Charlotte rolled her eyes but kept her voice low. "Stay here then, and I'll go check."

Nellie shook her head violently. "I'm not staying here alone."

"Gracious, Nellie, I'm only going around the corner. I could have already been there and back by now." Charlotte marched down the side of the barn with Flora beside her and Nellie so close behind she kept stepping on her dress. She rounded the corner and scanned the back of the barn. Dusk had arrived while they played with the kittens.

She shuffled forward, and Nellie bumped into her from behind. That was when Charlotte saw the driver, Mr. Pranger, lying on the ground bound and gagged just as Nellie let go of her and gasped. Charlotte went forward to untie the carriage driver. "Nellie run to the house and get Stuebing."

Charlotte knelt down to pull the cloth from Mr. Pranger's mouth. "Did you hear me, Nellie?" Charlotte turned, but Nellie was gone. She stood and ran to the corner of the barn where a man, his face covered with a bandana, had his hand over Nellie's mouth. He was dragging her as she kicked and squirmed in his arms. "Nellie!" Charlotte didn't take the time to think but ran after her sister. "Let her go!"

The man stopped. Charlotte slowed. That seemed a little too easy. He looked down at the flailing woman in his arms and back at her. Then he released her. Nellie started running away, and the man turned.

To Charlotte's horror, the abductor now was after her. Suddenly she understood why he had let her sister go. She had called her Nellie, and he realized he had the wrong woman. "Run to the house. Run to the house!"

Nellie took a sharp right and ran for the house with Charlotte trying as hard as she could to catch up and Flora right beside her.

Strong arms came from behind and grasped her around the waist, lifting her feet from the ground. Charlotte screamed. Flora growled and barked. Nellie tripped and swung around. "Charlotte! Charlotte!"

Charlotte jabbed her elbow back into the man's chest with all her strength. "Go! Get Stuebing!" Her words came out in gasps. Nellie hesitated as if uncertain of what to do, then sped toward the house.

Charlotte continued to struggle, but it didn't seem to slow down her attacker. As he neared the copse of trees, panic seized her. With darkness nearly upon them, if he got her into the woods, they'd never find her.

Flora growled and barked.

She kicked her legs and hammered her elbows into his chest and arms.

"Umph." He tightened his grip around her.

A thud sounded and then Flora let out a yipe.

Charlotte straightened her body and brought her elbow up and back as hard as she could. A deep thump and a low grunt let her know she had hurt him. He let go of her and, as her feet hit the ground she tried to run, but he held her arm. He jerked her back to him and raised his fist. Pain splintered through her cheek and she slid to the ground.

Chapter 30

They had tracked the traitor down to a brothel, but by the time they had arrived, he was nowhere to be found. Duncan and Tavis continued to search the area with no luck. But each day they got closer to finding him. And when they did, he would face justice in Britain.

Duncan saluted Tavis and rode away, leaving him at his house. Aberdeen was restless and wanted to take his lead. When he reached the outskirts of Charleston, Duncan allowed Aberdeen to take off at a gallop. The crisp wind hit his face as he thought back on the evening's events. The moss strewn oak trees standing majestically along the way allowed the sun to finger through the breeze blown branches, casting dancing shadows on the ground.

Once this mission was behind him, he could devote himself to Charlotte. He hoped she'd be willing to start a new life in Scotland. His gut churned. This mission had complicated his life. His beloved Scotland called to him daily. No Scottish man could recall gazing upon the lush green hills and not desire to return from whence he came. But would his wife feel the same?

As Aberdeen slowed his pace to a trot, Duncan sat back in the saddle and closed his eyes, bringing Charlotte's image forth. Would he change any of it—not marry her if he had a choice? Nay. He loved her more than he'd thought possible.

Perhaps fate would smile kindly on him and things would work themselves out. But what if it didn't? Did he love her enough to allow her to choose whether she came with him or stayed in America?

A small pub sat tucked back and away from where Duncan planned to turn left and head toward home. A niggling thought urged him to go in. He reined Aberdeen to a stop. He hadn't paid much attention to the place before. But it had gained his attention this time. With a new awareness, he examined the dilapidated building. A sign hung overhead by a single hook, Ale Before Ye Sail, swung in the cool evening breeze. Sea water and sun had weathered the unpainted clapboards. A single shutter clattered open and shut as if calling to its missing mate. Once he'd dismounted, Duncan led his horse over to a post and tied him.

He pulled on the rusty door handle and the hinges groaned. As he stepped in, he glanced around the empty room. An old man, bald on top and gray around the side, hobbled from a back room.

He ran his hand over his unkept beard. "Guid day tae ye. And what is it I can be getting ye?"

Duncan smiled. Had the tide changed? He allowed his heavy brogue free rein. "Och! Weel, 'tis thirsty I am. I'll ha'e a cup of yer ale."

The old man's bushy brows rose to near where his hairline used to be. "Hoot. Come sit a spell. 'Tis been a while since I blethered with a Scotsman."

Duncan pulled a stool up and sat. "Perhaps if ye hung a tartan oot, it'd draw more." The old man chuckled, and Duncan took advantage of the immediate camaraderie. "Do ye see many new faces from the homeland?"

The old man pulled a can over and spit in it. "Nay. Yer the first new brother in months."

Months? The timing could be about right. Did he dare get his hopes up? "Months, ye say? Ha'e ye seen the mon since?"

"Aye, he came in regularly up until aboot a week and a half ago."

"So, he's made America his home then, eh?"

"I'm no' too sure aboot that. He ne'er shared much. Dinna like anyone asking questions either. But then that's no' too uncommon in my business." The owner slid the drink across the bar.

Duncan grinned. "Nay, I'd think no'. 'Tis the nature of the business. Eh?"

"Oh, aye, that be so. But this fella, he was no' too friendly. And between you and me, I'll tell ye, I ha'e been in this business long enough to ken when a mon is hiding something, and he certainly was."

When Duncan left the little pub, excitement raced through his body. The owner had given him a description of the patron, one that fit his man. Finally, some solid evidence of the traitor. Now Duncan knew where to find him. He just needed to be patient.

When he crested the last hill before reaching his manor, the last rays of sun disappeared. The heavy blanket of dusk moved in. Duncan spurred Aberdeen on. There would be no moon tonight for light.

Distant screams reached his ears as his horse cantered down his road. They came from the direction of his home. He jabbed his heels into his mount, and Aberdeen began digging up the ground, throwing clods of dirt as he closed the distance to the manor.

Nellie stood on the steps yelling as Stuebing took off running. Duncan peered across his land searching in the direction his valet moved. Ice clamps seized his chest. Someone pulled his wife toward the woods. Aberdeen sensed the urgency and picked up speed. His feet thundered against the ground.

Charlotte's assailant glanced over his shoulder and then tossed her onto the ground like a rag doll before dashing into the woods.

This was it—he had his traitor. As he gained on the man, he kept his eyes on Charlotte. She didn't move. Her crumpled body cried to him with each of Aberdeen's strides. Like a baby bird that had fallen from its nest called to its mother, Charlotte's motionless body beckoned him. But if he stopped to check on her, he would lose his chance to end this right here and right now.

As he neared the wooded area, he could see the turncoat's hair and face were covered in cloth.

His country had put its trust in him. The thousand soldiers who had lost their lives and every family member who suffered because of this man weighed on his shoulders. They needed to see this man caught. He needed to catch this man. If the traitor was apprehended, not only Britain could put this behind them, but Charlotte and he could shut this door, never to open it again.

His gaze returned to his love against his will. Her stillness tore at him. He gained on her motionless body. With his sharp yank on the reins, Aberdeen rose up on hind legs. Duncan jumped off and ran the few steps to her.

He lifted her limp body into his arms and remounted. Britain forgive him, he'd find the turncoat again. And when he did, the man would pay for what he'd done to Charlotte and his country.

Nellie held the door for him as he rushed inside. He took the stairs two at a time and went to their room. Gingerly, he laid her on the bed and got his first look at her. Raging heat shot through him, and he clenched his teeth to control himself. A bluish-purple lump rose on her cheek. Though her eyes were shut, he knew when she woke her left eye wouldn't open for the swelling. "Get me some cold cloths."

Stuebing disappeared from the room. Duncan glanced around. Nellie stood near the door, Flora in her arms and tears streaming down her face.

"Help me get her out of these clothes."

Nellie put the puppy down, wiped her face with her sleeve and went to help him. They removed her dress, leaving just her chemise. After he felt her arms and legs and found no broken bones, Duncan let out the pent-up breath. He pulled the quilt up and tucked it around her shoulders.

Kirsten stood in the door. "What happened?"

"Someone tried to kidnap Charlotte." Duncan answered.

"Is she hurt?"

"Looks as if she was hit on the head."

Stuebing returned with a bowl of water and a cold cloth. Duncan took the cloth and began gently wiping Charlotte's face. She groaned.

Nellie picked up her sister's hand and kissed it. "Do you think she'll be all right?"

He dipped the cloth into the water and wrung it out before blotting her face again. "She's going to be sore."

Charlotte groaned. "Duncan."

"I'm right here." Duncan put his hand on her shoulder when she tried to sit up. "Relax dearling."

A tear trickled down her cheek. "Did you catch him?"

Duncan ran the back of his finger lightly over her cheek. "Nay. I had to choose between you and him. I chose you. I'll find him."

"Why did he want me?"

"I'm sure he wanted to get to me through you. Did you see his face?"

Charlotte tried again to sit up but winced and fell back down. "No, I never saw him. Why would anyone want to hurt you, Duncan?"

"Dinna fash aboot it. Just rest so you can get better."

Her eyes pleaded with him for answers.

He resituated her covers. "Stuebing." He spoke in a whisper.

"Here, sir." Stuebing's voice was equally as subdued.

"Where were my footman and groundsmen?"

"Miss Nellie came in and called for me. I ran out, and you rode up moments later."

Charlotte looked around the room. "How is Mr. Pranger?"

Nellie gasped. Everyone turned to her, and she continued to tremble. "I f-forgot to tell you." She wiped at the tears still streaming down her cheeks. "I was so worried about Charlotte. Mr. Pranger is still tied up behind the barn."

"Stuebing."

"I'm going, sir."

"And find oot why no one else came to my wife's rescue." Duncan waited for his valet to leave the room before turning his attention back to Charlotte. "You're going to have to lie around and let people take care of you for a few days while you heal."

He sat next to her, dabbing her cheek with the cool cloth until she drifted off to sleep. He sent Nellie to get some rest, with Vivian to accompany her. She was more shaken than his wife. He gazed down at Charlotte's bruised face. The traitor needed to be found.

Stuebing came back with a report a short time later. "The men went to town. Someone told them you gave them the night off. Pranger didn't want to go and stayed back."

So, he was still being watched. How else would anyone know he was gone? It wouldn't be hard to find out who was a part of this.

He sat beside the bed until sleep came to claim him. Giving in, he lay down beside his wife and wrapped his arms around her.

He woke in the same position he had fallen asleep. Charlotte's swollen cheek posed a grim reminder of the plight he had brought down on his wife. What was she going to think if she found out this had happened to her because of him? Not because someone disliked him, but because he drew closer to finding his adversary. Would she hate him? Could she forgive him more trespasses? Not many women would absolve their husband of such grievances two times. But then, he knew no other woman like Charlotte.

He stared at his brave and beautiful wife. She forgave him so he could understand God's forgiveness. Why was it so important to her? She saw God much differently than he did. He tried not to think about God. She saw Him as some wonderful Father that showed great mercy. He saw God as one who had favorites, and those were the ones He looked out for. The others had to take care of themselves.

He was glad God favored his wife. But looking down at her, he couldn't help but worry he had caused her to lose that favor. His whole life, God had turned his back on him. When Tavis moved away, he'd begged God to bring him back. He didn't. That was when he first knew God really didn't care. Later when he was older, one of his younger sisters got sick. The whole family prayed. He watched his da beg God to show mercy and let her live, but He didn't. The neighbor's child came down with the same illness and their child lived. God loved some more than others. He wasn't going to try to figure out why. He knew He did. Taking his brother was another in the list of Duncan's grievances with God. He couldn't bring his brother back, but he could ensure justice was served, and that was exactly what he intended to do.

Chapter 31

After several days abed, Charlotte's back ached. She insisted that Duncan let her get up, and he acquiesced...with stipulations. The swelling had gone down enough so that she could open her eye again. The bruising was still there, and the spot was tender.

With only a few days left to spend with Nellie, who was scheduled to leave on Sunday, she wanted to make the most of them. Mama would surely want Nellie's help getting ready for the holidays.

Duncan had ordered that the women were not allowed to leave the house without his permission and then, only with escorts. He'd been less than forthcoming with any information as to why someone might want to abduct her. Something niggled in the back of her mind about his secrecy, but she couldn't dwell on it. She didn't want to cause any friction between them. And if she started questioning things, she'd be stirring the pot. She had asked Kirsten about it, but Duncan's cousin didn't seem to know anything either.

Nellie had helped keep her mind occupied and off things she need not think about. Her sister had been so wonderful to her since she'd been confined to bed. She had barely left her side. Charlotte wanted to repay her, and her marriage to Duncan should afford her ways to do so. She glanced at Nellie, who sat in a chair with needlework. "I'd like to get out of this room and go to the parlor."

Nellie hopped up and put her hoop and thread on her chair. "Do you need my help getting up?"

"I can manage. I really need not be in bed anymore. I need a change of scenery."

She was happy to be out of her room and sitting in a comfortable chair with sunshine streaming through the window, giving both warmth and light. Glancing at her sister, whose nimble fingers sent the needle up and down through the tablecloth creating beautiful stitches, she smiled.

Charlotte appreciated the way Kirsten sensed when she needed time alone with her sister. She'd excused herself to go read in the library.

"What do you want to do more than anything?" Charlotte arranged the pillow behind her back.

Nellie glanced up from her work. "What do I want to do? I don't have much choice, do I?"

"But if you could, what would you do?"

Nellie set her work in her lap and let out a sigh. "Marry a man who loves me and raise a family."

"Nothing else? Not become a doctor, a nurse, or an accountant?"

Nellie laughed. "You jest. Can you see me as any of those things? That sounds more like Pearl, Effie, or even you. Besides, what's wrong with being a wife and a mother? That's what you are—a wife. And you will be a mother someday."

"Yes, but it wasn't my choice. Remember I wanted to be an accountant." She loved numbers and paper. "I don't want Papa to force you into anything like he did me. You need to seek your dreams, even if it's marrying a man you love. Don't let Papa keep you from it. You always have Duncan and me if you need us."

"Did that bump on your head affect your thinking?" Nellie had picked back up her handwork and busied herself with it.

Enjoying the welcomed warmth from sunshine, Charlotte leaned forward and pulled the other end of the fabric into her lap. Drawing out the thread and needle where she'd left it, she began to embroider at a much slower pace than her sister. "No. My mind is sound. I only wish for you to make your own decisions instead of having someone make them for you. Promise me you'll contact me if you ever feel Papa doesn't give you a choice."

Nellie shook her head and gave her a look that said she thought her brain was addled. "I promise."

The following day brought cold rain. Duncan stayed around the house, hovering over her and not letting her do much of anything. Kirsten and Duncan's bantering was a bright spot of entertainment to both her and Nellie on such a gloomy day.

Stuebing stepped into the parlor. "Excuse me, sir. A telegram for Miss Macleod."

He handed the missive to Kirsten. All eyes turned to her as she read it. Her hand went to her chest. Duncan stood and moved toward her.

"What is it, Kirs?"

"Da. He's fallen ill. I need to get back to him."

"I'm so sorry, Kirsten. I'll be praying for him." Charlotte's heart ached for her. From the pain on the woman's face, she could see she was close with her father.

"Thank you, Charlotte."

"I'll take you to the train station in the morning. There will no' be anything going oot tonight."

"If you dinna mind, I'm going to turn in." Kirsten pushed herself up and left the room.

Nellie turned to Charlotte. "I feel so bad for her. I can't imagine being so far away and getting that kind of news."

Charlotte nodded. "I pray whatever is wrong he will recover from. I'm sorry to see her go."

"Me too. I've enjoyed getting to know her," Nellie added.

"You'll be leaving in a few days. It's going to be quiet around here." Charlotte sighed.

Duncan stood. "'Tis time for bed. You need your rest to recover."

Charlotte frowned at him. "It is not that late, Duncan. And I am fine. You needn't coddle me."

He scooped her up into his arms, ignoring her protests. "Goodnight, Nellie."

"Goodnight."

Charlotte woke to the sound of rain hitting the window. The cold, wet rain seemed to have taken up residence in Charleston.

Duncan, dressed for the day, stood at the door. "'Tis a miserable day oot there, but I'm still going to take Kirsten to the train depot after she eats breakfast."

"I pray her father recovers."

"Aye, I hope so, too. I'll have her send me notice once she gets home."

Charlotte got up, and he rushed over to help.

"Duncan, I can take care of myself."

He chuckled. "Weel, I see the fire has returned. 'Tis a guid sign."

"I'll be down for breakfast shortly. Go sit with your cousin. She needs you right now."

"Aye, wife. I shall do your bidding. Be careful on the stairs."

Charlotte rolled her eyes. "I feel fine."

As she readied for the day, she avoided looking into the mirror, knowing the bruising would still be there. When she came down, Kirsten had finished her scone and tea and quietly visited with Nellie and Duncan at the table.

"How are you feeling this morning, Charlotte?" Kirsten reached over and squeezed her hand.

"I feel much better than I look, I am sure." Charlotte squeezed back.

"I'm sorry my time here was cut short. Maybe you and Duncan will be able to come visit us soon."

Charlotte turned to Duncan. "Can we?"

"Aye, I see no reason we can no'."

Charlotte turned back to Kirsten. "Then it is settled."

Nellie stuck her lip out. "I wish I could come."

"Duncan?" Kirsten grinned.

"Say no more. Nellie, you may come as well."

Nellie hugged Charlotte. "Oh, this will be fun."

"I did no' say when we will be going," Duncan said defensively.

"It doesn't matter. It gives me something to look forward to. You're the best brother-in-law, Duncan."

Charlotte laughed. "He is your only one."

Nellie gave a mischievous grin. "I know."

"Weel, cousin, we should be on our way." Duncan pushed away from the table.

Kirsten gave Charlotte a hug. "I wish my visit had no' been cut short."

"Yes, it was not long enough."

Kirsten then hugged Nellie. "I've enjoyed getting to ken you as weel."

"I'll look forward to our visit to Texas." Nellie's smile lit up her face.

With goodbyes said, Duncan and Kirsten headed for the train. Nellie and Charlotte went to the parlor, where Nellie picked up her needlework and Charlotte leaned back in the chair and rested.

Duncan returned later, having stayed with Kirsten until her train left.

The soggy weather kept them inside for several more days and gave them plenty of time for more needlework. Every evening Duncan would come into the parlor where they worked and insist the light wasn't good enough. Charlotte allowed herself to be swept away on her husband's arm. Nellie's giggling proved she believed not one word of her husband's excuse to get her alone.

On this particular night, Duncan made his entrance as they finished up the last few stitches. Charlotte folded the fine cotton cloth, now ready for the Thanksgiving and Christmas season, and laid it on the table beside her.

Duncan took a chair and stretched out his legs before him as he always did in the evening. "Weel, Nellie, 'tis sorry I am to see you have to leave us."

"I am sorry to go. It has been an adventure being here."

"I know Mother must be missing you. But not nearly as much as I will when you go."

"You sound as if she lives in Texas with Kirsten. The lass lives in Charleston and can come visit anytime."

Charlotte grinned. "I know. It has just been like old times having her here day and night. And once she goes home and with the holidays upon us, Mother will keep her busy."

♥♥♥

Call it vanity, but Charlotte could not make herself go to church with her face still bruised, albeit only yellowish-purple now. Instead, she stood on the top step and waved goodbye to Nellie as Tavis drove her off to church. She remained stationed on the step until the carriage faded from view behind the trees lining the drive before escaping back into the warmth of her house.

Already missing her sister, she settled into a parlor chair across from Duncan. She glanced at him, noticing he hadn't taken his eyes off her since she entered. While Nellie had been with them, it was easy to push aside questions about what all transpired, but now she wanted to know. "Did you find out where all the stable hands were when Mr. Pranger was tied up?"

Duncan got up and threw a log on the dying fire and reached for the poker. "Langley told them I gave them the evening off."

"Langley is one of your stable hands? And you didn't?"

"Aye, he is, and nay I dinna. And I dinna understand why they would think I would give all of them the night off. But I'm sure they looked at it like the old saying, 'Dinna look a gift horse in the mouth.'"

He poked the log, and sparks flew up the chimney. "Did you ask Mr. Langley why he'd tell such an untruth?"

"He has no' returned to work, and I'm sure does no' plan to."

"We know what he looks like, so he shouldn't be too hard to find."

"Och! I wish it were only that easy. I doubt verra much the mon is staying around Charleston. He's probably far from here by now."

Charlotte wiggled in her chair, attempting to get more comfortable. "Why exactly do you suppose Langley and the attacker wanted to abduct me?"

"I wish I ken."

"I think we should call in the police. Surely they could find the men. They're trained for this kind of thing."

Duncan grunted. "I told you, lass. I dinna think Langley is around the area anymore and, of the other, we have no name or description."

Charlotte frowned, then winced, quickly remembering the bruises. "But if we don't contact the authorities, we know they won't be found. What is the harm in talking with them?"

"I dinna like others in my business."

"This isn't business. We are talking about justice and keeping people safe. I don't want dangerous people walking the streets of Charleston. And I certainly don't want to have to worry about leaving my home or not being able to visit Nellie and my family."

Duncan returned the poker to the stand. "I have to check on Aberdeen. I dinna think he's feeling weel." Stopping next to her as he passed by, he bent over and dropped a kiss gently on her lips. "We can discuss this later."

♥♥♥

They hadn't discussed it later. A week passed, and they still hadn't called in the police. Every time she brought it up, he evaded the topic. With arms folded, Charlotte tapped her foot on the floor. There was a reason he didn't want people to know, but she hadn't figured it out. It left things once again strained between them. She was sure he avoided being alone with her to keep the subject at bay. He came to bed late and was gone when she awoke.

By the next Sunday the bruises were still visible, though the pain was gone. The thought of going to church and having dozens of questions tossed her way was more than she wished to endure. With that thought in mind, she decided to stay home one more Sunday. But Nellie would worry if she didn't hear from her.

She headed to Duncan's desk in the study in search of paper and pen to write Nellie a note. Stuebing met her as she turned to go into the room.

"A missive." He held out a white envelope with faded ink smears. "I believe that says Mrs., but one cannot be sure without opening it."

Charlotte took it from his hand and studied it closely. "Looks like it's been through a rainstorm or two. I hope the inside letter fared better. If it's for Duncan, I'll leave it on his desk." She started into the room and remembered she wanted to tell the valet something. "I'm penning my sister a letter. When I finish, could you see that it gets in the post?"

"Yes, ma'am."

Charlotte sat down at Duncan's desk and searched the oak top for a letter opener. Opening the center drawer, she spied one made of ivory. With a quick flick down the crease, the envelope opened, and she pulled out the letter. She had no recognition of the eloquent handwriting as the letter unfolded.

The first three words, *My Dearest Duncan*, caused her breath to catch in her throat. The letter wasn't for her. Her husband was the recipient. Conviction told her she should place it back in the envelope and give it to him, as she'd told Stuebing she'd do. But the letter's greeting kept her from it. She stood with the missive still in her hand and hurried to shut the door. With shaking fingers, she returned to the desk, willing herself to read. It was her right as a wife.

> *My Dearest Duncan,*
> *I miss you greatly. I wish I had hidden away with you when you sailed to America. You may have been angry when you first discovered, but you would have absolved me. You always do! I thought you were done with all these secret missions and we would once again have time to spend together. I would be mad at the queen*

for asking such a thing of you again, but that would not be loyal to the Crown. But enough of that.

Why don't you write me? It's terrible that I have to find out about you from someone else. I was saddened to hear you had married. Does this mean you will have no more time for me? Perhaps we can sneak away like old times. I've heard you were practically forced to marry for duty's sake. Is this true? And an American! Heavens! You poor thing. Do you think she will return with you when your mission is complete? Please write back soon. I wait with bated breath. I love you.

Always Yours,

Ailsa

Chapter 32

The note fell from Charlotte's fingers and drifted to the desktop. Her hands trembled as she stared at the offending words. *Wait with bated breath. I love you. Mission? Sent by the queen?* Duncan was a spy? This woman knew he forced her to marry. Her brain tried to process all the information. Her chest ached, and she struggled for breath. This couldn't be true. But that would explain so much. Why he hid the item in her bag. Why he forced the marriage. Why he left and returned at such strange hours. Pain stabbed at her heart—the enemy twisting a knife in her wound. He had a love in Scotland, and this woman, Ailsa, still loved him and wanted to spend time with him—regardless of his marriage. The man she loved didn't love her, but another. He didn't seek her hand in marriage because he desperately wanted her to be his wife, but because of duty. *Duty.* He didn't even plan to stay in America. When his mission was over, he planned to return to Scotland. Had he intended to leave her here when he finished whatever he came to do, or did he think to force her to go to Scotland?

A chill ran down her back, and she dropped the letter into her lap. If he was a spy on a mission in America, did that mean he planned to betray her country? But America and Scotland were on friendly terms. What to do? She could go home and tell Papa. But if Duncan was a spy, then she really didn't know him. If he discovered she'd told her family what she knew, he might harm them. No. She couldn't go home. She stood and began pacing the floor on wobbly legs. She needed to think. Make a clear plan.

If she got on the train, he could easily follow her within hours.

She nibbled on her bottom lip. She'd need money or things to trade for money. The amethyst and diamond necklace, silver brush set, and other gifts Duncan had given her would bring in some. The thistle pin that had caused her all this pain. Duncan said it was valuable. And there were funds in the wood box on Duncan's clothes chest. But where could she go and not be found?

Her eyes rested on the small wooden ship sitting on the mantle. That was it. *The Scottish Lass* was to sail this afternoon. She glanced at the clock. Duncan had said the ship planned to set sail at five o'clock. That would leave her plenty of time to get there. Duncan never came home until late, and by the time he discovered she was gone, if he figured out she left on the ship, which she doubted he would, it would be too late.

But the captain would never let her go with him. No, she'd have to sneak aboard and hide. She'd overheard Captain Maher telling Duncan *The Scottish Lass* would be making several stops along the way, going first up the South Carolina coast, then coming back down to stop by Savannah on their way to port cities in Florida. Once the boat docked, she'd get off and go find her aunt and uncle in Savannah. They were good Christian people and would help her decide what to do. Charlotte rushed out of the room and up the stairs. She'd worry about the details later. Right now she needed to get some clothes and money and leave.

Charlotte ran to the library and pulled the pin from the kilt. She turned to leave, glancing down at the pin in her hand. Duncan treasured the heirloom. She swung back around and replaced it. It wasn't hers to take. She hurried down to her room. The necklace and brush set lay on her bureau. She scooped them up and shoved them into her pocketbook. What should she bring for clothing? Gowns she could get on and off herself. She took out several and tossed them on the bed. With her mind still reeling, she pulled out other articles of clothing and went into Duncan's room.

A quick tug opened the chest drawer. She spied the wooden box and lifted it out. She couldn't think about what she was doing. She removed all the money. It wasn't stealing.

Hadn't Duncan told her she could use this money, should she ever need it? He just hadn't planned on it aiding her escape.

Now she needed a bag for her clothes. Hanging on a hook on the wall was a brown leather bag. Charlotte snatched it and returned to her room. Only one dress would fit inside. When she finished packing, she slipped out to the carriage and stashed the leather bag under the seat so Stuebing wouldn't see her leaving with it. She lay down on her bed to wait. It was too early to leave. She didn't want to wander around town waiting for the time to pass. The hands on the clock slowly moved. At two-thirty she opened up her door and called on Stuebing to ready the carriage.

She slipped on her coat and grabbed her pocketbook, then made her way down the stairs. The carriage arrived at the front door a short time later along with Stuebing. "May I ask where you are off to, miss? In case your husband should ask."

Charlotte sent up a quick prayer that she would not sound as frightened as she felt. "To town." That was the truth. "Duncan isn't due back until late."

"I see." Stuebing glanced around. "Doesn't Mr. Mackenzie wish you to be home before dark?"

"I'm a grown woman. I can take care of myself."

"I really must insist you stay, at least until he returns."

"Unless you plan to hold me here against my will, of which I will inform my husband, I need to be on my way."

Stuebing hesitated. "Where is your maid?"

She needed to avoid his questions and leave before he should ask her one she couldn't answer. "She is picking wildflowers alongside the road to put on the table. I wanted it to look nice when Duncan came home." That was the truth, only now it didn't matter. Charlotte almost let out a sob but caught herself.

"You should pass by her on the way to town. May I suggest you take her with you?"

"That is a good idea." Charlotte forced a smile. He could suggest it, but she wouldn't be doing it.

"Ah, very good. What time do you plan to return?"

"I don't know." Charlotte hurried down to the waiting carriage and climbed in with the help of the driver. "To town, Mr. Pranger."

Mr. Pranger gave a slight bow. "Where in town would that be?"

"Let me think on that. When we get closer, I'll decide where I'd like to stop." Charlotte adjusted her bustle behind her as she sat. The bag under the seat held her plainest dress and some incidentals. She stuffed her pocketbook in it.

Mr. Pranger climbed up on his seat and clucked to the horses. Charlotte leaned back, willing her heart to calm. She could do this. There really was no choice if she wished to have time to think.

What if Duncan came back early? He'd be traveling this same road. What would she tell him? She brushed the idea away. That wasn't going to happen. As Mama used to say, she borrowed trouble.

By the time they reached the outskirts of Charleston, Charlotte's muscles ached from the tension. Mr. Pranger slowed the carriage and yelled over his shoulder. "Do you know where you'd like to stop, Mrs. Mackenzie?"

She couldn't stop right at the ship, and she didn't want to stop too far from it and have to walk a long way. Captain Maher might set sail before she got there. "Such a chill in the air. I think I'll walk a bit to get the blood circulating. I'll have you stop up here just a bit."

Mr. Pranger looked over his shoulder with concern. "This isn't the best area, ma'am, with the sailors and riff-raff wandering around."

Charlotte peeked down the road. Another thing she hadn't thought of. Mr. Pranger would never let her depart the carriage if he thought it wasn't safe. "Perhaps you're right. Take me down to the corner of Market and Church Street."

"Much better, ma'am." He snapped the reins, and the horses picked up their pace.

That was only a few blocks over from the wharf where *The Scottish Lass* moored. She'd often heard Duncan speak of where he kept his ships. The church clock rang in the distance. She would have plenty of time to sneak on board and find a place to hide.

Mr. Pranger helped Charlotte down. She thanked him and assured him she would be fine, noting his clouded look when she pulled her large bag with her.

"I'm taking a dress in for mending."

Mr. Pranger's face eased. He smiled. "Ah. Would you like some help?"

"Thank you, but I can see to it. It's not heavy."

Once out of sight of the carriage, Charlotte made her way toward the wharf and her destination. Finding the ship, she stood back and searched the main deck until she spotted Captain Maher. The ship buzzed with activity. Crewman hustled around securing cargo while others scrambled aloft readying to unfurl the sails. Several sailors stood near the ropes that held the ship to the dock, waiting for orders to cast them off. Two couples walked up the dock and onboard. Captain Maher turned from his duties, speaking briefly with them, then strode away, returning to his responsibilities. The couple disappeared and then reappeared with another couple. They spoke with one of the crewmen and then left the ship. She waited until the captain went to the far side of the ship and started a conversation with one of his crew before she made a mad dash for the wooden planks that connected the dock to the ship. As she stepped aboard, a young boy intercepted her. "Can I help you ma'am?"

Chapter 33

"I'm sailing with you. I spoke with Captain Maher this week." Well, she did speak with him. "If you don't mind, I'd like to catch up with the other passengers."

The boy shifted nervously. He was so young she couldn't help but wonder if this was his first voyage, too. "I'm sorry, ma'am, but the other passengers stepped off after dropping their bags in their cabins. But they should be back soon as we set sail in an hour."

"Then I'll wait for them there." Charlotte prayed her nervous smile wouldn't give her away as she hurried in the direction she'd seen the couples disappear.

The captain yelled orders, and the men hustled about, taking no notice of her. If he saw her, he must have assumed she was one of the other guests sailing with them. With a quick glance around her, Charlotte found the stairs right where she had envisioned them and took them below the deck.

From Duncan's conversations with Captain Maher, she'd learned that only one room was used for guests that traveled. The men would be sleeping with the crew, and the ladies would share the one room. A light push opened the unlatched door. She stuck her head in and glanced around. The room stood empty other than a few bags sitting on the floor. Scanning the area, she saw there was no way to conceal her presence. She dropped her bag beside one of the bunks and sank down on the thin mattress.

Trying to console herself that what she was doing was right, she noted the crying of gulls. Their mournful sound summoned her heartache to the surface. Duncan had wanted to be the first to take her aboard his ship. Her battered heart wept. Here she was, preparing to sail on his pride and joy but running from him.

Scooting her bag up against the bed to make as much room as possible, she realized in all the rush to make a plan and leave, she'd never given any thought to food or how long the trip would take. That would be of no concern, she was sure, for when the other ladies discovered her, they would talk about it and within a day she felt certain the captain would discover her. By then it would be too late to turn back—she hoped. The thought of facing an angry Duncan, the spy, the man she really didn't know, sent a chill down her spine.

Charlotte curled up on the bed. What would Duncan do when he found her missing? Would he be angry, or would he care at all? The ache in her heart had no relief to be found.

The soft lapping of the water against the side of the ship and the gentle rocking as it went over the ocean's wakes lulled her to sleep. She woke to the chatter of women's voices and the bumping of the door. Sleepily, she sat up and smiled at the now silent women.

Charlotte swung her feet to the floor. "Hello."

The taller woman had a white streak running through her hair. She smiled. "Good afternoon."

She was accompanied by a shorter woman with black hair and eyes that almost matched. The woman didn't seem nearly as welcoming. "I wasn't aware we were to share accommodations."

Charlotte stretched and tried to act nonchalant. "It was a last-minute decision."

The black-haired woman humphed and moved her bag to one of the other beds. Her friend came forward. "I'm Mrs. Smith, and this is Mrs. Summerfield. It's nice to meet you."

It was good to see a smiling face. "I'm M—" Should she give her real name? The idea of being less than honest didn't sit well. But she'd been anything but truthful thus far. With each lie, she needed another it seemed. Just like her Mama had always warned her. Captain Maher would discover her soon enough, but no sense helping it along. "Mrs. Jackson."

Mrs. Summerfield sniffed. Mrs. Smith shifted her gaze to her and frowned before returning her attention back to

Charlotte. "Excuse my sister-in-law, Mrs. Jackson. She hasn't felt well since we've set sail and it has made her progressively more irritable."

"Don't speak as if I'm not here, Marilyn."

Mrs. Smith smiled.

"I'm glad to have company." Charlotte peeked around Mrs. Smith. "I hope you get to feeling better, Mrs. Summerfield."

She wasn't sure, but Charlotte thought the woman murmured a thank-you before collapsing on the bed with a moan. Time slipped by, and while Mrs. Summerfield tried to sleep, Charlotte and Mrs. Smith talked quietly. Startled by a knock on the door, Charlotte edged over to the end of her bed out of view of the opening door.

A deep voice resonated into the room as Mrs. Smith peered out. "I've come to get you and Mrs. Summerfield for supper."

"Ann is sleeping. She still isn't feeling well. I'm afraid the rocking of the ship has upset her stomach." Mrs. Smith kept her voice low.

"Would you like me to bring your meal to you?" The voice on the other side of the door asked.

"That would be wonderful. Thank you." She started to close the door and turned to Charlotte. "Would you like to eat in here tonight?"

Charlotte nodded.

Mrs. Smith stuck her head into the hall. "Mr. Smith, would you bring two plates, please?" She shut the door and took a seat on the only chair in the room.

By the time the meals arrived Charlotte was famished. Mrs. Smith's husband returned with a crew member and two plates and two cups of tea. As he handed his wife the plates, he glanced toward Charlotte's side of the room. There was no question he had seen her. His wide-eyed double-take said it all. She whispered a prayer.

Lord, I pray he doesn't speak to the captain tonight. She had hoped to get through at least the first night and next day.

When they finished the meal, Charlotte stretched her legs, walking back and forth in the short distance of the room. What she wouldn't give for some fresh air. And this was only her first day. Mrs. Smith looked to be dozing along with her sister-in-law.

The crew had quieted, and only an occasional order was bellowed out. She lowered herself to the bed and waited for time to pass.

Clicks on the wooden steps sent Charlotte's heart thrumming. They grew louder. She grasped the mattress edge.

"Are you sure there's another woman in there? I won't tolerate stowaways. Woman or not, she can scrub the deck during the day and sleep in the brig come night." Captain Maher's voice boomed from somewhere outside the room, confirming Charlotte's fears and causing her to jump.

She braced her feet apart on the floor and grasped the bed's edge as the ship hit a swell. She might get that fresh air sooner than she thought. How many times had her mother told her to be careful what she wished for? A sharp rap sounded on the door. She glanced at the still sleeping women. Drawing herself up, she squared her shoulders and clasped her hands in front of her. "Come in."

The door swung open with a little too much force, banging the wall. "I'll need—" Captain Maher's words seemed to be stuck in his throat. He gawked and shook his head as if to make the vision of her go away. "Mrs. Mackenzie?"

Charlotte smiled. The poor man. Seeing her there was quite a shock. "Hello, Captain."

He fumbled over his words. "C-Could I speak to you in private?"

Charlotte glanced over at Mrs. Smith, who now stood with mouth agape. Apparently, from the captain's reaction, she knew who owned the ship and had put two and two together. "I'll be right back."

The captain escorted her from her room and to his cabin. He shut the door and turned to her. "What are you *doing?*"

Charlotte kept her demeanor as unconcerned as possible. "I'm enjoying my first time at sea."

"Does Mr. Mackenzie know you're aboard?"

"I really don't know if he does or not."

He began to pace the room. "You left without his knowledge then? He'll have my job for this. What were you thinking? Why would you leave without telling him?"

Charlotte eyed him as he made sharp turns every few steps. "Quite obviously, sir, it is because I do not wish him to know where I am."

He ran his hand through his silvery brown hair. "Mr. Mackenzie is one of the finest men I've ever met. I'll not dishonor myself in his eyes. I'm bringing you back as soon as I drop off my cargo. You'll not go ashore."

Charlotte lifted her chin. "I most certainly will."

"If I let you off this ship, he will not only relieve me of my ship, but possibly my life."

She didn't know the man she married, and that was precisely why she was on this ship "Let me explain."

"There is no changing my mind. Your husband has been very good to me, and I *will* return the favor. You can go and get your belongings and bring them here. I'll vacate the cabin."

"I don't expect special treatment while I'm here. My room is comfortable enough."

Captain Maher walked over to his desk and began pulling papers from it. "Expect or not, you will be staying here. Mr. Mackenzie would demand it. I'll not argue with you."

Charlotte huffed and turned to go out of the room as the ship hit another large swell. The jolt set her off balance and bumping into the wall.

The captain straightened from his search through his papers. "It appears we are heading into a squall. When you get your things together, you'll need to stay in your cabin for safety's sake."

"But there was no storm when we left to sail a few hours ago."

"Look outside." He glared at her. "Things don't always go as we hope."

Charlotte winced at the kind captain's harsh words. If he was this unhappy, she shuddered to think how her husband would take it.

Mrs. Smith was in bed when Charlotte went to retrieve her things. She really would have preferred to stay with the other women instead of alone. But Captain Maher was already upset with her. She tiptoed out and back to her room, guilt eating at her over taking the captain's room. The rain began pelting the ship as she settled into the bed fully clothed. She pulled the blanket up over her shoulders, warding off the chill that slowly crept into the room.

Charlotte woke as she slammed to the floor of the ship. *The Scottish Lass* lurched to starboard. Outside her cabin the captain bellowed orders above the howl of the wind and pounding waves. Crawling on hands and knees, she felt her way across the room to the chair, which was secured to the deck.

The urgency in the captain's voice sent a shiver of dread down her spine. The ship tilted until she thought it lay on its side. Lord, have mercy on her. She didn't want to die—not without telling Duncan she was sorry.

Chapter 34

Finally. A break in the case. Duncan rode in much later than he had expected. After he'd come so close to catching the traitor at the brothel, he had doubled his efforts. But it always came to naught. But tonight it seemed that God had given him a break. Perhaps his pretty little wife's divine favor had rubbed off on him.

He slid off his horse and threw the reins to one of the stablemen who had come to take his horse. He bounded up the steps and was met at the door by Stuebing. He handed his valet his hat and began to slough off his coat.

Stuebing adjusted his weight from one foot to the other and cleared his throat. "You may want to leave that on, sir."

Duncan froze with one arm half in the sleeve. He eyed Stuebing. The man was never nervous. "And why would that be?"

"Your wife hasn't returned from town. I sent Gibson to see if the carriage has broken down or brigands set on it. He returned mere minutes before you. He—"

"Why has she gone to town?"

Stuebing raised his chin. "I tried to persuade her against going. I could do nothing short of tying her down."

"How long has she been gone?"

"Hours, sir."

Duncan shoved his arm back in his coat. "What did Gibson find oot?" Duncan snatched his hat back from Stuebing's hand.

"He found the carriage and Pranger in town, but Mrs. Mackenzie had not returned to it all afternoon. Mr. Pranger was beside himself, at a loss for not knowing what to do. He did go to the police and ask them to look for her. Gibson is rounding up the men to go to town and start searching."

"Do you have any idea why she would have left?"

"No. She seemed very much herself when I gave her the missive that had been delivered. Then the next time I saw her, she was heading out the door in a rush."

Duncan raised his brow. "In a hurry, you say?"

Stuebing nodded. "Yes, sir."

"Where is this letter she received?"

"I really couldn't say. I gave it to her as she headed into your study. She said she wished to write Miss Nellie a note and would want it posted."

"What time did Pranger last see her?"

"He thought it about three o'clock or perhaps a bit later."

Duncan turned away and headed for his study. He strode through the open door and to his desk. Six or more hours had passed since she'd been seen. The white linen paper lay on his desk. He recognized the smooth rounded letters as his sister's script. Note in hand, he sank into his chair and began to scan the words. Dread the weight of a lead ball dropped to his stomach as he carefully examined each word his sister had penned.

What Charlotte had read and presumed was more than obvious. She hadn't gone to town. She'd run away.

Relief flooded him. She would go home...to Nellie...to her parents.

"Stuebing!"

"Here, sir."

"I'm sure she has gone to her family. I'll ride into town and—"

"I'm sorry, sir, but she isn't at her family's estate. Gibson said Mr. Pranger informed him that was one of the first places he checked. He also asked them to send a messenger should she arrive there."

Where could she have gone if not to her family home? He'd never heard her talk of close friends. She loved church. Perhaps she'd gone there. "I'm going to check the church and the preacher's home. If she should come home or you hear something, I'll leave a mon stationed at the church where we can check in. And Stuebing, send someone to her parents to find out where her closest relatives live."

Stuebing shuffled his feet. He pushed his shoulders back and looked his employer in the eye. "If you don't mind, sir, I'd like to ride along with you."

Duncan had the urge to shake his head and have him repeat himself. Stuebing wanted to ride along? On a horse? The last time he rode he could barely walk when he got off. "It's raining."

Stuebing took a step forward. "I won't slow you down, sir. The young lady has grown on me."

Despite the circumstances, Duncan grinned. Charlotte had a way of doing that. "Send someone to speak with her parents, then get your coat and hat and meet me at the stable."

"Right away." Stuebing dashed from the room.

Once Duncan, Stuebing, Gibson, and two other hired hands were saddled up, they set out. By the time they reached the church, their clothes were drenched. Duncan slid off his horse, and Aberdeen snorted his protest. The whole group would be lucky if they didn't catch their deaths. And what of Charlotte? Was she in this bone-chilling downpour? No light shone through the church windows, but he pushed on the door anyway. It didn't move. He pounded his fist on the painted wood. No answer.

With meaningful strides he rushed across the patchy lawn to the parsonage and banged on the door. After a moment, a light appeared through the window. The door creaked open and Pastor Aldridge peered out. "Who's there?"

"'Tis Duncan Mackenzie. I'd be looking for my wife. Have you seen her?"

Eyes droopy and hair disheveled, Pastor Aldridge opened the door. Duncan hadn't thought about the late hour.

"Come in and get out of that rain." The light from the pastor's lamp, now in full view, filtered through the darkness.

"Nay. I just need to ken if you have seen her."

"No, I haven't seen Miss Charlotte in several weeks now. We've been missing her in church." He looked at Duncan accusingly.

He didn't have time to chat. "'Tis sorry I am to interrupt your sleep. Guid evening."

"Can I help with something?" He leaned out the door.

Duncan had already turned to go to his horse. He stopped. "If I could leave one of my men here to wait for word of her return, it would be most helpful."

"Say no more. I'll go get something for him to dry off with, and he can warm himself before the fire. And I shall pray."

Gibson stayed and the rest continued on to their mounts. The horses slogged through the muddy roads until they were south of Calhoun Street, where some of the roads were paved. Duncan turned off Meeting Street onto Market. Lights burned in many of the homes they passed. The carriage sat where they were told it would be, and with Mr. Pranger huddled on the seat.

Duncan reined his horse in beside him. "Have you heard anything?"

"No, sir. I've been afraid to go too far for fear the missus will return. I did dash down to the police department and the Jacksons'."

"Good thinking." Duncan turned to the group. "Spread out. Check the…" The thought of what he was about to say sent a chill down his spine. "The less than reputable areas. If she's been taken, I'm guessing it'll be to a place where people will turn their heads the other way. I'm going to ride o'er to Tavis's. He's guid at this kind of thing. Check back with Pranger when you can so we ken what's going on. Let him ken where you've been."

"Mr. Mackenzie, I've already contacted Mr. Dalzell. He's searching as we speak. He was the only other person I could think of to help, since I knew he was your confidant."

Duncan swelled with gratitude toward Pranger. His devotion to Charlotte was admirable. "Then I'll search with the rest of you. If any of you see Dalzell, fill him in."

The men split up. With each hour that passed and they came up empty, Duncan's heart darkened. Crevvens, this was his fault. His dishonesty jeopardized the person he loved most. Why hadn't he listened to Tavis when he told him he needed to come clean, that he had a wife to think about? He was a fool. He would re-earn her trust and win her back if it took the rest of his days.

He looked up to the heavens and wanted to shake his fist. *Lord, what do You have against me? Why do You constantly take away the ones I love and the things important to me?*

♥♥♥

Charlotte's beating heart crowded her throat for what seemed like hours now. She was alone in the captain's quarters and tossed about by waves that only seemed to grow in height and intensity. How were the other women faring? Surely, these ships saw tempests like this frequently. She tightened her hands on the chair and worked her way around it to sit. What was she doing out in the ocean without a soul knowing she was here? She closed her eyes, though the darkness both within and without remained the same.

"God, why didn't You answer my prayers? I didn't want to marry Duncan, and I asked You to free me from him. But You didn't, and now I love him, and he has hurt me over and over. Why are You doing this to me?"

Be strong. Trust me.

Charlotte opened her eyes and quickly glanced around, but everything remained black. The only sounds were the whistling wind, the crashing waves, and the creaking ship. Yet the words had been as clear as the moans of the ship. Was that wishful thinking or was God really trying to tell her something? Maybe there was a chance she would live through this storm.

Hope crashed in as fast as the waves hitting the ship. Hope that she'd live to see another day. Hope that she'd be there for her sisters. Hope for her marriage.

The ship jerked and she tightened her grip on the chair.

How long could a ship take such a beating? Her stomach reeled against the tossing and pitching of the ship. Each wave seemed to pound the wooden frame with more force than the last. "God, I don't want to die here alone, in this deep ocean where I will never be found."

Maybe this storm was her fault. Like Jonah, she was running from God's will. And as with Jonah, God sent a storm. Would He allow her to live through it as He had His prophet? Would it take a life-threatening storm to make her realize that she would rather return to her husband than perish in her rebellion? God never promised things would be easy. Maybe she should have tried talking to Duncan instead of running from him. If she lived through this, she would have to trust the Lord's leading in her and her husband's lives.

The large ship groaned as the tempest pounded against it. The imminent danger of drowning gave her pause. She closed her eyes and held tight to the chair. If she perished with Duncan's ship, he would never know the sea was her grave. He would continue to believe she had run away from the marriage and never returned. A tear slipped down her face.

The ship careened, throwing Charlotte to the floor like a rag doll. Her knees hit the wooden planks, sending shards of pain through them. To keep herself from sailing across the small cabin, she reached out and grasped the chair she'd been thrown from. "God, if You let me live, I will go back to Duncan." A wave crashed onto the hull. The ship tilted to larboard. Water gushed under the door, soaking her cotton dress. She shivered. Whether it was from the cold water or the icy grip of death, she didn't ponder long. If she remained here, she would surely drown.

The door flung open and more water gushed into the cabin. She crawled to the door and pulled herself up, using the bulkhead to keep herself upright.

She had heard that drowning wasn't a bad way to die. It was like going to sleep. But how could anyone know? If they had drowned, they wouldn't be around to tell about it.

The wind howled, muffling the sound of the frantic crew. She glanced up toward the top of the stairs but couldn't see anyone. The ship lunged, and she fell against the bulkhead. Holding onto the sides, she made her way up the tilted stairs—lower rooms would fill with water first, so she needed to go higher.

Rain beat down with relentless anger, working together with the storm surge to fill *The Scottish Lass*.

Above, bolts of lightning gave her a glimpse of men scrambling in front of her on a water-slick deck to clear the rigging—their faces contorted with fear.

A strong hand grasped Charlotte's shoulder, and she swung around. Concern etched the captain's face as another fork of lightning lit up the sky. "Go back to your cabin and stay there," he yelled over the drumming rain and crashing thunder. He turned and barked orders to his men.

The schooner pitched to larboard, sending her skidding across the quarterdeck and slamming into the rail. Her hands tightened on the wooden bar.

"Get down below," the captain bellowed.

She shook her head. Letting go was as good as wishing death upon herself. Besides, if the ship went down, she had no desire to be trapped below. One thing she did know, if it came to a sinking ship, it was every man for himself. She'd stay up here and look for something that would float.

Another wave washed over her as the vessel tilted again and she watched the black sea rise up to meet her. This spot was definitely not safe. When the ship righted, she loosened her grip and with quick, careful steps made her way over to the capstan and away from the raging dark ocean. She clutched the wooden structure, willing the sea to calm.

It refused. The surge continued to rise and wash over the schooner and her crew. Raindrops fell with such force they felt like hundreds of bees were stinging her skin and tearing at her clothes. Men slipped, fell, and pulled themselves back up to finish their mission. A cry escaped her lips, but the tempest's howling wind drowned the sound as they left her lips. Waves collided violently with the ship's hull as she teetered back and forth. The captain stomped toward her.

An earsplitting crack rent the air as another wave crashed over the quarterdeck. The ship groaned and strained as the torrent of wind hit the mast.

A swell of water rose from the starboard side. Instead of crashing over them, it continued to grow until it became a solid black wall towering over the vessel.

This was it. But she didn't want to die. Not like this.

Charlotte clung to the capstan, her anchor, waiting for the water to crash down on her.

The wall of water lifted the ship and caused it to tilt, then hurtled onto the deck knocking her from the capstan and onto her backside. Her body rose from the deck. Lightning flashed. She glimpsed the captain's fearful face as he now rushed toward her. The sensation of falling sent a splinter of fear through her body as the force swept her over the side. Charlotte reached out to grab at the captain's extended hand and came up with nothing. She grasped for anything that could stop her descent over the side, but her hands came up empty. Her body plunged into the dark ocean. Her sodden clothes tangled around her limbs and pulled her down.

She sent up another plea for help as the ocean swallowed her. *Please God, save me.* A board from the foundering ship struck her shoulder, sending a bolt of pain through it and down into her arm. She grasped it like a lifeline, though it pulled her farther into the depths of the sea. The abrupt movement sent more agony through her arm. She opened her mouth to let out a cry. Water filled her lungs. She choked and drew in more water. The long wooden plank stopped its downward descent and began to climb upward, taking her with it. When she broke through the water to the surface, she gasped for air. Before she could take a second breath, another wave crashed down on her, and the piece of wood she clung to slipped from her hands.

Her gown tangled around her legs, dragging her down. She fought to kick her feet and propel herself upward. The last gulp of air she had managed to suck in burned her chest. Fear such as she had never known pierced her body. She twisted and tugged at her skirt, trying to free her legs, but the effort only worked against her. Exhaustion threatened. Muscles weakened and each movement slowed. She let out a small amount of air to ease the ache in her lungs. How much longer could she fight the inevitable? The desire to draw in a new breath warred with her senses, since brine would be all she would take in. The temptation to give up was great, but she couldn't die here in this watery grave. Duncan would never know. She needed to tell him God loved him, she loved him, and that she was sorry for running away.

Something or someone pushed her. She could no longer tell what was up or down. Her mind grew tired, her strength was gone. Another nudge. It didn't matter. She just wanted to sleep. Cold air hit her face. She gasped for breath as she broke through the surface of water. Again a nudge, this time on the back of her shoulder. She turned to feel for the person who had guided her upward. She reached over and her hands wrapped around a plank, her salvation. She clung to it as she coughed and searched the sea for her rescuer, but there was nothing but blackness. Her chest burned. Everywhere she turned, a dark void consumed the horizon. The wind slapped at her face stealing her breath and letting loose an eerie growl. Once again the sky lit up, and she scanned the water, but no one was there. The sea continued to pelt droplets into her face as the waves lifted and tossed her like flotsam. Her eyes stung from the salty water, and she squeezed them shut, then blinked rapidly upon opening them. Darkness surrounded her. She called to her rescuer, but there was no answer. The wind continued to roar like an angry animal. A wave crashed over her as she opened her mouth to call again. Coughing and choking, she spit out the tangy mix and tightened her grip on the board.

The night sky was as black as she had ever seen it. She looked down at the piece of wood but couldn't make out her hands. She took a deep breath. "Is anyone there?"

The wind snatched the words as they left her mouth. She could barely hear them herself. "Help! Can anyone hear me?"

The words disappeared into the nothingness that surrounded her.

Something brushed her leg, and her mind traveled to the stories she had heard as a child. Sharks. What if she survived the storm only to have sharks feast on her body? A tremor shot through her. With all her strength she pulled herself up and onto the timber, wrapping her arms and legs around it.

She laid her head on the beam. She was alone like never before. If she survived this, she would never again listen to her heart without seeking God. Following her own will and her selfish prayers had gotten her where she was this stormy night. If she survived, it was only by the grace of God.

Another wave came crashing down on her. She tightened her grip, not willing to let her lifeline slip away again. Up and down she rode the waves. Her stomach churned from the endless rocking and her belly full of saltwater. The aching in her muscles and hands weakened her grip. The cold jaws of icy sea served a grim reminder that she must hold on.

Chapter 35

Tired though he was, Duncan hadn't tried to sleep. They had scoured the area where Charlotte was last seen and most of the seedier areas along the wharf, but to no avail. The storm had passed hours ago, leaving him and his men soaked. Tavis caught up with him, and they walked along the strip of warehouses.

A vagrant with wrinkled trousers and a torn brown shirt crouched under a store awning.

"You lookin' for the girl?"

Duncan spun around. "What would you ken aboot that?"

"Some others were askin' of her. But you look like you can pay for what I saw."

Duncan gazed down at the man, who was desperately in need of a bath, a shave, and probably a good meal. "Have you seen her?"

"Maybe." The man shrugged.

Duncan pulled out a silver dollar and held it before the man's nose. "What might you like to tell us?"

The man reached to grab it, and Duncan pulled it back. "No' until I hear whether your information is worth anything."

The man eyed him. "I seen her yesterday, I did. She looked out of place. She kept watching a ship. Then she ran and got on it."

Duncan's heart stalled. "What did she look like?" The man's observation was hardly proof the woman he'd seen had actually been Charlotte.

"Purty little thing. Light color hair. Carried a brown leather bag, she did."

"That could be half the women in Charleston," Tavis said.

Duncan squatted down in front of the man. "Do you ken what ship she got on?"

"It was…now let me think here. I seen the ship before, a schooner, I'm thinking. Name was *The Scottish Girl.*"

Duncan's pulse began to race. "Was she alone?" He waved the coin in front of the man's face.

"Yep. Just her and her bag."

"That could still be half the women in Charleston," Tavis repeated.

Duncan flipped the coin to the man and stood, facing Tavis. "No' getting on my ship alone. It had to be Charlotte."

"Now what?"

"We let the others ken that the search is off—at least here. I'm going over to the telegraph office and have the man send a message to all the ports she's supposed to stop at. One of the missives will catch up with Captain Maher. You can go down to *The Moor* and have them prepare to set sail. Then I'll go home and get into dry clothes before heading oot. I want to speak with Captain Gilbert before he sails."

Tavis sidestepped one of the many puddles on the road and fell in beside Duncan as he strode back to his horse. "You should get some rest before you start out again."

"I would no' be able to sleep."

"And I wouldn't be a good friend if I didn't insist that you go home, get into some warm clothes, and get a couple hours' sleep before leaving. What is your profit if we get back to the docks before they're ready to sail?"

"The sooner I get on the road, the sooner I get to Savannah."

"Take the train to Savannah. It's faster."

"'Tis faster but doesn't leave for hours. I'll be in Savannah before the train."

Duncan took the horse's reins in his hand and climbed into the saddle. He was too tired to argue. "Where's your horse?"

"Over a few streets. I'll swing by my place and pick up some clothes and meet you on the road."

Duncan found the telegraph office and woke the man who lived above it. He ordered messages sent to all of *The Scottish Lass*'s port stops. When he finished and stepped outside, the lack of sleep hit him. Drained of energy, he climbed on his horse and started home. A few hours' sleep sounded good, but Charlotte held the only importance right now. He had to convince her that she had misconstrued the letter. It would take a miracle from God for her to forgive him this time. And well he knew that God didn't do anything good for him. What he got, he got on his own.

He was almost home when the thumping of horse hooves overtook him. He glanced over his shoulder and slowed Aberdeen to allow Tavis to catch up.

Tavis came alongside, his clothes dry and looking better than Duncan felt. Tavis grinned. "You sure are a sorry sight."

Duncan glared at him.

Tavis nodded his understanding. "You need to rest."

"Dinna be after me aboot that again. I'll no' give God more time to turn the lass against me."

"Whoa, there, friend. I haven't said much to you because I know how you feel about God, but I can't sit here and say nothing if you think you are in some kind of competition with the Almighty. This is not God exacting punishment for something."

"God has his favorites, and I'd no' be one of them. He'd no' be caring aboot my prayers *if* I had any."

Tavis rested his hands on the saddle horn. "God doesn't have favorites. Have you not heard the verse in Proverbs? 'The Lord is far from the wicked: but He heareth the prayer of the righteous.' 'Tis only a matter of if you are right with God."

Duncan snorted. "Sounds more like 'tis saying I'm wicked. And that is why God does no' hear me and why He takes the ones I love from me."

"Och! You twist the words in your anger. Peter speaks in Acts saying, 'Of a truth I perceive that God is no respecter of persons: But in every nation he that feareth Him, and worketh righteousness, is accepted with Him.' No respecter. Do you hear that?"

Duncan gritted his teeth and looked ahead. "It means nothing to me. *Righteous.* I keep hearing that word. I ken some of the Bible, and it says no mon is blameless. So these scriptures you recite only contradict others."

"You are wrong. We are righteous through Jesus Christ. Through His blood. 'Tis time you stop blaming God and get right with Him. Your bitterness has blinded you. You've spent all these years angry with Him and hurting when you could have called on Him and been blanketed in His peace."

"Are you saying if I had no' gotten angry with God, my brother would no' have died? Charlotte would no' have run from me?"

"Nay. You know better than that. I don't tell you that all will be rosy. Don't forget, I lost my brother as well. We live in a fallen world, but we have God to pray to, and He'll help us through."

"God does no' care."

Tavis heaved a heavy sigh. "You can't believe that. You say that out of your anger. Your wife doesn't feel that way. She loves the Lord."

They crested the hill, and Duncan looked upon home, then nudged Aberdeen to a trot. "Aye, she does. But He loves her. 'Tis easier to love when one is loved in return."

Tavis sighed again. "God loves you as much as He does her."

"God is guid to her, no' me. I dinna ken how you can say that."

"From where you stand, it may seem like that, but I can assure you that from where Charlotte sits, it doesn't seem so wonderful. You blackmailed her into a marriage she didn't want. Her father forced her to follow through. She discovered the man she wed married for other purposes, and I imagine she thinks you don't love her. And right now, she is on a ship sailing away from all the people she cares about. How pretty do you think that picture looks to her?"

Duncan pulled on the reins, and Aberdeen slowed his pace. "I'm sure no' too guid right now, but I hope to change that."

"That's not my point, Duncan. The fact is that good and bad things happen to all of us. It's all about how we handle those things. Do we blame God or call on God? I would be willing to bet Charlotte is praying right this minute. Two things I know about your wife are these, that she knows God and she prays."

"Then let's hope she does no' pray that I dinna find her."

Tavis let out a growl, then clamped his mouth shut. It was just as well because the conversation had worn itself out.

By the time they arrived at the stable, the men who had rode on ahead while he posted the telegrams had already changed into dry clothes and were finishing brushing down their mounts. Duncan jumped off his horse and led Aberdeen into a stall, then hustled to the house, leaving instructions for the extra care of his horse to a groom.

With Stuebing just returning as well, Duncan saw to his own clothes, then sat down by the fireplace, allowing the fire's warmth to seep into his aching body.

He hadn't planned to sleep, only to sit for a few minutes and rest his weary bones. The next thing he knew, hours had passed. He stomped down the stairs.

Tavis met him in the hall. "Did you have a good rest?"

Duncan walked past him.

Och! Why'd he let him sleep? He'd told him he wanted to get back on the road. Now two hours had passed. He needed to speak with Charlotte before she could talk herself into never letting him back in her life. He couldn't bear the thought of them being apart. She touched his life more than he realized. As the old saying went, her eyes were indeed the mirror to her soul. They twinkled when she teased, longed for him when he returned from a long day's work, and flamed with indignation when she was angry. Crevvens. He missed her.

What would his life be without her now that he had experienced the fullness of marriage with her? His life would be worthless—a drudgery. His gut knotted. He had to get her back. Stopping by the kitchen to grab something to eat, he took the time to throw some food in a small cloth bag, then went out the kitchen door into the side yard.

The click of heels on the flagstone sidewalk quickened. "You sure are ornery." Tavis strode behind him.

"I told you I did no' want to sleep."

"You needed your rest, my friend. I'm not going to stand by watching you kill yourself. I've worked too hard keeping you alive to let you put yourself into an early grave."

"What is that supposed to mean?"

Tavis swatted the air with his hand. "Nothing. Forget it. A few hours isn't going to make any difference. She'll be there when we arrive. You sent a telegram ahead. Trust the Lord to take care of the rest."

Duncan grunted. "I dinna have that kind of faith. I prefer to take care of things myself."

"You are a stubborn man, Duncan Mackenzie, but God can bring you to your knees if that's what it takes."

Duncan ignored Tavis's remark. He had too much to think about. *The Moor* should have docked and received the message they would be heading back out to sea. And by the time they got to his ship, the cargo should be off. He would check in with Captain Gilbert, then go to the telegraph office and see if Captain Maher had sent a return message. Message or not, he would be on his way within a few hours.

The autumn morning sun shone down, warming the air and drying the ground. Travel slowed in areas where the water had puddled and turned to mud. As they reached the south end of town, Duncan chose the crushed shell roads where they were easily navigated. Once they crossed over Calhoun, they made good time on the city's newly constructed brick roads.

They turned on Elliot Street and then crossed over East Bay, riding between the warehouses to get to the wharf where his ship was docked.

The Moor sat quietly in the water, crewman lounging around. Duncan strode up the wooden planks and onto the ship, where he was met by Captain Gilbert. Duncan glanced around the ship taking note of its readiness to sail. "Sorry aboot the change of plans. I ken your men were ready to spend the week on land. I'll make this trip worth their while. I'll meet you in Savannah at port."

The wind picked up, and Captain Gilbert tugged his black hat further down on his head. "Someone dropped this off for you." He reached in his pocket and pulled out a folded telegram and handed it to Duncan.

Duncan unfolded the paper.

Found wife aboard ship STOP Squall hit STOP Wife washed overboard STOP Searching Savannah area STOP Awaiting other instructions

Chapter 36

Charlotte dead? Duncan scanned the telegram, a second time, then looked up at Gilbert. "We go to Savannah and we leave now. Look for me when you arrive. As you travel, keep your eyes open for anything…" He choked. "Watch for my wife." He had to keep hope that she had somehow survived. He showed Tavis the missive, then stuffed it into his pocket. The two dashed off the schooner and retrieved their mounts. The captain began shouting orders, and sailors tossed the ropes from the ship, separating it from the dock.

Duncan swung up on Aberdeen. What had Charlotte been doing on deck during a storm, and why had Maher allowed it? When he got his hands on the man…but that was the least of his worries right now. Searching for his wife came first. What were the chances that he'd find her alive?

"Does the lass know how to swim?" Tavis interrupted his thoughts as he settled into the saddle.

"I dinna ken. But to be tossed into the sea in the midst of a tempest…" Duncan choked. "The weight of her sodden dress alone could pull her down. Then add the crashing of waves. Even a seasoned swimmer would be lucky to survive."

"But didn't you tell me that God watches over her? He favors her?"

"I ken what you are trying to do—give me hope. But I'm no fool. I begin to think I'm cursed." Duncan shoved his hand through his hair as the horses picked up speed.

"Och! You are not cursed," Tavis yelled as they moved along at a fast clip. "You are a man who let a boy's anger at God grow into blaming God for everything. The Lord has the lass in His hands, whether it be here on earth or in heaven. Do you think that if Charlotte is in heaven, standing in the glory of the Lord or walking the streets of gold, that she is sad? 'Tis yourself you feel sorry for. If God has called Charlotte home, she is rejoicing right now. If you want to be sure to see her again, then get right with God."

Duncan tried to block out Tavis's words and focus on his wife. How would he live with himself if something happened to her? He had to find her, had to hold her one more time.

♥♥♥

Charlotte burrowed down deeper under the covers. The chair beside her bed creaked, and she pulled the blanket down and peeked out. Wrinkles covered her rescuer's leather-like skin. Bushy white eyebrows furrowed over blue eyes that stared back at her.

The man rubbed his calloused hand over his whiskered chin, making a scratching sound. "How are you feeling?"

Charlotte tried to sit up, but pain shot through both her arms, and she collapsed back onto the bed. "Very sore."

"And I imagine you will be for a few days. You're lucky to be alive. That storm was fierce."

She jerked up and winced. "The ship." The room tilted as if she were still sailing. She gripped the sheets with both hands, waiting for the bed to right. "Did it go down?"

He cocked his head. "I didn't see anything like that. Only you and a board."

"How did you find me? What were you doing in the ocean in the middle of a storm?"

"I might ask you the same thing." He leaned forward. "As for me, the storm had passed when I went to fish early this morning. The sun hadn't yet come up, but I could see your dark outline as you washed up on shore. I carried you here. Don't you remember asking me my name?"

She nodded at the memory. *Titus.* That was all she remembered. She looked down at the thin gown she wore, and heat shot to her face. His facial features softened, and he seemed to read her thoughts.

"My wife put you in dry clothes and checked on you through the day. If you're up to eating, she's fixed you a light meal."

"What time is it?"

"It's after six."

"In the evening?" She'd slept the whole day away. "Where am I?"

"You're north of the mouth of the Savannah River." He pushed himself up from his chair and slowly straightened, placing his hands on his lower back. She couldn't help but wonder if the weight of carrying her had caused his pain. He stopped before exiting the room. "I'll tell the missus to bring you something to eat. Then we'll see about finding your family. I'm sure they're worried."

She forced a smile. "Yes. I need to contact my husband."

How would she explain her actions to Duncan? Her home was with him, and she had to return. Marriage was sacred, and God had never told her to leave. She'd done that on her own. Somewhere amidst thinking she would die, God impressed upon her to trust Him and to be strong. She'd been so busy trying to do what she wanted that she never stopped to listen to God. They could make their marriage work. She needed to be strong and tell Duncan how she felt when she didn't agree with him. With her decision to trust God in all areas of her life came an overwhelming sense of freedom. Her life was now in God's hands.

Titus's wife brought in fresh bread and a bowl of chicken soup and introduced herself. "Please call me Martha."

Charlotte ate a few bites of bread and a few swallows of soup. With all the salt water she'd swallowed, her stomach rebelled against the food. She handed the tray to Martha. The old woman glanced from the bowl to Charlotte, then felt her forehead.

"You're hot as coals." She turned and set the food on the bedside table. "Scoot back down and get some sleep. I'll be back in a minute." She disappeared from the room.

Charlotte lay down. The room spun. A moan escaped her lips. She closed her eyes and gave in to sleep.

When she awoke, the light from a candle illuminated the dark room. Martha sat beside her in a chair, wiping a damp cloth across her forehead and crooning a prayer. Charlotte's eyes drooped and she fought to keep them open. The exhaustion won and she gave in to a fitful sleep.

♥♥♥

Midafternoon brought a stiff wind off the ocean to the Savannah River. Duncan refused to give up. He rode alone along the shore while Tavis set off in the opposite direction, searching along the beach. Duncan worked his way toward the docks and *The Scottish Lass,* for he couldn't waste any time. Hopefully this was unnecessary and upon finding the captain, he would learn the man had found his wife.

He'd scour all the shores of Georgia looking for Charlotte if he had to. He'd search every town along its coast. Returning to Charleston without his wife wasn't an option for him.

Every log or piece of debris that had drifted ashore tightened Duncan's gut into a knot. He'd spot driftwood or rocks in the distance, spur Aberdeen to them, wanting to find her, but fearful it *was* her. As the light faded, Duncan looked over the vast ocean and the endless shoreline. How would he ever find her? Not wanting to waste a second of light, he quickened the pace.

When darkness finally stole the light and surrounded him, he glanced at the moon over the choppy waters to lay eyes on *The Scottish Lass.* He'd know her anywhere.

Hoof falls on sand told him Tavis had returned as well.

"Perhaps Maher has guid news," Duncan said hopefully.

Tavis gave a low whistle. "I hope its good news, for his sake."

Reflections from the ship's lanterns danced on the ocean waves, sparkling like diamonds on a black velvet cloth. Usually the beauty of it would mesmerize him, but tonight it was only a reminder that he had never shared it with Charlotte. And now that beguiling beauty could well have swallowed up the greatest love of his life.

Maher sailed the ship toward the docks, and Tavis and Duncan headed that way as well. "'Tis an overwhelming feeling to ken Charlotte could be anywhere. When I look around me, both on shore and sea, my gut twists like I have never known. 'Tis so much I need to say to my wife. So much forgiveness I need to ask."

Tavis listened and didn't preach to him this night, for which Duncan was glad. His heart was heavy, and he had so many regrets. If he'd not forced her into marriage, she would be home, safe with her family right now. The knot in his gut tightened, and he almost wished Tavis would rail at him. He deserved it. He'd had everything he wanted growing up. Things came easy to him, success, friends, women. He shook his head and sniffed. He was spoiled. And he couldn't take no for an answer, and look what it had gotten him. If God would just this once hear his prayer and spare his wife, he'd promise to be a better husband, to treat her fairly.

Upon reaching the ship, they climbed aboard *The Scottish Lass,* where the undertone of hushed voices didn't bode well. Captain Maher greeted them.

"Have you found her?" Looking at Maher's troubled expression, he hoped they hadn't. At least then there would still be a chance.

"I put every able body on this shore. We searched miles in both directions from where she swept off the ship. I'm sorry, but we've come up empty. I went on into Savannah and have some of the men asking people if they've heard of anyone washing ashore."

"We go back oot in the morning before the sun rises." Duncan shoved his hand through his hair and looked toward land.

Tavis rubbed his shoulder. "Come now Duncan, if they've already searched for miles…"

"It can no' hurt to go over the shore one more time. Maybe they missed something." Duncan turned to Maher. "I want to speak to you in your cabin."

Maher nodded and started toward it. Tavis fell into step. "Mind if I come along?"

He didn't answer, and Tavis followed. As soon as they entered the room, Duncan slammed the door and swung around. "I want to hear every word of how this happened."

By the time Captain Maher had finished his story, Duncan's anger had dissolved. He'd been angry with Maher, blaming him for Charlotte's disappearance like he blamed God for everything that went wrong in his life. Maher wasn't at fault. If anyone was guilty, it was he. None of this would have happened had he been honest with her from the beginning.

Duncan walked out into the night air. He gazed over the ocean and land. Such an impossible task, searching every inch of it. Yet how could he not? If only he had God's vision and could see where to go. The night sky, twinkling stars, and glimmering full moon bragged of His greatness. In contrast, Duncan suddenly felt insignificant.

Tavis stepped up behind him. "A penny for your thoughts."

"They are no' worth that much." Duncan leaned against the railing, appreciating the calming effect of water lapping at the sides of the ship.

"They are to me, my friend." Tavis slapped his hand on Duncan's shoulder and squeezed. "Now, what's going through that head of yours?"

"When I look up at the endless universe, I realize why God has no time for me. I am but what? A piece of dust in this world He has created. Then I look upon the ocean as it stretches along the shore as far as the eye can see, and I waver in my belief that I will find my wife. I am helpless, and I have nowhere to turn."

Tavis smiled. "Don't you know that when you finally reach the end, when you come to the point where you can't do it yourself, that is when you free God to work? You have to surrender yourself to Him in order for Him to be able to do a good work in you. I know God has been calling you, and you have been too stubborn to answer."

"I dinna think I can find her myself. But I'm no' sure I believe He will help me. I do ken that with Charlotte gone I feel empty."

"I can't promise you the Lord will give Charlotte back."

Duncan tightened his hands on the rail. "Then why would I want to surrender my will to Him?"

A sharp wind blew across the ship, and Tavis tugged his coat lapels together. "Because if you do, He will help you get through whatever happens."

"I want her back. If I kent He would give her back to me…"

"You can't go to Him on a bargain. You have to come to Him because you know you need Him. We all have sinned. You've spent all these years blaming God for everything. No one is immune to unhappiness. Only God can fill the emptiness you are feeling. Finding Charlotte won't do it, though it may seem to temporarily."

Duncan wiped his hand down his face. "I have never felt so helpless."

"Go to the foot of the cross, my friend." Tavis turned away from the railing. "I'll leave you and the Lord to work things out."

What exactly did one say to God when you hadn't spoken to Him for over a dozen years?

Duncan stared over the endless waves. "God, it is Duncan here. After not speaking to You for so long and blaming You for all the things that have gone wrong in my life, I'm no' sure You really want to hear from me, but Tavis assures me You do. I ken I have done so much wrong in my life. I have tried to do all things by myself, and I dinna take nay for an answer, like when I forced Charlotte to marry me. I judged Sorrel, but the truth is, my behavior was nay better than his. I trusted only in myself, believing I was in control. I've sought pleasure to fill this emptiness inside me and found it only to be temporary. I need Your forgiveness for all I've done wrong, for all the times I have disappointed You. Lord, I need the peace that Tavis speaks of, the peace that will get me through if You have taken my beautiful wife home. I dinna ken why you would allow Your Son to die for someone like me, but I put my trust in Him and ask that I will see Charlotte again either here on earth or in Heaven."

The moonlight glistened on the water peaks. Duncan didn't feel a lot different, but what he did feel was peace. The knot in his gut dissolved and though he feared he'd never see Charlotte again, he knew God was in control and he could trust Him.

♥♥♥

The dark abyss pulled Charlotte down. She looked up and tried to swim to the light, but with each stroke, she tired more. She couldn't breathe. The water pressed upon her chest, making it difficult to draw in air. The chill of the water sank deep into her bones, stealing her strength. She trembled. If she gave in, she'd never see the light. Summoning up the last of her energy, she used her arms and legs to free herself from the cold black chasm that held her.

Strong hands grasped her arms and legs. A melodic voice, a long way away, sang a song that she should know, but couldn't bring the words to mind. It calmed her. Heavy covers wrapped around her, returning her warmth. The darkness fled, and she returned to nothingness.

What was wrong with her? She couldn't open her eyes. The voices were back, whispering from far away, but she couldn't make out what they were saying. They sounded worried. Why couldn't she understand them? Hot. The room was hot. She wanted to wipe her brow, but her arms wouldn't cooperate. They were too heavy to lift.

Gentle hands and a cool cloth touched her forehead and passed over her cheeks, as if their owner had read her mind and given her a brief respite from the heat. The cloth disappeared. She burned. The room must be on fire. She must make herself get up—still, nothing obeyed. The hands came back with the cool cloth, bathing her skin. This time humming accompanied them. If only she could remember the song.

♥♥♥

Duncan stood on the dock overlooking the Savannah River. Two crews and four days of endless searching had turned up no sign of Charlotte. The clank of the hoisting-crane had stopped for the night. Ships sat at the dock waiting for morning and their loads of the precious white gold. The last of the year's cotton sat in piles heaped all along the waterfront, soon to be shipped all over the world. Captain Gilbert had secured a load on *The Moor* and had sailed early in the morning up the coast.

A week ago, he'd have been throwing people out of his way in his frantic search, but since the night Tavis had left him alone on the deck of *The Scottish Lass,* things had changed. He not only had surrendered to Jesus' lordship, he also had found some peace amidst the turmoil. He'd sent the men from both of his ships searching the shores, scouring the city, and talking to travelers. All for naught. He'd finally allowed Gilbert to take his crew and sail north.

Trusting the Lord certainly sounded much easier than accomplishing it. Tavis had told him he needed to give Charlotte to the Lord. And so he had. But now he found himself wanting to take her back. Not that it would help. He snorted. He was still doing everything he could to find her. *The Moor* had deadlines to keep. In a step of faith, he let her sail. God didn't need those crewmen to find Charlotte. But now that the ship traveled out to sea, taking many able-bodied searchers, he struggled with allowing them to go. He wanted to order them back.

The uncertainty of Charlotte's fate loomed as big as the fathomless ocean that had taken his beloved, and as big as the God who alone could restore her to him from the depths of the blue. His mind told him she was lost forever. Strong sailors rarely survived when tossed overboard amidst a storm. The chances of Charlotte surviving wearing a heavy sodden gown were not in his favor.

His chest constricted. He needed to put every thought into a plan for finding Charlotte, dead or alive. He never knew he could love so deeply. And he'd never said those three words to her. Such simple words, yet he chose not to say them. *God, please give me the chance to tell her.*

He had to get back to Charleston. *The Scottish Lass* also had deadlines to meet. Three more days. That's what he gave himself to find her.

Chapter 37

This must be what it was like to die of thirst. Charlotte tried to open her mouth, but it stuck together. Her parched tongue wouldn't run along her cracked lips. Why was she so thirsty? Her attempts to speak only came out a groan.

She opened her eyes. The fire's light flickered on the ceiling.

"You've decided to come back to us, have you?" A smallish woman with gray hair pulled back into a tight, low bun pushed herself up from an old rocker. A glass sat on the table, and she picked it up, lifting Charlotte's head and pressing the drink to her lips. Charlotte took deep gulps of the cool liquid.

The old woman tsked. "Slow down. I'm not going to take it from you."

Charlotte emptied the water. The woman laid Charlotte's head back down and went to a pitcher, where she refilled the glass and returned. "You can have more after you let that settle a bit."

"Do I know you?" Charlotte's voice came out raspy. She tried to clear the fog from her head, but it held on like the clouds in a storm.

The old woman chuckled. "No, I don't suppose you remember me. You were very sick and talking out of your head when you did come to. My name is Martha, and Titus is my husband."

Charlotte reached back into her memory. What did she remember? The letter for Duncan. Her heart sank. What else? She sailed aboard Duncan's ship. Then the storm. Nearly drowning. The old man rescuing her. She coughed, and fire burned within her chest. Yes, she remembered some, but the

recollection stopped there. "How long have I been here?" She
forced the words out.

The woman ticked days off on her fingers. "Seven days."
She chuckled. "And my husband will be glad you're doing
better. I wouldn't let him go to town for fear you'd need the
doctor and I'd have no way to send for him." She shook her
head. "I'm out of flour, and he misses his bread." She waddled
over to the door and called for Titus.

Blue eyes peeked around the frame, followed by a
checkerboard grin. "You're looking mighty purty this
morning."

Charlotte brought her hand to her hair and felt the mats. A
smile tickled her cracked lips at his kindhearted flattery.
"Thank you for rescuing me."

"No reason to thank me. I'm glad you're doing better. You
gave us quite a scare."

"I'm sorry I've been such a burden." Her words were a
struggle to get out. If she'd been here a full week, she'd
already been a huge inconvenience for this couple. But she
needed to get word to Duncan. She'd pay them for their
kindness as soon as she returned home. "Would you—" She
ran her already parched tongue over her sore lips. "—be going
to town today, by chance?"

"He'll be going in now that we know you're going to be
fine. I'll bet you want to let someone know you're here."
Martha shuffled over to the bed and patted Charlotte's
shoulder.

"Yes, ma'am. My husband must be—" What would he be?
"Wondering where I am." She hoped he was concerned and
that he didn't find her disappearance a relief. After the letter
she'd read and the way she fled, she wasn't too certain.

Martha frowned. "I'll go get something for you to write
on. Titus doesn't have that good of a memory anymore. He's
liable to get there and forget half of what you tell him." She
walked away grumbling. "I would hope that husband of yours
is more than wondering where you're at. He should have
worried himself sick by now. If he hasn't, then he…" Charlotte

strained to hear the rest of Martha's complaints against Duncan but could make no more out of her murmuring. The old woman's concern warmed her.

She returned and Charlotte took the paper, pencil, and a flat board to write on. What should she say? She rolled the pencil between her fingers. "Where am I?"

"You're in Savannah, sweetie."

Charlotte glanced down at the paper. She'd keep it simple.

> *I'm in Savannah. No money. Please advise.*
>
> > *Sincerely,*
> > *Charlotte*

❤❤❤

Duncan stood on deck praying. He had to get the ship back and his affairs at home in order—he'd left in a hurry. His heart ripped apart with the tug-of-war going on inside him. He longed to stay and search for Charlotte, but he had to think about the crew. He couldn't think of this as abandoning her.

He turned his back on the dock as the sailors pulled up the planks to depart. He'd return as quickly as possible to continue the search. He strode toward his quarters. He didn't want to see Savannah fade from view along with his hope for finding his wife.

"Stop! Wait!"

Duncan swung around as a middle-aged man half-ran, half-limped down the dock, waving his arms above his head.

Captain Maher stepped over. "That's the telegrapher. I recognize him from when I sent you the missive."

What now? He didn't need any more problems. Especially with his other ship. When the man reached where they docked, he bent over, bracing his hands on his thighs, and gasped for breath.

"I hope it isn't bad news." Tavis stepped next to Duncan and Captain Maher.

"Aye, my mind went down the same track." Duncan moved to the rail. "What can I help you with?"

The man straightened up, still panting. "I have a..." He gulped more air. "...message for Duncan Mackenzie."

"I figured as much. Who sent the missive?" He prayed it wasn't something that would require him to stay home longer than he'd planned.

"'Tis from...a Miss Charlotte."

Duncan's knees nearly gave out. He grasped the railing as weakness swept through his body. "Are you sure?"

"Yes sir. It's written right here." He waved the paper in the air.

The wooden boards were thrown back down, and Duncan dashed to the dock. He snatched the paper from the telegrapher's hand and read the nine words.

Praise be to God. *He kept her safe.* "Do you ken who brought this?" The note was in Charlotte's handwriting.

He shook his head. "I didn't take the message. I had stepped out when it came, but my wife will have that information back at the office."

"Lead the way." Duncan fell in step beside the telegrapher. "'Tis thankful I am that when Captain Maher sent me the first message, he told you what had happened. Otherwise you'd no' have known to come here, and the message would have ended up in Charleston. I'd have arrived home before I learned she is alive."

"Yes, sir. Someone is looking after you."

By the time they got the sender's name and directions on where to go and had rented a carriage, Tavis had caught up with him, and Duncan had already said a half-dozen prayers, thanking the Lord for Charlotte's life. Over an hour after leaving the ship, they finally arrived at a cottage surrounded by flower gardens and a neatly kept yard. Too anxious to wait, Duncan launched himself out of the moving carriage and dashed up the steps. He gave three sharp raps and waited. The door creaked open, and a weathered old man peeked out. "Can I help you?"

"I'm Duncan Mackenzie. I believe my wife is here?" He attempted to tamp down the anxiety in his voice, but there was no help for it. He had tried to have faith, but it waxed and waned like a seafarer's moon. Thank the Lord, doubting didn't keep Him from answering his prayer.

"Come in." The old man opened the door wide and led him down a short hall to a door. When he looked in the room, his breath caught in his throat. Charlotte sat in a wooden rocker, struggling to catch her breath. Duncan glanced from the unmade bed to where she sat—a distance of not more than four feet. She lifted her head and smiled. His heart clenched. She'd lost weight. Her beautiful glistening eyes, now cloudy, had sunk into a gaunt face. Her smile, revealing bloody, cracked lips, gave welcome but tore at his very soul as he moved toward her.

He fell to one knee in front of her. "You are a bonnie sight, lass." His eyes drank in her presence. He wanted to say so much more. Tavis stood inside the door with the old man. Arms crossed and eyes narrowed, an elderly woman stood by the bed. She didn't appear any too happy to see him. What had Charlotte said to them? It mattered not. What was important was that she was alive. He would make things right when he got her home. "How are you?"

She took a swallow from the glass sitting on the bedside table, wetting her dry lips. "I'm doing well." She glanced from the man to the woman. "Titus and Martha saved my life." Murmurs of disagreement came from both sides of the room. Charlotte looked to them with fondness. "You know it's true. I owe you my life."

She snapped her attention back to Duncan. "And I owe them for the telegram they sent you." She leaned forward and whispered. "It'd be nice to give them some money for taking care of me, too."

Duncan nodded. "Dinna fash yourself with it. I'll see they are graciously compensated. I am forever in their debt."

"How did you arrive here so quickly? Titus sent—" She stopped. "Have you been introduced to my rescuers?"

"No' formally."

Charlotte introduced the couple to Tavis and Duncan.

Martha stood stiff as a soldier. "How *did* you get here so quickly?" She glared at Duncan.

He set his gaze on Charlotte. "I have been searching a week for you. Two of my ships were here, and I put the crews of both to work seeking your whereaboots."

Charlotte's eyes lit up.

"We searched every inch of shoreline and river edge for miles. When we had exhausted that route, we went to town and began asking questions. No one had heard of a lass washing ashore. *The Moor* sailed three days ago, and I was aboard *The Scottish Lass* preparing to leave when I got your telegram."

He had said something to disappoint her, for her shoulders dropped, and she lowered her head.

"You were leaving then. I guess I should be thankful that Titus caught you before you had to waste a second trip."

"Och! Lass, I was no' giving up. I had left in such a rush, I needed to return for a few days to take care of things, and then I planned to return and resume the search. I had determined I would no' give up till I found you."

Her smile returned, though uncertain. "I'm glad you found me. I'm ready to go home." She quickly glanced at her hosts. "Please forgive me. You've been more than wonderful to me. I just want to go home and see my family."

Martha swatted the air. "Think nothing of it. I would be anxious to be home too if I had spent a week away and lain on my deathbed." She eyed Duncan, relaxing her stance.

"Deathbed?" Duncan tensed.

The old woman nodded. "She was a sick woman—ran a ferocious fever."

"Are you able to travel, love?" Duncan tucked the stray hairs behind her ear. Oh, how much he missed doing that.

"Not that you're asking, but I think she needs to stay here and recuperate. Her fever broke this morning." Martha sniffed and folded her arms in front of her. Her gaze met Charlotte's and softened. "Sorry, child. I know you want to get home, but I worry for your health."

Duncan wanted to snatch Charlotte up and leave. "'Tis up to you, love. If you need to stay a few more days, we'll stay."

"You'll stay too? What of the matters at home?" Her tone was uncertain.

He smiled. "Aye, I'll stay. I'm no' letting you oot of my sight. You need no' fash yourself aboot anything but getting weel."

A smile wavered on her lips. "I'm well enough, but I'll need help to the carriage."

With no belongings to gather, Duncan paid the couple what he had on him and promised to send a fisherman's wages for a year—despite their hearty protests. It was the least he could do for their kindness. He thanked them again, and he and Charlotte were on their way. Charlotte slept through the carriage ride. He carried her aboard ship and tucked her into bed in his cabin without her waking.

Tavis checked on their horses while he sat in a chair and guarded over her as she slept. Her breaths were broken occasionally by coughs, which sent him to the edge of the bed wanting to do something for her. Each time she settled back down, not once opening her eyes.

Never had he wanted so much to wrap her in his arms and hold her tightly to him, but he contented himself with watching. Heaven only knew how much he loved her. The hours ticked away as he watched over her. Halfway through the journey to Charleston, he moved over to the edge of her bed and felt her forehead. No fever, thank the Lord. The illness and ordeal must have exhausted her.

Her eyes flickered open. She shivered. "It's cold in here." Her gaze swept the small room.

Duncan stretched out beside her and encompassed her in his arms. He kissed her forehead and tugged the covers over them. "That better?"

Charlotte nodded, snuggling against his chest. "Much."

"We need to talk, love. There is much I would ken and much to tell."

"Can it wait? I'm so tired." Her eyes fluttered shut.

"Aye, it can wait." He stroked the back of her hair. "You just get weel right now. We have the rest of our lives." He hoped she felt the same way when he told her all of his secrets.

Chapter 38

Flora snuggled up next to Charlotte, demanding every bit of her attention as she sat in bed with pillows propped behind her back. The early morning sun streamed through the unshuttered window. Duncan wouldn't allow her to leave the room for anything other than necessities. She'd slept through the entire trip. Upon arriving home, she ate a bowl of chicken soup at Duncan's insistence and went back to sleep. Vivian stood guard to be sure she obeyed her husband's order.

"I'm really feeling much better today. What I need is to get up and stretch my legs."

"I'm sorry, but I have my orders. Mr. Mackenzie warned me I was not to give in to your pleas." Vivian's eyes implored Charlotte's understanding.

Charlotte smiled. "He is a commanding man, is he not?"

Vivian giggled. "That's to be sure, ma'am."

"Is he with Tavis?"

"Yes, ma'am."

"How much longer did he say he'd be? I grow weary of waiting when I'm allowed to do nothing but lounge around." Charlotte brushed the hair away from her face and clasped her hands in her lap.

"Shortly, I'm sure. He told me as soon as you awaken and have eaten to send for him, which I have."

"And have you eaten, lass?" Duncan stood in the doorway, broad shoulders filling the frame. His brow rose toward his wind-blown hair, and he folded his arms in front of him.

"I have, if you must know." She smiled and winced. Picking up the handkerchief next to her, she dabbed at the blood on her lips.

Duncan rushed forward. "Your lips—" He took the cloth from her and dipped it in the glass of water beside the bed and applied it to her sores. Without turning his attention away, he spoke to Vivian. "Go and find some ointment."

Vivian curtseyed and left the room.

"I'm fine, Duncan. Really. I'm much improved from even yesterday."

"And I will have you back to your healthy self. How do you feel?"

Charlotte's cheeks burned. She'd seen her reflection in the mirror. With no bath in over a week, her hair a mess, and the loss of weight made her look like an unkempt orphan. Of course he didn't think she was healthy. "I'm doing well. What I need is a nice hot bath."

"Then you shall have it." He went to the hallway and gave some orders and returned to her bedside. Vivian followed him into the room and handed him the jar of petroleum jelly.

Duncan dipped his finger in the ointment and gently rubbed it on her lips, leaving them tingling from his touch.

Flora nudged her way between them, her tail wagging vigorously.

"Och! What is this ball of fur doing on our bed? Did I no' say a dog's place in on the floor, no' in my bed?"

Charlotte pulled Flora to her chest. "Shh. You'll hurt her feelings. She could barely contain herself when she saw me, and she won't leave my side now. Surely you wouldn't deny her or me that comfort."

As if on cue, Flora turned to Duncan and barked.

Duncan shook his head. "Lass, I could no' deny you anything that would give you comfort." He sighed. "But I do hope I will no' have to share my bed with the critter tonight."

Charlotte grinned. Awaiting her bath to be drawn, she hoped he would bring up the discussion he had wanted to have with her. But the bath was soon prepared, and he carried her to it.

Vivian saw to her bathing. Once she was dried and dressed, the lady's maid called in Duncan. He scooped her up again.

"Duncan, I am not an invalid. I'm quite capable of walking."

"You fit nicely right where you are. Let a mon redeem himself, will you?" He sat her on the bed.

She scooted back against the headboard where Flora once again snuggled in tightly. "Do you feel better now that you have proven your strength?"

Duncan grinned. "Och! It was just an excuse to carry you." His smile faded as fast as it had appeared on his face.

"Is something wrong?"

"Nay. I was just thinking how much I missed you and your sweet nature. We have been through much in our short marriage."

Charlotte held her breath, knowing what would come. The conversation needed to happen, but she wasn't sure she was ready for it or sure what would happen because of it. "I'm sure every marriage has its challenging times. Ours just came early."

Duncan took her hand. Deep jade eyes stared back at her. Two small creases formed between his brows. "We must talk aboot those things. There is much I wish to explain to you."

His eyes held a vulnerability she'd never seen before. His strong jaw relaxed, and his self-assurance fell to the wayside. Her heart fluttered. Would God mend their marriage and make it whole again? Something was different about him, but so much had passed—so many deceptions, lies, and secrets. She sent up a silent prayer. *Help me to be more like you, Lord. Help me to forgive with my heart, not just my words.* "I'm listening."

"I would like to say first that what I told you before was all true. The reason I paid a few men to dance with you, as well as the reason I tricked you into marrying me. But it was that which I lacked that drew me to you. You dinna hide behind falsehoods, pretending to be something you were no'. Your determination and fire made me want you more. I did all I ken to get your attention, but alas, everything I did seemed to push you further away from me and into Sorrell's arms. I was at my wit's end when the idea of hiding the pin in your bag came to me. I ken it was wrong to blackmail you into marriage."

"Are you saying you're sorry?" An apology was all well and good, but actions always said so much more. There were transgressions more than these she wanted answers to.

"Aye. I am sorry, lass, for how I went aboot it, no' for the results."

As her insides quivered, Charlotte lifted her chin. "And what of..." Her mind fought through the tangled web of words.

Duncan came to her rescue. He slid his hand under her chin and captured her gaze. "The letter?"

Charlotte nodded.

"'Tis true. I'm here on a mission in search of a traitor—a mon who betrayed no' only my country and our soldiers, but my brother as well. The queen kens my family and understood that the death of my brother would drive me as much as love for my country. I dinna boast when I tell you I am verra guid at what I do."

His thumb began to caress her cheek interrupting her concentration. "Have you found this man?" No, that wasn't what she wanted to know. Was he going to leave her and return to Scotland—could he tell her that?

"Nay, but I have been distracted by our problems. Something I usually would no' allow to happen."

"And when you do find him, you will return to Scotland?" She lifted her chin a little more, even though he continued to hold and stroke it. She wouldn't let him know how much his touch affected her.

Duncan let his hand fall. "That is the plan. I must bring him home to face charges."

She felt the loss as soon as his touch left. So nothing had changed. But why should she think it had? Didn't the letter imply that his mistress awaited him with open arms, regardless of his marriage?

"And what did you plan to do with me?" The thought suddenly hit her. Mayhap he had searched for her so diligently only because of guilt or worse, to have proof she had died, thus freeing him.

"I hoped you would return with me, lass. You are my wife."

Charlotte felt less and less forgiving. He would tear her away from her family, her sisters, Nellie? To a place she had never been and where she knew not a soul? And for what? So she could compete with another woman? The idea didn't sound at all enticing. "Why would you desire to bring me along? It surely isn't because of religious conviction. I see you have none of that." Was that a wince she saw? Surely not. He'd hardly spoken of God since they'd married.

"Nay, I would no' have taken you to be my wife had I no' wanted you. I wish you to sail to my beloved homeland with me."

How could he suggest such a thing? She would live the rest of her life alone before she'd allow him to flaunt another woman over her. She shook her head. "No, I'm not willing to share my husband with another woman."

His brows furrowed, and he seemed to search her face. "Another woman?"

Oh, the nerve of him. Did he think she missed all those endearing words? "Let me refresh your memory. *My Dearest Duncan, I miss you greatly. Always Yours, Ailsa.*"

A smile quivered on the corner of his mouth. He looked as if he fought it. How could he find that so funny? Heat shot through her, and she pursed her lips despite the pain.

Duncan burst out laughing. "You are jealous."

She narrowed her eyes. "No. I'm just not going to share a husband. *Any* husband."

"Say it. You are jealous. I can see it on your face." He chuckled again.

She sat unflinching, her anger growing.

Duncan's smile faded. "Och, lass. Sorry I am. I should no' tease you, but happy I am to see you care enough for me to be jealous. Ailsa is my baby sister. She has much the same spirit as me, and we have been verra close since she learned to walk."

Relief and a bit of chagrin swept over her. "Your sister?"

"Aye, my sister. So will you come home with me? That is, after I have found the traitor I seek?"

He didn't have a lover. He wanted her to go with him. What of her sisters? They were the reason she'd married. Who would be here to see that they didn't have to marry someone they didn't love or help them reach their dreams? But as a wife, God called her to go with her husband. Oh, Lord have mercy on her. How could she say yes? How could she say no? "I have a request before I make my decision. Will you consider it?"

"If it will ease your mind."

"I don't wish for my sisters to be forced into loveless marriages or be denied a fulfilling career, if that is what they wish. I would ask that, should they need money, being a reasonable amount, of course, I could send it."

Duncan nodded.

"And if they need me for something I deem necessary, I would be allowed to come to them."

He stopped nodding and rubbed the side of his jaw. "I dinna mind helping your sisters should they need money. I can no' say the same for sailing back across the sea. I would have to agree that it is necessary and important enough to take such a long journey."

Charlotte frowned.

"I could deceive you, lass, and say aye. But I'll be doing no more of that. I have gotten my life right with God, and I'll no' be saying things to get my way. His will should be in this one way or another."

Did she hear him right? Did she dare believe? "Did you say *His will?*"

He nodded.

She threw her arms around him, nearly knocking him off balance and the edge of the bed. "I knew there was something different about you."

Duncan wrapped his arms around her. "Aye. When I thought I had lost you—" He choked.

She leaned back, tears streaming down her face. "You could not have said anything that would make me happier." She brushed her cracked lips lightly over his soft ones.

"If I'd have known it made you this happy, I would have told you that first." They both laughed. "Does that mean you will come with me?"

Charlotte swallowed, knowing what she was sacrificing. Aching to think she might not see her family for a very long time. But he was her husband and a Christian and had told her many times he cared for her. If he only loved her, it would make it so much easier. "Yes, Duncan. I'll go."

Chapter 39

"You have made me a verra happy mon." Duncan thought to pinch himself to see if he was dreaming. She had agreed to go home to Scotland with him. Her lips turned up in a smile. He gazed into her large eyes, where, despite her smile, sadness lingered. Once she saw his Scotland, she'd love it as much as he did. How could she resist the heather that spread across the hillsides or the castles that overlooked the sea?

His family would adore her, though she would never believe that after Ailsa claimed to feel pity for him marrying an American. When he got his hands on that little imp of a sister, he would give her a good thrashing. He'd always told her to watch her tongue or it would get her into trouble. And wasn't he right? She now had a sister-in-law to win over. But she would do it. She had a way of winning hearts. She and Charlotte would end up best of friends.

"How long do you think it will take to catch this man you search for?"

"No' long. I'll double my efforts. Tavis and I have made great strides in flushing him oot. I'm verra thankful that we ran into each other. He has been a blessing. I see now how the Lord's hand has been upon our friendship all along."

Charlotte leaned back against the pillows and smiled. "How will you two find the traitor? Do you know him?"

Duncan rose and walked to the window and glanced out. "Nay. I dinna ken him, but I have been trained in this, and he is no' the first mon I have had to smoke oot."

"Then you know his name?" Charlotte sat on the bed with a puzzled look.

"Nay, I ken no' his name, either. But I'm close to finding him. He kens it, too."

"And how is it you're so sure of this?"

"That's why he has sent me warnings. He used your attempted kidnapping as a ploy. He kens whether he succeeded in taking you or no' I would get the message. No' to mention the missive he had delivered." Duncan regretted mentioning the note as soon as the words left his lips. Charlotte didn't know about that threat. He wished he hadn't told her.

Her brows rose. "Message? What did it say?"

"Telling me to leave be. But I canno' do that. I dinna understand why he stays in this city when he kens that I am hot on his trail, but it matters no' why. He makes my job easier by it. I will find him, and I will bring him to justice, this scarred traitor."

"Scarred?"

"'Tis one of the few things I ken of him. He is scarred, and he has a cross with a thistle tattooed on his right upper arm."

Charlotte gasped and the color drained from her face.

Charlotte's head spun. Surely she heard wrong. Duncan and Mr. Ferguson were friends. Yes, it was her imagination running away from her. Probably from the sickness and exhaustion. A few days ago, he'd spent a week with Mr. Ferguson on a ship. If a tattoo was what he looked for, he would have seen it.

Duncan sat down on the bed and framed her face in his hands. "What's wrong, lass? Are you feeling ill?"

Charlotte shook herself. "I thought you said the traitor had a cross tattoo on his arm." She tried to give a short laugh.

"Why would that disturb you? 'Tis indeed what I said."

Her heart galloped. What were the chances of two men having a cross tattooed on their upper arm and having a scar? Not likely.

"I ken you weel enough to see something is amiss. What troubles you?"

Charlotte's voice trembled. "Duncan, I'm sorry."

"Sweeting, dinna be upset. You have nothing to be sorry for." He ran his thumb over her cheek.

"But I'm sorry for what I have to tell you." She drew in a shaky breath.

"Och! You can say nothing to change the way I feel aboot you. Now tell me what it is."

"The day that I was nearly kidnapped. It happened that day."

"What happened." His voice came out low, and he caressed her cheek. It gave her the courage to continue.

"I was on my way to my room, and I had my scissors in my hand. As I passed the room Mr. Ferguson stayed in, I thought to check and see if his bedding had been changed. It had, and I left the room. Later when I needed my scissors I tried to remember where I had put them. Then I recalled going into his room, so I hurried back. The door stood ajar and I pushed on the door and walked in, thinking he had gone to town. I didn't think to knock. I should have." Her cheeks burned as she remembered seeing the man shirtless. "He dressed in the room, and when I burst in, he swung around, with his shirt off."

Duncan's thumb ceased moving.

"I-I left right away, terribly embarrassed, and not wanting anyone to know how I'd foolishly entered without knocking."

"Tell me love, what did you see?"

Charlotte swallowed the lump in her throat. "I saw a cross with a thistle tattooed on his arm."

♥♥♥

"Was the thistle on his upper arm?" Duncan asked.

"Yes."

"Did you see a bullet wound to his shoulder?"

"No. But I was so embarrassed I quickly looked down and backed out of the room."

"Weel, there are many men who wear a similar tattoo. The scar is what will give my traitor away." Duncan didn't want her to worry.

"But what if it is him? He may be dangerous."

"Nay, if it were him and he wished to harm me, he had many a chance." He'd look into it.

Charlotte shook her head fretfully. "You're a threat to him now. You weren't before."

"Lass, you think too much." This wife of his would not be one he could sneak things by. "I'll be verra careful." Duncan leaned over and brushed his lips across hers.

He got up and strode across the room, pulled the door open, and bellowed for Vivian. She appeared before him and curtseyed. He ushered her into the room. "Keep my wife to bed. I dinna want her up for anything until I return." He stepped into the hall and turned back. "Even if you must sit on her." He closed the door on Charlotte's gasp.

He hadn't made it to the stairs when Stuebing rounded the corner. "How is the missus, sir?"

"Improving."

"Ah, glad to hear sir. For an American, she has rather grown on me."

Duncan stared at his stuffed-shirt valet. "Dinna let anyone in or oot of this room until I return, and I mean *anyone*."

Stuebing drew his shoulders back. "As you say, sir."

"And, Stuebing, thank you for coming with me that rainy night she disappeared."

"It was my honor, sir."

Frustrated, Duncan went outside to get some fresh air. His traitor was a hair's breadth away. He could feel it. Walking away from the house, he startled one of the kittens, and it ran for the barn. Duncan kept walking. How did the traitor stay ahead of him the whole way? It was as if he was privy to Duncan's information.

But that was impossible. He'd kept most everyone in the dark, aside from Tavis and Stuebing. Duncan didn't like where his thoughts were going. Stuebing had been with him since he was nearly a boy. He could rule his valet out of the running. The man might be stealthy, but he was not a traitor to his country.

What did he really know about Tavis? He grew up a child of missionaries and traveled to many countries. Other than that, they had shown up in the States around the same time. But Tavis was his friend.

Friend or not, Tavis might not have the loyalty to Scotland like he had. The man had grown up all over the world with missionary parents. His frequent gesture of rubbing his shoulder flitted through his mind. He'd said he'd taken a fall from his horse, but perhaps it was a bullet wound that ailed him.

Duncan stopped at the spot where Charlotte had almost been abducted. He closed his eyes, trying to remember anything about the man. The morning sun rose in the sky, sending away the early chill. Duncan breathed in the fresh air. It had been too dark to see anything that night. And when they had searched the woods the following morning, they found nothing of significance. He glanced at the woods, wishing for another chance to catch the perpetrator.

He spun around and marched back toward the house. A colorful glint caught his eye. Duncan walked over to it, thinking Charlotte had lost one of her trinkets. Reaching down, he saw it wasn't anything of his wife's, but a knife. Snatching it up he ran his hand over the jeweled handle. A memory flashed through his mind—Ferguson had closed his jacket, and Duncan eyed the knife tucked beneath this belt. Ferguson must have dropped it while helping them search the woods for the traitor. Duncan continued toward the house.

His feet froze on the ground. Ferguson wasn't there to help with the search.

Chapter 40

So how did he lose his knife? What did he know about the man? He'd lost his family. His sister had to stay in Scotland while he came to America to make a living. He hadn't been here long. Duncan ran his fingers over the colorful handle, then gently ran his thumb across the curved blade. A blade that could nicely slice a man's throat. Hadn't Ferguson ridden up shortly after they had found the body in the abandoned building? And hadn't Duncan distrusted him from the beginning? He did the one thing he knew never to do. He'd allowed himself to be distracted. Distracted by his desire for Charlotte.

He hurried back to the house. After leaving specific instructions with Stuebing that Alan Ferguson was not to be allowed in the house, he found Tavis and they headed for Ferguson's. When they reached his residence, Duncan knocked on the door. Ferguson answered.

The looks on their faces must have warned Ferguson, because he turned to run. Duncan pulled out his pistol. "Dinna think aboot running. I will use this if I have to."

Ferguson turned back around. His shoulders fell.

Duncan narrowed his eyes. "Why? Why did you do it?"

He shook his head. "I never meant for all those men to die. My father was accused of selling information to Afghanistan, and though there was no proof, he still lost his job. He spent all his money trying to prove his innocence. He couldn't live with the scorn and accusations, so he took his life. My mother grieved herself to death months later."

Duncan nodded. "Go on."

"Shortly after my parents died, I was approached by a man who claimed he could prove my father's innocence. I needed to give him information about the troops. I never knew they were going to massacre them in a surprise attack."

"You ken that your actions took my brother's and Tavis's brother's lives?"

"Aye, I ken. And it has grieved me. I pledge to you I dinna ken their evil plans."

Duncan shoved the gun back in his jacket. "I wish I could believe you. But after you've killed two innocent people here in America to cover your tracks, I am forced to question your motives."

Ferguson's eyes grew wide. "I dinna kill no one."

Ferguson came with them without a fight. He was locked in one of the guest bedrooms under guard and waiting to be returned to Scotland. He truly appeared to be grieved by the devastation his actions had caused. But Duncan still had to return the man to his accusers.

Tavis sat beside Duncan, and the two stared into the flickering flames in the fireplace.

"I never would have thought Ferguson was the man we searched for." Tavis stretched his long legs in front of him and crossed his ankles.

"Weel, I dinna at first either. I ken there were things aboot the mon that troubled me, but I was no' able to put a finger on it. At one point I even considered you and Stuebing."

"Me?" Tavis's brows drew down to form a *V*.

"Aye. You kept rubbing that shoulder, and I began to think that you hid a gunshot wound. You did show up here around the same time as me."

"I told you I fell from my horse. If I was going to make up a lie to cover myself, I'd not have picked such a humiliating one."

Duncan chuckled. "I did tell you I'd give you riding lessons."

Tavis let out a snort. "And why Stuebing, for heaven sake? Stuebing is…well…Stuebing."

"The mon can disappear and reappear withoot one even kenning he's entered the room. No' too many men have that ability. I begin to think that perhaps he had been trained as a spy."

"Ah, I will take that as a compliment, sir." Stuebing stood behind them, his nose in the air.

Duncan jumped from his chair and spun around. "See what I mean?"

Tavis laughed.

"You wished me to inform you when your wife woke from her nap. She is asking about you. If you will excuse me, I have duties to see to." Stuebing turned and headed for the door.

"Back to Ferguson. So now what are you going to do?" Tavis lifted lazy eyes.

Duncan felt much the same way. He could finally relax now that his job was done. "I will have to return him to Scotland as soon as *The Scottish Lass* returns. 'Tis sad. But perhaps I can say a word to the queen, and the punishment won't be so harsh."

"So you believe him?"

"Aye. I do. Ferguson acted out of anger towards the men who had accused his father and allowed the grief over his father's death to cloud his thinking. I canno' blame him for wanting to clear his family's name. The irony though—he sought to clear his father of treason and in the process, he committed it."

"What of the murders? If Ferguson didn't kill those men, who did?"

"That I dinna ken. That is left to the American police. Perhaps they are no' even related to this case. I have found the man I sought, and I will return him to face charges."

"But what if the murders are somehow tied to Ferguson?"

"Then perhaps the queen will ask your help. Once I deliver Ferguson, I am retired from espionage. And then I plan to live a quiet life with my wife and hopefully a passel of bairns."

A chortle escaped Tavis's lips. "If you are wanting a passel of bairns, I don't think there will be anything quiet about that."

Duncan rose from the chair. "I best be getting to Charlotte. Dinna want to keep her waiting."

Charlotte's willingness to leave her family and follow him troubled him. She had yet to tell him she loved him, but didn't her actions speak for her? How else could he decipher that sacrifice? Yet he longed to hear those three words come from her sweet lips.

He had hoped she would be the first to say it. She very well might feel the same way. Och! He would have to swallow his pride and tell her—and pray she would repeat the words.

When he got to their room Vivian sat beside the bed chattering like an early morning bird, while Charlotte nodded and smiled. Duncan cleared his throat and Vivian jumped up from the chair. "Will you be staying, sir?"

"Aye. You can leave."

She curtseyed. "Yes, sir."

"And Vivian?"

She turned to look at him. She'd become devoted to his wife in a short period of time. "Thank you. I ken your assistance to my wife goes beyond service. I wish you to ken it does no' go unnoticed."

"Thank you, sir." She pulled the door shut.

Duncan sat on the bed where Charlotte lounged, watching him.

"How are you feeling, love?" He tucked a lock of hair behind her ear and was shocked at the desire the small action instilled in him.

"Quite well, and I think if *someone* would allow me to get up, I could show him."

"You are a sassy thing."

Charlotte tipped her nose up. "You, sir, bring it out of me."

What this woman did to him. He could spend the rest of his life staring into those deep brown eyes, which could put chocolate to shame for the richness of their color. He scooped her up and sat in a chair near the window, situating her on his lap. "We need to talk."

♥♥♥

Charlotte turned to face him. "First I'd like to know about Ferguson."

"I think sometimes you enjoy being obstinate."

With heavy concentration, she slowly raised her right brow. Duncan burst out laughing. "Och! What is this, lassie? Would ye be trying to intimidate me?"

"Ah-ha! So you were using that as intimidation. I knew it." Charlotte ran her tongue over her lips to moisten the cracked skin.

"Now, dearling, I dinna ken what you are referring to."

"You are impossible. Tell me about Ferguson."

Duncan heaved a sigh. "Weel, I have to say in my defense, that I have never missed so many signs in all my years. You had me so distracted that I am afraid I somehow missed all the cues I normally would have picked up on." He continued to spend the next few minutes telling her what had transpired between him and his former friend.

Charlotte rested her head against Duncan's chest. "I feel sorry for him."

"Aye, it is a sad situation. But what he did was wrong, and he must stand accountable. I will try and put in a guid word for him."

"Does this mean we will be leaving for Scotland right away?"

"'Tis what I wish to talk with you aboot. Now if you will permit me to continue." He lightly clipped her chin with his finger.

"By all means, go ahead. You have my complete attention." Charlotte nestled down on his lap.

"Do you want to go to Scotland, lass?"

"Of course I want to go. A wife's place is with her husband."

"Aye, I agree. But what if your husband would agree to stay in America?"

Charlotte raised her head so she could see him. He loved his homeland. "Are you thinking of staying?"

"Aye, I am. I dinna want to take you away from your family and especially Nellie. I ken what kind of a bond you have with her. 'Tis the same as I shared with my brother before he died."

"I'm sorry Duncan." Charlotte wrapped her arms around his neck and kissed him. "Although I've never lost a sibling, I can only imagine how terrible it'd be to lose someone that close."

"But God is healing me. I will always miss my brother, but I'm finding strength in the Lord."

"You cannot know how good it does my heart to hear you speak of God in a positive way."

Duncan ran his thumb over her cheek. "You dinna answer my question."

"If I said I didn't want to stay, it'd be a lie, Duncan. But I want you to know that I will go willingly to wherever you choose."

"I ken that. But when I thought aboot the sacrifice that Christ made for me because He loves me, I realized I wanted to make this sacrifice for you because I love you. You mean more to me than my homeland. I dinna want to take away any of your joy, and I ken that if you leave your family, 'twould be difficult for you."

Her hands moved from behind his neck to his cheeks, framing his face. She searched his eyes. "Did I hear you correctly? You love me?"

"I love you with all my heart."

Tears welled in her eyes. "You really love me?" She wiped the tears that rolled down her cheek and laughed. "I love you, too."

His eyes sparkled. "We will take the trip to Scotland with Ferguson, and you can meet my family and my infamous sister, Ailsa. You will love her, I promise. The trip can be our honeymoon. I will show you the land I love, and then we will return to Charleston…to our home and the land we both love."

He pulled her to him.

"Oh, Duncan, you may have blackmailed me into marriage, but there's no trickery in that offer."

"Aye lass, nothing but love." He brushed his lips over hers before deepening the kiss.

Debbie Lynne Costello has been writing since the young age of eight. She went to college for journalism. She enjoys medieval settings and settings set in nineteenth century Charleston, South Carolina. She loves the Lord and hopes to touch people's lives through her stories. Debbie Lynne lives in the beautiful state of South Carolina with her husband of 40 years, their 4 children, 2 Tennessee Walking horses, 2 Arabians, miniature donkey, 6 ducks, and 3 dogs.

If you enjoyed reading *Bride by Blackmail* you might enjoy ***Shattered Memories*** set in the 1880's during the Charleston Earthquake.

If you enjoy medieval time periods, look up ***Sword of Forgiveness*** and the rest of the **Winds of Change Series.**

One of the best ways to let me know you enjoyed ***Bride by Blackmail*** and say "thank you" is to write a favorable review on Amazon, Bookbub, Goodreads as well as other sites! Thank you so much!

I love hearing from my readers. If you have any comments or questions please feel free to contact me at debbielynnecostello@hotmail.com.

Catch me online at:
My website: DebbieLynneCostello.com
Facebook: https://www.facebook.com/debbielynnecostello
Twitter: https://twitter.com/DebiLynCostello
Newsletter:
https://mailchi.mp/276616916748/debbielynnecostello

Other Books by Debbie Lynne Costello

WINDS OF CHANGE SERIES:
SWORD OF FORGIVENESS
SWORD OF THE MATCHMAKER
THE PERFECT BRIDE
SWORD OF TRUTH (COMING SOON)

SHATTERED MEMORIES

Made in the USA
Middletown, DE
16 October 2020